A WORLD TURNED UPSIDE DOWN

World War II is over—yet their greatest struggle still lies ahead. Their ancient land of China has new rulers, bent on destroying the past. Those who once had so much now must flee with nothing but their courage and desire, and the fierce determination not only to survive but to triumph.

This is their story . . . the story of men and women caught up in a great tidal wave of change that casts them on America's distant shore . . . the story of their intertwined lives, their loves, their struggles . . . the story of the passion and price of making their deepest dreams come true.

ON WINGS OF DESTINY

With my best regards

Oct. 1992

ON WINGS OF DESTINY

BY

Ching Yun Bezine

A SIGNET BOOK

SIGNET
Published by the Penguin Group
Penguin Books USA Inc., 375 Hudson Street,
New York, New York 10014, U.S.A.
Penguin Books Ltd, 27 Wrights Lane,
London W8 5TZ, England
Penguin Books Australia Ltd, Ringwood,
Victoria, Australia
Penguin Books Canada Ltd, 10 Alcorn Avenue,
Toronto, Ontario, Canada M4V 3B2
Penguin Books (N.Z.) Ltd, 182-190 Wairau Road,
Auckland 10, New Zealand

Penguin Books Ltd, Registered Offices:
Harmondsworth, Middlesex, England
First published by Signet, an imprint of New American Library,
a division of Penguin Books USA Inc.

First Printing, October, 1992
10 9 8 7 6 5 4 3 2 1

Printed in the United States of America

PUBLISHER'S NOTE
This is a work of fiction. Names, characters, places, and incidents either are the product of the author's imagination or are used fictitiously, and any resemblance to actual persons, living or dead, events, or locales is entirely coincidental.

My Crystal:
Until I can hold you in my arms again,
I'll continue to hold you in my heart,
and leave a few more footprints on the sand.

My husband:
The Wings of Destiny brought us together,
and together we have crawled,
but now it's time for us to fly.

To Audrey LaFehr, my editor:
If each of my books is a flower,
then your encouragement is the sun
and your criticism the rain.

To all my friends:
Here is our third book.
I hope you like it,
As you did the first two.

Destiny is a beautiful crane,
Descending from white clouds to yellow sand.
It carries me on its back,
Soaring through the sky.
I beg it to fly toward my heart's desire;
My tradition gives it a different command.
The crane ignores me and my tradition,
And flaps its wings toward an unknown land.

PART I

1

October 1949

In south China the autumn sun set slowly over the eternal Pearl River, turning the flowing water into a multicolored ribbon, glistening as it coursed its way through many ancient villages.

In White Stone a flock of sparrows sensed the ending of another day and left the riverbank. They headed for their nests, fluttering their wings, painted gold by the sun's last shimmering rays. Their homes were in old trees on top of a hill where the ghost of a headless lord was said to roam, where white marble stones were piled, giving the town its name.

The older and wiser sparrows noticed a disturbance in the usually peaceful air; they soared higher. The younger, less-experienced ones followed habitually.

When they reached the town square, they were all frightened by the noisy crowd. They levitated into the high drifting clouds and flapped their wings faster. They hurried for the hilltop without making their routine stop at the Ma house, although they saw a little girl in her walled garden, waiting in the middle of a bridge curved over a lotus pond.

The girl had on a pink pajama suit. Her long hair was braided into two pigtails tied with red silk ribbons. Her pretty face was heart-shaped and small. Her large black eyes contrasted with her pale skin. Her mouth was narrow and her thin lips parted as she looked in puzzlement at the fleeing birds.

"Aren't you hungry today, my friends?" Ma Qing asked, gazing after the sparrows.

Ma Qing was nine years old. She had learned from her grandmother to relish the magnificent view of each setting sun. They used to walk hand-in-hand while a maid followed with a basketful of leftover rice. They had always come to the pond and crossed to the center of the bridge, then waited for the sparrows to come.

In the past year Qing's grandmother had become too weak to visit the garden. Qing had continued to feed the birds on her own. She had grown tired of the company of her maid and ordered the woman to fetch her the rice, then leave her alone.

The birds' strange behavior surprised Qing and she asked them a few questions. "Did you steal from the farmers or the fishermen? Were you not afraid of being caught and turned into their dinner? Or did some other girl give you her leftover rice and you're not hungry for mine?"

Qing looked at the last dot of a departing bird, then murmured doubtfully, "But the servants say that outside our garden walls everyone is starving and no one has a single grain of rice to spare.''

Qing knew very little of the world outside her grandfather's compound. When she was six and should have gone to the public school, her grandmother had insisted that she must not be placed in the company of village children. A scholar had been hired to come to the Ma house every day to teach Qing in the richly furnished study.

The sun's rays weakened and the sky turned gray. The Ma family dined late. Qing still had about an hour to play before the maid would come looking for her. She left the bridge and walked around the pond in the stillness of twilight, listening to cricket song.

She squatted when she heard the chant rising from underneath the rocks piled in the shape of a crouching lion. She removed a moss-covered flat stone and looked for the singing insects.

In the dim light she saw several small brown crickets scattering in all directions. She cupped a hand over the largest cricket, using the other hand to take a silk handkerchief out of her pocket. She wrapped the handkerchief loosely around the cricket, then looked for more. Later she would bring all of them to her room, where several cricket cages stood in a line on the windowsill. Each cage was carved out of teakwood into a miniature pagoda. The imprisoned crickets would sing for her alone in what remained of their lives.

''When I wake up in the middle of the night, I can listen to you and feel less lonely,'' she whispered to her musician friends.

Loneliness apprehended Qing frequently. Within her grandfather's garden walls lived many people. Qing's grandmother favored Qing over all others, and the old lady's attitude created a jealousy so strong that the other children refused to play with Qing.

Although too young to know the value of monetary things, Qing's cousins were influenced by their parents' words: "When the old lady dies, she will leave all her money and jewelry to her favorite, Qing, and you will receive nothing!"

Qing didn't like living in an environment filled with animosity, but she had no choice. As she searched for more crickets, she thought of her home in Shanghai, where at one time she and her younger brother, Te, had lived happily together with their parents.

Qing's father had gone from White Stone to Shanghai, where he met and married her mother. When Qing was four and Te three, her parents had brought both children back to visit the paternal grandparents. Qing's grandmother had become attached to Qing immediately.

"Leave her with me and I'll regain my health," the fragile old woman had said. "The laughter of a child will bring back youth to an aged heart."

Qing's father had answered without hesitation, "Since you put it that way, Mama, if I don't leave my daughter with you, people will say I am a cruel son."

Qing had cried and refused to be left behind. She had run to her mother and held on to her mother's hand. But her mother had pried Qing's fingers away. "I love you, my daughter, but there is nothing I can do. I am only a woman, and I must obey my man. Besides, if we don't let your grandmother keep you, she may take your brother. Your Baba and I can't part from our son."

Qing's mother had continued with a practical smile, "Just stay with the old woman and try your best to please her. When she dies, she'll leave you so much money and jewelry that you'll have more dowry than any other girl in the Ma family."

Qing had cried every day after her parents and brother were gone, until she grew to love her grandmother without ever thinking about what the old lady could give her.

She only wished that her grandmother was in better health so they could have more chances to play together and Qing wouldn't be so lonely.

Qing stood holding her handkerchief gently, then said to the captured crickets, "When Grandmama wakes up, you'll sing her your best songs. Perhaps that can chase away her illness and make her well again."

She stopped at the gate shaped like a full moon when she heard loud noises coming from the front of the house.

It sounded like the front doors were being banged and kicked. But who would dare do such a thing? Her grandfather was the richest and most powerful man in White Stone—he was untouchable.

"Time for Fan Shen!" a man's voice shouted.

"Fan Shen! Fan Shen!" many other voices followed in a chant.

Ma Qing cocked her head to one side and listened carefully. Fan Shen meant Turning Over, making the upside down and the downside up.

Why would people knock on the door and shout those silly words? she asked herself.

"Time for the filthy rich to get down on their knees!" the leader's voice cried.

"Down with the filthy rich!" the crowd echoed in an ear-shattering roar.

Qing relaxed when she hard her grandfather ordering the Ma servants to grab hold of sticks and knives to stop the intruders.

Qing's worries vanished when she heard the footsteps of the servants running toward the front door. She knew the threatening mob would be chased away. She began to walk toward her grandmother's courtyard once again.

Qing froze.

"We are no longer slaves to the feudalistic pigs!" yelled the servants who had served the Ma family for years.

The next moment the Ma mansion was filled with the cheering voices of the intruders as the servants opened the doors for them, welcoming the trespassers into their master's domain.

"We poor must unite as one!" the villagers shouted as they stormed through the front yard alongside the servants.

Qing was confused. How could the servants be disloyal to her family? Didn't her grandfather say servants were like dogs, owned by the Ma family, whose sole purpose was to carry out their master's commands?

"My comrades, we the deprived must rise to power!" the familiar voice boomed.

"We shall stay in power forever!" the followers chanted.

Qing heard numerous tramping feet moving

into the first courtyard, followed by an enormous crashing sound.

She moved away from the moon gate, peeked, and saw a mob rushing in, sweeping aside everything that stood in their way. Flowerpots in the hall were thrown to the floor. Paintings and scrolls were torn from the walls and stepped on.

Qing gasped and took a few steps back, then retreated soundlessly into the garden.

She heard the intruders advancing into the second courtyard and passing the moon gate. She hid behind the thick trunk of an old willow and peered out from the deep shadow. She saw a man leading the rebels, and she recognized him.

He was the gravedigger Fan Yu. Qing had seen him many times before when she went with the grown-ups to the graveyard to burn incense for the dead.

Fan Yu had discarded his peasant clothes and put on a dark green uniform. In the middle of his cap shone a red star. He held a large shovel, a tool he had used all his life and could handle well. The heavy shovel seemed weightless in his big hands as he raised it threateningly. Behind him a swarm of villagers trailed, holding clubs, sickles, and axes, waving their weapons violently.

They charged toward the inner living quarters. Qing thought of her grandmother sleeping in one of the rooms.

"Poor Grandmama, your weak heart cannot take such disturbance," she whispered and began to cry.

She raised her hands to cover her mouth and dropped her knotted handkerchief. At the same time she saw that a few of the villagers had left the others to enter the garden. She moved to the shadow of a larger willow, but didn't have time to pick up her handkerchief.

The villagers trampled the silk bundle, crushing the poor crickets and putting an end to their unfinished song.

Qing moved quietly from the shadow of one tree to another, until she was once again at the lotus pond. She squatted beside the crouching lion made of rocks, and from a distance she looked like a small bush fluttering in the night wind.

The small bush trembled harder, although the night wind was gentle. Qing shivered violently when she heard the sound of clubs and sticks hitting against human flesh as people were slapped and beaten in the main house.

Qing collapsed to the ground when she heard the villagers screaming at her weeping aunts and moaning uncles. "You lazy fools! We'll teach you how to become more useful human beings!"

"What a dirty, tricky old man! I'm glad you lived long enough to fall into our hands!" someone yelled at her grandfather. As the old man shrieked and begged for mercy, Qing clamped her teeth together and squeezed her eyes shut.

"Such a fat, ugly old pig! We'll have fun with you when the time comes!" another person crowed, and then Qing's grandmother's shrill wail pierced the garden.

Qing forgot her own safety and stood up. She took one step toward the moon gate, then hesitated at the sight of the chaotic battle. The cries and moans of her family were accompanied by the yells and bellows of the servants and villagers. She brought her arms up and pressed them against her drumming heart. Her legs were weak and her throat dry.

Thick clouds covered a half-moon; the garden was shrouded by the deepening dusk. Qing stood in the shadow, staring helplessly as the mob flowed out of the main house and into the garden. They did not see her yet, but soon would if she didn't find a better place to hide. Her eyes explored the garden for a place to conceal herself.

She looked at the edge of the pond and hesitated. When she heard once again a loud slap followed by one of her cousins screaming pitifully, she stepped into the water.

The heat of the day still lingered in the pond. The water was warm. Qing walked along the shallow bank where the water reached her chest, holding on to the tough bamboo stalks.

A gust of wind tossed aside the clouds, revealing the half-moon. Qing was frightened at being discovered in the moonlight. She moved quietly until she was under the curved bridge. The next moment the invaders charged over the bridge, their heavy footsteps pounding above Qing's head.

"I don't see anybody here, do you?" one of them asked.

"No," another answered. "Let's go back to the house."

Then the villagers ran back. Qing didn't understand why the people of White Stone hated the Ma family. She couldn't believe the torturers of her relatives were the same people who had always bowed and smiled humbly and obediently.

Qing forgot how her cousins had always resented her. Mentally she received each blow that landed on them. Her anguish was so excruciating that she had trouble breathing. She raised a hand to her throat.

"I'm choking. I feel someone's icy fingers strangling me," she mumbled as she looked at the water.

She screamed when she realized she was standing in the haunted pond where, according to everyone, her Aunt Melin's ghost dwelled.

"Aunt Melin, are you with me?" she asked, then quickly covered her mouth with her shaking hands.

Qing remembered what the servants had whispered about her aunt's suicide.

"Melin was the most beautiful girl in White Stone. When she was still a young woman, one night she climbed up the lion rocks in the moonlight and jumped into the lotus pond. Her body was found the following morning, her hands and face floating among the blooming lotus flowers, her feet tangled in the strong lotus roots.

"Ever since then, whenever the moon shines over the pond, Melin will appear. Many of us saw her rising in a thin mist, wearing lotus flowers and roots. She looked as beautiful as she always did, although her white face was half-covered with mud. She whispers a name each time she appears . . . the name of a young man."

The water had suddenly lost the heat of the sun. The pond had become chilly in the last few minutes. "Please, Aunt Melin, don't hurt me . . ." Qing pleaded, her whole body shaking violently. Her mother had said there was an amazing resemblance between Qing and Aunt Melin. Without the age difference, they could have been twins.

Her grandmother had stared at her and sighed, "Are you Qing or Melin? If you are Melin, please listen to me: Mama loves you very much and she is sorry. Please forgive her."

Qing whispered softly to the rippling water. "Aunt Melin, since I look like you, will you protect me?"

As Qing waited for her aunt to answer, an owl flew out of its hiding place and crossed the garden. It left a strange cry that sounded like a woman laughing sarcastically. The noise lingered in the air, terrorizing Qing. She closed her eyes, was certain that if she opened them she would see her Aunt Melin rising from the pond . . . no longer beautiful, but glaring at her through the empty sockets of a decayed skull.

"Baba and Mama, why didn't you take me with you to Taiwan?" Qing kept her eyes closed and sobbed feebly.

Her voice rode on the night wind that swept over the garden ". . . take me with you . . ." it echoed, faded, then died—just like the hope she had had a month ago.

Her parents had arrived in White Stone with her younger brother, Te, and this time her mother had looked very sad.

Her mother had held her close and said, "Qing, after this visit we may not be able to see you for a long while. Your Baba and I are taking Te away from Shanghai. We'll sail across the ocean for a faraway island called Taiwan. We don't know how long it will be before we can come back."

"Why are you going?" Qing had asked.

"Because the communists are taking over China, and your Baba says a communist country is very dangerous for the rich," her mother had explained.

"My grandparents are also rich. Shouldn't they leave China too?" Qing had asked.

"They should," her mother had said, "and so should all the Chinese who cannot survive the rule of a communist government. But among our friends and relatives, your Baba and I are the only ones willing to uproot ourselves."

Her mother had paused and then sighed. "Many people think the way your grandfather does. He argues that if even the Japanese didn't harm him and his family, how can the Chinese communists?"

Qing had begged not to be left behind.

A few tears had fallen from Qing's mother's eyes, but the woman had been firm. "Qing, we must do what has been done before by our ancestors. There has always been war in China, and at times the younger generation is forced to run away while the old stays. The young choose among their children a baby girl to be left behind to keep the old people company. Your grandmama has requested that you be left with her. We cannot say no. . . ."

Someone screamed in the house. Qing opened her eyes. She saw herself standing in the pond, buried to her chest in water. She looked up and saw the bridge curving over her head.

She peered around the bridge and stared at the glowing moon. She whispered to it, "Are you also shining over an island called Taiwan? Can you tell my parents that they should have taken me with them, even though I am only a girl?" She stopped.

"Due-na-ma!" Gravedigger Fan's angry voice roared from the house. It reverberated in the garden, hushed the crickets, and made Qing flinch. The owl left its perching post and flew away, cackling as it soared into the night's shadowland.

"You can keep your filthy money!" Fan shouted. "What you aristocrats did to the poor cannot be erased with a few dollars! I am thirty-six years old. My mother was raped thirty-seven years ago by one of the men who worked for your father. Yes, the walking dogs of the rich are just as bad as the rich themselves. My mother lost her mind after she was raped. Her father married her to a miller. The miller treated her badly when he discovered that she was not a virgin. I was born a few months later. I called the miller Baba, but he beat me and kicked me every day. I lived a miserable life until both the miller and my mother died. My misery is caused by you! I am here for revenge!"

The pond water was now icy cold. Qing's feet and legs were numb. Her teeth clattered so loudly that she was certain the people could hear her all the way to the house. She clenched her hands into fists, then pushed a fist in between her upper and lower teeth. She chewed on her knuckles and tasted the salt from her tears that had streamed down her face and fallen on her fist.

"Destroy everything that is useless, but do not damage the house! In the new China we do not need vain artifacts, but our people can always use some living space!'' Gravedigger Fan ordered.

Immediately the racket of glass shattering and wood splintering reached the courtyard. Qing visualized the destruction of antiques and art collections treasured by the Ma family. She sank her teeth deeper into her knuckles and tasted blood.

''My comrades, when the poor of China sold their children to buy rice, the rich were wasting a fortune on expensive toys. Now that the toys are destroyed, we can take their owners to prison!'' Fan cried triumphantly.

Qing peeked from under the bridge and saw her family members tied to a long rope, one following another. The villagers and servants kicked them and hit them with clubs and sticks, forcing them out of the house. Dragging at the end of the procession was Qing's grandmother, whose large body was being pulled and pushed like a pig on its way to the chopping block.

The Ma family was herded into the street. Their footsteps turned at the corner and moved toward the town square. When the last of their wailing died away, the only sound that remained was the front door, left open and forgotten, banging against its frame.

2

October 1949, Taiwan

THE SUN EMERGED from the horizon, slowly reddening the East China Sea. Mighty waves washed the north shore of a leaf-shaped island, rolling up the sandy beach.

Along the shoreline, soldiers were posted every few yards. Having stood fully armed throughout the night, following the searchlights with their eyes and scanning every inch of the water, they were now very tired. As daylight appeared, they knew their replacements would soon arrive. They relaxed a little.

"Keep your eyes open!" their sergeant shouted. "The frogmen from the mainland will sneak ashore and cut your lazy throats!"

The soldiers shivered and became alert again. They were Chiang Kai-shek's men. They had lost the entire mainland so quickly that they were now afraid of losing the last bit of land in their control. They continued to stare at the whitecaps, believing that behind each swell could be an enemy.

Fear of a Red Army invasion was ingrained in their minds, just as it was planted in the hearts of all the civilians. The entire island of Taiwan was heavily guarded against both Chinese Communist troops and spies.

One of the soldiers heard a sound from the water. He quickly aimed his rifle at it. His abrupt movement caused all the others to turn toward the same direction. The sergeant was ready to give the order to fire when a white bird flapped its wings and took flight from the sea, carrying a fish in its beak.

"*Ta-ma-de!*" the sergeant cursed in Mandarin. "You stupid bird! I thought you were Bandit Mao's man invading our great President Chiang's domain!"

No one dared to laugh. They watched the bird soaring into the sky, thanked it silently, and relaxed a little.

The bird perched on top of a palm tree, ate its breakfast quickly, then continued its journey toward the south of the island and the city of Taipei. It flew high over the crowded streets, then gradually lowered itself when quiet lanes came into view.

At the end of one of the narrow lanes stood a small house surrounded by tropical trees and flowers. The bird circled the treetops until it found its target—a young boy.

The boy had on brown shorts, a brown short-sleeved shirt, and a black tie. He wore knee-high black socks and white tennis shoes to complete his uniform. His crewcut made his face look perfectly round. His large almond eyes searched the sky as he held his hands out with a bowl of left-over rice.

"Where are you, my feathered friends? You better come soon, or I'll be late for school," called Ma Te.

The bird spread its wings and sailed to the ground. The eight-year-old boy smiled at it happily. He threw the rice over the yard and watched the bird eat. Another bird soon joined the first one, and then another, until the yard was filled with birds.

From behind Te, the sliding door opened and a young woman appeared.

"Your breakfast is getting cold," she said, frowning at the birds. "You're feeding them again! Can't you see their droppings are hard to clean? We don't have the servants we had in Shanghai, and your poor mama has to do everything," she complained, but took Te's hand lovingly as she led him to the dining room.

"Qing learned to feed the birds from Grandmama, and then taught me," Ma Te said to his mother. "Every time I feed the birds, I think of Qing. I really miss her, Mama."

"I miss her too," the woman said, and sighed.

Food was already on the table. A man, a little older than the woman, folded away his newspaper.

Mrs. Ma sipped her rice gruel as she looked from her husband to their son. She felt sad that although Te mentioned his sister frequently, her husband seemed to have forgotten that they had left a daughter on the mainland in White Stone.

Soon after the Nationalists were defeated in the

civil war and retreated to Taiwan, Chiang Kai-shek had become president of the tiny island. He refused to admit he was overthrown, and claimed that Mao Tze-dung's rule of the mainland was only temporary. He proclaimed many new laws, and one of them was to forbid that his people communicate with anyone on the mainland. Mrs. Ma often worried about Qing's well-being. Tradition had forced her to leave the girl with her in-laws, but it couldn't stop her from thinking about her daughter.

"Ma Te!" a boy called from outside the front door. "Time to go!"

Ma Te tilted his bowl, swallowed the rest of the rice gruel in one large gulp, then reached across the table and grabbed two steamed buns.

"Tan Yen is here. I have to go. Good-bye, Baba, good-bye, Mama," he said on his way to the door.

His mother stood up and followed him, handed him his book satchel and lunch box. She then leaned against the open door and watched him talking animatedly to the other little boy.

The two wore the same kind of uniform and haircut. They were the same height, had the same round face and the same large almond eyes.

"Why, our Te looks so much like that Taiwanese boy," Mrs. Ma said, shaking her head. "No wonder they are such good friends. Maybe they use each other for a mirror." She turned to her husband, but he didn't seem to have heard her. He had finished eating and had his face buried in the newspaper again.

She came back to the table. Her husband didn't

look up from his reading. He was frowning over the section on the stock market. He had brought a large sum of money to Taiwan, but had made a few bad investments and lost most of it. He must do better from now on. To make money and protect his wealth were the only goals in his life. He had no time to miss his daughter, to watch his son grow, or to notice his wife's regret.

His wife understood his worry. She didn't talk anymore, but stood up to clear the breakfast dishes.

"Do your Baba and Mama mind my coming to your house every morning, since I am Taiwanese?" Yen asked as he and Te zigzagged through the vegetable vendors who were setting up their stands.

"No, they do not. My Mama lets me do whatever I want as long as I don't get hurt. My Baba is too busy to pay much attention to me," Te answered, giving his friend one of the two hot buns. "Do your Baba and Mama mind your playing with me, a mainland boy?"

Yen took a large bite of the bun. "My Baba said I can play with you all I want, and you are welcome to my house anytime."

Yen added hesitantly, "But my uncle doesn't like you in my house. Every time I talk about you, he reminds me once again that your people killed many of our people in 1947 . . . only two years ago."

Yen jumped over a puddle of water, gave Te a helping hand. "My uncle keeps talking about revenge," he said.

They had finished their buns, and Yen took out

of his satchel an orange, broke it in two, and gave half to Te. They ate the orange and threw the peels hard, competing as to whose landed the farthest.

Te said as he threw a peel, "Revenge? President Chiang says you Taiwanese refused to let him come here after he lost the mainland, and you killed many of us mainlanders."

Yen shook his head, "According to my uncle, Chiang Kai-shek is a liar . . ." He couldn't continue because his mouth was suddenly covered by Te's hand.

"Hush!" Te kept his friend's mouth clamped tightly shut. "Anyone who dares to call President Chiang by his full name can be arrested for showing disrespect. And now you call him a liar on top of using his name. You want to go to jail and be tortured to death?"

Yen's dark eyes filled with fear as he glanced around. He was relieved to see that all the people around them were too busy to eavesdrop. Te slowly removed his hand from his friend's mouth. Yen smiled as they walked through a rocky lane, both chattering happily until they heard shouting from behind them. "You dirty Taiwanese! You stupid Taiwanese lover!"

They stopped, turned, and gasped at the sight of half a dozen big mainland boys approaching aggressively.

"One thing I can't stand is to see a mainlander befriend a dirty Taiwanese." The biggest boy sneered, glaring at Te. "My friends and I will show you the right way to treat the islanders!"

Two of the boys charged toward Yen, each taking one of his arms. The third boy scooped up handfuls of dirt and rubbed it into Yen's face. Yen closed his eyes and thrashed his head from side to side, but couldn't break free. The bullies laughed and their leader nodded with satisfaction. "Now it's your turn," he said, pointing a taunting finger at Te. "We can't let you go unpunished."

They let go of Yen and came toward Te. Before they could grab him, Te quickly picked up several rocks and threw them at the approaching boys. He aimed well and in rapid succession hit three in the face. He heard their cries but didn't pause. "Run! Hurry!" he yelled, sprinting in one direction as Yen charged in another.

The big boys cursed as they chased after first Te, then Yen. Their confusion gave the advantage to the two smaller boys. Te and Yen lost their attackers and made their way to school by different routes. They met again near the school wall. They smiled at each other and shook hands.

"You saved my life," Yen said.

"We form a good team." Te held Yen's hand tightly. "Let's always fight side by side, no matter who our enemies are."

Before Yen could say anything, a bugle blared, announcing the start of a new school day.

"Hurry!" Te shouted, and began to run. "We're late! We'd better make it to the assembly before the bugler's last note!"

"I'm hurrying," Yen answered, running fast beside Te. "I don't want my palms to be whacked by a ruler again!"

They barely slipped into Taipei First Elementary School before the two tall iron gates were closed by a janitor. Children appeared from every direction, all converging on the school's open field.

Facing a flagpole, lines formed quickly and neatly according to each child's height. Te and Yen found their places in the correct line just as the bugler blew his last note.

The flag-raising ceremony began with the Taiwanese national anthem, and was followed by the shouting of slogans.

"May our great President Chiang live to be ten thousand! May the mainland be liberated from oppression! May Bandit Mao be destroyed without mercy!"

After the rousing patriotic assembly, the daily exercise began. For the next twenty minutes all teachers and students jogged in place, jumped, turned, and bent in the warm island sun. The sweaty students then marched to various classrooms to wait for their teachers.

Te and Yen and the other third-graders talked in small groups. The Taiwanese children spoke in a dialect known only to the islanders. Each mainland child spoke a different dialect, according to his origin. They hushed immediately when a young man, their geography teacher, entered.

"Open your books to the section on Taiwan," the teacher said. "Trace the map and memorize everything about it, including its size."

Te and Yen sat beside each other, working diligently on the map. They both liked geography, and shared the dream of seeing the world when they were grown.

The teacher walked between the aisles as he lectured. "Taiwan is very large, almost half the size of the entire Chinese mainland. Living on such a big, powerful island, you should have absolute faith in our winning the war against the bandits."

Yen elbowed Te. "According to my uncle, Taiwan is only a tiny dot, a fraction of the size of the mainland. Chiang Kai-shek changed our textbooks because he wants his people to think he is still ruling a large territory."

Te looked at the teacher and saw a troubled look on the young man's face. The teacher met Te's eyes and turned away. "Maybe your uncle is right," Te whispered in puzzlement. "Our teacher has the guilty look of a grown-up who is forced to lie."

After geography was history. The class was told to memorize all the important dates when great events took place during the Chinese dynasty they were studying.

In mathematics the students were told to memorize several complicted formulas. And in Chinese literature the class read loudly as one voice, repeating word by word until they remembered every word in an ancient poem, without comprehending its meaning.

At last it was lunchtime. Te and Yen took their lunch boxes to a far corner of the schoolyard, near the bomb shelters. All public buildings had bomb shelters because Chiang Kai-shek said that Mao's Communists might invade Taiwan at any time. Te and Yen crawled into one of the large concrete tubes and sat on the ground, eating their lunches as they talked.

"How come your food is so different from mine?" Te took a small fish and a piece of pickled radish from his friend's lunch box. "Always rice, fish, and some pickled vegetables."

"We Taiwanese are more Japanese than Chinese in many ways." Yen helped himself to the pork and beef in Te's box. "My uncle said we lived under Japanese rule for fifty years, because one of the Chinese emperors gave Taiwan to Japan to pay off a war debt. We learned to like their food and their clothes and many other things." Yen laughed. "But I like meat much better than fish and vegetables."

"And I like vegetables and fish better than meat," Te said. "Let's trade."

They exchanged their lunch boxes and ate heartily, then returned for their afternoon classes. They marched in military training, ran in physical education, sang patriotic songs in music, and drew patriotic posters in art. When they left school, it was five o'clock.

"Something looks strange," Te said, pointing at the street.

"There are so many soldiers, and they're all carrying rifles," Yen observed. "Would you like to come to my home for a while? Maybe the soldiers will be gone soon."

They crossed a few streets and were in front of a Japanese-style house as big as a mansion.

Te followed his friend's example to remove his shoes in the entrance hall. He looked up and pointed at a high place in the middle of a wall. "Why is the word 'patience' framed and hung facing the door?" he asked curiously.

Before Yen could answer, a young man appeared. He glanced at Te, then glared at Yen. He was Yen's uncle.

"I see you have brought your mainlander friend home regardless of how I feel," he said to Yen, then turned to Te. "The word 'patience' is formed by drawing a sword over a heart. Besides patience, it also means endurance. You will find this symbol in every home, store, or business owned by a Taiwanese."

He pointed a finger at Te's forehead and said through clenched teeth. "We endure your presence like a man tolerates a sword pointed over his heart. We have no choice but be patient right now, but someday we'll chase you off our land." He turned and charged out the door.

Te said hesitantly, "Perhaps I should go home."

"Never mind my uncle. He is angry all the time." Yen took his friend's hand. "Come in with me and let's play."

The Tan house contained many paper screens and straw mats, but very few pieces of furniture. It was an excellent playground for two little boys. Te was surprised to see there was no bed in Yen's bedroom. Yen told him it was the Taiwanese way to sleep on a mat over thick bedding that was rolled up and put away during the day. They did somersaults and then wrestled. Te soon forgot all about the soldiers outside and the unpleasant encounter with Yen's uncle at the door.

When it was time for snacks, they went to the living room. Yen's gentle mother served tea and sweets on a low table. Yen's dignified father joined them to sit cross-legged on the mat. Yen's sister, a pretty little girl of about five, sat next to Te, smiling at him shyly.

"I must tell you what happened this morning on the way to school," Yen said, then told his family about the big boys. "Te saved my life," he said with some exaggeration. "They would have killed me, I'm sure."

Mrs. Tan's eyes filled with tears of gratitude as she served Te more tea. Mr. Tan bowed to Te and thanked Te formally. Yen's sister looked at Te with wide eyes and said in a trembling little voice, "Thank you for saving my brother's life . . ." Her voice trailed off and she began to cry. She bowed to the others, then stood and left the room.

"Yimi cries a lot," Yen said, shaking his head. "Now she cries because she is touched by your bravery. She definitely likes you," he teased. "I can tell by her silly tears."

The only girl Te had ever liked was his sister, Qing. He didn't like other girls, especially the crying ones. But he decided that if he should ever change his mind, he would like Yimi.

Throughout the tea and snacks, Mr. and Mrs. Tan treated Te like an honored guest. He was embarrassed. "I didn't really fight the big boys. I didn't even try. All I did was throw some rocks . . ." he mumbled, and was relieved when they returned to play on their own.

Te didn't leave the Tan house until it was getting dark. He walked in the twilight, saw soldiers everywhere. They didn't seem to have anyplace to go, but lingered on the streets, staring at the vendors viciously, as if ready to pick fights.

There were both mainlander and Taiwanese vendors. Te could tell them apart easily, by the obvious differences in language and clothing and by what they wore on their feet. The mainlanders preferred shoes, the islanders sandals. Te noticed that Chiang's soldiers picked on only the Taiwanese vendors.

One soldier picked up a Taiwanese fruit vendor's oranges, squeezed them one by one until they were all smashed. The other soldiers laughed.

The orange vendor was a young man. He clenched his teeth and glared at the uniformed men but didn't utter a sound. Te saw hanging from the cart a sign with the word "patience" written in black ink.

Another soldier took a pair of new leather shoes from a Taiwanese shoe vendor, then undid his boots and tried the shoes on. He walked into all the puddles he could find, jumped in the mud until the brand-new shoes were ruined. He then took off the shoes and gave them back to the vendor with a mocking little bow.

The aged vendor didn't say anything, but Te could see fury in the old man's eyes.

Near the end of the street that led to Te's home, he saw a group of soldiers surrounding an old woman selling cigarettes from a dingy little stand. He hid behind a tall palm tree to avoid a confrontation with the soldiers.

"You should give us free cigarettes," a soldier said, taking a pack of cigarettes from the woman.

"Why?" the old woman challenged. "I don't get these wares for free."

"President Chiang has instructed us true Chinese to put you Taiwanese in your place. You must bow to us to show your total submission. Giving us free cigarettes is only another way of bowing."

"That's right," said a second soldier as he snatched two packs of cigarettes from the woman. "You Taiwanese have not been behaving properly. Your attitude needs improving. We are here to teach you some manners.''

With that the man waved a hand and swept all the cigarettes off the stand, including a small plaque that bore the word ''patience.''

The other soldiers stepped on the scattered cigarettes and ground them into the mud. The old woman cried and tried to pick up the means of her livelihood. When she saw that none of the merchandise could be saved, she suddenly stopped crying, stood up, and screamed out her rage in Taiwanese. The soldiers didn't understand her, but Te had learned some of the dialect from Yen.

She said, ''How dare you bastards come and take over our island? We suffered Japanese rule until we became adjusted to it. Now the Japanese are gone and it is our turn to rule our own home. You slaughtered us when you forced your way in, and now—'' She never had a chance to finish.

A soldier took out his handgun and whacked her over the head with its butt. Another soldier joined him. Te watched the blood pour out of the old woman's head. She fell to the ground, where she was pummeled with savage kicks. Her head became a smashed melon, her screams turned into a low moan, and then she was completely silent.

''She's dead,'' one soldier said casually, nudging the still body with the toe of his boot. ''An example has been set, a mission accomplished. A few more examples, and the Taiwanese will readily bow to our every wish.'' With that they sauntered away.

Te came out from behind the tree, shaking badly. The old woman lay crumpled on her back, her crushed face covered with blood, her eyes open and staring at the darkening sky.

Te tiptoed through the bloodstained cigarettes and ran toward home as fast as he could.

3

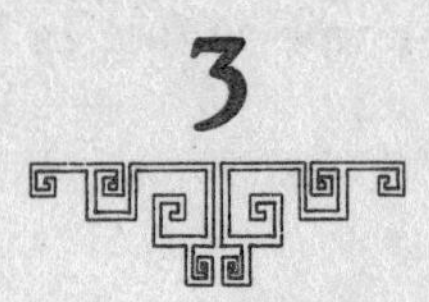

THE WIND STOPPED. Clouds gathered over the half-moon, shielding the world from its glow. The garden became as black as ink.

Ma Qing listened carefully. The crickets resumed singing. The owl settled in another tree. Far away, a dog barked.

Qing turned in the pond. The water wobbled, reverberated like someone gargling. It made her stop moving immediately. She looked nervously in the direction of the main house.

They must have left someone guarding the place, she thought. When they discovered she was here they would come for her, to beat her and take her to jail.

Minutes passed. Qing strained her eyes and ears. Except for the hooting owl and the chanting crickets, nothing stirred. Qing had not eaten since noon and was ravenous. Her growling stomach ordered her to cast away her fear and emerge from hiding.

She climbed out of the pond. Her pajama suit was now a coat of mud glued to her freezing body like a second layer of skin. With each step she left a muddy puddle. She had lost her shoes and the ribbons on her pigtails. She stumbled forward on bare feet, peeking through the dripping hair that fell over her eyes.

Clutching her trembling body with her thin arms, she tried to stop her teeth from chattering. She moved toward the moon gate, wide-eyed, her heart pounding with fright.

In her eyes, every tree changed into a giant with many arms, and each large rock resembled a crouching demon. Would attackers suddenly appear from inside the pagoda? Did she detect an enemy peering from behind one of the posts of the gazebo? She walked more quickly and tried to keep her eyes straight ahead.

Electricity was a luxury in White Stone. The villagers still used oil lamps. The mob didn't know the existence of light switches, so the house was left without light. The darkness inside was even grimmer than in the garden.

Qing felt sharp pain in her foot as soon as she entered the living room. She squatted and reached out a hand. Her fingers touched broken glass on the floor. She stood up, stayed still, and waited for her eyes to become adjusted to the blackness.

She made her way to a light switch.

She couldn't recognize the living room. Chairs were broken, sofas slashed. Curtains were torn from the rods, the large hanging lamp in the middle of the ceiling smashed. Ivory figurines were shattered, Ming vases lying in tiny pieces.

As Qing moved her eyes from one item to another, in her mind's vision she saw the room in its former magnificence. She heard her grandmother's voice saying proudly as the brocade curtains were being hung, "When you pull the four panels together, you'll see a completed mural of the flowing Pearl River."

She went to the hall, turning all the lights on as she moved toward the kitchen. Every court was in disarray, each room in ruins. It seemed that the mob had taken whatever valuables they hadn't destroyed. Trunks were opened, drawers pulled out. Mattresses were thrown from the beds and pillows slashed, because they were the two favorite hiding places for those with money and jewelry.

The kitchen was separated from the main house. The family couldn't be disturbed by the odor of hot grease and the shrieks of dying animals. Qing had never been inside the kitchen before.

She hesitated, hearing her grandmother's voice in her imagination: "Qing, a young lady never enters the servants' domain. You'll lose your appetite when you see your food when it's still alive. You'll come out of the kitchen smelling like a lowly maid."

"Grandmama, they had better give you a jail room that's far from the kitchen," she whispered, then pushed open the kitchen door.

She didn't know there were areas in her home that were not carpeted. The dirt floor was uneven, covered with spit, droppings, fish scales, and animal bones. A bunch of dead eels lay tangled in the sink. A headless duck, still wearing all its feathers, stretched on the blood-soaked chopping block.

Qing's eyes brightened when she saw a rattan basket filled with leftover rice.

The rice had hardened. Each grain was like

gravel. Qing scooped it up with her hands, pushed it into her mouth, then swallowed without chewing.

"Manners are extremely important for a young lady," Grandmama's voice echoed in her ears. "Always act like you don't have any appetite. Frown at the sight of the most expensive foods, so that people will know you have had them so frequently you are bored to see them again."

Qing emptied the whole basket, then picked the few grains of rice glued to her chin and licked them off her fingers.

She was thirsty. She found a kettle of cold tea, drank directly from the heavy container in large gulps.

"A lady sips her tea from tiny cups, and enjoys every drop, like a scholar savors each word in a poem," her grandmother had taught her. "Swallowing tea by the mouthful will make you a peasant. Reciting a poem in one long breath shows you do not understand its finer meaning."

"Forgive me, Grandmama," Qing murmured as she left the kitchen and returned to the main house. She stopped at her grandmother's room, gasped beside the open door. She shivered at the blood on her grandmother's clothes that were flung all over the floor. Her own room was next to her grandmother's. Her closet was open and her things scattered around, but not everything was shredded. She found a set of green pajamas and took them to the bathroom.

She turned the brass faucets and filled the white ceramic tub with hot water. This was the first time she had ever drawn her own bath. She soaked herself for a long time, washed her hair. She dressed, put a bandage over her cut foot. She braided her long hair into two pigtails all by herself, also for the first time, then tied them with silk ribbons. She went to bed.

Her ceiling was covered with large tiles, each bearing a yellow chrysanthemum. She looked at the flowers and told herself that what she had gone through was unreal, that when she opened her eyes again her maid would be there with a tray of hot breakfast and talking to her softly: "Qing Sheo-jay, it's time to get up. Your grandmother is waiting for you."

"Grandmama, I'll tell you my nightmare." She closed her eyes. "You won't believe how horrible it was . . ."

It seemed to Qing that she had slept only a few minutes when she heard a bang.

Her maid was standing a few feet from her bed, opening the closet door and dresser drawers, talking to four shabbily clothed children. None of them had noticed Qing's small frame under the large heavy quilt.

"We'll take over this room. It's our home now," the woman said to her three girls and a boy. "Whatever clothes you can wear are yours. The things you see and like, grab them before the others can put their greedy hands on them."

A man, older than the woman, appeared at the door. He saw Qing right away, pointed a finger at her, and shouted. "There is one of them left!"

Qing jumped out of bed, tried to run, but they were already on top of her. She was yanked out of her room by six pairs of hands, dragged to the Ma courtyard that now swarmed with villagers.

Men, women, old folks, and children rushed in and out of various rooms, each carrying bundles of clothes and household items.

One woman said proudly to another, "We were fast. We beat all others and got ourselves a big room." She then frowned. "But there was a strange type of quilt nailed to the floor. It took my old man a lot of work to tear it off."

The other woman answered happily. "We were not all that slow either. Our room is big too." She shook her head. "But the rich folks are strange in many ways. They had fancy sheets hanging over every window to block off the sun. It took me some work to yank them down!"

They stopped moving and became silent when they saw Qing.

"This is the Ma family's granddaughter." Qing's former maid pushed Qing to the center of the courtyard and jammed a finger to her head. "She is a brat! She used to order me around and wouldn't do one single thing for herself!"

A circle was quickly formed around Qing. Many filthy, coarse hands reached out to pull her hair or pinch her face. She tried to break through the circle, but her former maid grabbed her and pulled her back.

Qing began to cry. Everyone laughed. Their laughter hurt Qing's pride. She bit her lip and tried to keep her tears from falling.

"So you don't want to cry in front of us lowly peasants? So you still think you are a noble young lady?" The maid's husband slapped Qing hard across the face.

Qing had never been slapped in her life. She stumbled at the impact. The sun-filled courtyard turned black in her eyes and it seemed that a million bees had suddenly appeared. Her ears were filled with their buzzing noise.

She struggled to regain her balance. Fire touched her face with incredible heat, then bit into her skin with sharp teeth. She felt something dripping from the corner of her mouth. She licked it and tasted blood.

"That was for ordering my woman around," said the maid's husband. He raised his hand again and slapped Qing on the other cheek, harder than the first time. "This is for feeding the leftover rice to the silly birds instead of letting my woman bring it home!"

Qing lost her balance. She fell to the stone floor. Once again her vision blurred and her ears rang. Needles stung her blazing cheeks, stirring up an unbearable pain. Her mouth was filled with blood. She moved her tongue and touched a loose tooth. She struggled to stand up, but several hands landed on her at the same time, knocking her down. Her blouse was torn and her knees scraped. She gave up struggling, stayed down and closed her eyes, waited for her end to come.

"Let's give her a good thrashing," one woman suggested, grinning broadly. "Then take her to jail."

"But we don't have the time," a man said. "Comrade Fan Yu told us to get settled in our new home as quickly as possible, then go to the town hall for a meeting."

"That's right," another woman agreed. "Comrade Fan Yu also said that the rooms and things we can take this morning will be ours to keep . . ."

The woman rushed away, but her words reminded the others that they, too, had more urgent things to attend to than torturing a little girl. They followed the woman's example and hastened in various directions.

"Let's not waste time on her right now," Qing's former maid said, pulling her husband toward the house. "The good days are over for her kind. She is but a little mouse in a world of cats from now on."

The maid's husband kicked Qing's back. "You'd better scram before we change our mind!"

The powerful kick landed on Qing's lower spine. She screamed, opening her mouth wide. When she caught her breath, she cringed for the next blow. It didn't come, and she realized that she had been left alone. Free to escape.

Trembling in agony, she stayed on the ground. She couldn't move. She was certain that her back was broken.

She lay back and closed her eyes, and after what seemed like a long time, the pain finally eased away a little. She was relieved that the man had not cracked her backbone. She looked up and saw a deserted courtyard. She could hear the villagers arguing inside the house, fighting over better rooms and the more valuable possessions. Qing tried to stand up, and was surprised when she made it to her feet. She hurried to the front door and ran out of it without looking back.

The gravel road twisted before her in the autumn sun. Qing was not certain where it led, but she didn't stop to think. She must get as far from the house as she could, no matter where she went.

Each step jarred her aching back, but she kept running.

She didn't know that she had no shoes until she felt the pain on her feet.

She looked over her shoulder and saw no pursuer. She slowed down.

Tall willows lined the narrow path. A familiar old oak told her she was quite far from her home now. She sat on a tree stump and rested, looking at the far end of the road, where a few rooftops were silhouetted against a pale blue sky.

"The town square, the many shops . . . I know where I can find a hiding place," she told herself, and stood up.

Several years ago a fire had destroyed most of the White Stone Temple. Only a small room remained standing. Its walls were charred and its windows smashed. It was little more than a dark skeleton.

Qing knew the existence of this room because her grandmother had brought her there many times, always riding in a wagon.

"When I was young, this temple was the most grand . . ." her grandmother had said with tears in her aged eyes.

Qing didn't know it would take her so long to reach the temple on foot, especially when she had to duck behind rocks or trees every time some villagers appeared on the road. The sun was high when she started the journey. When she stood in the remains of the temple at last, a pale moon had surfaced among the faint stars.

Qing entered the ghastly room, fell to the floor immediately. She was exhausted. Her wounded feet hurt terribly. She looked out the broken window and saw a half-moon that looked like a broken rice bowl. She could hear the autumn wind blowing, traveling through a bamboo grove, rubbing one bamboo stalk against another and creating a haunting sound. The cicadas seemed to know that the cold days were coming; they sang mournfully their last few chanting songs.

As Qing's eyelids became heavier, she called to her grandmother, her parents, and her brother, Te. She loved all of them so much, and had thought that at least one of them would always be beside her. She was too tired and hurt to cry, and soon fell asleep.

From the deep foliage of many ancient willows, birds chirped at sunrise. Their songs traveled through the broken windows and woke Qing. She didn't open her eyes, but lingered in her dreamland and thought she was in her bed. She felt cold. She tried to pull up the quilt, but her fingers touched hard earth. She came fully awake the next second and sat up.

She gasped at the sight of the room. Then she realized where she was and what had happened to her. Soon after that, she felt hunger. Her stomach growled and ached.

She looked at the spiderwebs everywhere. The fat spiders were busy consuming flies and other insects caught during the night. Qing wished she could also spin a web and catch some food.

She heard a squeaking sound, looked down, and saw a large rat peeking at her from inside one of the many holes on the wall. She stared at her roommate. "You look as fat as the spiders. Can you teach me a lesson or two in finding food?"

The rat tilted its head to one side, studied Qing for a moment, then disappeared. Qing sighed, stood up, stretched her aching body. She walked out of the room and entered the garden, which was overgrown with weeds. Near the center of it was an old well. Qing lowered the slimy moss-covered wooden bucket until she heard it hit water. She brought up the bucket, used the chilly water to wash her face and rinse her mouth. She cupped her hands and drank the well water, which tasted faintly of mud. She then brushed her tattered clothes and combed her long hair with her fingers. She braided it into two pigtails and tied them with straws. She had lost her ribbons and doubted if she would ever return to her silk-ribbon days again.

"A Ma girl must look her best when she is to appear before her inferiors," her grandmother had told her more than once.

Qing whispered, "My dear grandmama, this Ma girl is about to appear before the lowly villagers to beg for food now."

She roamed the town square carefully, stopping at the open door of a teahouse.

Steam rose from a large pot of soybean milk over the stove. The owner's wife was ladling it out, adding either sugar or salt to each bowl according to the customer's taste.

The owner, a middle-aged man, was kneading a large piece of dough. When the dough was ready, he broke it into small portions, pulled each segment into a long strip, then dropped it into a pot of hot oil. When each strip puffed up and turned brown, it became a fried devil, an inexpensive breakfast favored by the average Chinese.

Qing's mouth watered at the aroma of the fried devils, although it was considered commoners' food and seldom appeared on the Mas' breakfast table.

She stepped forward and bowed to the teahouse owner. ''Sian-san, I am very hungry—'' she didn't have a chance to finish.

''Go away!'' the man hollered at her as he looked at her with deep hatred. ''Your grandfather charged me such high rent on this shack that I had to sell my youngest daughter to keep it! She must be about fifteen now!''

The owner's wife thrust her ladle at Qing. ''Because of your family, my baby girl is suffering somewhere in a whorehouse! You want to eat? Go to the slave trader and ask him to take you to join my daughter!''

The couple's voices turned the heads of their customers. A man said, ''I must say that Great Buddha is impartial to us mortals. He sees to it that we all take turns suffering. The Ma girl! A princess! Now she looks like a beggar! Shall we throw a fried devil at her? How about letting her lick our bowls?''

As the villagers jeered, some broke off small pieces of their fried devils and aimed them at Qing. The pieces fell to the ground, but hunger forced Qing to pick them out of the dirt and put them in her mouth. She heard the villagers ridicule her, and her eyes burned with tears. She bit her lip and fled as the people continued to laugh and jeer.

Her hunger was only sharpened by the few morsels. She circled the town square, from one food stand to another. Her begging was rejected again and again.

"In order to pay the rent to your grandfather, I couldn't afford to buy medicine for my sick mother, and she died!" a small man shouted, then came into the street, picked up a rock, and threw it at Qing.

Qing ran from the town square. She reached the grass-roofed and earth-walled huts around the rice fields.

The peasants never closed their doors during the day, especially when the husbands were in the field and the wives were home alone. A woman must protect her reputation by leaving her front door open, showing the world that she had nothing to hide.

Qing saw a woman in a one-room hut, making a pot of thin rice gruel.

"I am very hungry," she said shyly. "May I have some of that rice gruel? Just a small bowl, please?"

The woman charged toward Qing immediately. "You want my rice gruel? I'll give it to you!" she spat at Qing. "Both my family and my husband's family leased the Ma land. Until only two days ago we were tenant farmers to your grandfather. We worked in the rice fields from before sunrise to after sunset, but had to give most of the crops to that greedy old man so he could ship the rice to large cities to sell at high prices."

The woman grabbed hold of Qing's arm, slapped her hard on both cheeks. "When the year was bad and we could collect no rice at all, your grandfather still demanded to be paid. Several years ago there was a drought. Your grandfather sent the slave trader over and he took my oldest boy away. A year ago we had a flood. The same man came again, by your grandfather's order, and took my youngest girl."

The woman raised her hand once more. Qing freed herself with a jerk and ran from her. She heard the woman shouting after her, "The Great Buddha is not blind after all! Now you and your family will rot like dogs!"

Qing kept running until her lungs were about to explode. She was at the bank of the Pearl River now. She collapsed beside a tall willow, rubbed her throbbing cheeks with her trembling hands.

Through her tears she saw many women on the riverbank with lunch pails in their hands, waiting for their men, who had been fishing since dawn.

"If I don't risk being slapped again, I'll starve to death," she said as she stumbled forward.

"Please . . ." Qing bowed to a middle-aged woman and asked for a small portion of the food in the pail.

"You are the Ma girl! How dare you ask me to give you my man's lunch?" The woman spat at Qing. "Your family charged us high rent on the boat but never repaired it when the work was needed!"

All the fishermen's wives came after Qing. Qing ran for her life. When she returned to the village, she fell on the ground beside a small hut. She had no strength left at all. She felt dizzy. Cold sweat stood on her forehead and her face. The sharp pain in her stomach had become a dull ache.

A delicious aroma wafted over her, and when she raised her head and looked through the open door of the shack, she saw a family having lunch.

She stood up slowly, holding on to a low-hanging willow branch. Hunger and exhaustion nailed her feet to the ground. She stared at them, forgetting her fear. Her eyes followed their chopsticks, moving from bowls to mouths. She licked her lips unknowingly.

"That's the Ma girl," an old man said. "The poor thing is starved. Surely we can spare a bowl of rice."

A young man hesitated. "Will we get in trouble with Comrade Fan? He is in charge of things in our village now, and he hates the Ma family."

The old man raised his voice. "I am the oldest in this family, and I am the master under my own roof. I say we'll feed the girl."

An old woman filled a chipped bowl with rice and ladled some vegetables over it, then gave Qing a pair of chopsticks. Qing pushed every bit of the coarse rice and bug-eaten vegetables into her mouth, and it tasted better than any delicacy she had ever had.

She returned the bowl and chopsticks to the old woman, bowed deeply to everyone in the family.

"We'll feed you only this once," the young man said with a warning look. "Don't you dare come back!"

Qing hurried away, returning to the town square. She ducked behind a tree when she saw the gravedigger Fan Yu walking with a group of men in dark green uniforms like his.

"We'll give them a trial right here tomorrow morning . . ." he said to the men as they walked toward the jail.

Qing shivered as she looked up at the high walls topped with barbed wire. Her entire family was behind those walls. She could not imagine what it was like.

Once her grandfather had pointed at the two thick prison doors and told her that those who went in seldom came out alive, and if alive, wouldn't be without the marks of torture. He had said, "But, my child, you needn't be afraid of that place. The Ma family puts people in jail, not the other way around!"

The prison doors closed behind Fan and his followers, and Qing made her way carefully away from the town square, avoiding people. She went through back alleys to reach the temple. She didn't mind returning to the company of spiders and rats, since they were so much friendlier than humans.

She was near the temple when she heard banging and smelled dust. She hastened, turned the corner, and saw the remaining room of the temple being torn down.

"We must get rid of the last trace of Buddhism, because we, the citizens of the People's Republic of China, don't need anything to remind us of the old feudalism!" a man in a green uniform shouted as he supervised the others to level the walls to the ground.

Qing stared in disbelief as she watched her hiding place being demolished. It went brick by brick, and then was completely gone.

4

Hawaii, 1949

THE SHORELINE of Hanauma Bay curved like the rim of a rice bowl, keeping the roaring Pacific from disturbing the peaceful water in a precious container. Within its shelter, tropical fish of the most brilliant colors lived in a sanctuary, unafraid of fishermen's hooks—fishing within the bay was forbidden by Hawaiian law.

In the radiant sun the water gleamed turquoise. It washed against the shore, bringing in shells and leaving them on the sand. Among the various kinds of shells was a tiny white one with a touch of lavender and pink to adorn its fringe; its Hawaiian name was puka.

The word "puka" means "hole." In the center of every puka shell is a hole created by nature, just large enough for a needle to pass through.

"Puka, puka, where are you?" murmured a young man on the beach. He combed the sand on his hands and knees, wearing only a pair of shorts.

Paala Nihoa was fourteen. Swimming and surfing had filled his free hours since he was five; they had molded his body beautifully. His shoulders were broad, his waist narrow. His arms and legs were strong and lean with muscle.

His strikingly handsome face went well with his body. His hair was black and curly. His dark brown eyes were deep and surrounded by thick black lashes. His skin was smooth and brown in sharp contrast to his white teeth. Among Paala's ancestors were Samoans, Portuguese, Japanese, Irish, and Americans. Within his veins flowed the blood of many races, and each had contributed its best.

Beside Paala was a coconut shell, half-filled with the pukas he had gathered. He glanced at it and shook his head.

"It's far from enough to make her a necklace—" He looked up abruptly when he heard someone calling his name.

"Paala!" The call came from the top of a narrow path that wound down through a grove of flowering trees to connect the beach with the road high above.

Paala stood. Happiness and excitement shone in his eyes.

"Sumiko," he said softly. His eyes sparkled like water in the sun. His lips parted in a bright smile.

Sumiko Yamada was too far from Paala to hear his gentle call, but the sight of him was enough to bring joy to the heart of an eleven-year-old girl. She quickened her steps, wanting to fly to his side.

"Be careful!" Paala shouted. He frowned at the possibility of her tumbling down the steep path and getting hurt. The frown turned into laughter when he saw the way she ran.

It was Friday, the Aloha Day, and a day for the island women to wear the muumuu, or long dress. Sumiko's white muumuu splashed with red flowers was long enough to cover her feet. It was designed for a young lady to stay still or move slowly, certainly not for racing down hills. Sumiko gathered the troublesome skirt in her hands and held it around her thighs, revealing her slender legs and occasional glimpses of lace-trimmed pink underpants.

The breeze carried the taste of ocean to Sumiko, together with the sound of Paala's laughter. Sumiko licked her lips to relish the saltiness of the sea, savored the ring of Paala's chuckle within her heart. She loved the ocean as much she did Paala; both were important elements in her life.

Sumiko's mother, Mrs. Yamada, was an attorney. Paala's father worked for Mrs. Yamada as a gardener; his mother was Mrs. Yamada's housekeeper. The Nihoa family had moved into an apartment over the garage in the Yamada house three years ago. Paala, Sumiko, and Sumiko's two brothers had grown up together. To the Yamada boys, Paala was only a playmate, but to Sumiko he was much more—he was her first love.

Sumiko's natural parents were Japanese. Her father had been killed while serving in the U.S. Air Force. Sumiko, her older brother, Kitaro, and their mother had been sent to a detention camp in Arizona during World War II. Their mother had died in the camp and Sumiko and Kitaro had been adopted by Mrs. Yamada, a prisoner in the same camp. When the war ended, Mrs. Yamada had brought Sumiko and Kitaro to Hawaii, and treated them the same as she did her own son, Genkai.

The boys had forgotten the unpleasant days easily. For the gentle and sensitive Sumiko it hadn't worked that way. Sumiko had been just four when she was taken to the camp, and freed when she was seven. But the years behind barbed-wire fences were a dark cloud that came and went and could easily cast a shadow over Sumiko's most joyful moment. Only with Paala was the cloud completely driven away. She didn't know why she needed Paala as the island flowers needed the sun. She only knew that that was the unchangeable truth.

As Sumiko ran toward Paala her hair was caught by a low-hanging branch, and she lost the band around her ponytail. She ran the rest of the way with her long hair flying behind her, the silken strands brushing through the flower petals that clung to the low-hanging boughs.

Paala raised a hand to his eyebrows, shielding his eyes from the setting sun to adore Sumiko's beauty that transcended her young age.

Her face was round like a porcelain doll's, her features drawn by the hand of a master. She never tanned regardless of the island sun. Her almond eyes slanted up to meet slim curved eyebrows. Her nose was straight and narrow, her mouth small. Two dimples danced in her cheeks at the first sign of a smile, creating twin wells of sweet innocence.

"Paala!" She smiled delightedly, pausing at the edge of the beach to kick off her shoes. She left the shoes there and raced across the sand, still holding her muumuu in her hands. "I'm so happy!"

"What makes you happy this time?" Paala asked in the tone of voice used by an adult talking to a treasured child. He was only three years older than she, but a head taller and much more mature—the son of a gardener and housekeeper had far more contact with the world than did a well-protected daughter of a prosperous lawyer.

"Because the weekend has just begun!" Sumiko let down her muumuu, put her hands in Paala's, and jumped up and down. "I had to go for my piano lesson after school, and then directly to my ballet class. But that's all over now. No school, no lessons, no practicing . . . nothing but playing with you for the next two whole days!"

"May Queen Pali help me. What did I do to deserve two whole days with a spoiled brat?" Paala teased. He held her hands over her head and gave her body a gentle turn. He spun her around like a top, making her giggle with pleasure.

"I'm not a spoiled brat, and the queen of all volcanoes will not help you at all." Sumiko laughed as she twirled. Her hair sailed in the air and the flower petals fell to the sand. "You're making me dizzy!"

Paala stopped instantly. "Don't you dare throw up on me!" he said, holding her in his arms to steady her. He then brought her closer to him and pressed her face against his heart to let her rest.

Sumiko rested only a few seconds, when she saw the coconut shell on the ground. She left Paala's embracing arms immediately.

"Puka shells! You gathered so many!" She knelt down, dipped a hand into the coconut container. "Are they for me?" she asked, taking a handful of the shells, then pouring them back into the coconut, watching them sparkle like a white stream as they fell.

"Who else would I break my back for?" Paala squatted beside her. "I want to make you a necklace. Each shell has to be perfect, and strung in order of size. I saw a necklace like that selling for two hundred dollars. If I were a rich man, I would have bought it for you."

There were still two shells left in Sumiko's hands. She brought them to her lips, kissed them gently. "Thank you, Paala, for gathering them. They are so hard to find. Like you said, it's a backbreaking job. Paala, you are so good to me."

She looked at him, her eyes sparkling with unshed tears. "My necklace will be worth two thousand dollars. No, twenty thousand . . . no, two million!" She kissed the shells again and her young voice trembled. "I'll never part with my necklace. Even if someone offers me all the money in this world. I'll still tell him that a gift from my Paala will never be for sale." She was so filled with emotion that she could not go on.

Paala became worried. Loving her as much as he did, he disliked it when she cried. "This is the fastest inflation I ever heard," Paala said, pulling her to her feet. "Let's go find more pukas while there is still enough daylight. I believe I've taken everything from this side of the beach. Let's try the other side."

They ran hand in hand along the curved shoreline. The fast-setting sun was halfway below the horizon now. The enclosed water in the bay turned into a bowl of golden wine, rich with an intoxicating power. A few white birds perched on a protruding rock sipped the wine and became tipsy. They saw Sumiko and Paala but didn't fly away, only cocked their heads and studied the boy and girl curiously.

A wave washed over the shore, leaving a layer of white foam and a few strands of seaweed on Sumiko and Paala's feet. Paala looked at Sumiko's delicate toes with delight, then bent and picked up a puka abandoned by the breaker.

"The largest and finest puka in this world," he said. "More beautiful than a pearl. I'll use it for the centerpiece of your necklace." He brushed off the sand and put the shell in Sumiko's hand. "Look at the lavender rim. And it has not only a touch of pink but also a yellow glow. It's very unusual."

Sumiko looked at the shell wide-eyed. "A gift from the sea. The Sea God left it right on my feet. That means he likes me." She took Paala's hand and tried to put the shell in his palm. "You keep it. A gift from the Sea God has magic power. It'll bring you good luck."

Paala pushed her hand away and laughed. "I am a kamaaina, an Island Son and a child of all the Hawaiian gods. I have my own magic power, and I'm in control of my luck. Besides, when a kamaaina gives someone a present, he can never take it back."

Looking into Sumiko's bright eyes, Paala whispered softly, "Together with the shell, I've given you my love, Sumiko, and I'll never take that back either."

Paala didn't think Sumiko would understand what he meant, for he was a man, and she a child, and he must wait patiently for her to grow up. But Sumiko did understand—maybe not love between a man and a woman, but certainly the love between her and her Paala.

Tears brimmed in her eyes just as they had a short time ago. She stood on tiptoe to kiss Paala on the cheek. "I'll treasure both of them forever . . . the puka, and especially your love."

Quickly Paala pointed at the ocean and changed the subject. "Our island is so beautiful—" He stopped in mid-sentence.

The tree-lined path used by Sumiko to descend the hill was known only to the islanders. Near the path was a paved road for cars, used by tourists and newcomers to Hawaii. Now four young men appeared on that road, dressed in jeans and gaudy shirts worn only by the white Hawaiians. Their blaring voices drove away the tranquillity of the beach, sent the perching birds flying high.

"Do you see what I see?" one of them bellowed. "Two local monkeys standing on our section of the beach!"

"Not only standing there, but also stealing our valuable seashells, I bet!" another shouted. "Well, we can't allow this to happen. We must teach the two local monkeys a good lesson!"

"Let's take care of the boy first, and while doing that, the girl can watch," one said as they all hurried down the road.

"Stupid haoles! Look at their ugly white skins! They're good for nothing but shark bait!" Paala cursed.

Sumiko looked at him and gasped at the change

in his expression. All softness was gone. The love in his eyes had been replaced by hatred.

"Damn haole pigs!" Paala cursed again.

In Hawaiian the word "haole" means "outsider." It has nothing to do with race, but in common usage a haole is a white person who has disturbed the island's peace and harmony—rude transgressor.

The four white Hawaiians marched across the beach in large steps, their heavy stride making deep tracks on the smooth sand. The kamaainas never did that. They considered the beach the bosom of Mother Earth and always walked on it softly.

"You little monkeys! If you have any sense, you'll get off our beach and run for your lives!" the tallest of the four yelled as he and his friends neared the two children.

Sumiko pulled Paala's hand. "Let's run, Paala, I'm scared!"

Sumiko felt she was pulling a deeply rooted tree. Paala wouldn't move. He raised his voice and shouted at the four approaching young men, "This is our island, and our beach! It's you who should go away, you ignorant haoles!"

The four young men stopped to look at one another.

"A disrespectful little brown bastard!" one of them said. "How dare he! Has he not learned from the missionaries that we white Christians are the saviors of all the colored heathens of the world?"

"A rude native boy!" said another. "When Christianity reached the Hawaiian islands many years ago and civilized all the islanders, it must have passed his ancestors without knocking any sense into their thick brown heads."

"You leave my ancestors alone!" Paala said through clenched teeth, then raised his voice. "You know as well as I that your ancestors came to Hawaii and disguised themselves as missionaries, then stole the land from my forefathers. You have no right to impose your religion on us, nor do you have any claim to our beach or our seashells!"

"Listen to that! Are we going to stand here and listen to this child's nonsense?" one of the men took a folding knife out of his pants pocket.

"Of course not," another man answered as he also revealed a pocketknife.

Sumiko begged Paala, "Please, let's run, hurry!"

Paala pried off Sumiko's pulling hand, but kept his eyes on the advancing men. The youngest among them was about eighteen. Paala was strong and solid and could probably beat any of these haoles barehanded, but to fight all four at the same time when they had knives and he had not even a stick? He was not sure of the result.

He said without looking away from the men, "Sumiko, you must run away from here."

Sumiko was crying now. "I won't go without you, Paala. If you must fight them, I'll help."

"You'll give me a lot of trouble, but not any help," he said impatiently. "Listen to me. Run up the hill and go to the nearest phone booth. Do you have any coins?"

She nodded. "I have my bus fare in my pocket."

The men were only a few yards away now.

Paala spoke quickly. "Call your mother. Ask her to drive my father over. Tell her what's happening here . . ."

He stopped. The white men were intrigued by Sumiko's pretty face. They stared at her, and voiced their opinions as if they were talking about a tree or a rock.

"Cute little doll. Rather pale for a native," one said, then shouted at Paala with a grin, "Is she your sister?"

"That's none of your business!" Paala hated the way the white men looked at Sumiko. Something filthy glittered in their eyes. It was as if they had undressed Sumiko and were hungrily touching her innocent body.

"If she's your sister, then we won't beat you up, provided you persuade her to be real nice to us . . . I mean *real* nice." The tallest man took a step closer to Sumiko. "They say all the native girls mature early, that some are married at nine or ten. I can see this little flower is at least that old, and is definitely ready to be plucked from the flowering tree."

They moved closer in large steps while laughing and staring at Sumiko. They had forgotten the territorial feud and the seashell dispute. The impolite native boy was no longer their target. The lovely little native girl had become the center of their attention.

Paala knew he must save Sumiko and bring the attackers' attention back to himself. He pushed Sumiko so hard that she stumbled. He raised a hand as if he was going to slap her.

"Run as fast as you can, and run right this second!'' he yelled at Sumiko threateningly without looking away from the four young men.

Sumiko turned and ran. When she reached the foot of the ascending path, she heard an angry bellow. She realized instantly the sound had come from her Paala's throat. She looked over her shoulder and saw that the four men had Paala surrounded. Her heart sank. Among the white men's tall frames, her Paala looked helplessly small.

She turned and raced back, shouting ''I'm coming back to help you, whether you want me or not, my Paala!''

Paala didn't look at her, but kept his eyes on the four men ready to attack him, and hollered, ''Go! Sumiko, don't you *dare* come back!''

She stopped abruptly, not knowing whether to listen to herself or to Paala.

''I have a good idea,'' one of the four men said loudly to the others. ''I'm going to catch that little doll. She can watch us beat up her brother, and then he can learn a few things while we pluck our little island flower!'' Without waiting for his friends to answer, he began to run toward Sumiko.

His words helped Sumiko make her choice. She turned once again and fled toward the hill, her pursuer charging not far behind.

The man's words also set Paala in motion. He couldn't wait for the white men to make the first move. He bellowed in rage and rushed the nearest man, punching him in the lower abdomen. His enemy doubled over in pain.

One of the other two men called after Sumiko's

hunter, ''Forget the girl! The brown beast here is stronger than we thought!''

Sumiko lost her tracker but not her fear. She flew up the path, parting tree branches with her arms and hands. She didn't feel any pain when the thorns on the low-hanging vines cut into her skin. Her only thought was to reach the road and the nearest phone booth. She turned only once to peer back through the trees. The glimpse was like a piercing sword through her heart: Paala was pinned down by the haoles and his face was covered with blood.

5

QING WAS HUNGRY AGAIN. She could no longer depend on begging. She wandered around the town square, searching hard for food.

Dozens of strangers had arrived in White Stone. They were wearing the same thing Gravedigger Fan had on: green pants and jacket, a green cap with a red star in its center. When a group of them headed Qing's way at the edge of the square, she quickly climbed up a huge willow tree.

The tree was so old that the massive trunk had split and created a crater the size of a cradle. Qing saw the hollow area and dropped herself into it. She pulled more branches around her, covered herself with the thick foliage.

"Now I have another hiding place," she said to herself.

For many hours she was forced to stay in the tree. Fan Yu and his men lingered on in the square, worked all afternoon nailing wood boards together. Their hammering overpowered their voices, so Qing couldn't hear what they were saying. She wondered what they were building. When the men left at twilight, there was a platform like a stage standing not far from her hiding place.

Qing climbed down the tree when the square was deserted. She searched laboriously and found a few rotted cabbage leaves left beside the vegetable vendor's stand. She picked them up, then dashed toward a bunch of small carrots lying in the gutter. She lifted them out of the muddy water, held them tightly, feeling rich as she returned to her tree house.

When night fell and a moon brightened the sky, Qing felt secure enough to eat her dinner without worry that the crunching sound might lead people to her. She used her clothes to rub the carrots clean, but they still tasted strange. She knew that the gutter was a toilet bowl for the peasants, but she tried to block off that unpleasant knowledge.

She looked up at the moon on a cloudless sky, and remembered that on warm nights like this her grandmother frequently suggested a snack in the gazebo. The servants would carry many delicacies there, together with hot tea and sweet wine. Her grandmother would dip the tip of a chopstick into the wine, then let Qing suck the sweet liquor—that was the maximum amount of wine children were allowed to have.

"Sweet wine, sweet life," her grandmother used to say. "May the Great Buddha watch over my sweet granddaughter all the time."

Qing squinted to look at the faraway prison wall. She whispered softly to the barbed wire that glistened in the moonlight. "When these awful days are over, Grandmama, you and I will have our picnic under the moon again. Please let me drink a whole cup of that sweet wine, so the funny taste in my mouth will be washed away."

She was still hungry when she finished the last

carrot, so she ate the rotted cabbage leaves. She checked to make sure that no one was around, then climbed down the willow. Like a peasant, she used the gutter as a bathroom, then returned to her tree home.

The prison doors were still visible in the moonlight. "Good night, Grandmama," she said. "We are not that far apart from each other."

The clouds gathered during the night, and then the moon faded away. Large drops of rain woke Qing. She was soon drenched. The rain kept falling, the wind began to blow. The branches were tossed in all directions, slapping Qing whichever way they went.

In the darkness the tree seemed to have grown taller and the ground miles away from her hiding place. Qing felt stranded in midair, and could fall at any moment and break her neck.

She held on to the tree trunk. Fright and freezing cold made her shake uncontrollably. When the rain and wind finally stopped at dawn, Qing was so exhausted that she fell asleep in the rising sun.

In her sleep she heard sounds from far away, like waves of the Pearl River splashing against shore.

"Chin Shwan! Chin Shwan! Chin Shwan!"

She turned without opening her eyes. Chin Shwan—count thoroughly. Why would people repeat those two words endlessly?

"Chin Shwan! Chin Shwan!" There was such hatred in the two words.

Qing opened her eyes. The storm had bundled the willow branches around her, covered her securely. She peered down and saw the square crowded with villagers and men in uniform, raising their fists and shouting at the newly built stage.

On the stage four soldiers stood two at each side, guarding a group of people gathered in the center of the platform. Qing looked at those people and screamed, but her voice was lost in the continued shrilling of the crowd, "Chin Shwan!"

Her grandparents, uncles and aunts, and all her cousins were kneeling with their hands tied behind their backs. Their clothes were torn, their hair a mess. They had bruises on their faces; their eyes were filled with fear.

Fan Yu appeared from the crowd, jumped up onto the stage. The crowd hushed when he began to talk.

"White Stone has been liberated for a week now, and more Liberation Army soldiers have moved in. A new China will soon be established for the people who have been deprived for five thousand years. But first we must remove those who have deprived us. Today is our big day. On this day we will give the imperialistic pigs a good Chin Shwan." He pointed at Qing's grandfather. "We will begin with this old pig. We will count thoroughly all the crimes he has committed in his life."

The soldiers went to Qing's grandfather and dragged him forward. They kept him kneeling as they kicked him and hit him on the head with the butts of their handguns. The old man's already swollen face was soon covered with blood. One of the soldiers grabbed his white hair and forced him to look up, while Fan Yu pointed at him and listed his misconducts.

". . . and he cooperated with the Japanese

when our village was under enemy rule, then bribed the Nationalist officials and was never arrested as a collaborator." Fan concluded the long list with a question. "Is there any more?"

Several villagers raised their hands. When Fan Yu gave them chances to talk, they added more to the list of crimes committed by the old man.

"My grandfather didn't do all those bad things," Qing sobbed from the deep foliage of the willow. "No, he didn't."

Fan Yu and the uniformed men sentenced her grandfather to a public whipping, followed by life in prison, first in White Stone jail and then in a labor camp in the far north.

One soldier stripped the old man of his tattered shirt; another raised a bullwhip. The old man jerked his head up and screamed when the whip landed on his naked back, then continued to shriek for mercy. His voice gradually became hoarse as the whipping went on, eventually faded to a whimper.

When he fainted, a villager brought a bucketful of water up and splashed it on his face. He regained his senses and the soldier resumed the whipping. Toward the end the old man's back was a bleeding mess. He was hardly breathing, but lying there convulsing semiconsciously.

"Bring the old woman!" Fan Yu ordered.

"No! Not my grandmother!" Qing's voice was overpowered by the voices of a cheering crowd.

After listing her crime as being her husband's aid in every evil thing he did, the crowd agreed upon the same sentence for her. The kneeling old woman's blouse was removed, her soft white flesh exposed.

The crowd roared. "What a pig!"

Qing saw her grandmother lifting a tearstained face to heaven, those frightened old eyes searching for help. For a brief moment Qing thought her grandmother had seen through the willow leaves and found her, but then a soldier turned the old woman around to let the crowd view the bare back that was to be whipped.

When the first blow landed, the cracking sound was so loud that it overpowered the old woman's feeble cry. At the second thrash a shrilling outcry escaped the old woman's throat. The third lash sent her sprawling forward. The soldiers pulled her by the hair to make her kneel again, but she fell to the ground once more.

She took the rest of the beating lying flat, kicking her legs and flapping her arms in pain, drumming her feet and hands against the stage floor helplessly. When the whipping was almost over she stopped screaming, and soon after that ceased moving.

"Cold water for the fat old pig!" Fan Yu ordered at the end of the whipping. "She fainted, I think."

Water was dumped on the old woman, but she didn't stir. She was turned on her back and another bucket of water was splashed over her, yet she remained still.

Fan Yu squatted beside the old woman and put a hand in front of her nose to feel her breath. He then tried to find her pulse and heartbeat. After a while he stood up and faced the crowd, and a faint trace of guilt flashed over his face before he could hide it. "She is dead," he announced in a trembling voice.

"Grandmama!" Qing screamed again from the tree, and again her voice was unheard, because the entire town square was filled with the sound of people shouting out their delight at seeing old Mrs. Ma dead.

Two villagers went up to carry Qing's grandmother off the stage. They loaded the body on a waiting wagon hitched to a water buffalo. A village boy drove the wagon from the town square.

"Grandmama!" Qing cried, climbing down the willow tree. "I'm coming with you!"

The crowd was totally involved with the trial of the rest of the Ma family so no one noticed Qing. She chased after the wagon until she was about ten feet from it, then followed it toward the graveyard.

From behind her the swarm of people continued to applaud as another imperialistic pig was whipped. Qing heard the cry of one of her uncles and covered her ears with her hands until she was much farther from the town square. When she listened again, she heard nothing but the cicadas, the crickets, and the frogs in a nearby pond.

The wagon rattled from side to side on a dirt road. The rear of the wagon was but a few pieces of board nailed together, without any railing to protect its cargo. Qing saw her grandmother lying facedown, being jolted all around. Her bare feet stuck over the edge of the wagon, and one arm hung limply, almost touching the ground. No one had put poor Grandmama's blouse back on. Crisscross red lines marked her white skin.

"Grandmama! You're about to fall!" Qing cried, and ran closer to the wagon.

The boy heard her and slowed down, but Qing

paid no attention to him. She caught up to the wagon, grabbed the old woman's dangling arm, and ran alongside, holding on to the hand that was so dear to her. She then pressed it against her face and cried, "Grandmama, your hand is so cold!"

The boy stopped the wagon, jumped off the seat, and came to Qing. He was a head taller than she, his face much darker than hers, his expression the look of a much older person.

"I am Fan Kuei, the gravedigger's son," he said.

Qing screamed, dropped her grandmother's hand, and turned to run.

The boy caught her, put his arms around her, and said softly, "Don't be afraid. I won't hurt you."

Qing struggled in his tight embrace. When she couldn't get away, she turned to look at her grandmother's body and said, "His father killed you, and now he is going to kill me. We'll be together again soon, Grandmama."

Fan Kuei shook his head and sighed. "I'll not hurt you. I promise. You can ride with your grandmother if you like." To reassure her, he smiled and revealed his crooked teeth.

Qing studied the boy's face with distrust. He resembled his father, but there was no hatred in his eyes. "Where are you taking my grandmother?" she asked with doubt.

"To the burial ground," Fan Kuei said. "My Baba told me to get the wagon ready and wait by the platform, because some of the imperialistic pigs . . . I mean, the rich folks, may not survive the Chin Shwan. I'm sorry it has to be your grandmother."

He looked at the tears on Qing's face. He kept one hand on her arm, raised the other hand to dry her tears. But when she flinched, he dropped his hand. "I won't hurt you, really. Would you like to help me bury your grandmother?"

Qing looked at him in puzzlement. "Bury her? So soon? What about the funeral? Have you never seen a burial before? We need to burn paper things, to hire professional mourners and monks and nuns . . . and so many other things to do before getting around to the burial."

The boy shook his head and sighed once again. "I've seen plenty of burials, believe me. But China has changed, my little girl."

He continued to talk as if he were a grown-up and Qing a child. "I heard Baba and the other comrades talking last night. They said that in the new China there will be no funerals, no professional mourners, no monks or nuns. The dead will be cremated without ceremony."

He pushed Qing toward the wagon. "I think we should hurry and have your grandmother buried before they have the cremation place ready."

Qing shivered at the thought of having her grandmother burned to ashes. That would blister Grandmama's delicate skin and hurt a lot.

"All right, I'll help you bury her," she said, then climbed up on the back of the wagon to sit beside her grandmother. "Her face . . ." she muttered. "It's touching the dirty board. She hates to be touched by anything dirty."

Fan Kuei helped Qing to turn her grandmother's body over, so the old woman could lie on her back. They also moved the body away from the edge of the wagon so the old lady wouldn't fall. Kuei then returned to the driver's seat and whistled for the water buffalo to move on.

Qing sat with her back against the driver's seat, rested her grandmother's head on her lap. She tried her best to cover her grandmother's exposed breasts, then cradled the dear old woman's face in her hands. She bent forward and said softly, "Grandmama, they cannot hurt you anymore. You will sleep and forget what happened . . ." She was crying too hard to continue.

Her tears fell on the deceased woman's cheeks, gathered, and then streamed down slowly. It looked like her dead grandmother was crying with living tears. "Don't cry, please don't. They can't whip you anymore," Qing sobbed.

Fan Kuei turned, saw the tears running down the dead woman's face. He shivered. He tried to make conversation as the wagon headed slowly toward the graveyard.

"I can see your grandmother was very dear to you. My mother was dear to me too. But I can't remember her very well. She died when I was young. Baba raised me by himself. I am fourteen now. I've helped to dig graves since I was ten."

He made a fist with his left hand, curled his left arm to show Qing his muscle. "See? My arms are strong like the arms of a big man."

Qing looked at him from the corner of her eye. She wondered if he could be a nice person, since he was that mean man's son. She decided it would be safer not to talk to him.

But Fan Kuei went on talking, "We can bury your grandmother first and then look for some paper to fold a thing or two, and burn them for her. I know how to fold paper tables and chairs. Yes, after we burn them, your grandmother will have some furniture to use in the other world. But soon after that I must drive the wagon back to the town square. Baba told me to go back right away, because there may be more bodies, and the weather is very warm during the day."

Qing still wouldn't talk to him, although she was no longer afraid of him. Anyone who knew the art of paper-folding couldn't be that bad, she was sure.

She talked to her grandmother instead. "I'll make a paper bed for you, and burn it right away." She squeezed her grandmother's cold hand tightly, but didn't feel it squeezing back as it always had. She continued to whisper. "I'm holding you, but not the entire you. Something in you is missing, Grandmama."

She stared at the expressionless face. "Grandmama, you are like a lamp after the fire is blown out. Your light is gone, and you are no longer warm. Where are your light and warmth now, my dear grandmama? They must be somewhere. High above in heaven? In the temple of the moon? Wherever you are, I know you can hear me and see me. If only I could also see you and hear you . . ." She talked until they were at the graveyard.

The wagon stopped beside the Ma-family plot and Fan Kuei spread a mat on the ground next to the wagon. Qing carried her grandmother's head, Kuei took the feet. They unloaded the dead woman to the mat, nearly dropped the extremely heavy load. They both pulled the mat forward, gradually moved the body past the many tombstones, marble statues, and large incense burners.

While puffing, Qing pointed at the newest grave of them all. "This is my Aunt Melin's grave. My grandmama would want to be buried beside her favorite daughter."

Kuei nodded and went to look for the shovel. He came back and began to dig with the force of a grown man. A hole gradually appeared in the ground. When it was large and deep, he told Qing it was time for the burial.

She looked at him in disbelief. "Where is the coffin?"

"Baba and the other comrades also said there will be no coffins in the new China. They said it's a waste of time for carpenters to build boxes for the dead, when their labor could be used in building things for the living."

When Qing hesitated, Kuei reminded her once more that they needed to hurry. Qing nodded reluctantly. The thought of having her dear grandmother lying half-naked in a mudhole bothered her so much that she felt her heart was torn.

"Grandmama, I'm so sorry"—she looked at her own ragged clothes—"I don't have anything to wrap around you."

Fan Kuei jumped into the hole, reached up to grab one end of the mat, then pulled it toward him. Qing held the mat's other end, guided her grandmother's body toward the grave. The old woman's feet went down first, then the rest of her. Kuei then moved the mat from under her, covered her body with it.

Fan Kuei climbed out of the hole. He and Qing pushed the piled dirt back to the grave, covered the old lady's body one part at a time. The most difficult moment came for Qing when her grandmother's face began to disappear in front of her eyes.

"Grandmama!" She sank to her knees and leaned toward the grave. "Will you be scared down there? Will you be cold when winter comes? What about all the worms? They are so dirty and you are so clean . . ." She choked and couldn't go on. She collapsed on the ground.

Kuei finished the burial quickly, then carried the shovel under his arm, came to Qing and pulled her up. "Come," he said in the firm voice of a man. "You better come home with me. We'll fold the paper things for your grandmother there."

"No!" Qing tried to free her hand from his strong hold. "Your father will kill me!"

"He will not." Kuei held her tighter and said angrily. "My father is a good man. He has a grudge against your family. But deep inside he is very kind. You need to look at him the way I do."

He dragged Qing back to the wagon and continued in a softer voice, "If you don't come home with me, where can you go?"

"Go back to the willow tree . . ." Qing sobbed as she described her hiding place.

"You can't go back there. Sooner or later someone will find you. You'll be tried and whipped, then kept in our prison until you're sent to a labor camp—just like the rest of your family," Fan Kuei said as he lifted her up, placed her on the wagon seat, then jumped up to sit beside her. He never let go of her hand. He whistled and the water buffalo began to pull the wagon forward. Qing struggled once more, but his fingers were made of iron, just like his shovel, she thought.

"My Baba can save you from that horrible fate, you know," Fan Kuei said again.

Qing looked at him doubtfully. "Why would he want to save me? I am a Ma girl, and he hates all the Mas."

Fan Kuei smiled confidently. "Because I am my Baba's only son. Communist or no Communist, no man can refuse his only son's request."

Qing still didn't believe Fan Kuei. But she couldn't run away from him. She had no choice but to stay on the wagon.

The wagon stopped at the foot of a hill with white marbles piled on its top.

"This is my home." Fan Kuei pointed at a little house and helped Qing down.

The red bricks had turned black with time. The once-painted wooden door was now naked and cracked. Old trees surrounded three sides of the house, some dead and some hung with aged vines. Forsythias had grown wild through the past decades and formed a messy jungle.

Kuei took Qing inside, showed her three small rooms, then brought her to the kitchen, seated her on a wooden chair.

"I'll heat up some water so you can take a bath," he said, sniffed, and made a face. "You smell like a pig."

He gave her a pair of pants, a shirt, and a pair of shoes that had been his when he was much younger. When the water was heated, he took a wooden tub to the next room, filled it with hot water, diluted it with the cold.

"You'll feel better after the bath," he said as he

closed the door behind him. "I'll cook something for you to eat."

Qing bathed and washed her hair. To her own surprise, she did feel much better. She had wanted to die with her grandmother, but now believed it was better to be alive than dead, no matter how difficult life was.

She came to the kitchen dressed like a boy. Kuei smiled at her fondly. "I can give you a haircut and make you look like a real boy."

He seated her at a small table and gave her a large bowl of plain noodles in steaming hot soup. Qing ate so quickly that she burned her lips and tongue. She tilted the bowl to finish every drop of the soup, then looked at the pot on the stove.

Kuei laughed. "We better save some for Baba, to put him in a good mood," he said. "And I believe with one more bite your little stomach will burst—" He stopped.

The front door was opened and a man's voice thundered in the outer room. "Kuei, how come you didn't come back to the town square? You're lucky that no one else died. It's not like you to be so irresponsible!"

Fan Yu stopped at the kitchen door. He stared at Qing. "You are the Ma girl! Why are you in my home?"

Qing slid off the chair and backed away from the frightful man until her back touched the wall. She trembled as she stared at him wide-eyed. She lost her voice.

Kuei said calmly, "Baba, I brought her here. She helped me to bury her grandmother. She has no place to go. Baba, don't you think it's a good idea to keep her in our house?"

"Good idea? Have you gone mad?" Fan Yu shouted. "How can I, the organizer of the town's Chin Shwan operation, shelter the granddaughter of this operation's number-one target? Besides, a senior party member is arriving tomorrow. He will rule the entire village. I can't ask his permission to keep this girl out of prison, after what happened to the rest of her family . . ." He continued to talk.

Qing cringed when she heard that every one of her uncles and aunts and cousins had been whipped severely. She winced as she learned that her entire family, except for her grandmother, were back in prison again. She grimaced when she realized that the Mas would stay in the small White Stone jail indefinitely—it would take months if not years for them to be sent to the far north to work in labor camps. She quivered when she understood that the duration of their jail terms varied from ten to thirty years.

Because Qing was staring at Fan Yu and listening to him, it was beyond her ability to hear and see Fan Yu's mixed emotion.

Driven by anger at his mother's doomed fate, Fan Yu had joined the Communist party several years ago. He was determined to avenge his mother. But as he had tortured the Ma family, something soft inside him bothered him deeply. In front of the others, he had to act the tough and fearless party member. But when alone with his son, he was free to relinquish his pretense and become an ordinary man again.

Fan Kuei knew his father well. He had no fear of his loving Baba. "Baba," Kuei asked with a smile, "what does Fan Shen mean?"

Fan Yu frowned. "You know very well it means to turn things upside down."

"That's it!" Fan Kuei clapped his hands. "The best example of Fan Shen is to turn the landlord's granddaughter into a servant in the gravedigger's home. You are a bachelor and I am a boy. We can use someone to cook and clean and wash clothes. You tell that to the senior party member, and he'll have nothing to say. If he dares to object, then you can say he is standing in the way of carrying out the great Chairman Mao's Fan Shen principle."

Fan Yu looked at Qing's frightened face. Surely this little girl had had nothing to do with his mother's tragic fate. He had revenge enough. He then looked at his son's pleading eyes. The poor motherless boy worked hard and seldom asked for any favor.

Fan Yu thought for a long while, then sighed. He said to his son, "I guess I can say that the girl is only a child and can't be much use in a labor camp. I can even ask permission to spare her the public whipping by telling them that we need to put her to work immediately, and a sore back just won't do."

He then glared at Qing and raised his voice. "You better know your place and work hard! If not, I'll take you off to prison!"

6

SOMEONE TURNED ON Te's bedside lamp in the middle of the night. He opened his eyes, squinted, and saw his mother standing in front of his bed, her face distorted by fear.

"Get up and get dressed," she said in a quivering voice. "We need to run away."

"Away from what?" Te asked, rubbing his eyes.

"From the Taiwanese." His mother gave him his clothes and began to help him dress. "Hurry! A mob of them are going from house to house, searching for mainlanders and killing them. They are avenging the deaths of the cigarette woman and many other local vendors."

Te became wide awake. "Where can we go?" he asked as he dressed quickly.

"We don't know. Your Baba is trying to bolt the front door. I wish our house was more solidly built." Te's mother shook her head.

The houses in Taiwan were of lightweight materials and had been influenced by the old Japanese architecture. The sliding doors were thin, the garden walls low.

"Maybe we can hide in the space under the house—" She stopped.

There was a banging on the front door. Te and his mother jumped. They held each other, stood shaking until Te's father entered the room.

"The bolted door can keep them out for only a few minutes longer," he said. "Let's hurry out the back door and hide in the garden."

Te's mother asked, "Can we jump over the wall and run to the police station?"

Te's father shook his head. "There are Taiwanese all over the streets. I peeked out the front door before I shut it, and saw them holding torches and clubs."

The banging became louder, accompanied by shouting. The Ma family rushed toward the back door.

Te stopped suddenly and tilted his head to one side to listen. A smile lit his face.

"Wait," he said, pulling his parents' hands.

"Te! You had better—" his father stopped.

They could all hear a child's voice calling. "Ma Te, it's me and my Baba. We're here to help. Please open the door for us!"

"It's Tan Yen," Te said and began to run toward the front door.

His father grabbed him. "We can't trust a Taiwanese!"

Te struggled in his father's grasp. "Yen is my best friend!"

"But he has his father with him!" Te's father forced Te toward the back door.

"Yen and his Baba are here to save us, I know! Please believe me!" Te continued to struggle.

Te's father held on to him and continued for the back door.

The banging became louder and Yen's voice was

clearer. "Te! Baba and I are here to help you and your parents. Please trust us, or it'll be too late!"

Te's mother put a hand on her husband's arm. It was not her habit to disagree with him, but at this moment her fear for her family's safety overpowered her fear of her husband. "Wait," she said in a trembling voice. "Maybe our son is right."

"Stupid woman, are you out of your mind?" Te's father continued to pull the boy toward the back door.

"Please." Te's mother stood between her husband and the door. "Stop and think. Our garden is small. The crawl space is open. They'll find us anyway. We may as well trust our son's friend."

Te's father thought, then let go of Te's arm. He glared at his wife. "I hope you are not wrong."

Te ran to the front door, his parents following. He unbolted the door with his father's help. The streetlamp shone on Tan Yen and his father. The two boys exchanged a quick smile. Yen gave his hand to Te, and the two began to run down the lane, disappearing into the darkness. They didn't even take the time to introduce the three adults to one another.

"Please come with me," Yen's father said to the Ma couple as he turned from the door and led the way.

Te's parents hesitated only one second, then followed the stranger.

The three adults found the two boys waiting in the shadow of a tree. Then the five of them rushed forward together. After a few yards they saw in the distance a house with a crashed door. People were screaming inside, their cries gradually dying away. Then a group of men rushed out, holding torches and sticks and metal bars. The boys and their parents dived into the shadow of a row of garbage cans and held their breath.

They could see blood on the weapons in the mob's hands, could read the word "Revenge" in red ink on the white bandanna wrapped around each man's head.

The horde passed them, marched toward the next house, checked its street number against a list held by their leader, then began to bash in the door.

Yen whispered, "They know exactly which houses belong to the mainlanders."

Te shivered; this house was only a few doors from his own.

When the five of them reached the main road, there were many groups of men holding torches and weapons, combing the streets. Each group was led by a man with a list in his hands, and all members wore bandannas bearing the word "Revenge."

Te suddenly realized it was impossible for anyone to escape the searching eyes of so many. He turned to look at his parents, found their faces white in the light of a nearby lamp. They must have thought of the same thing.

Yen's father seemed to have read their minds. "Don't worry. Just come with me," he said in a tone of confidence, leading them toward a row of tall palm trees.

Each palm towered over thirty feet, with a girth as thick as a water buffalo's middle. Behind the trees, large rocks were heaped high. Yen's father got to his hands and knees, crawled into a crack on the rock pile. Yen stood beside the crack and urged the others to go on. Te and his parents crawled into the hole with Yen following them. After a few yards they could stand up, and found themselves in an alley they hadn't known existed.

Yen's father explained in a whisper, "When Taiwan was first ruled by the Japanese, there were constant battles between them and us. We built many alleys like this as escape paths for our guerrilla fighters. Then we learned to live under Japanese rule and stopped fighting them. But these alleys were never destroyed."

The way was so narrow that they had to move in single file. They didn't run into anyone, but could hear cries and screams and crashing sounds clearly, coming from outside.

The alley was a maze, turning every few steps. After one last turn they came out of it under a grape arbor.

"Welcome to my humble home," Yen's father said, leading them through a Japanese garden.

The garden was brightened by colorful paper lanterns gleaming on low carved wood posts. The five of them walked on stepping-stones across a manicured lawn, past a field covered with white gravel and adorned with flowers and a statue of Buddha.

At the edge of the garden two sliding doors parted soundlessly. A young woman and a little girl bowed deeply with their hands on their knees.

"My wife and daughter," Yen's father said, but didn't stop. He led the Ma family into the entrance hall, stopped at the gateway to take off his shoes. After Te and his parents did the same,

Yen's mother hid their shoes behind a bamboo screen.

They all entered a large room, one wall of which was covered by eight panels of paper sliding doors. Beautiful scenes in watercolor started on the first panel and continued on to the last. Yen's father pushed a panel that depicted a fisherman and a small boat. The door slid aside, revealing a deep, high closet.

Mr. Tan squatted to let Yen climb on his back and stand on his shoulders. Then he stood and Yen climbed to the upper section of the closet. The boy removed a board exposing an opening in the ceiling.

"You have plenty of space up there to hide, and two air vents to give you fresh air," Yen's father said.

First the Ma couple and then Te stepped onto Yen's father and climbed up. Yen replaced the board after Te and climbed down. His father closed the closet door. At that moment a group of men entered the room.

"It's the voice of Yen's uncle!" Te whispered to his parents. "He is not like Yen . . ." He shuddered.

Sitting in the darkness, Te and his parents could hear clearly the voices in the room below. The conversation was in Taiwanese and the elder Mas couldn't understand, but Te had learned the dialect from Yen.

"We covered all the mainlanders' houses on my list and got almost all of them," Yen's uncle said. "The strange thing is, Yen, we couldn't find anyone in your friend's home. We are positive they had no place to go. We searched the garden and the space under the house, but they were not there. You had nothing to do with their disappearance, I hope?"

"Of course not," Yen said evenly. And then, sarcasm coloring his young voice: "Why would I want to save the life of my best friend?"

"There is no friendship between us and the mainlanders. If you saved any of them, my nephew, then you've betrayed your own people."

Yen raised his voice. "I am not a traitor! But Te is not my enemy either! He—"

Yen was interrupted by his father, who asked quickly how well the revenge had gone.

The men gave a detailed report of their success. Te quivered as the description went on. He was glad his parents would never know what his best friend's uncle had done. He even wished that he had not learned the Taiwan dialect.

Te's parents felt him trembling and guessed that what he had heard was horrible. They wanted to hold him, but were afraid to move, so each of them merely reached for one of his hands and held it tightly.

Finally the conversation came to an end. Yen's uncle went to sleep in another room and his friends left the house. The room beneath the Ma family was empty, but Te and his parents forced themselves to stay awake, for fear that they might snore or turn over and make a sound.

They dozed off now and then, and finally knew morning had arrived when the blackness beyond the air vents turned gray. Their bodies were stiff and sore. They heard sounds when the Tan family got up, and then they smelled breakfast. They were hungry and needed to go to the bathroom, but didn't dare leave their hiding place.

Near noon, bright sunlight poured through the vents and their hiding place became unbearably warm. Now, worse than their hunger and need to relieve themselves was their thirst.

Soft footsteps padded across the room below. The Mas tensed and held their breath.

"Ma Te," Yen called in a whisper. "You can move the panel to one side just a little bit."

Te did and saw his friend standing in front of the open closet. The boy held a plateful of buns in one hand, and in his other hand he had a water pitcher and an empty tin pot.

"I'll throw the buns up one at a time." Yen smiled up at Te. "Catch them well, just like when we play ball."

Te caught the hot buns and handed them to his parents.

"Now, the pitcher of water," Yen said, and threw up a rope whose other end was tied to the handle of a pitcher. Te caught the rope, pulled carefully, and brought the water up without spilling a drop.

"Now the bulkiest item of all, the tin pot!" Yen said. "You must need it very badly by now."

Yen threw, and Te caught. "Great catch!" Yen congratulated his friend. "Your needs are temporarily taken care of," he whispered with a bright smile. "But you can't come down yet. My uncle is—"

Yen's smile froze at the roar that came from behind him: "My nephew is a traitor!"

Yen's uncle scowled up at the ceiling. "How dare you betray your own people?" he shouted as he charged toward Yen. He slapped Yen across the cheek and raised his hand again, just as Yen's father appeared.

"Stop!" Yen's father ran across the room and grabbed his younger brother's hand in midair. "You have no right to strike my son when I'm still alive!"

"Everyone has a right to punish a traitor!" The younger brother tried to free himself but couldn't. He screamed furiously, "I never thought you'd be on the mainlanders' side! How can you forget what they did to your own people?"

"I've forgotten nothing. That's why, although I knew it was wrong of you to take revenge on innocent people, I didn't stop you. But I won't allow you to hurt either my son or his best friend." Yen's father let go of his brother's arm but stood protectively in front of his son.

"I don't need your permission to carry out justice!" the younger brother hissed, then pointed a finger toward the Ma family. "My friends will be here any minute now. Just wait and see what they do to these mainlanders!"

His last word still lingered in the air when a group of men rushed into the room. They hadn't even taken off their shoes, and looked ashen-faced, both furious and scared.

"My brother is hiding some mainlanders in his—" Yen's uncle began, but they interrupted him.

Without looking at Te and his parents, all the men began to talk at the same time.

"What are they saying?" Te's father asked in a shaking voice.

"Are they looking for ways to torture us?" Te's mother cried helplessly.

"No, they don't have time to deal with us at all," Te answered.

He listened a while longer, then translated: "It's their turn to run for their lives now. The Nationalist Army has received an order to put an end to the revolt by massacring the Taiwanese."

Te's face turned white as he listened. "Baba and Mama, it's awful! The soldiers are coming this way with rifles and machine guns. The Taiwanese only revolted in the city of Taipei, but the Nationalist soldiers are killing the Taiwanese all over the island, including those who had nothing to do with last night's revolt. They have already killed many people, and have lists similar to what the Taiwanese had—they know exactly which houses belong to Taiwanese families. Baba, now it's our turn to save my best friend and his family!"

A slow grin appeared on Te's father's face. He sighed with relief and said slowly, "My son, you don't really expect your Baba to risk his life for the Taiwanese traitors, do you?"

Te stared openmouthed at his father. "Baba! Of course we must save Yen and his family. It's only fair!"

Te's mother knew her husband better than did her son, and was aware that an appeal to fairness was not the way to reach him. She touched his arm and said gently, "Please listen, my husband. If this is a contest to the death, then we don't know which side will be the winner—not yet. We had better not align ourselves with one side only—it just might be the wrong side. We don't want to make a fatal mistake, my clever husband."

Te's father stared at his wife for a moment, then smiled. "Woman, you're not as stupid as I thought." He turned to Te. "All right, we'll help your friend and his family!"

As the Ma family climbed down from their hiding place, they could already hear the roar of military trucks in the distance, and the sound was getting louder.

Yen's uncle's friends rushed away. Yen's father wouldn't let his younger brother go with them. The five Yens and three Mas entered the garden. Yen's father parted the grape vines and revealed the opening and they entered the narrow alley.

They moved forward in the mazelike passage. When they were halfway through, they heard shooting in the street. After a few more yards they could hear the voices of soldiers coming from a truck stopped in the nearest lane.

They exited from the alley, then ducked quickly behind the large palm trees. Several open trucks were going by, each carrying a few soldiers and many prisoners.

The captured young men already wore marks of beating on their faces and looks of fury in their eyes. Several of them had been wounded by bullets and were bleeding badly. Each had his hands tied behind his back, and all of them were tied together to a long rope. Several of the faces looked familiar to Te. He recognized them as the young people he had seen only a while ago in Yen's house.

"My friends!" Yen's uncle stepped forward. "They arrested all my friends!"

Yen's father held his younger brother tightly.

"You can't help them. You must live for the spirits of our parents."

Yen's uncle struggled. "But I can't be a coward! I must go to my friends!"

"You are a son to our parents first, then a friend to them." Yen's father continued to hold his brother down.

Te had never seen a grown-up cry. He watched Yen's uncle sobbing. He felt sorry for the man he used to fear. He looked at Yen and saw his friend crying silently. He took his friend's hand and squeezed it. Both boys felt the bond of friendship and knew it would last a lifetime.

The group stayed in hiding until the last truck was out of sight. Once they reached Te's home, Mr. Ma moved quickly, dragging a square table to the middle of the living room, setting four chairs around it.

He said to his wife, "Boil water for tea!"

He turned to Te and Yen. "You two go gather all the sweets and nuts, cookies and crackers, then put them in dishes and scatter them all over the living room. Eat all you can while you work, and be sure to throw the wrappings and shells everywhere."

He turned away from the puzzled boys and began to set up a mah-jongg table. "You, you, and you"—he pointed at Yen's father, mother, and uncle—"sit with me and act like we've gambled throughout the night."

He said to the three children. "If anyone asks, just say that you slept, then woke up and played and ate the nuts and sweets. You have not paid any attention to the grown-ups, and have no idea what they have talked about."

The knocking came thirty minutes later. Te's mother answered it. An aged captain looked at the sheets of paper in his hands, then looked at the woman.

"According to my list, a family from Shanghai lives in this house . . ." He watched her closely and waited for her to respond.

"Yes, my husband and I are both from Shanghai," Mrs. Ma answered calmly. In mandarin, the word "I" was pronounced as Wol, but in Shanghai dialect it was A-la. She used A-la to show her origins and it convinced the captain.

He asked what damage the Taiwanese had done to her family last night. She shook her head and answered innocently, "Taiwanese? We don't know any of them. We wouldn't want the barbaric islanders in our house. How could they come and damage anything?"

"There was a revolt . . ." The captain shook his head. He had seen much bloodshed. In every disaster, there were always a few unaware but lucky people. They made him wonder if there was actually a Buddha somewhere, protecting the fortunate ones. He said to the ignorant-looking woman, "All your mainlander neighbors' homes were broken into. You must have heard them scream when they were beaten."

Mrs. Ma was very composed. "My husband, our friends, and I played mah-jongg all night. We took turns to check on the three children, of course. It's my turn to watch over the little monsters now, and that's why I'm not playing. Anyway, the little ones were arguing and making a lot of noise. And we also had the record player on, turned way up because my husband loves that silly old opera. You know, the one about the white sneak. We played the same record over and over . . ."

She rattled on for a while and then said, "We didn't hear a thing. The game is still on. We turned off the record player a while ago or I wouldn't even have heard you at the door."

The captain mumbled, "If you had been listening to the radio instead, you would have heard about the revolt." He shook his head again. "I would like to take a look inside."

"Come in," Mrs. Ma said, and opened the door wide.

The captain looked at the four players. None of them paid any attention to him. The three men and one woman were banging the tiles against the table, cracking seeds, chewing nuts, sucking on candy, and drinking tea. It was a relaxed and typical mah-jongg scene.

The captain glanced at the two boys and the girl playing on the floor among candy wrappers and nutshells. It was a picture of peace and harmony.

The captain looked at the players again and frowned.

The young man must have lost a lot of money, because he looked angry. The young woman must have wanted to win very badly, because her hand shook nervously as she held a tile in midair.

The captain's observant eyes also took in the dark skin of three of these people—could they be Taiwanese? But a mainlander couple would never have invited three Taiwanese for a game of mah-jongg. Besides, even if the dark-skinned ones were Taiwanese, since it was obvious that they had played mah-jongg all night, of course they couldn't have been involved in the bloody revolt.

The captain ordered his men to leave the house. It was not that he had found nothing questionable. But he was convinced that no mainlander would help the Taiwanese—just as it was true the other way around.

As soon as the men were gone, the door was bolted from inside. The mah-jongg players left the table instantly. The adults stood shakily, and the children ran to their parents.

Te went to his mother first. "Mama! I didn't know you were an actress! You were great!"

He then told his father, "Baba, we fooled them! We won! You were so brave and clever!"

His father answered in a low, unsteady voice, "Clever? That was the dumbest thing I ever did in my entire life! My son, I will never act so recklessly again, not even for you, my one and only son! And you would do well to remember that!"

7

1952, Honolulu

WAIKIKI BEACH changed its appearance drastically after sunset. When nature's beauty was shrouded by darkness, city lights gave the island an artificial glow, turning the paradise into a man-made stage.

In the gleam of the first neon light, a noisy group appeared on Kalakawa Avenue, the broad street that ran parallel to the ocean. They were long-haired island boys in tight jeans and colorful shirts, with brown complexions and dark hair. They talked loudly as they dominated the sidewalk and forced other pedestrians into detouring around them. Their hatred for the haoles was clearly visible—when they elbowed white people out of their way, they smiled at one another in victory.

Among them was Paala Nihoa, a seventeen-year-old young man. His clothes and hairstyle resembled his friends', but his body was noticeably well-built and his face extremely handsome. He stood out from the group like a tall tree in a clump of shrubbery. People couldn't help looking at him. But he returned their admiration with angry glares.

An elderly woman, obviously a tourist, looked at Paala's striking young face and smiled at him with a visitor's innocent adoration for all the beautiful things on the paradise island. Her white skin brought instant detestation to Paala's eyes. He abruptly stopped moving, and his group stopped with him.

He faced the woman, stared at her. "Are you looking at the scar on my face?" His voice was cold as ice and sharp as a knife. "For your information, it was left there by the hands of four men of your own kind!" He leaned close to the woman and enjoyed her shocked expression.

The woman quickly walked away. Paala's group laughed. Halaki, a fourteen-year-old boy and the youngest of the group, pulled Paala's arm and said hesitantly, "Paala, you don't really believe what you said to her, do you? Because there is no scar on your face . . ." He looked up at Paala, then added sincerely, "No scar at all."

Paala threw his head back and laughed. "I know, little Halaki." He tousled his younger friend's black hair fondly. "Three years may be long enough to erase the knife mark from my face, but not the scar from my heart." He hit his palm with his fist, saying through clenched teeth, "I'll always remember that day on the beach, and I'll hate the white bastards forever!"

Paala and his friends were all children from families with various problems. Halaki's parents were dead, and his relatives were not very kind to him. The weak younger boy looked up to Paala and seldom disagreed with anything Paala said, but now he frowned and said in a low voice, "I don't think Sumiko likes you to hate anyone so much . . ." Halaki blushed and stopped. He had met Sumiko only a few times, but had developed a crush on her.

"Who cares what Sumiko thinks? She is but a girl!" Paala shrugged.

As he spoke those words, Paala felt guilty. He quickened his steps, and his thick brows furrowed deeper. His parents had moved to Maui Island, and he had stayed in Oahu just to be near Sumiko. He loved her even more deeply now than he had three years ago. But he would not tell her. He wanted to be a big tough man in her eyes instead of a soft little sissy to be toyed with by a girl's delicate fingers. The mere fact that Halaki had mentioned Sumiko bothered Paala. Was it so obvious that he was in love? He turned to Halaki and repeated loudly, "Sumiko is but a girl, and I have plenty of girls following me around!"

At Paala's raised voice, Halaki lowered his eyes. But the skinny boy was stubborn. Paala's anger couldn't stop him from murmuring, "Sumiko is much more than just a girl. She is more beautiful than any other girl in the world. And she is also the sweetest and nicest girl I've ever met."

Halaki's comment brought a mumbled agreement from the crowd. "Sumiko Yamada is all right. But her mother, that lawyer Mrs. Yamada, is a bitch!"

Paala bit his lip at the mention of Mrs. Yamada. How he hated that woman!

Three years ago, when Paala had opened his eyes in the hospital, it was Mrs. Yamada's face that he saw first. She had just become a state prosecutor at the time. She had promised Paala that she would do her best to bring the four arrested white men to justice, but had warned Paala that when he left the hospital he must not think of personal revenge.

"Racial differences can be settled only through tolerance and understanding. I can't allow you, Sumiko, or my two boys to be involved in a racially motivated gang fight."

Paala had cast aside Mrs. Yamada's warning as soon as he left the hospital. He had formed a group of island boys who called themselves the Oahu Hawks. They had fought all the haoles they could corner, then began to do much more. They had pressured some store owners into giving them weekly payoffs, and petrified tourists on deserted beaches into surrendering their purses and billfolds.

Two years ago, when Paala's actions had been discovered by Mrs. Yamada, she moved the Nihoas out of her servants' quarters to sever the bond between Paala and Sumiko. She had fired Paala's parents and the Nihoas moved back to their home island to live in a small hut. Paala had become a homeless boy on Oahu Island.

For two years now Paala had been living on his own. He had been toughened by life and hardened by struggle, and each time he was beaten by the cold world he blamed the defeat on Mrs. Yamada. Some of the other gang members had encountered the state prosecutor in unpleasant situations, and all agreed with Paala's assessment of the unbending iron lady.

"Yes, that Yamada woman is a bitch!" Paala agreed, then said a hasty good-bye to the other Oahu Hawks.

He headed toward Hotel Street, was soon at the edge of Chinatown.

Honolulu's Chinatown had once been known for its filth, its dwellings notorious for their disease-carrying rats. The white men had given orders to burn down the whole area, and started a fire in the center of this district. While the dying rats screeched, the Chinese screamed and managed to save a few buildings that bordered the zone. Through the years new structures had replaced burned ones, but the salvaged ones become the affordable rooming houses for the poor.

Paala hurried toward a two-story wooden building. A yellow streetlamp shone on the old house. The whole structure was tilted to one side and looked ready to crumble at any time. The outside had not been painted for several decades, and its roof still showed traces of that old fire. The inside had received minimal maintenance to satisfy the health department.

An unpleasant odor greeted Paala as soon as he entered the front door. He ran through a dark narrow hall with closed doors on both sides, climbed an even darker stairway. The second floor was identical to the first, but smelled even worse. He fumbled for his key as he counted the doors to his left.

His room was pitch black. Paala waved his hand in the air, found a dangling string. A naked bulb lighted up, revealing a windowless closet-size room that contained nothing but a cot. Paala knelt beside the cot and pulled out a cardboard box. Inside was his entire wardrobe. He grabbed a set of clean clothes including underwear and socks, then left his room and raced to the public bathroom at the end of the hall.

There was never any hot water. Standing under the weak cold shower, Paala closed his eyes and whispered, "Sumiko, I love you. I'm sure you know how I feel about you, even without my ever telling you."

Twenty minutes later, Paala, scrubbed clean, was on a bus to Thomas Square.

Thomas Square was a small area embraced by banyan trees, with a water fountain and several white benches. It stood undisturbed by the night traffic on Beretania Street, a peaceful island floating in a rushing sea. Across from the square was a brightly lighted stone building with a tile roof—the Honolulu Academy of Arts.

The many exhibition halls were surrounded by a large garden. At the west end a banana grove stood as a backdrop for the marble statues of a young Oriental warrior and a woman.

Myriad lights shone on the handsome man clothed in uniform and the beautiful woman in a long robe. He was about to touch her, one of his strong hands only an inch from her shoulder. Her head was turned to look at him with a mystic smile, as if to say that she would always be beyond his reach. She was in the process of changing into one of the grove's banana trees. Her flying long hair already resembled a leaf; one of her pretty legs exposed by her parted garment was almost a tree trunk.

Sumiko Yamada stood staring at the statues, recalling the sad story. He was a Japanese prince, she a peasant girl. He wanted her as one of his many ladies-in-waiting, but she didn't want to be his; she was in love with a peasant boy. When he was about to catch her, she willed herself to become a banana tree.

"If anyone takes me from Paala, I'll try to turn into a tree," Sumiko said with a sigh.

In the past three years she had grown taller and much thinner. Her round face had become oval. Her cheekbones were more prominent and her almond eyes larger. Three years ago she had smiled a lot, two dimples always dancing beside her narrow mouth. Now her lips were frequently a tight line and she often frowned.

She frowned again when she looked at her watch. Paala was late again. "Roaming the streets with the Hawks? Doing things you won't tell me about? Why do you treat me like this when you know I love you so much?" she murmured.

Sumiko's mother wanted her daughter to have all the things she herself had never had as a child, so arranged many activities for Sumiko, including dancing and piano lessons, plus weekly art lessons at the academy. On Wednesday nights Sumiko always managed to meet Paala in the academy, although he usually kept her waiting.

She looked at her watch again. "Paala, you're not arrested again?"

His voice came from behind her, "Of course I am not arrested! Do you think I'm dumber than the stupid police?"

Sumiko turned, and all her misery was gone. She threw her arms around Paala, hugged him tightly, and leaned her face against his heart. "Paala!" She closed her eyes. He never liked to see her cry, but she couldn't keep her voice from trembling. "I've missed you so much since last Wednesday."

Paala tightened his embrace on Sumiko. He had missed her too, but he wouldn't tell her. She would cry, and then he would have to spend their brief moments together drying her tears.

"I have good news," he said, and held her away from him to look at her beautiful face. "I will start on a good job next week."

"A good job? Better than all the others? What will you do this time?" Sumiko didn't sound enthusiastic.

In the past years, besides getting money from the store owners and tourists, Paala had worked on many jobs. None of them had been more than common labor, and the pay had never been sufficient for his rent and food.

Paala said, "I'll be working with Halaki."

"In a band?" Sumiko's eyes brightened. Halaki was the drummer in an unknown small band formed by island teenagers to play in nightclubs. Sumiko liked the shy and soft-spoken Halaki—he was the only member of the Oahu Hawks that didn't frighten her.

"Yes. I'll play guitar in the background," Paala said. "The guitar player quit. Halaki took me to the bandleader, and I got the job." He smiled proudly. He had taught himself to play the old guitar he'd bought at the Goodwill Store.

"Will they pay you very well?" Sumiko asked eagerly.

"No, but I'll be doing what I like. And I'll learn more about music. Who knows? Maybe someday I'll become rich and famous." He shrugged, then went on to tell Sumiko that the band would be playing in a small nightclub in a second-rate hotel. "It'll be great if you can come to hear me . . . us, I mean. Because I don't have any solo part, not yet." He shook her softly. "Please try to come. Make an excuse. Lie a little. Bring your brothers if you must. That kind of nightclub is not very strict—even minors can get in."

"I'll do my best," Sumiko promised with a bright smile. Then her smile faded as she looked at her watch again.

Sumiko wanted to avoid trouble, and there would be plenty of trouble if her art teacher told Mrs. Yamada that she was late for her lesson.

They looked at each other and felt the deep sorrow of parting, although Paala tried to hide it. Their time together was always so short. After Paala's last arrest, Mrs. Yamada had bailed him out of prison but had forbidden Sumiko to see him ever again. Now they could meet only once a week for a few minutes.

Paala squared his broad shoulders and acted unconcerned as he walked Sumiko to her classroom. They parted with a quick kiss, and when Sumiko turned at the door to wave, Paala was already gone.

Outside the classroom window, from the deep shadow of the trees, Paala watched her for a while, then walked away slowly, his heart aching with sorrow and despair.

The stage was small. The young lead singer held the microphone to his lips, but still his voice was almost drowned by the customers, who never stopped talking or placing orders. They were called Hamburger Tourists by the islanders because they came to visit Hawaii on a tight budget. The first-class nightclubs featuring famous entertainers were beyond their reach, so they were in this place. But they were not truly entertained by the amateur musicians, so they continued to talk.

''I can't make out a word. Is he singing in English?''

''Look at the band members. Some of them look like children!''

Their voices reached Sumiko's ears. She wanted to stand up and scream for them to shut up. But a true lady must never scream, so Sumiko whispered instead, ''Please lower your voices. Soon you'll hear my Paala playing his guitar. He is very good, really.'' She was almost crying because she could see how angry Paala was onstage, standing in the shadow of a big cello, in the band uniform of white pants and an ''Aloha'' shirt.

''You dragged us here to hear this?'' her older brother, Kitaro, asked. ''Where is our ex-gardener's son? I can't even find him!''

''Over there.'' Sumiko pointed at the big cello. ''And don't call him our ex-gardener's son. The four of us used to play together as children, and you know very well his name is Paala!''

''Is he playing? I can't hear a note!'' her younger brother, Genkai, said, and laughed. ''From his expression, it looks like he is about to pick a fight with his audience instead of serenading them!''

Tears fell from Sumiko's eyes. She should have known better than to expect the boys to be nice to Paala. But without them she would never have received permission from her mother to come out at night. Mrs. Yamada didn't want her daughter to know the dangerous world or the sugarcane field that had been a part of her own life.

Kitaro saw her tears and softened his voice. "Sumiko, you really should forget Paala." He took his sister's hand in his. "We are not children anymore. Our playing days are over."

"No!" Sumiko shook her head. More tears fell from her large eyes.

"Listen to me," Kitaro said while drying Sumiko's tears with a napkin. "When we were children, we were equal to one another even though Paala was the son of our gardener and housekeeper. Our unequal status began when he went off in the wrong direction—"

Sumiko interrupted her brother. "By wrong direction, you mean he doesn't want to be a doctor like you or an attorney like Genkai."

Kitaro shook his head. "No. If Paala wants to be a musician, that's all right too. But he should take music lessons and aim at becoming a composer or performer. And then we'll be equals again. . . ." He continued to lecture his younger sister.

Kitaro was only fifteen, Genkai thirteen. Like most Japanese and Chinese boys in Hawaii, they knew exactly what they wanted out of life: to study hard and enter a profession, then work diligently and become rich and important.

The two boys ignored the music. They talked about a business tycoon on the island, a Chinese named Sung Quanming, who was very close to the Yamada family.

Kitaro said, "In Mr. Sung's generation, and even the generation of our mother, things were much tougher for the Asians. Now we can be anything we want to be, as long as we work hard." He looked at his sister with love. "Our mother has great plans for you. Genkai and I can't let you throw away a good life for Paala. We all love you."

Sumiko bowed her head. She felt helpless when her mother or brothers used the word "love" to persuade her.

Kitaro picked up the bill and stood. Genkai followed him. They waited for Sumiko. "Let's go," Kitaro said. "We are too young to be in a place like this."

Sumiko didn't want to go. But she stood up anyway. She never fought with her brothers. She didn't know how. She wished Paala could fight for her. She looked at him onstage, found him far away from her, shadowed by that big cello. She raised a hand to wave good-bye.

After the three well-dressed young people walked out of the club, the other customers stopped talking and turned to look at the guitar player.

The good-looking young Hawaiian suddenly drummed his fingers over the guitar strings so loudly that his notes overpowered the band and the singer. His sad and angry face was so forceful that it stirred up confusion in even the most nonchalant hearts.

The nightclub manager stared at the young man and began to speculate on ways to bring in more customers.

PART II

8

Spring 1955

THE BIRDS LEFT their nests when the night sky showed the first glimpse of morning gray. Qing heard them chirping and opened her eyes. She sat up on her cot, reached into the darkness for the clothes piled on a stool.

The baggy pants were rough against her bare legs, the loose blouse coarse. As she dressed quickly, for a fleeting moment she recalled her days in silk. But those days had become as unclear as the objects in this unlit room. She was no longer certain if at one time she had actually been the granddaughter of the wealthiest man in White Stone.

Her hands touched a strip of worn cloth sewn into a wide armband. She sighed as she put her left hand through it. "Yes, it's written on this band: 'Descendant of a Filthy Landlord'—that's who I am, and I was indeed rich at one time."

She had been wearing this very same black armband for almost six years now. She had grown, and the once loose band was now tight. It had been torn and patched together many times. But the party had not given permission for her to stop wearing it, and she dared not remove it on her own.

Qing lit an oil lamp, carried it to the kitchen, and started breakfast. As she washed the rice in a bamboo colander, she remembered the day that Fan Yu had returned from the town hall and said to her and Kuei, "The senior party member granted my request to keep Qing in our house. The jail is crowded with the older imperialistic pigs, so there is no room for all their children. He likes the idea of making her an example of Fan Shen and he will do the same to about two dozen other children of the filthy rich."

Two dozen black armbands had been made, each bearing white characters to identify their wearers' shameful status. The descendants of the people's enemies had been ordered to live in the streets, exist on scraps of food, carry out the hardest labor. More than half of them had died. The survivors were all in poor health and treated viciously by the villagers. Each time Qing saw one, she realized how lucky she was.

Qing began to make the rice gruel. Six years ago she hadn't known how to do anything, but Kuei had taught her patiently to cook, to wash, and to clean.

When the rice gruel began to boil, Qing steamed some vegetables and dished out a small salted fish from a tightly sealed jar. She was cutting the hard-boiled duck eggs into small wedges when she glanced at the window. The outside darkness had turned the glass into a mirror.

She stared at a fifteen-year-old girl with a heart-shaped face, very large eyes, and a rather narrow mouth. Her hair was short, her body thin, her legs long. Although the window was not a real mirror, Qing could still tell that her skin was tanned a deep brown.

"Kuei was only trying to be nice when he said I was pretty," Qing whispered with a sigh. "If my grandmother could see me, she would tell me that I am not a pale and beautiful lady, but a dark and ugly peasant."

She sighed again at the thought of her deceased grandmother. She had never returned to the graveyard to burn anything. Burial was outlawed, the burning of paper representations forbidden. All the dead had been cremated, and Fan Yu was no longer a gravedigger. He worked in the town hall as an assistant to the party members of much higher rank.

Qing poured boiling water into the teapot, and the steam moistened her eyes. She blinked, but her eyes became misty again at the thought of her living family kept in the local prison all these years. According to Fan Yu, a lot of paperwork was needed to transport them to the labor camps in the north. With the weight of bureaucracy, paperwork dragged to almost a standstill.

Qing was never allowed to visit them, but had heard that all the prisoners were at the mercy of the guards, who enjoyed torturing people.

She dried her eyes quickly when Fan Yu and Kuei appeared.

The three ate in silence. Qing did all the serving. When the men's rice bowls or teacups were empty, she stood up quickly.

When she refilled Kuei's rice bowl once more, he smiled at her. "It's nice to have you here. I've almost forgotten the days when Baba and I had to cook and serve ourselves."

Fan Yu nodded at Qing approvingly. "And I cannot believe that at one time you were rich and useless. Talking about being rich and useless, I have to tell you something about your family."

Qing held her breath. She watched Fan Yu drink more tea. She waited patiently.

Fan Yu put down his teacup. "When I came home from the town hall last night, it was near midnight and you were already asleep." He looked at Qing. "Your family is leaving White Stone today. Your grandfather is going to an iron mine in Inner Mongolia, the rest of them to the desert land in Xinjiang."

Qing shivered. It was common knowledge to the Pearl River people that only the northern barbarians were tough enough to endure the freezing weather in Inner Mongolia and Xinjiang. The delicate southerners would not last long.

They finished eating and Qing did the dishes quickly. The three walked to the town square. Fan Yu went to the town hall, Qing and Kuei to the temple grounds.

The remains of the temple had been knocked down six years ago, and the villagers had just now begun to level the land and turn it into a rice field. Everything had moved in slow motion in the past years. The government had created many new policies, and each policy had turned the villagers in a different direction. None of the policies had improved living conditions, but each year the White Stone people started something new. This year's aim was to save the new China with a Land Reform Policy.

Qing and Kuei worked side by side. She used her hands to dig out the bricks and stones; he carried them away to the dumping ground. Kuei was twenty. The other men in the field were either his age or much older. When China had joined the Korean War five years ago, many of the White Stone young men had been sent to North Korea and died there. Kuei was considered too young then, and his father too old.

Everyone worked in silence, but the air was far from silent. A loudspeaker installed on a post in the middle of the field blared: "May Chairman Mao live to be ten thousand! May the People's Republic of China live forever! May Taiwan be liberated soon!" The same words were screamed out every few minutes, followed by one of the patriotic songs.

The morning sun moved to mid-sky. Qing's fingers were raw. Her legs had gone to sleep and her back was sore. She clenched her teeth and worked on. From the corner of her eye she saw that the others were also exhausted, including those who had farmed all their lives.

In between the slogans and songs she heard an old farmer say, "When we farmed for the landlords, we were free to stretch or yawn or take a break. Now we work for the government and don't dare to stop for one minute. There is no telling who will report us to the party, and then we will be criticized in the next meeting . . ." He realized he was in danger and hushed in mid-sentence.

Qing felt a soft tap on her back and looked up to see Kuei. He smiled at her, then continued with his work, carrying a long pole over his shoulder, balancing two large baskets full of gravel. That single gentle tap eased away Qing's misery. Her back didn't hurt so much anymore. Her eyes followed Kuei, and she thought that he was the best-looking man in White Stone.

"My brother, my friend, my teacher, and my protector . . ." she called softly.

There was a sudden silence. Everyone stopped working, straightened, and waited anxiously. When the loudspeaker was turned off, it meant there would be an announcement. The people of White Stone were afraid of announcements these days—usually the signal that their already impossible lives were to become even more miserable.

"My people in White Stone, listen carefully," a male voice droned. "You will go to the train station now to see the imperialist pigs leaving your village. This will be your last chance to Chin Shwan them and to get even with them for their evil deeds."

The prisoners were led out of jail, ordered to march in single file. One of the comrades had decided to make it more dramatic by having a young man lead the procession and bang on a gong.

"Down with the feudal lords! Gone are the filthy rich! Equality for everyone in the People's Republic!" shouted the party members as they raised their fists.

The villagers repeated every word, without truly understanding what they were shouting about. Qing raised a fist also. As she shouted, she searched for her family.

It wasn't easy to tell one prisoner from another. The jail had melted away everyone's individuality. They walked with their heads bowed and shoulders hunched, dragging their heavy feet, dangling their stiff arms, showing no expression either on their numb faces or in their dull eyes.

At first Qing thought they were all men, then realized it was because their heads were shaved and they were all dressed the same—in gray pants and matching sleeveless shirts with large numbers stamped on the back.

"My grandfather?" Qing said, staring at the profile of one of the prisoners.

The man turned. Qing saw his full face and she gasped. Six years ago her grandfather had been in his mid-fifties. Now he looked more than eighty. He had always been pleasantly plump; this aged person was a skeleton.

"His eye!" she screamed. "They blinded one of his eyes!" She began to run toward the procession.

"Stop!" Fan Kuei grabbed her hand, his fingers like a handcuff. "Do you want to go to Inner Mongolia with him?"

Qing stood still and cried helplessly. In her blurred vision appeared the rest of her family. Her uncles and aunts and cousins had changed just as much as her grandfather. Even her cousins had gone from childhood directly into middle age.

"Hurry up and join the others!" Kuei let go of her wrist, nudged her with his elbow. "Pick up a rock!"

As rocks were thrown at the prisoners by the bystanders, several uniformed men watched hawk-eyed to see who was not participating.

"Hurry!" Kuei pushed a rock into Qing's hand.

She took the rock, looked at its sharp edges, and hesitated. How could she?

"The comrade is looking at you now. Do it or you'll get in trouble!" Kuei urged as he continued to throw one rock after another.

Qing closed her eyes when she threw the rock.

She opened her eyes just in time to see her grandfather being hit on the side of the head. He stumbled, raised a hand to cover his wound, then struggled on. Just before he was out of Qing's sight, she saw blood oozing from between his fingers, streaming down the back of his hand.

Qing screamed, "I hit him!"

Guilt stabbed her. She pressed a hand against her heart but couldn't stop the pain.

Fear chilled her and made her shake. According to tradition, those who raised a hand to their elders would be struck by lightning and electrocuted.

"You didn't hurt him. Your rock fell ten feet from him," Kuei said, and picked up two more rocks, one for himself and the other for her. "Now, shout something!"

Qing's eyes met the observing eyes of the comrade. "Down with the filthy landlord!" she screamed, tears streaming down her face, and then threw the rock.

"You're doing better now. Keep up the good work," Fan Kuei said, giving Qing more rocks.

Qing soon discovered that the banging gong and the jeering crowd were so loud that as long as she pretended to shout, no one could hear her soft-spoken words.

"I'm sorry, Grandfather!" she whispered as she threw the next rock.

"Try your best to survive, my uncles and aunts," she murmured with the following rock.

"Maybe we'll meet again, my dear cousins," she mumbled as she threw the last rock.

9

PALI MOUNTAIN was shaped like a giant pagoda, its peak proudly in the clouds.

A winding road led to the mountaintop, where a gazebo stood. The nearby flowering trees were much older than the gazebo. Their branches embraced the building like loving arms, offering the gazebo bouquets of fragrant blossoms.

A small white car zigzagged up the road, passed through the low-flying clouds, stopped at the rim of the peak. A young girl got out, wearing a short pink skirt and a sleeveless white blouse.

Sumiko Yamada had not been driving long. She was only seventeen. She turned her head to see if she had parked properly, then continued to walk toward the gazebo.

The evening sun shone on her slender figure. Her face was porcelain white, small, with a pointed chin and prominent cheekbones. Her large and slanted almond eyes were frequently filled with sorrow, her dark and softly curved eyebrows often gathered in a frown.

A smile appeared on her sad face when she saw the beautiful flowers on the plumeria trees. Two dimples appeared on each side of her narrow mouth. Those dimples became twin wells filled with enchanting dreams, and her face glowed with expectation: she would see her Paala soon.

She raced to the gazebo, was immediately surrounded by an ocean of her most favorite flowers. She wore no jewelry. She wanted to pick a plumeria to adorn her long straight hair, which was hanging loose. She debated among the multicolored petals. Pink, white, yellow, lavender . . . She was not very good at making decisions. It took her a long time to decide on pink.

She searched until her eyes stopped at the most perfectly shaped one. But it was just beyond her reach. She stood on her toes and extended her arm.

"I see that you can use some help," a low voice came from behind her.

She turned and saw Paala only a few yards away, walking toward her in the golden sunlight.

He had grown much taller in the past few years. He was now six-foot-one. Besides working in the band, he had continued to swim and surf. His body was sculptured to remind Sumiko of the classical statues in the academy.

Unlike the marble statues, Paala had on a red sport shirt and faded jeans. The shirt was skintight and revealed shoulders that were solid and broad, a chest that was thick and wide. His muscled arms filled the short sleeves that were rolled even shorter. His long legs seemed choked in his snug-fit jeans. Imitation gold glistened on his chest; many thick chains could be seen through the low opening of his shirt collar.

His rich black hair was long enough to curl around the nape of his neck. He had on mirrored sunglasses but removed them when he was closer to Sumiko. A wild look shone in his eyes and a twisted smile curved his lips.

"Paala!" Sumiko threw her arms around him, kissed him on the mouth. "You have to be especially good to me today. My mother gave me a hard time again."

"What does she want now?" He held her tightly, kissed her tenderly.

She sighed. "She brought up the same threat again—she wants me to go to San Francisco to some of her old friends."

Paala was immediately angry. "Why does your mother want to put an ocean between us? Why is she still so strongly against me? I stopped seeing the Oahu Hawks boys over a year ago."

Sumiko gave him a kiss instead of an answer. She touched his face lovingly. Sorrow returned to her eyes. Paala had stopped seeing the gang when his father died. His mother had died six months after that. Now Paala had no one but her. Sumiko vaguely remembered the deaths of her natural parents. Mrs. Yamada had adopted her and been good to her, which made it even more difficult for Sumiko to do things against her wishes.

"That woman still sees me as a ruthless avenger." Paala held Sumiko's face in his large palms and looked into her eyes.

Sumiko nodded. "She doesn't believe you've changed. Give her time, and she will see you the way I do, really."

Paala sighed. For the past year he had tried his best to stay out of trouble. In one more year Sumiko would be eighteen. By then he would need Mrs. Yamada's permission to marry Sumiko. How could he produce such a miracle in a year's time?

He reached easily for the flower Sumiko had been unable to pick and helped her pin it to her hair.

They left the gazebo and walked to the fringe of the mountaintop. Clouds surrounded them, showered them with a fine mist. Wind wrapped them in strong arms, rocked them back and forth singing a haunting lullaby.

Beneath their eyes, the island lay in the setting sun, and beyond that, the ocean glittered in the slanting golden rays.

Paala said firmly, "When you are eighteen, we'll be married, with or without her approval." He held her with one arm, waved the other arm to point at the scene below. "Somewhere down there is a little home for us. Maybe at the foot of that little hill. Or perhaps right beside that rippling stream. I'll earn enough money to buy a piece of land, and then build you a house with my love and my hands."

He turned to face her, held her in his arms. "You don't mind living in a house that has only one room, do you? That'll be all I can afford, as long as I'm still one of the many unknown entertainers on this island."

"I don't mind if it's a tree house in one of these plumeria trees. We'll be happy, and so will our children . . . there will be many of them." Sumiko leaned her face against his heart.

There was no one on top of the mountain but the two of them. He kissed her harder, and gradually they lowered themselves to the grass-covered ground. It had rained the night before, and the ground was softened by moisture. For a brief moment Sumiko worried about the grass staining her skirt; then those worries were pushed away by Paala's more passionate kisses.

"A year is a long time . . . almost an eternity," Paala said between kisses, breathing hard. At age twenty he had a fair amount of sexual experience, but never with Sumiko. "You are special to me . . . so very special that I've been waiting for our wedding night . . . but it's been such a painful wait. I'm not sure I can live through another year."

With her eyes tightly closed, Sumiko felt Paala's warm hands burning through her clothes, branding her flesh. They touched her breasts first, then moved to her thighs. She heard a voice calling her back to her senses; it was the voice of her mother, the forever cool and sensible Mrs. Yamada. *But, Mama, I'll be Paala's wife sooner or later,* Sumiko argued silently, and the voice of her mother faded away.

Sumiko opened her eyes and saw herself and Paala wrapped in a thick mist. She was dazed by the beautiful scene. She whispered, "Paala, look. An unseen hand has reached down from heaven and made our wedding bed. It gave us a mattress of clouds, then covered us with a quilt of vapor to shield us from all observing eyes. We are married, Paala—I feel it so strongly I know it's true!"

Her words convinced Paala, made him feel the same as she did—that they were already husband and wife. He undressed her gently, then hurriedly removed his own clothes. The warm wind caressed their naked bodies, awoke from within them the hunger that had been long suppressed. They felt like two island youths of many centuries ago, freed from civilized conventions. He entered her swiftly and they became one. Her soft cry of pain soon melted away. When his desire was satisfied, he made love to her again, and this time he showed her patiently the joy of pillowing. Gradually she relaxed and moaned faintly with delight.

"You are my wife now," Paala said. "Shall we tell the world about our marriage, or keep it to ourselves for another year?"

Sumiko answered hesitantly, "Let's wait. The world won't accept our marriage without a ceremony. And we must not hurt my mother's feelings . . ." She stopped when she saw him frown disapprovingly.

Paala gave Sumiko her clothes when the wind turned cold. They had to leave the beautiful spot before the sun sank below the horizon. They walked with their arms around each other, passed the gazebo, and reached the two parked cars. She got into the new white car, he into the rusted old one. She followed him down the mountain road. At the foot of Pali Mountain they turned in opposite directions, she toward Aiea Heights, he toward downtown Honolulu.

Sumiko walked into the living room, where her mother and two brothers were watching television.

Mrs. Yamada looked at the wall clock immediately. "So you were with him again."

Sumiko answered in a low voice tinged with guilt. "Yes, Mama. Paala and I love each other. We have to meet. And we . . ." She wanted to tell the truth, but looked at her mother's face and left her sentence unfinished.

Two years ago Sumiko had gathered enough courage to confess to her mother that she had never stopped seeing Paala. She had further declared that she must continue to see him. Mrs. Yamada had been greatly distressed, yet agreed that Sumiko was no longer a child. She had allowed Sumiko to meet Paala now and then, but insisted on a detailed report each time.

Mrs. Yamada said, "Where did you go and what did you do?" She examined Sumiko's clothes with sharp eyes. Her heart sank when she noticed Sumiko's wrinkled skirt.

"We went to the Pali lookout, talked, and then I came home," Sumiko answered vaguely, then tried to walk away.

Genkai stood up, turned off the TV. Kitaro joined him. They came to Sumiko, looked at her from head to foot and back to head—a team of examiners eager to know if Paala had damaged their precious sister. But their boyish eyes detected nothing.

"You're very beautiful, sis," the sixteen-year-old Genkai said. "It's a shame that instead of going to a fancy restaurant to eat an expensive dinner, you went to the Pali to swallow wind."

"That's right, Sumiko." The eighteen-year-old Kitaro nodded his agreement. "You should date one of the young lawyers Mama brings home for you, or one of my friends in premed."

Sumiko's eyes were filled with tears. She stared at her brothers, but didn't know how to fight them. She walked away from her family, entered the music room, closed the door.

She didn't hear the hushed gasp from her mother. Mrs. Yamada had noticed the stained skirt and observed the unnatural way Sumiko moved her legs.

Mrs. Yamada didn't say anything to her sons. She remained seated and thought deeply. She knew what Sumiko and Paala must have done, although she couldn't prove it. Mrs. Yamada didn't believe that a girl must marry the same man who took her virginity. She had always felt certain that Paala was wrong for Sumiko, and was now determined to separate the lovers before it was really too late.

Sumiko sat on the piano bench, began to play. She played well. Her teachers had told her so. Mrs. Yamada wished for her to be a music major, but she wanted to go to nursing school. She had always liked the idea of being a nurse. When Paala and she were married next year, could she still ask her mother to put her through nursing school? She considered the possibility as she played, and smiled deeply when she imagined the bright future waiting for her and Paala. She was his woman now. Now she never needed to worry about losing him to another beautiful girl. She and Paala would soon have a warm home and many children.

Sumiko continued to play as her thoughts drifted to a year ago, when Paala had mentioned marriage for the first time. It was her sixteenth birthday. He had taken her to a nice dinner. She had on her first formal. The white lace was gathered at her waist with a pale blue ribbon. She and Paala had left the restaurant and gone to the beach and walked on the deserted Waikiki. A full moon had glistened over them, the tide whispered nearby. He had held her face in his hands, looked into her eyes for a long time. He had then kissed her on the mouth, the way a man would kiss a woman. It had been hard for them to curb their desire for each other even then. Now Sumiko whispered as she blushed deeply, "If we hadn't waited, then I could have known the ultimate pleasure of life much earlier."

The dressing room was the size of a closet. Paala took off his jeans and shirt, put on a pair of white satin pants and a matching white shirt adorned with glass beads.

As he combed his hair, he could hear the band playing onstage, especially the fast-beating drum of his best friend, Halaki, who was also his current roommate and the only member of the Oahu Hawks he still saw. He felt guilty that he was now the lead singer and Halaki was still just a backup drummer. Soon after Paala had begun to play in the band, he had caught the attention of the manager and been given a solo guitar part. A year later, when the lead singer was absent, Paala had taken his place, and the audience had applauded him. He had been singing in this little place ever since.

Paala picked up his guitar and headed for the stage. Before he reached the microphone, he was stopped by a waiter.

"From the same lady," the waiter said, giving him a folded sheet of paper, then pointing at a large middle-aged woman in the audience.

Paala opened the note: "Want to have dinner with me?" It was unsigned.

"Tell her to go to hell!" Paala crumpled the note and threw it to the floor.

The band played softly as his backup. He played a few notes on his guitar, then began to sing. He couldn't avoid seeing the woman with dyed blond hair, because she was sitting by herself at a table front-row-center.

Tonight she wore a short tight green dress. Her perfume was so strong that the musicians on the bandstand were choked by it. She smiled broadly, didn't seem to be bothered by Paala's newest refusal. For about a week now she had appeared every night, and each night she had sent Paala a note with a similar request.

Paala continued to sing, and thought of Pali Mountain. It was heavenly to hold Sumiko in his arms and make her completely his. He closed his eyes. The audience disappeared. Once again he felt the clouds and heard the wind. He raised his voice.

It was a song for him and Sumiko alone; it was their wedding song. He sang with his heart, composed the words and melody as he went. The band members were young and unknown islanders, but talented. They managed to follow him. When the song reached its end, Paala opened his eyes. He was drowned in a sea of applause.

When he bowed, he noticed the woman in green was gone.

Paala returned to his apartment after midnight. He and Halaki now shared a room in a building much better than their old place. He showered and went to sleep, didn't pay any attention to Halaki's empty bed: Halaki was a careful young man who could do nothing worse than going with the other musicians for a nightcap.

Paala slept soundly until someone banged on his door. He glanced at the clock on his way to answer it; it was only eight.

Two of his musician friends entered the apartment, a saxophonist and a guitarist. Their faces were wet with tears, their jaws tightened, their hands clenched into fists.

"They killed Halaki!" the saxophonist said.

"What?" Paala stared at them.

"Haole soldiers killed Halaki!" said the guitarist.

"Impossible!" Paala shook his head quickly. "Halaki has nothing to do with them. He doesn't even know any of them."

The saxophonist said, "They killed him anyway. They said he asked an officer's wife to go for a walk on the beach, then suddenly attacked her. The soldiers were on leave. They passed the two and saw them struggle. They helped the woman. Halaki fought with them and drew a knife. They killed him in self-defense."

"But Halaki didn't even own a knife! And he would never attack a woman. He was so shy that I don't believe he would ask any woman for a walk on the beach!" Paala stopped abruptly. His eyes opened wide. "Did anyone see Halaki leaving the club with a woman?"

The guitarist said, "Halaki talked to me before he left with her. He said she sent him a note, and he felt it rude to refuse a lady, although she was about twice his age."

The saxophonist said, "I saw them leave. I recognized the woman. You might have noticed her too. A big blond woman sitting at the center table every night, and tonight she wore a green dress."

Paala said through clenched teeth, "Yes, I noticed her!"

The death of his friend began to sink in. He tilted his head back and screamed, "Halaki! I can't let you die like this!"

The saxophonist extended a hand toward Paala. "Neither can we. That's why we are here."

The guitarist also gave his hand to Paala. "We came to see you as soon as we heard the news. We know you feel exactly the way we do. Let's go gather more kamaainas. We must show the haoles we can't be stepped on like ants."

Paala stared at the hands of his two friends. He remembered how he had sworn by his father's deathbed that he would never fight again. He could see Sumiko's face brighten when he had told her about his promise. He hesitated. But then he saw in his imagination the face of Halaki, and heard the boy's voice calling faintly, "Paala, I didn't attack her. She attacked me. The others came, and she lied. Paala, my friend, please avenge me."

Sumiko's face faded away. Paala took the hands of his friends, shook them firmly.

As the three charged out the door, Sumiko's face appeared in Paala's mind one more time. Paala opened his mouth to say something to his friends, but he could never back away from a handshake.

Sumiko was in the living room, watching the late news with her family.

The announcer had a serious face to match his voice. "On the west end of Oahu a group of island youth attacked three off-duty Caucasian soldiers. The unarmed military men were all seriously wounded. The attackers are now in police custody. The prosecutor is waiting for doctors to release reports on the condition of the victims, to decide whether to charge the accused with aggravated assault, manslaughter, or premeditated murder. . . ."

As the names of the accused were delivered, their faces appeared on the screen. Paala stared out at Sumiko, his eyes narrowed against the harsh light.

10

December 1955

WINTER WAS NOT severe in Taiwan. Even in December the weather stayed mild and the days began early. At a little past five, the city of Taipei was already bathed in bright sunlight.

Ma Te pushed his bicycle out of the house, carrying a heavy book satchel on his back. He was fourteen now, and in the ninth grade.

He had on his uniform: gray pants and matching shirt, plus a gray cap over his crewcut hair. Like most of the students in Taiwan, he was nearsighted and wearing glasses.

It was not yet six o'clock, but already many students were on their way to school, each carrying a bulky book satchel. From a distance they looked like midgets toting heavy loads—their bodies were scrawny but their burdens enormous, and one of their shoulders was weighed down by the massive books.

Te pedaled on his bicycle, passed a girl who was walking and studying at the same time. She glanced at her book quickly, then muttered some words as she moved on.

". . . a fleet was sent to Besika Bay in 1877 . . .

1877 . . . Besika Bay . . ." She repeated the same words again and again.

Te became worried because he didn't know anything about that year and that place with a strange-sounding name. As soon as he reached school he would have to find out about it and memorize it. The high-school entrance examination was only six months away. According to his teachers, there would be many multiple-choice questions designed mainly for the sake of finding out if the students knew everything there was to know.

He slowed his pedaling, wanted to turn back and ask the girl from which volume of the history books he could learn about Besika Bay.

"No," he told himself. "She will never tell me because she can't afford to share such valuable information." He pedaled on.

The students in Taiwan needed to guard every ounce of their knowledge for the many entrance examinations. The competition was so stiff and the end result so crucial that each student was forced to treat the others as enemies.

"Everyone is fighting for life," Te mumbled as he continued for school. "But Tan Yen and I are fighting side by side."

The thought of his best friend waiting for him urged him to pedal faster. But he slowed down again when he saw another girl walking ahead of him along the road. He had enjoyed looking at girls since a year ago. He couldn't control his eyes, although all rules and regulations told him it was a wrong thing to do.

From a distance he couldn't see any difference between this girl and all others. All girls, no matter what school they were in, wore the same uniform—black skirt and white blouse, white socks and tennis shoes. Their hair was straight and short. No trace of makeup could be found on their faces. Not even nail polish or perfume was allowed. The government said that before graduating from high school, no girl should waste any valuable time on grooming herself.

When Te was closer to the girl, he noticed that from the back this girl looked prettier than the others. Her skirt reached her calves, according to rules, but the belt around her waist was pulled tight, giving her a willowy look and a beautiful swing as she took each step.

Te stopped pedaling and cruised behind her. The sound of his bicycle alerted her and she turned. Her face was as beautiful as her figure.

"Good morning," Te said, smiling and nodding politely. He wished very much to be her friend.

All her beauty was chased away by an angry frown. "Get lost," she hissed, "or I'll copy down your registration number!" She glanced at his shirt threateningly.

Te raised his right hand to cover his left breast. Over his shirt pocket a seven-digit number was embroidered in black.

Upon entering a new school level, each student was given a new number, to be embroidered on the assigned place in a prominent color. All students were encouraged to wear uniforms at all times, including weekends. Thus when a student misbehaved, his identity could be easily found.

Te pedaled away from the girl as fast as he could. If she reported him to the authorities, he could be punished severely. The government didn't like for young minds to be affected by romantic thoughts. Boys and girls were ordered to attend different schools from the seventh grade on.

Te passed several other attractive girls, but he didn't look at them. It was better to avoid trouble.

Te reached school. High walls surrounded the building. An iron gate, guarded by a security man, was locked between seven-thirty and five. Late arrivals were taken to the military training instructor's office to be questioned, and early departure was not allowed without the instructor's written permission.

"Ma Te!" Tan Yen waved at him from the shade of a banyan tree. He, too, was wearing glasses now.

Te locked his bike and joined his friend.

"How many pages did you memorize last night?" Yen asked.

"Very few. Only seventy or so," Te sighed while opening his book satchel. "I fell asleep in my chair before midnight. I woke up at three and tried to memorize more, but I couldn't keep my eyes open, so I went to bed and set the alarm for four. I didn't even hear it buzz. I slept until past five." He took out a huge three-ring binder. "How about you?"

"I managed eighty-five pages by two in the morning. I got up at four-thirty and memorized fifteen more." Yen pointed at a binder as thick as Te's. "I'm memorizing this thing for the fourth time."

"The fifth for me," Te said.

The two boys sat beneath the banyan tree and

studied for a while; then their eyes met over the rims of their binders. They shouldn't waste time talking, but they couldn't help it.

"If we are both lucky enough to enter high school, we should enjoy life for at least a whole month," Te said. "No books, only play. We should watch three movies every day."

"Only ten percent of the middle-school graduates can be admitted into high school. If we're that lucky, of course we'll celebrate. But we can't afford to play for a whole month," Yen said seriously, "because as soon as we are in high school, we'll be studying for the college-entrance exam."

Te put his hands over his ears and screamed. "You're no fun! You're not the Tan Yen I knew six years ago!"

Yen put down his heavy binder and gave his thick glasses a push. "Six years ago we were different. Before the revolt and massacre we were children. After that we were old men."

"Yen . . ." Te didn't know how to comfort his friend. The Nationalist government had proclaimed martial law six years ago and punished the uprising Taiwanese by killing twenty thousand of them, until their rebel leaders surrendered and the rest of them became totally submissive.

"You mainlanders have taken over our island. We Taiwanese must leave home if we want a better life," Yen continued in the voice of a forty-year-old. "I must study hard so I can enter college, graduate, pass the qualifying exam for going abroad, and then . . ." He waved a hand around and shouted sarcastically, "Good-bye, my poor invaded homeland!"

"We'll survive all the exams and graduate from college. Then we'll leave this impossible island together," Te said, and put his hand on Yen's.

Yen's harsh expression softened a little. He nodded and picked up the binder. "We better work hard or our palms won't even survive today's trashing!"

But it was difficult for two young hearts to continue such concentration. Once in a while they would look up from their binders and talk about things unrelated to study, especially their dreams of going abroad—they both wanted to go to the United States.

"Just imagine that in America we can ask our teachers questions," Te said. "According to Mr. Lee, the American teachers like students to understand things thoroughly."

Mr. Lee had been their seventh-grade social-studies teacher and had studied in the USA. He had been fired a year ago for refusing to follow the lesson plan designed by the Taiwan school board.

"And according to Mr. Lee, if we were in America we wouldn't have to memorize answers," Yen said. "He said that the American teachers like to give essay questions and ask each student to give a different answer according to his own opinion." He shook his head in disbelief.

They forced their wandering thoughts back to their binders, although they both knew that a large part of the things they were memorizing were but distortions the government wished to force on all the citizens.

An hour later they put away their binders and

took from their satchels two English-Chinese dictionaries.

They had begun to learn English when they were in the seventh grade. "The best way to learn is to memorize the dictionary," all the teachers had said.

They took turns calling out the words in English, spelling them, then giving their definitions in Chinese. When it was Te's turn to give the answers and he didn't have to hold a dictionary, he used his free hands to carve on the banyan tree with a pocketknife. When it was Yen's turn to answer, he took over the carving.

Words appeared on the aged tree trunk, the strokes unsteady, the calligraphy far from perfect. But the meaning was clear: "Ma Te and Tan Yen—Forever Friends."

At seven-thirty a bugler called the students to assemble. The flag-raising ceremony was the same all over the island in all levels of school, and the students of all ages shouted the same pledge: "May the great President Chiang live to be ten thousand!"

Te and Yen left school at five, pedaling their bicycles in the setting sun, toward Mr. Lee's home.

They had to squeeze the little horns on their handlebars to alert pedestrians. The population in Taiwan had soared in the past years because of the government's disapproval of birth control.

On both sides of the street, tall buildings now stood in place of the low houses. The government encouraged private enterprise.

Te and Yen zigzagged through rickshaws and

pedicabs, taxicabs and private cars, trucks and ox carts. The streets of Taipei were a museum of all means of transportation, from the very old to the very new.

"Look." Te pointed to the right. "Remember our old homes?" he asked with a smile. To him the childhood he had shared with Yen meant warmth and brotherly love, regardless of all the unpleasantness.

Sorrow appeared on Yen's face as he looked toward the changed neighborhood. Both the Ma house and the Tan house were gone. Commercial buildings had taken over the area.

Te's father had become wealthy and the Ma family had moved from their little house to a big one. On the contrary, Yen's father had lost a lot of money and the Tan family had sold their big house and moved into a shabby one.

"The secret alley is no longer there. If you and your parents should ever need to escape again, my Baba wouldn't be able to help you anymore," Yen said with a sarcastic smile.

Te said with a shrug, "The Taiwanese and mainlanders have learned to live in harmony. That secret alley is no longer needed, since there will never be another bloodbath."

Yen shook his head. "Harmony? For your information, we Taiwanese still keep the enlarged word 'Patience' on our walls."

They pedaled on. Mr. Lee's place was a shack, the walls cracked, the roof leaky. The only furniture was a bamboo bed and a wooden table. Mr. Lee was in his mid-thirties, tall and thin, wearing a white shirt and a pair of blue pants. His features were ordinary except his eyes, which glittered with wisdom and enthusiasm.

Unable to find another teaching job, Mr. Lee lived on the money he could make from private tutoring and writing short stories. Te and Yen were among many of his former students who visited him whenever they could squeeze some time out of their tight schedule—at times it meant shortening their sleep that night.

Te and Yen opened their book satchels and took out the books they had borrowed from Mr. Lee a week ago. All of Mr. Lee's books were covered by brown paper. On Te's was written: *Little Women;* on Yen's: *Jane Eyre.* But underneath the wrappings Te had *A Tale of Two Cities* and Yen had *Anna Karenina.*

The government censored books according to a very strict rule, especially those translated from foreign languages. Tolstoy's books were forbidden because he was a Russian. *A Tale of Two Cities* was prohibited because it concerned the masses revolting against authority.

Mr. Lee had his ways of smuggling free books from Hong Kong, which he lent to his young visitors free of charge. Under his bed was a library—books stacked in wooden crates.

"How did you like your books?" Mr. Lee asked Yen and Te.

"I didn't understand it," Te said honestly. "I had time enough to read only a few pages here and there."

Yen was very excited. "*Two Cities* made my blood boil. I shared the feelings of the people. The aristocrats got what they deserved."

Mr. Lee patted Yen on the back. "You'd better cool your blood before getting into trouble."

Soon after Te and Yen had joined Mr. Lee's other visitors sitting on the ground, the guest speaker arrived.

He was in his forties, bald, slightly overweight, and wearing the kind of long robe no longer worn by anyone in China. Mr. Lee introduced him. "We're honored to have with us Mr. Boi Yong, a writer who has quit his teaching job in the USA for his homeland."

Te and Yen exchanged a thrilled glance.

Boi Yong began to talk. "Many of you dream of going to America. I want to warn you that your dreamland has many faults, and you must be prepared before you go." He cleared his throat, glanced over the eager young faces. "The Americans know very little about China. Let me tell you how little."

He said with a twisted smile, "They believe President Chiang Kai-shek is great and kind, and that Madame is sweet and thoughtful to us common people. They are convinced that we people in Taiwan have all the freedom there is to have and that this tiny island is a land of liberty which should represent the whole of China in the United Nations."

He lowered his voice. "There are two reasons for the Americans to think this way. The first is that Chiang Kai-shek is spending a fortune in the USA to support a public-relations campaign. The second is, there is a crazy American named McCarthy persecuting people who dare to be negative about any government which is anti-communist—"

Mr. Lee cleared his throat, stepped forward, and whispered something into Boi Yong's ear. The speaker nodded and changed his tone of voice. "Well, the USA is a fun place to be. The movies are great . . ." He carried out the rest of his speech without mentioning politics.

The meeting was over. Te and Yen rode their bikes through the streets which were brightened by neon lights.

"I'm not going to America if they worship Chiang Kai-shek, a tyrant who has killed so many of my people and is still killing us," Yen said loudly. "Maybe I will go to England or Japan."

Even in the midst of the raucous city sound, Te was afraid that his friend would be overheard. "Lower your voice!" He reached over to cover his friend's mouth. "Will you never learn to be careful?"

Yen pushed Te's hand away forcefully and the two bikes swung from one side of the street to the other. "Ma Te, I'm tired of your cautiousness. Sometimes you act like a coward."

Te was hurt by the comment. "When we were children, you were grateful when I covered your big mouth for you."

"We are not children anymore," Yen said curtly. "People change, and you and I are changing in different directions."

"What do you mean?" Te moved closer.

"You are thoroughly tamed by the government. You even believe in their lies. For instance, I know you still want to go to America after what we have heard."

"What we've heard was only one man's opinion . . ." Te stopped.

On the sidewalk a teenage boy had been caught by two policemen. The boy's arms were held behind his back and his cap was thrown to the ground. One of the policemen began to run his fingers through the boy's hair.

Te and Yen jumped off their bikes and watched as the policeman took from his pocket a pair of clippers.

Taiwan policemen had the right to measure the students' hair at all times and in all places. A girl's hair was considered too long when it reached her earlobes. For a boy, it was when his hair could cover the fingers that ran through his crewcut.

"Don't! Please!" the boy screamed.

The policeman laughed.

The boy tried to free himself, but the two policemen slapped him, kicked him, then punched him on the chest and stomach until he doubled over in pain. One lifted the boy's head roughly and held it in place while the other began to shave his head. The boy sobbed loudly but was no longer struggling.

A crowd gathered to watch the compulsory haircut. Everyone was entertained by the boy's misery and no one was sympathetic. Among the crowd were Taiwanese as well as mainlanders.

"My beautiful island is turned into a land of terror, and my people are changed into heartless animals," Yen said in a shaking voice. "We used to feel sorry for those who suffer. Now, copying your example, we have all become selfish and cruel."

Te was shocked by the deep hatred in his friend's voice. He looked at the multicolored neon lights shining on Yen's face. Red, blue, orange, purple, and red again. With each different color, his friend looked like a new stranger: an angry man, a sad man, a sneering man, and then a vengeful man. Suddenly, all the lights flashed on, and Yen's many faces combined into one. Te trembled when he realized that the many faces were but one—the face of his oldest, dearest, and best friend.

"Yen . . ." He held his bike with one hand, used the other hand to grab the hand of his friend. "Please don't change. The world has nothing to do with us, not really. Everything around us can grow old, but please let you and me stay as little boys." He pleaded with tears in his eyes, "Yen, I want to be your best friend, always."

Without looking at Te, Yen shook off Te's placating hand, then jumped back on his bike and pedaled away without looking back.

11

WINTER ARRIVED IN White Stone. Qing remained miserable. Day after day she was haunted by the last sight of her family. She could never forgive herself for casting rocks at them.

On a sunny day at lunch hour, the temple ground was deserted. Qing didn't feel like eating. She stood alone for a while, then collapsed to the ground, leaned her face against the earth. She dug her fingers into the soil and cried until she saw the feet of two people coming toward her. She looked up, stared at Fan Yu and Kuei.

"Qing," Fan Yu said slowly, squatting beside her, "I know you are tortured by guilt. But I've done much more to your family than you. Compared to my guilt, yours is nothing. Will you ever forgive me?" He didn't wait for her answer. He turned abruptly and walked away.

Fan Yu had never asked Qing for forgiveness. She sat up, called after him, "Uncle Fan, it's not your fault."

This was the first time she had called him uncle. He heard her clearly, but didn't turn. He only waved a hand as he continued toward the town hall. His back was hunched and his shoulders dropped. He no longer looked like a firm believer in the party. His eagerness to avenge his mother had died away.

As Qing stared after Fan Yu, Kuei pulled her to her feet. "Let's go for a walk."

They walked for a long time, to the edge of White Stone. Beside the dirt road stood a tall tree that had died three years ago during a drought that killed many people along the Pearl River. At the root of the dead tree was a flat rock. "Sit with me." Kuei pulled Qing's hand gently.

The soft breeze dried Qing's tears. The call of a whippoorwill from a distant valley carried her thoughts away from reality. The winter sun in south China was a warm hand caressing her tenderly. She felt a little better.

"It's a beautiful day, no matter what . . ." she said, then stopped. She saw Kuei bending forward, staring at the ground, using his fingers to part the grass and sweep away the old leaves. "What are you looking for?"

Kuei didn't answer, but kept searching. "Ah! I found one!" he finally said, sat up straight, and smiled at Qing proudly.

He took Qing's hand, put something in the middle of her palm. She looked and saw a bead smaller than her fingernail, bright red, and shaped like a heart.

"It grows on this tree," Kuei said. "Although the tree is long dead, its beads will never rot. They will stay red forever." He pointed at the bead in Qing's palm, "This one fell from the tree at least three years ago. Look how beautiful it still is."

"What's the bead's name?" Qing asked, rubbing it gently.

"Lover's teardrop," Kuei answered.

"What a beautiful name. There must be a story behind it," Qing said. "My grandmother told me many stories, but never this one. Will you tell it to me?"

Kuei didn't like to tell stories. He cleared his throat and frowned. "Well, it's just one of those old legends. There are two lovers. He is gone and she waits for him under a tall tree. He doesn't come back as promised, so she cries day and night. Her teardrops become drops of blood, falling all over the ground, covering the tree's root. When her lover finally returns, she is dead. He bangs his head against the tree trunk, and red beads begin to fall from the tree, and keep falling until he is buried. His spirit joins hers in heaven, and the tree continues to produce heart-shaped red beads." He looked at Qing and said, "Why are you crying? My story can't be that bad."

Qing smiled through her tears. "It's a beautiful story, but it's so sad." She looked down at the bead again. "Will you drill a tiny hole through it for me? Then I'll put a fishing line through the hole and tie the bead around my neck. I'll wear it forever, to remember this day."

Kuei squeezed her arm. "Why is this day worth remembering?" He hesitated. "You've been sad since the departure of your family, and today you seemed sadder than ever. I didn't think you would like to remember—"

Qing interrupted him. "I stopped hating your father today. It feels good to have no more hate in my heart." She stood up, and he followed her.

As they walked back to the village, Qing held the bead tightly against her heart and said, "And today I feel I'm all grown-up. I feel I am a woman, and you . . ." She looked Kuei straight in the eye. "A man."

Kuei took her hand. They walked silently in the weak sunlight, and the whippoorwill called softly from a valley far away.

The Pearl River water turned warm when the spring of 1956 arrived in White Stone. The days became long, so even after Qing and Kuei finished working in the field, returned home, had supper, night was still far away. They usually played checkers; most of the time Kuei let Qing win.

When they were bored with the game, Kuei used bamboo sticks to make two flutes, then taught Qing to play the songs handed down by the peasants along the Pearl River.

Qing returned his music lessons with lessons in poetry—her knowledge was greater than his in this area. He could read and write very little, but she had taken years of lessons from a scholar and knew many poems by heart. The years of difficult life had not erased those poems from her memory. When reciting them, she still could feel their beauty.

Qing and Kuei ran out of things to do one evening, so they walked to the Pearl and watched the children swim. "It looks like fun," Qing said, watching the swimmers with envy.

"Let's join them," Kuei said, and began to unbutton his shirt and kick off his shoes.

"I can't swim," Qing said, shaking her head.

"You can't?" Kuei stared at her incredulously. "What have you been doing all these years? All children of the Pearl swim like fish. Come, I'll teach you."

Standing barefoot and naked from the waist up, he reached over to undress her.

"No!" She turned to run.

"You come back here!" He caught her in just a few steps.

He carried her to the water as she struggled, yelling at him and screaming for help.

There were grown-ups and children at the riverbank, but none was willing to come to her aid. They all laughed as they watched a former gravedigger's son forcing a previous landlord's granddaughter into the water.

"Don't! I'm afraid of the water! I'll drown! I'll never speak to you again! You big ugly bully! Let me go!" Qing kicked as Kuei carried her toward the river.

She shrieked when he let go, and then her voice became a gurgling sound when her head went under. He pulled her by the hair to bring her up, then put a hand under her chin.

"Kick your feet and beat the water with your hands," he said as he swam beside her.

Qing had no choice but to do as he said. She kicked hard and beat the water with all the strength she had. She was surprised to see the trees on the riverbank moving and to find herself going past the people on shore.

"I'm swimming!" she shouted, sank immediately, and swallowed more muddy water.

He carried her out of the river when she was too exhausted to move her arms and legs. He dropped her on the grass, lay beside her, and laughed. "You look like a drowned rat!"

Qing looked at herself and blushed. Her clothes seemed to have become another layer of skin. The red bead hanging from her neck rose and fell as she breathed hard. She crossed her arms in front of her breasts.

Her crimson face and bashful gesture called Kuei's attention to her curved figure. His face turned red also. He looked at the other young men sitting on the riverbank, and found their eyes all glued to Qing. He glared at them angrily, then looked around but could find nothing to shield Qing. He pulled her up from the grass. "Let's go back to the river."

This time Qing didn't bother to argue. She ran toward the water with her arms crossed in front of her, stepped into the river quickly. They began to swim. After a while she was able to keep her head above water without Kuei's hand under her chin. He then swam in front of her and kept his legs low, so she could wrap her arms around his waist and follow him around.

"This is fun," she said, leaning her face against his back. "Why didn't you teach me earlier?"

They didn't notice that night was growing deep and people were leaving the riverbank. They kept swimming in the peaceful Pearl, moving softly because they didn't want to disturb the moon's reflection.

When they finally decided to go home, the entire village was in a quiet slumber. They held hands but didn't talk. Both of their hearts were filled with words, but neither of them knew how to get the words out of their mouths.

When they neared the hill they saw something sparkling on the ground. They raced home and saw Fan Yu kneeling beside a recently built fire.

Beside the fire were piled their kettle and wok,

their cleaver and saw, and many other metal items.

"Uncle Fan, what are you doing?" Qing asked.

Fan Yu sighed without looking up. "I've just come home from another meeting. The government's Five-Year Plan is not being carried out fast enough. My superiors are very upset. You two had better help me gather more pots and pans, and anything else that's made of brass, iron, or steel."

Without questioning, Kuei and Qing went to work. They found very few pots and pans. After those were gathered, they removed doorknobs, pulled out nails, and brought everything to one pile.

According to the Five-Year Plan, China was to become an industrial country within five years. Steel and iron industries must be developed, and every individual must contribute. Fan Yu said, "We'll melt everything, turn things into one big lump of metal. The metal lumps from villages like White Stone will go to the city of Kwangchow to be used in the iron and steel factories there."

Kuei looked at the doorknobs and nails, asked doubtfully, "Can this pile really help our industry? It looks more like a pile of junk to me."

His father shook his head. "I don't think it'll help in developing the industry of China, but it will definitely help in saving the skin of the Fan family. If we don't give them a large lump of melted metal tomorrow, we'll be classified as anti-revolutionaries."

"Uncle Fan, how can I cook without wok and frying pan?" Qing asked apologetically. "I'm sorry about our industry, but I'm more directly involved with tomorrow's breakfast. I need the kettle to boil water for tea, and the wok to cook our rice gruel."

The fire glowed on Uncle Fan's wrinkled face. The middle-aged man looked old and tired. He sighed helplessly and answered, "I don't know how you can cook from now on. I only know you won't be the only person with a problem. All the pots and pans and woks will be melted away in the next few days. Not one woman in White Stone will have a piece of metal in her kitchen."

Qing saved from the fire a large rusted can, and for the next three months she used it to cook their daily meals. Kuei drilled two holes on top of the can and attached a wooden handle to it. Qing was very proud of her strange-shaped utensil.

After three months the government had to admit that the melted metal would never help the nation's industry, and allowed the citizens to own pots and pans again. But Qing kept the can as a souvenir.

She treasured everything made for her by Kuei because she knew she loved him as much as he loved her. He was now twenty-one and she sixteen. He was no longer merely her brother, friend, teacher, and protector. He was now her man, and she couldn't wait to become his woman.

12

SUMIKO COULD SEE the prison wall from the highway. The barbed wire on its top stood dark against the clear sky. Hawaiian skies were always blue, but in spring they looked transparent.

"This is your first spring behind those walls, Paala," she whispered as she took the exit. "Four more after this and you'll be free."

She made a turn, passed a pineapple farm. A grass hut, maybe an outhouse for the field workers, stood at the corner of the field. "I'll wait for you to come out and build us a home. We'll be happy even if it's only a small hut," she whispered again, and the world became a blur to her misty eyes.

Since Paala's jail term had begun, her days had become longer. Each second moved in slow motion, and sometimes time stood still. How could she spend almost fifteen hundred more days without him? "I shouldn't complain," she mumbled when she thought how much worse it must be for him.

She blinked. Tears fell on her bright yellow muumuu. She always wore bright colors when visiting him, to brighten his days if she could.

"Paala is like the wind that must soar freely. It's so cruel to confine him in a cell."

She had spoken her thoughts to her mother. "Please defend him," she had begged. "If he goes to jail, a large part of me will be jailed with him."

Mrs. Yamada had said with a sigh, "I'm afraid I can't help him this time. He and his buddies crippled an innocent soldier, you know."

Sumiko was in the courtroom when Paala was sentenced. She had wanted to run to him, but her mother and two brothers had held her down. Paala had turned toward her and their eyes had locked on each other until two guards took him by the arms and guided him away.

The parking lot was already filled with cars. Sumiko exchanged greetings with a woman who was always there on visiting days. Each time Sumiko looked at the woman, the same thought occurred: If Paala and I were married, the time would go faster.

That thought was still with Sumiko when she was in the visiting room, sitting on one of the stools on one side of the wall and waiting for Paala to appear on the other side.

Through the safety glass she saw a door open and a line of prisoners enter. The sight of Paala drove the slightest doubts away from her contemplation; she made a decision.

"Paala!" she called, reached for him, but touched only the hard glass.

No more tight jeans and red shirts for Paala. His uniform was gray and baggy. No more long hair for him either. They had given him a crewcut. He showed no signs of torture, but the mere change in his clothes and hair was enough to bring pain to Sumiko's heart.

"My Paala!" she called again, and pressed her warm forehead against the cold glass.

On the glass, small round holes provided a passage of sound between a prisoner and his visitor. Paala settled his large frame on a stool and said through the hole, "Didn't I tell you not to come this week?"

"Yes, you did." Sumiko studied him carefully. He had become thinner and paler since the last visit. "Do they feed you properly? Did you like the food I brought you? Do they keep you inside all the time? Haven't you been in the sun at all?" She asked the same questions each time.

"They feed me well. I liked the food you brought, and shared it with others. It was enough for ten. I'm not surfing or swimming, but I do spend enough time outdoors. We must exercise, you know," he answered patiently, then said, "Sumiko, please don't come every week."

"Why?" she asked. "It's not too long a drive."

"It's too much for you." He hesitated. "And I don't mean the driving."

"I live for the visiting days," Sumiko said, her eyes glistening with tears. She mustn't trouble Paala with her sorrow. She forced herself to smile, and changed the subject. "I brought you another basket of food. I gave it to them at the entrance. After checking it, they should give it to you. Please eat the things yourself instead of giving them away." A horrible thought hit her. "Do the others take food from you by force? Is that why you're becoming thinner?"

Paala smiled. "You've watched too many movies. No, no one treats me like that. We have plenty to eat. We have job-training programs and classes. There is even a music class taught by volunteers from outside. I would like to learn to read music, and my case worker encourages me to do so—''

Sumiko interrupted him. ''Paala, let's get married.''

''What?'' He stared at her.

''You and I should get married. It's allowed, I know. I read it somewhere. Two prisoners can marry each other, and a prisoner can marry a free person. You always said you'll marry me when I'm eighteen. I'm eighteen now. I'll graduate in less than two months.''

''You're out of your mind!'' He raised his voice. There were four armed guards at the corners of the room. They turned their eyes on him immediately.

''I'll ask Mama the proper procedure. We'll marry, and they should allow us to spend a few moments together without this stupid wall between us.'' She blushed. ''They may still keep an eye on us, and we may not be able to do anything . . . I mean, you may not have a chance to give me a baby. But I'll be Mrs. Nihoa, and that alone will make the waiting easier. You don't know how I envy the woman who comes to visit her husband.''

''Stop that! You're talking nonsense!'' He lowered his voice when he became aware of the guards' interest. But he didn't stop shaking his head. ''If we married, what would you say when people ask what your husband does? 'He is in prison!' Can you say those four words proudly?''

''Yes!'' Sumiko answered positively. ''It'll be

very easy for me to be proud, because I can show them your picture and let them see how handsome you are. I'll take pride in telling them my husband didn't do anything wrong, that he only bravely avenged the death of a friend."

Paala frowned. "But I was wrong, Sumiko. I've had a lot of time to think things over. It was wrong of me and my kamaaina friends to hurt three innocent men only because they were haoles. At times I have to admit I deserve to be here."

"All right. So I'll tell them my man did a crazy foolish thing, and then I'll show them the picture of my handsome wonderful husband," Sumiko said with determination. "I'll go home and talk to Mama. You must start from your end too. Talk to someone in charge . . . who will that be? The warden? A minister? The social worker? Oh, no! Not her!" She brought a hand to her open mouth.

One of Sumiko's previous visits had been interrupted by a pretty young girl holding a stack of papers. The girl had walked in through the door on Paala's side, tapped Paala on the shoulder. Then she had talked to him familiarly and added a few words to a file she had.

When Sumiko asked who the girl was, Paala had answered casually, "My case worker. She is trying to place me in one of the rehabilitation programs. She comes to talk to me every day."

"You don't need your case worker's permission to get married, do you?" Sumiko asked, unable to hide her anger. "I don't like her!"

"You're crazy," Paala said. "I never notice any other girl and you ought to know it. I just don't want my Sumiko to marry a prisoner, not even when that prisoner is me."

But as he spoke, his voice softened, his eyes brightened, and he smiled. He would very much like to marry his Sumiko. It was silly of her to worry about any pretty social worker, but only sensible for him to be troubled by the fact that outside these prison walls there were many eligible young men. How he had stared at the barred window in his cell and wondered if by the time he was free Sumiko would have already become someone else's wife. Yes, if they were married, the next few years would go much faster.

Visiting time was over before he could tell her that he would apply for marriage permission immediately. But she must know that he had never been able to say no to any of her wishes since they were children.

He had always pretended to be cheerful during her visits, then lowered his head and dragged his feet once he was out of her sight. Today he walked back to his cell with light steps and high spirits. Now there was a touch of light and happiness in a life that was darker and more miserable than he had ever admitted to Sumiko.

"Come with me," the guard said, pointing a finger at Paala. "You!"

Paala left his three cellmates and followed the guard down the hall. He wondered if his marriage application had been approved. He had talked with the warden the day after Sumiko's visit two days ago. Could things work so fast in this place?

He was led to a small room next to the warden's office, where there were a long table and four chairs; Mrs. Yamada was sitting on one of them.

''Do you want me to stay?'' the guard asked her.

''No. I want to talk to Paala alone.'' She waited for the guard to leave and close the door, then gestured Paala to sit. ''Paala, why do you want to hurt Sumiko?'' She leaned forward and looked into his eyes.

''Hurt her? I only want to marry her.'' Paala took a deep breath, then let it out slowly. Control your temper, he warned himself.

''That's the same thing,'' Mrs. Yamada said. ''She told me it was her suggestion. But I don't believe her. I know it's you who put the crazy idea into her head. She is very naive, Paala. How can you be so selfish? You're taking advantage of her innocence. Do you think by becoming the son-in-law of an attorney you'll get out of here sooner?''

Anger flashed in Paala's eyes. He opened his mouth, then used all his willpower to swallow his words. He told himself to be calm. This woman was not a bad person, but she would protect her daughter as fiercely as a lioness would protect a cub.

She waited for his answer. He ignored what she had said and explained patiently, ''Mrs. Yamada, you don't like me, I know. But Sumiko and I love each other. We want to be married so we can both feel more secure. She'll have to live in your home as she does now. I can't support her for a while. But as soon as I'm free I'll find a job—''

She interrupted him. ''Doing what?''

''Entertaining.'' He didn't like her tone of voice at all. ''You don't think much of a singing career. Your two sons will become professionals. That's wonderful, but it would be a boring world if everyone became either a doctor or a lawyer. The world needs entertainers too—"

"The world also needs garbage collectors, but they will not marry my daughter!" She glared at him.

Paala breathed deeply once again, then answered slowly, "Garbage collectors are called sanitation workers now. If one of them could make Sumiko happy, why would you want to stand in the way?"

Mrs. Yamada said coldly. "You are not a sanitation worker or an entertainer. You are sentenced to five years and won't be free for a long time."

"A long time is not forever, Mrs. Yamada. With good behavior, I'll be out on parole in twenty months—"

She interrupted him again, her voice hard and unforgiving. "With your temper, you'll fight with someone within the next few days. You'll never pass the parole board."

"For Sumiko, I'll hold my temper."

"I watched you grow up. I know you well. Perhaps even better than you know yourself. You promised Sumiko many times never to fight. You broke your promise each time."

"This time it's different."

She stood up. "I don't have time to argue." She looked at Paala's young face and her voice softened. "Paala, your parents were good people. When you were little, I liked you. I still hold no grudge against you. I'm here as Sumiko's mother, pleading with you."

She patted Paala gently on the shoulder.

"Paala, please think for Sumiko. I know you have already made love to her. You don't have to deny it. I don't blame you, because I do believe that you love her in your own way. But, Paala, do you really believe her marrying you right now is good for her?"

Paala stared at Mrs. Yamada. His head knew the answer to her question, but his heart refused to accept it and his lips were unwilling to say the words.

Mrs. Yamada walked to the door, then stopped. She turned to face Paala and looked at him with tears in her eyes. "I was young once, and I haven't forgotten what young love is . . . it's to sacrifice oneself for the loved one. Sumiko is willing to sacrifice herself for you. Paala, why are you not man enough to do the same thing?"

Paala's face turned white. Mrs. Yamada's words exploded in the tiny room. Every word became many pieces of shrapnel, each piece piercing through both his heart and his brain.

"I *am* man enough . . ." His trembling voice died before he could finish the sentence. It was too painful to say what he had just realized.

Mrs. Yamada walked back to Paala, put a hand on his arm. "Then you'll do what a man must do." She squeezed his arm tenderly, then walked away once again and knocked on the closed door.

The guard appeared and Mrs. Yamada looked at Paala one last time. "The spirits of your parents are watching over you, Paala. Please make them proud." With that she started to walk away.

"Wait!" Paala called in a shaking voice.

Mrs. Yamada turned.

"I never did tell Sumiko that I would marry

her," Paala said, his eyes filled with tears and his lips trembling. "I will not marry her until I am out of jail and can provide for her well—this I promise."

"I don't want to marry you, and I don't want you to visit me anymore," Paala felt he was once again onstage, hiding his true feelings from an audience. The years in a nightclub had been good training.

"Why?" Sumiko couldn't believe her ears.

Paala shrugged lightly. "Your visits disturb me. I enrolled in the learning program they have. I want to study music. I have almost five years for it, so I can learn a lot if I concentrate."

Fear filled Sumiko. She looked like a drowning person unable to reach the only piece of nearby driftwood. She reached for Paala, only to slam her fingers against the glass. "I won't disturb you, I promise. Please let me come. I won't mention marriage again, I promise that too."

She shook violently when she thought of her life without these visiting days. "I must see you. If I don't have even that, what else is there to live for?"

Paala couldn't stand it any longer. He stood up. "Good-bye, Sumiko. I'll see you four and a half years from now."

"No! Paala! No!" She threw herself against the glass. One of the guards on the visitors' side came and tapped her on the shoulder.

Paala turned from her, his voice barely audible when he said to one of the guards, "Please let me go back to my cell now."

"Paala! I love you! Please forgive me if I did

anything wrong! But if you don't let me see you, I'll die!" Sumiko pounded on the glass in frustration, and the guard had to force her out of the visiting room.

Paala had not cried since the deaths of his parents. He cried now. As soon as the door shielded him from Sumiko's view, he leaned against the hallway wall, covered his face with his hands, and sobbed like a child.

In the Yamadas' living room Sumiko crouched on a small sofa, her face pale and her eyes swollen, her lips bloodless and her hands lifeless in her lap. "Paala will change his mind!" she said again and again. "He and I love each other. We belong together." She looked at her mother. "You simply don't understand."

"Yes I do," Mrs. Yamada said. She didn't want her daughter to know just how much she knew and how much she had done. "But still I insist that you must leave Hawaii for a while. There's no need for you to stay here, since Paala won't see you. You're torturing yourself, and you can't take this much longer."

Mrs. Yamada looked worriedly at Sumiko. The girl was near a breakdown, she was afraid. She leaned closer to Sumiko. "My daughter, let's make a deal. If you go to San Francisco, I'll forward any letter from Paala to you. In four years you'll be graduated from nursing school, and Paala will be free. If he can find a decent job and you two still love each other, I won't stand in your way."

Sumiko considered her mother's words. "Perhaps you are right. Maybe it will be easier to live across the ocean from Paala . . ." She changed her mind and shook her head. "I don't want to go to the mainland all by myself. I'm afraid to live among strangers."

Mrs. Yamada said, "You won't be in San Francisco alone. I'll put you on the plane and the Sungs will meet its arrival. You'll live in the home of your Uncle Hwa, who saved your brother's life many years ago." She shook her head at the memory. "Sumiko, you'll be happier in San Francisco."

"I'll never be happy again anywhere without my Paala." Sumiko teared up once again. "Mama, let me try once again to visit Paala . . . just once."

Mrs. Yamada thought for a few moments, then nodded. She couldn't drag a grown girl to the airport and force her into a plane. Even if she did, Sumiko could fly back to Hawaii as soon as she wanted to. "All right, you can go one more time. But if Paala doesn't want to see you, then we'll leave Hawaii the next day."

It was not a scheduled visiting day. Sumiko made a special request to the warden, making sure that the warden knew she was the daughter of Mrs. Yamada, a well-known attorney.

When permission was granted, Sumiko asked the guard to be sure to tell Paala that she was leaving for the mainland the next day. "Please tell him that I don't have to go, that all my plans can be changed by one word from him. And also please tell him that if he doesn't see me now, I just may never come back again."

The guard was gone quite a while. He came back with a puzzled expression. "Paala Nihoa doesn't want to see you, but he wishes you good luck on the mainland."

Tears fell as Sumiko asked in a trembling voice, "How does Paala look? Is he thin? Did he get any color back on his face?"

The guard said, "He seems to be all right. I didn't really look at his face, so I can't tell you if he is thin or fat, pale or tanned. He was sitting with his case worker, discussing something. His back was turned toward me . . ."

Sumiko ran from the room. The guard never had a chance to finish telling her what had puzzled him. Why would Paala refuse to see Sumiko, whom he obviously loved? When he heard that she was leaving for the mainland, his back had shivered and his shoulders had heaved. The guard had had to wait a long time before Paala was able to talk.

13

Spring 1958, Taiwan

IT WAS AZALEA time again. The Yong-ming Mountain was a sea of flowers. Petals of red, pink, and white glistened in the sun, filling the air with sweet fragrance.

On the first Sunday in March, many people left the crowded city and crammed onto the mountain, jammed against one another as they walked from hill to hill. Among the swarm were Ma Te, Tan Yen, and his sister, Tan Yimi.

Te and Yen were almost eighteen and in their last year of high school. Yimi was nearly fifteen. She had started school at five and finished ninth grade last summer. In the autumn of last year, as usual, the result of the high-school-entrance examination had been announced in the newspaper. The names of those who had passed were disclosed, but Yimi's name was not among them. Her parents and brother had comforted her with their love. Te had tried his best to reassure her.

Now, six months later, her gloomy mood had actually deepened. She cried every day, didn't eat or sleep much. She spent most of her time staring into space. The worst was when her two girlfriends who had also failed the exam visited her. The three would form a circle by putting their arms around one another, then bow their heads toward the center of the circle and murmur, "We've shamed our families and ancestors. We have no face left, no place in this world."

When Te and Yen overheard this, they were deeply concerned. They needed to work hard for their college qualifying examination, which was to take place soon, but they had taken this Sunday off from studying and dragged Yimi with them to the Yong-ming Mountain.

They stopped beside a cluster of magnificent flowers. Te cleared his throat and said hesitantly, "Yimi, I have a sister on the mainland, but I don't even know what she looks like now. I've watched you grow up in the past nine years . . . no, almost ten. You are like a sister to me."

Her dark eyes met his. She didn't look away. Her thin lips trembled, but she didn't open her mouth.

Te continued. "Yimi, the azaleas will bloom every spring, and the qualifying examination is held every summer. You must eat and sleep and stay healthy, so when summer comes again you can take the exam once more. This time you will pass it."

Yimi looked at Te sadly, then shook her head and sighed without uttering a word.

Yen put his hands on his sister's shoulders and shook her gently. "Look, Yimi, these azaleas are like a beautiful young girl. They are blooming, and so are you. Why let an examination ruin everything? It's not worth it."

Yimi didn't argue with her brother. She looked

at him and tears gradually filled her beautiful eyes. She didn't bother to wipe them away when they streamed down her pale cheeks.

"Please, my baby sister, please cheer up." Yen sighed and dried her tears for her. Yimi didn't move. When Yen and Te resumed walking, she walked between them silently.

The boys continued to talk to her from one blooming hill to another. When the bus that had brought them to the mountain was ready to return to the city, they had to admit that they had failed to bring Yimi out of her depression.

"She needs a little more time, and then she'll recover," Yen said.

Te agreed.

The next day was Monday. Te and Yen went to school and Mr. Tan went to work. Yimi's two girlfriends came to visit her again, and the three left the house at noon. Yimi's mother thought this would be good for her. When it was night and still they had not returned, the Tan family contacted the families of the other two girls. The other girls were also missing. The three families searched everywhere and then returned to their homes to find policemen waiting.

Yimi and her girlfriends had gone to the northern seashore. The three had left letters of apology on the beach and then waded into the deep sea. There were soldiers and lifeguards on the beach, but when they noticed the three small dots struggling to float in the powerful waves some distance away, it was already too late.

Te was with the Tan family the day Yimi was buried. When he watched her coffin being lowered into a hole in the ground, he sobbed as he remembered the little girl he had met almost ten years ago.

Through the burial Yen kept his lips sealed and his eyes dry. When it was over, he walked quickly away from the graveyard.

A week after Yimi's death, Te and Yen met again early in the morning in the schoolyard. They sat on the flat rock beneath a tall tree, and each took out a thick book containing materials for the college qualifying examination.

Te found the folded page and began to memorize, reading out loud as usual. When he didn't hear Yen's voice, he looked and found Yen staring at his book satchel. Te followed his friend's eyes and saw Yen's embroidered name on the flap. It was delicate work done by Yimi.

"Where Yimi is, there is no entrance examination," Te said, putting a hand on Yen's. "She is luckier than we."

"Stupid system! Senseless pressure! Yimi was only a child!" Yen shook off Te's hand furiously. "It's all you mainlanders' fault!"

Te had learned to ignore Yen's blaming everything on the mainlanders, but he couldn't figure out why the mainlanders were responsible for Yimi's death.

Yen continued in a cold voice. "My uncle is right. He said there used to be enough schools and jobs for everyone on our sparsely populated island. Then you mainlanders poured in by the millions. New schools are being built too slowly, and so are new businesses to provide jobs. It is impossible for us to make a decent living without a college degree, so we compete. The competition killed my sister." Yen glared at Te, daring him to deny the responsibility.

Te was angry, but swallowed his wrathful words. "Perhaps we mainlanders *are* to blame," he murmured softly. "But the main problem is our tradition. We are born to fulfill obligations and live up to expectations. If we are unable to do that, we are too ashamed to live."

Te then tried to turn his friend away from sorrow by reminding him of the reality. "Let's study, Yen. Yimi could have tried again, but we can't. If we don't enter college, we'll become soldiers."

"The brutal law! The crazy government!" Yen pounded an angry fist on the rock, skinned his knuckles, but didn't seem to feel the pain.

Te shared Yen's anger. According to the law, a boy who was not admitted to college was drafted into the army for three years. But Te was more worried than angry. If they went into the army, it would be impossible to find time to study, and after three years in the service, college would be forever beyond their reach.

Then Te's eyes brightened as he remembered something. He reached into his book satchel and took out a thick book. "I went to a bookstore last night. A salesman showed me this expensive book, *The Door to Universities,* and guaranteed it's the most detailed one ever printed. He said if I memorized every page, I'd pass the examination for sure." He smiled at Yen, "I'll tear it in two so we can both study it at the same time. Would you rather have the first half or the last?"

Yen said without expression, "The first half, if you don't mind."

It wasn't easy to tear the thick book. Te used so

much force that when the book tore his elbow knocked Yen's satchel to the ground. Books fell out and scattered. One of them was the very same book Te had just torn in two—*The Door to Universities*.

Yen took his time in gathering all his books and putting them back. He never bothered to explain or to meet Te's eyes.

Te shivered in the warm sunlight. He couldn't hide the hurt in his voice as he said, "Do me a favor, my friend. From now on, if I offer you a book you already have, please let me know so I won't tear up any more of my brand-new books."

Yen shrugged. "Your family is rich. You can afford to tear up many new books."

"Stop it!" Te put his hands on Yen's arms and shook him. "Is there no end to your bitterness? The financial situation of our families has never had anything to do with our friendship."

Yen jerked from Te's grasp and stared at him coldly. "My father is an honest businessman. He doesn't know how to deal with tricky mainlanders like your father. During recent years your father has made a fortune and my father has lost one. I'm not so certain it shouldn't affect our friendship."

Te's voice shook, "You are being ridiculous. My father never cheated your father. They aren't even in the same business."

Yen picked up his book satchel. "Perhaps you shouldn't be in the company of a ridiculous person." He moved away in large strides without looking back.

"Wait!" Te shouted, gathering his things in a hurry. "You always walk away from me. One of these days I'll just let you go and that'll be the end of our friendship!''

Yen didn't slow down.

On a warm July morning Te jumped on his bike and pedaled happily toward Yen's home.

They had graduated at the end of May and had studied hard for the past two months. Te had gone to Yen's house often, but Yen had never returned his visits.

Te passed the new streets and reached an old alley. He stopped at a small house, so unlike the big house the Tans used to have. Te could still visualize the large garden with all the lanterns and a grape harbor that led to a secret passage. Now the Tans had no garden at all. Yen's father had lost his family business, now worked long and unsteady hours for someone else. Yen's mother opened the door.

She had lost her youth within a few months of Yimi's death. She seemed senile as she stared at Te without recognizing him. Yen's uncle rushed by. He didn't return Te's greeting, but threw an angry look in Te's direction before he was gone.

''Yen!'' Te called as he entered the small room shared by Yen and his uncle. ''I have great news!''

Surrounded by books and notebooks, Yen sat on the naked floor of an empty room, leaning against a peeling wall. He was wearing only a pair of shorts, but still his face was beaded with sweat. He looked up from his book but didn't speak.

''I may not have to take the qualifying examination after all,'' Te dropped to the floor and sat beside his friend. He waited for Yen to ask questions and couldn't conceal his excitement.

Yen asked no questions, but continued to stare at Te bleakly.

Te couldn't wait any longer. "My father just bought stock in an IBM company," he said proudly. "You know, a company that deals with international business machines. Since Taiwan has become the most prosperous place in southeast Asia next to Japan, business machines are in great demand. My father's new company buys machines from many foreign countries, including the USA—"

Yen interrupted Te coldly. "I am not interested in your honorable father's booming business."

Te ignored Yen's acid tone. He continued, "Being the majority stockholder, Baba has the right to name the buying agents for the company. He will name me."

Te went on to explain that with the right connection and a solid company backing him, the government would close its eyes to the fact that the buying agent was only a young high-school graduate. When he received a passport from the Chinese government, the American consulate general would not hesitate to give him a visa.

Te said, "My father already had a long talk with his business associates in San Francisco. They promised to help me change my status when I arrive. They said that I can register in a college and receive a student visa, and then I can stay in the States as long as I don't drop out of school. Yen, when I'm in America, you'll soon be there too."

Te waited for Yen to jump up and hold him, then dance around the room and cheer for their happiness. But Yen didn't move at all.

When Yen finally spoke, his voice was sarcastic and frosty. "Well, well, congratulations, Ma Te. So your rich father has oiled the corrupted back doors for you, and you are going to the land of the white devils who think highly of Chiang, the killer of us Taiwanese. You'll sneak away just like the other sons and daughters of the rich and important. When you arrive in the USA, are you going to demonstrate typing on one of the business machines and find a wife among the Chinese-American viewers? I'm afraid you won't look too good holding an embroidery needle."

Te's eyes filled with tears. "How can you compare me with . . . ?" His voice trembled so that he couldn't talk.

A year ago the daughter of the Taiwan police chief had left for the States to demonstrate embroidery. One brave reporter had taken a picture of the young girl smiling and waving good-bye at the airport and written an article to tell the story behind the scene—the police chief had bought a great deal of finished needlework for his daughter, who didn't know how to embroider at all.

A few months later the same reporter had written a follow-up: in Los Angeles the girl had dressed in her fine silk and jewelry to host an embroidery show, for the purpose of finding a Chinese-American husband. Her mission was quickly accomplished; she was married and would never have to return to Taiwan again.

"It's easy for me to compare you with her." Yen laughed bitterly. "There is no difference between you!"

"Tan Yen, you are hateful!" Te pointed a finger at his friend. "I think of you as a brother, but you treat me as an enemy—" He was interrupted by Yen's uncle. "Boi Yong was arrested by the government!" The uncle ignored Te but gestured Yen to go with him. "There is a meeting at my friend's place. We'll try to find a way to save Boi Yong. Mr. Lee will be there too. We must go immediately."

Yen jumped up and raced out of the door with his uncle.

Te forgot his anger and hurt, followed them, and said, "I'm going with you. Mr. Lee was my most favorite teacher and I like Boi Yong's writings."

Yen's uncle said without turning or stopping, "For your information, this journey may not be too good for your health."

Te froze at the hinted message. He should have known: Yen and his uncle were involved with the Taiwan Independent Movement!

Since 1949 the Nationalist government had had two prominent enemies—the Communists and the Taiwan Independent Movement. In Taiwan, a person found to be a member of either had no chance to escape imprisonment and torture, followed by life in prison or execution.

"I promised Baba that I'd never go near danger," Te mumbled as he stood planted to the ground, and watched the other two going down the lane.

"I knew you wouldn't come with us. You are but a mainlander who pretends to be our friend. Deep inside, you are no different from the rest of them. Besides that, you are your parents' crybaby and a coward!" Yen threw these words back at

Te, then laughed as he disappeared at the end of the narrow alley.

Yen's biting snicker lingered in the air. It bothered Te so much that he started to chase after his friend. Again and again he stopped at the memory of his father's words—"Tread softly, my son, if you want to survive"—and the frequent stopping kept him far behind the other two men.

Te watched Yen and his uncle enter a house with a walled garden. He quickened his steps. "You'll be so proud of me when you see . . ." he said, then stopped.

Several military policemen jumped out from behind the walls, grabbed Yen and his uncle, then disappeared inside again. Their action was so fast that for a moment Te thought he was seeing things. Then a scream came from inside the house, so piercing that he couldn't tell if it had been a man or a woman. It sounded like an animal in pain, and it sent Te stumbling several steps backward. Instinct sent him hiding behind a lamppost. He was still shivering when another young man approached the house. The same thing happened once again: the military police grabbed the man, and soon after that the scream was repeated.

Te dug his fingernails into his palms. "How am I to save you, Yen?" he whispered shakily. "I'm coming to join you."

Te came out from behind the lamppost, but at that very moment the door opened. Te jumped back to his hiding place as a long line of men was paraded out of the house with their arms bent behind them and their hands cuffed. He recognized Mr. Lee, and then several of the people who used to visit the house. Yen appeared with his uncle, both bleeding from fresh wounds delivered by the policemen's clubs. Yen's face was a portrait of anger, his uncle's a picture of fury.

"You're not taking me to a cage and locking me up!" Yen's shouting reached Te's ears. "You're not torturing me like you did my comrades!"

One of the policemen raised his club. The sound of it landing on Yen's head pushed Te further into hiding.

"Do you think we've waited long enough in the trap?" Te heard one policeman asking another. "Could we have captured more if we'd waited longer?"

"I think we've got them all. There can't be more fools like these on Taiwan!"

Just then, Yen began to run. The police took pistols from their holsters and aimed at Yen's back. Te heard a series of shots, then saw Yen fall to the ground. He heard a scream coming from his own throat, but it was drowned out by the screams of Yen's uncle and the other captured men.

"It's all right." A policeman bent over Yen's still-convulsing body and kicked the dying man hard. "He is only one of the young fools who don't know much. Their leaders are the ones we must keep alive."

One policeman dragged Yen's body toward a truck parked at a distance, passing Te's hiding place. By now a crowd had gathered, and the police didn't notice Te among them. Te looked down at Yen's lifeless face and began to sob. He covered his mouth so no one could hear him.

He mumbled from behind his shaking fingers,

"They should at least remove your handcuffs. You wanted freedom so much."

The next morning Te's father read out loud the headline on the *Daily News:* "LEADERS OF TAIWAN INDEPENDENT MOVEMENT CAPTURED TOGETHER WITH THEIR FOLLOWERS."

Mr. Ma put down the paper and looked at his son. "They'll arrest everyone connected to these thirty-five people! Relatives, friends . . . you should have stopped seeing that Tan boy a long time ago!" Mr. Ma pointed a finger at his son and warned Te firmly, "Keep away from the Tan house. Don't ever go near your friend's parents!"

"But my bike is still there . . ." Te wanted to find an excuse to go comfort the Tans.

"Forget your bike. You won't need it for long anyway. I'll do my best to get you away from Taiwan as soon as possible."

While Te's parents were busy arranging his escape to the USA, he locked himself in his room and dwelled on Yen's last words—that Te was his parents' crybaby and a coward.

"I will prove to Yen's spirit that I am neither a crybaby nor a coward anymore," Te said to his reflection in the mirror as he watched the childlike look disappearing from his eyes. "When I reach the USA, I'll become a fighter. If I see injustices, I'll fight against them . . . I owe those battles to my dearest friend!"

The day before Te's departure, he went to the middle school he and Yen had attended. He found the old banyan tree and saw on the aged trunk the words carved by two boys: "Ma Te and Tan Yen—Forever Friends."

14

Autumn 1958

SUMIKO YAMADA stood in a well-groomed garden in San Francisco and looked at the western sky.

White clouds moved slowly in the soft wind, like ladies with fluffy skirts dancing invisible steps. It would take the clouds a long time to fly across the Pacific to the peak of the Pali Mountain. The clouds would become raindrops before reaching Oahu.

"Will either the clouds or I ever see Paala again?" she asked the autumn sky.

She had been in San Francisco two years now. In the beginning she had written Paala almost every day.

"I've quieted down from my anger and hurt. I've thought things over and decided it has to be my imagination—about you and your case worker," she had written. "The love between us is so strong. The prison wall cannot possibly cut it off."

She had expected him to explain why he had refused to marry her and then to see her. "Say you still love me and I'll fly back to you," she had said in each of those letters. "I'll drop out of nursing school and come home."

He never answered any of her letters. No matter how deep her love was, it was difficult to talk to oneself. She reduced her letters gradually from one a week to one a month. When still there was no answer, she wrote even less.

Her letter of three months ago had been returned unopened with a note scratched on the envelope by the warden: Paala Nihoa was no longer in prison because he had been paroled.

Sumiko had asked her mother for Paala's new address. Mrs. Yamada had acquired an address from Paala's parole officer; it was on Maui island, where Paala's family was from, a small place called Hana that had been Paala's hometown. Sumiko had mailed two letters to Paala in the past two months, but had received no response.

"What can he do in Hana?" she asked the floating clouds as she remembered the quiet town she had visited once on a field trip. Paala must be desperately in need of the comfort of his hometown people for him to remain there.

"Sumi! What are you doing in the garden?" a woman called as she approached. She was in her mid-thirties, with a plump figure and a cheerful face.

"I'm looking at the clouds, Aunt Sung," Sumiko answered. The Chinese woman, as usual, had skipped the last syllable of Sumiko's name. Chinese names had only two syllables, while Japanese names could have three or more. It was difficult for Mrs. Sung to make the transition.

Before Sumiko had come to San Francisco to live with the Sungs, she was instructed by her mother to call Sung Hwa "Uncle," and Lu-an, Sung Hwa's wife, "Aunt." In the past two years Sung Hwa and Sung Lu-an had taken care of her not only as an uncle and aunt but also as a father and mother.

"What can you see in the stupid clouds?" The woman stopped and looked up at the sky with a totally confused expression. "I never bother to look at them at all."

Sumiko sighed as she stared at Mrs. Sung. The woman wore silk clothes, gold chains, and many pieces of antique jade. Her hair was piled high above her head by the skillful hands of a beautician. There was no fault in her features, but no beauty either. Her eyes were too dull to excite people, and the unchanging smile that kept her lips permanently parted gave her a rather dumb look.

"The clouds make me homesick, Aunt Sung."

"Then you should stop looking at them." Mrs. Sung continued walking, picking her way carefully across the lawn that had been watered by the gardener only minutes ago. "It's very silly of you to torture yourself."

"I'm not trying to torture myself, Aunt Sung. I don't like to miss my home, my family, or anyone else. But at times my feelings are beyond my control. Sometimes, Aunt Sung, I feel empty." Sumiko looked at Mrs. Sung's well-painted face. There was not one line around Sung Lu-an's eyes or on her forehead. At thirty-six, her skin was as smooth as that of any twenty-year-old. Perhaps the secret of eternal youth was to block off unpleasant thoughts such as one's husband's infidelity, Sumiko thought.

"Empty? You must be hungry." Mrs. Sung stopped on the last stepping-stone. She couldn't go farther without staining her satin shoes. "Come with me, Sumi." She gave a hand to the girl. "Let's go have something to eat. You had hardly any lunch. Of course you'll feel empty by now." She looked at her gold watch. "It's almost three!"

Sumiko took the woman's hand, walked toward the big house that stood at the other end of the large garden. She looked at the beautiful mansion and thought of the things she had heard.

The house had been a wedding present from Sung Hwa's mother. It was said that Sung Hwa had returned from the war a determined bachelor for reasons unknown. His mother had brought many beautiful young girls to him but he had refused to look at any of them. When he was thirty-two his mother had become seriously ill. She had pleaded with him with her supposed-to-be dying breath until he gave his consent to marry.

The bride was picked by the mother, and the son didn't seem to care. The wedding brought such magical curing power to the mother that she lived on.

Lu-an was a third-generation Chinatowner, a good old-fashioned girl. Her family owned several laundries and she had helped in one of the stores since quitting school after the sixth grade. She had pleased her mother-in-law tremendously with a virtue that was rare in these modern days. After keeping himself away from all women for many years, Sung Hwa had started to take mistresses right after he married, but Lu-an never showed either anger or jealousy.

However, the good relationship between Lu-an and her mother-in-law had ended two years later, when it was discovered by a doctor that Lu-an could never have children. The old Mrs. Sung had insisted that her son take his wife back to her father and have the marriage annulled. Sung Hwa had refused to do so. The old Mrs. Sung soon died. The young Mrs. Sung was so grateful to her husband for keeping her that she not only ignored his adultery but also treated him as a royal guest whenever he honored her with an occasional visit.

"I don't think your Uncle Sung will visit us today," Mrs. Sung Lu-an said with an ageless smile. "We can eat the dim-sum I saved for him."

Sumiko felt sad for her Aunt Sung. Every day the woman waited for her husband to come home and told the cook to make his favorite dim-sum. The food was left untouched until midafternoon. Only after that was Mrs. Sung forced to accept that Sung Hwa was once again too busy with his social life to visit his wife.

"Very good dim-sum. Steamed buns, spring rolls, shrimp dumplings . . . all the favorites of people from the Pearl River area . . ." Mrs. Sung rattled on.

Just when Sumiko was ready to leave the house, Sung Hwa walked in. At forty, the prosperous businessman looked trim and fit and dashing. But his handsome face always wore a sad expression. Sumiko didn't remember ever seeing him smile. She remembered overhearing him and her mother talking about the old days. It seemed that Uncle Hwa had lost his first love during the war; a beautiful girl in China had killed herself for some complicated reason.

"Good afternoon, Uncle Sung." Sumiko bowed to the man politely.

"Good afternoon." Sung Hwa paused, looking at Sumiko's pale blue uniform with white stockings and shoes and a net to confine her long hair. "Are you a student nurse already? Has time flown that fast without my knowing it?"

"No, Uncle Hwa, I am not a nurse yet," Sumiko said. "One of my professors assigned the second-year nursing students to work in the hospital a few hours every week so we can get the feel of being nurses. We are not paid, and we are lower in rank than the student nurses . . . even they can give us orders."

Lu-an was excited about her husband's rare visit, and Sumiko said good-bye to Sung Hwa quickly. She didn't want to be in the way. "Maybe my poor Aunt Lu-an can win her husband's heart back by some miracle," she said as she left the house.

"You're late," one of the student nurses said as soon as Sumiko walked out of the elevator.

Sumiko looked at the wall clock behind the nursing station. "Only by one minute. I waited a long time for the elevator."

"Don't argue with me!" said the girl in white uniform. "Room 304 has rested his finger on the call button for the past ten minutes. You better go see what the old grouch wants."

Sumiko bit her lip as she walked down the hall. She soon heard an angry shout: "I am an orderly, not a slave! You treat me this way because I am

Chinese! I will go to the administrator and protest!'' It was a man's voice, heavily accented and trembling with emotion.

She turned at the corner to go to Room 304, and saw a young man in the blue uniform of an orderly, arguing with an interning doctor in white.

Sumiko stared at the man in blue. He was at least a head shorter than Paala, much smaller in every way, his face pale, his hair cropped close to his skull. There was no resemblance between the two at all, yet this man reminded her strongly of Paala.

Could it be the angry look in his eyes? She had never seen another man in such deep fury.

The intern said to the orderly, ''Yung Zhang, go ahead. It'll be a miracle if the administrator has time for a lowly orderly's complaint!'' The intern marched away triumphantly.

''Due-na-ma!'' The orderly cursed in a language Sumiko couldn't understand but knew to be Cantonese.

She couldn't take her eyes from his face as she walked toward him. Something in this young man attracted her powerfully; for some reason beyond her comprehension, she felt she was walking toward her Paala.

''Don't let him bother you,'' she said with a shy smile. ''Interning doctors and student nurses don't know how to make themselves look big, so they pick on us to show their authority.'' She hesitated, then gave him her hand. ''My name is Sumiko Yamada.''

After a brief pause he took her hand. His own hand was shaking, his grasp tight and clenching—

like Paala's when he was upset and in need of her comfort.

"My name is Yung Zhang." His voice was low but deep. His nostrils flared and his lips trembled with anger. Hostility and distrust lingered in his deep-set eyes. "I don't agree with you. I think that intern was mean to me because he knew I was Chinese and very poor. Had I been either white or rich, he would have treated me with respect."

His words took Sumiko back to the days after Paala was beaten by the four haole men. How she had tried to straighten Paala's hate-twisted point of view. Now she recognized another troubled mind. She stared at Yung Zhang and her heart beat fast. All her love for Paala was stored in her heart. Perhaps she could give it to this young medical student who reminded her of Paala in too many ways.

Sumiko did something she had never done before. "When will you be off-duty?" she asked bashfully.

"In two more hours."

"I'll also be off by then," Sumiko mumbled. "Would you like to meet me in the cafeteria?"

Yung Zhang narrowed his eyes, studied Sumiko carefully. "Well, I suppose so," he finally answered.

Sumiko worked for the next two hours with a smile on her face. She seldom smiled these days—it was awful to be an ocean away from home. She often stood beside San Francisco Bay, looked at the waves, and pretended they were the same waves that hit the shores of Hawaii. She could look at the anger on Yung Zhang's face now and pretend it was the anger of her Paala.

Before rushing to the cafeteria, Sumiko took off her hair net and applied new lipstick. Yung Zhang was waiting for her at the entrance, and they took a corner table.

"What does 'Sumiko' mean?" Yung Zhang asked while eating.

" 'Girl of Beauty and Purity,' " Sumiko answered. "What does 'Zhang' mean?"

" 'Mountain,' " he said, then looked out the window with a frown. "I was named after a mountain in Kwangdung, which was called Canton when I was born. I was born in a small village called Jasmine Valley, a beautiful place the Pearl River flows through."

He put down his utensils and looked deeply into Sumiko's eyes. He didn't look away even when she began to blush. "You are very kind to me. In my life, not many people have shown me such kindness . . ."

He went on to tell her his story in his unique, attractive, low and deep voice. He was born out of wedlock in 1938. At that time and in a small village, an unwed mother had no right to continue her life. His mother drowned herself in the Pearl soon after he was born, leaving him at the doorstep of the local teahouse. The owner, an aged woman named Yung, took him in, fed him, and clothed him until she died of old age. While dying, she sent Zhang to Hong Kong to live with her stepdaughter, who was married to a wealthy jeweler named David Cohen, thinking that Meiping Cohen could raise Zhang in comfort and luxury.

Yung Zhang shook his head slowly. "But the Cohens and I didn't get along. They said I caused too much trouble. They put me in an orphanage, and I grew up there."

Sumiko reached across the table to take his hand. She said comfortingly, "I was also an orphan. I lost my parents during the war. But I was luckier than you. My adopted mother loves me and is very kind to me. And I also have two brothers . . ." She continued to tell him her story, and as she talked, she felt a bond developing between her and this young medical student. They were both far from home. She needed someone, and he obviously did too.

Zhang listened with his full attention, then told her more about himself. "I finished high school in Hong Kong. Mrs. Cohen was impressed by my grades and got me a scholarship in the United States. She also paid my way here. But Mrs. Cohen soon died and I was on my own. I'm in the last year of premed. I work in the hospital and everyone gives me a hard time. Mrs. Cohen's son has a home in San Francisco, but I am not welcome there."

It was Sumiko's turn to talk again. She told him everything about herself and Paala, but was too shy to mention the lovemaking on top of the Pali Mountain. ". . . now I live in the house of Mr. and Mrs. Sung Hwa. My mother and Sung Hwa were friends at one time—"

He interrupted her. "Is this Sung Hwa the same man who owns many businesses, including the largest restaurant in Chinatown?"

"Why, yes." Sumiko nodded.

"Sung Hwa is known to be one of the wealthiest men in San Francisco! And you live in his house?" Yung Zhang asked with disbelief.

Sumiko nodded again. She sensed Yung Zhang's deep interest in Sung Hwa's business, so she told him about how it was started years ago. "Uncle Sung came home from the war, didn't do much of anything for a long time. Then one day he saw in Chinatown an old restaurant called Yung Fa being torn down. Its original owners had died, and their son was uninterested in the restaurant business. Uncle Sung bought the lot and built a new restaurant on it. He called it Jade Garden because of an old poem."

Yung Zhang's eyes brightened. "I know the poem!" He then recited it: " 'Promises of love can be carried off by the wind, dreams of passion fade with time. Jade gardens will turn to ashes, and beautiful girls must die.' "

Yung Zhang then smiled at Sumiko for the first time since they had met, and that smile illuminated his sad face and made it handsome. "Only six months ago I went to Jade Garden to look for a job. The manager didn't want me as a waiter. Maybe you and I can go there as customers. I bet the manager will treat us nicely now." He waited anxiously for her to answer.

Sumiko had never gone out with a man in the past two years. Now she smiled at Yung Zhang and said, "All right. It's a date."

Sumiko drove away from the hospital toward the school of music, where she had enrolled in some music-appreciation courses. She was allowed to use their music rooms, but had never dared touch any of the pianos. Tonight she must find out if without Paala there could be music in her heart.

When she was in one of the piano rooms, her hands trembled as she uncovered the keyboard. Under that lid were not only eighty-eight keys but also her girlhood days. "If I can play the old tunes without shedding tears, then I can also face the old memories while starting a new life," she said, and took a deep breath.

She warmed her stiff fingers by doing the scales, then went to a sonatina, and after that a waltz by Chopin. She had forgotten the written music, but her fingers still knew where to go. All the music belonged to the days when she and Paala were together. As she played, she could almost hear Paala whistling outside as he waited for her. She was washed by a warm nostalgia, but the tears never came, and when she finished, she stood up and shut the piano lid firmly.

"That chapter of my life is finished, and a new chapter is about to begin," she said to herself.

She went from the music room to the student center's post office to buy stamps. A young man was ahead of her, talking to the postal clerk in stilted English. "Why no letter to China?" he asked.

"Because the People's Republic and the USA are not on friendly terms," the clerk explained patiently.

"But I want to find my sister," the young man insisted loudly. "I have not seen her for so many years now. They wouldn't let me write to her when I was in Taiwan. In your country people are supposed to be free to do everything. Why can't I write to my sister?"

"You are free to write to her, but she will not receive your letters." The postal worker looked at Sumiko, then said to the young man, "It's too hard to explain. If you'll excuse me, I must wait on the next customer."

The young man was unwilling to move aside. He raised his voice even higher, as if he were ready to fight. "Nine years ago my sister, Qing, lived in White Stone, near the capital of Kwangdung province. I want to mail a letter to her, addressed to that place. Your American airplanes fly to all places in the world. You have to put my letter on one of those planes!"

The mail clerk sighed. "The only solution is for you to find a person to transfer your letters. Do you know anyone in England, Canada, or Hong Kong?" He looked at Sumiko again. "Perhaps you can explain this to him."

The stubborn young man turned away from the window and faced Sumiko. His face was a study in anger and confusion.

Sumiko's nursing instinct stirred within her. She gave him a friendly smile. "If you can wait a few minutes, I would like to talk to you."

The man returned her smile, then quickly stepped aside to wait for her.

15

THE AUTUMN MOON was almost full. It shone on the Pearl River, changed the water into an endless bolt of silk flung out by a proud merchant to display its silver splendor.

The ripples glistened quietly, as if they were afraid to be heard—just like the three people on the riverbank.

"Baba, I am twenty-three, and Qing is eighteen. The party should not forbid us to marry. What reason can there be?" Fan Kuei asked, lowering his voice to a whisper.

"The party doesn't need a reason," Fan Yu sighed, "although in this case they do have a very good reason to turn down your marriage application: Qing has a Black Background."

They were standing under a weeping willow, surrounded by its many hanging branches. But Ma Qing looked around to make sure no one was hiding behind the other willows that lined the bank of the Pearl. "My Black Element family is no longer in White Stone. I don't even know where they are. Does the party still count me as one of them?"

Fan Yu sighed once more. "We'll know by tomorrow, when the five senior party members arrive from Kwangchow. They'll be here to supervise the Great Leap Forward Movement. The final decision on granting marriage permission is in their hands. They outrank all party members in White Stone. I'll be only their errand boy."

Qing and Kuei looked at each other in the moonlight. They had lived under the same roof for nine years now, and felt they had loved each other for a lifetime. The marriage law in the new China required the groom to be at least twenty and the bride eighteen. Now that Qing had reached marriageable age, they hoped to marry immediately.

When Qing and Kuei looked at Fan Yu, all the problems in their young hearts were replaced by compassion for a dear father who had become old before his time.

The former gravedigger had aged unbelievably in the past three years. The once-patriotic young comrade was now a disappointed old man. The fire in him had died when reality was splashed upon him like buckets of ice water. His position in White Stone had declined with the arrival of each new party official. This was 1958, only nine years after the liberation. But as he had just said, he could not even give his own son the permission to marry.

Birds stirred in the willow tree. The three of them jumped. Fan Yu's tired eyes filled with fear as he looked around. "Let's go home," he whispered. "If someone sees us, we can be accused of forming a gang and plotting against the party."

Qing and Kuei followed Fan Yu wordlessly. As soon as they were out of the protection of the willows, they parted from one another. In the past three years many new rules had been proclaimed in the new China. One of them was that when a group of people walked together, they were expected to keep at least five feet away from one another.

They moved quickly across an empty field. The moon was behind them, throwing their shadows on the ground. They looked at the phantom replicas of themselves, shared the same sorrow: they couldn't take their own shadows in their hands, nor could they grasp the happiness that was supposed to be theirs to hold.

Fan Yu lamented, "It's almost Mid-Autumn Festival. In the old days, all families would celebrate, and it would be the perfect time for my son to marry."

From a distance Qing and Kuei heard the deep sorrow in the old man's voice. They ignored the need for caution and moved to Fan Yu's side. "Baba, it's all right. Qing and I have waited many years. We can wait a little longer."

Qing put a hand on Fan Yu's arm, then rubbed her face against his shoulder. She could hardly believe that at one time she had hated this man with all her heart for what he had done to her family. Everything changed at high speed in the new China: a hunter could become the quarry, and hatred could turn into love.

"Please don't worry, Baba." She addressed him as Kuei did. "After Mid-Autumn is New Year, so there will be plenty of festivals for us to marry."

Fan Yu patted Qing's head. "I'll be very happy to have you as a daughter-in-law. Maybe your grandmother's spirit will forgive me then." He shivered as the wind tossed a thick cloud over the moon and the world was wrapped in a cold shroud of darkness.

They moved away from one another when the village houses came in sight. They walked the rest of the way home without exchanging one single word.

"Chairman Mao says if we have the willpower, we can do twenty years' work in one!" one of the five men on the platform shouted. His voice, greatly enlarged by the loudspeaker, was enough to shatter the eardrums of the villagers gathered in the town square.

The man continued. "In the cities, our people are speeding toward industrialization. Since White Stone is a farming and fishing village, we must increase our agricultural productivity and raise the amount of fish we catch!"

Qing and Kuei stood far from the platform, waited for the five new top men of the village to finish speaking.

"Do you think we'll find a chance today to apply for permission to marry?" Qing whispered.

"I don't know," Kuei answered. "They've been going on for half a day now, repeating not only themselves but also what the others have already said many times before."

"And they're repeating things that don't even make sense." Qing's voice was barely audible. "How can the fishermen catch more fish and the farmers grow more rice at Chairman Mao's command? If it could be done, it would have been done hundreds of years ago in one of the dynasties long before Chairman Mao was born."

The speaker raised his voice to a scream. "The

young people of White Stone will fish and farm diligently. But the old folks and children will also give their best to the movement." He paused. He had heard the low murmuring, and it bothered him. His audience kept their mouths tightly sealed when he and his comrades searched for those who had dared to whisper.

In the dead silence, the man continued. "The old and the young will become helpers to the farmers. They will be in charge of getting rid of the number-one enemy of the rice planters: the birds."

A mumbling sound rose from the puzzled villagers. "But the birds eat the insects . . ."

The speaker tapped on the microphone. The villagers jumped at the noise and the murmuring died down. The man on stage cleared his throat. "Chairman Mao says all birds must be destroyed. Those of you either too old or too young to work will carry pots and pans, stones and rocks at all times. If you see birds perched on high places, you'll make noise to scare them away. When you find birds within your reach, you must throw things at them to kill the destructive creatures. Chairman Mao calculates that half the seeds are eaten by birds during every planting season. Without the birds, the harvest will double."

He went on to repeat the same command twice more. After that, another speaker restated the identical order three more times. When the last speaker finished stressing the same idea in similar words a few times more, the villagers were allowed to leave the town square.

The fisherman headed for the Pearl River, to the boats that now belonged to the government. The farmers hurried toward the rice fields, to the plows and tools that had also become state property.

Those too old or too young to farm and fish didn't dare to tarry. They gathered pots and pans, searched for rocks and stones, then started to destroy the birds.

Chairman Mao's order was followed by villagers all over the new China; no one wanted to risk his own life for the life of a little bird. The Pearl River delta soon became a land with no birdsong.

In the winter of 1958 Qing and Kuei were allowed to marry.

"In the old days, even the poor had music on their wedding day. But we won't even have one songbird to sing for us today," Qing said sadly.

Qing and Kuei walked toward the town hall beside Fan Yu. They all had on old clothes and torn shoes. Qing still wore the single red bead around her neck. Other than that, the only ornament among them was a red flower in Qing's hair. It was a wild winter blossom that bloomed every December along the Pearl. Since wildflowers were pulled to make room for more useful plants, Kuei had had to search all morning to find one bud to adorn his bride's hair.

Kuei saw the tears in his bride's eyes and realized how she must feel: in the old days, the Ma family's granddaughter would have had a wedding grand enough for a princess. "If you want music, I'll be your songbird," he said cheerfully, and began to sing: " 'We'll have good luck and prosperity in our new life to come—' "

"Stop that!" Fan Yu said nervously. "Don't

you know you're singing a forbidden song? In the new China, it's considered superstitious to count on luck, and feudalistic to wish for prosperity." He looked around to make sure that no one had heard his careless son.

Quickly Kuei changed to a different song: " 'The sky is red. Bright is the sun rising from the eastern horizon. The world is rejoicing. Brilliant is the man born to the land of the east: our great leader Mao Tze-dung—' "

"Enough!" Qing covered her ears with her hands. "We hear that song from the loudspeakers one hundred times a day. Please spare me from it on our wedding day."

They reached the town hall, entered a small office. The only furniture was a filing cabinet and a desk. A senior party member was sitting behind the desk on the only chair, reading a paper and drinking tea.

Kuei took from his pocket the marriage permission he had received only yesterday after waiting for three months. He handed it to the man respectfully.

The man put down his teacup, studied the permission for a long time. "Ma Qing, are you the bride?" He narrowed his eyes, stared at the girl's loveliness, which couldn't be shattered by her shabby clothes and chopped-off hair.

"Yes," Qing answered, wondering at the question, since she was the only woman in the room.

The man put down the permission and opened the top drawer on his filing cabinet. He searched until he found a folder. He went through each sheet slowly while the three people stood waiting anxiously.

"Your background is as black as ink." He glared at Qing when he finished reading the last page.

Qing's face turned white. "I . . ." She didn't know the safe answer. She turned to look at Kuei.

Kuei stepped forward. "We reported everything honestly and in detail in our application form. Whoever granted us permission to marry must have accepted my future wife's background."

"Hm!" The man didn't conceal his anger. The permission had been granted to Fan Kuei and Ma Qing by someone of higher rank than he. He couldn't overrule the decision. But . . .

He glanced from the former gravedigger's son to the previous landlord's granddaughter, then picked up a rubber stamp. He knew how to handle this. "I'm ready to marry you now," he said as he grinned.

The ceremony was a series of filling out forms, rubber-stamping, and fingerprinting. An hour later Qing, Kuei, and his father walked away from the town hall with inkstained fingers but without one single word of congratulation from anyone.

The new father-in-law told the bride and groom, "I'm going to the cremation building to help the comrades. You know how it is. There are always so many bodies to be burned. And the family of the deceased always linger around the stove, trying to make sure that the dead doesn't feel pain while being charred. Their crying and screaming makes work almost impossible. I won't have time to come home for supper. I may even have to spend the night there on a cot beside the stove. You children just run along."

* * *

Qing busied herself with the supper. The rice bucket was almost empty. She scraped a handful of rice out of it, then put half of the grains back. She filled the pot with water, washed a sweet potato, cut it into small pieces, and dropped them into the pot.

She stayed in the kitchen and waited for the water to boil. She looked around, hoping to find something appetizing for her wedding feast. Her mouth watered at the memory of the delicacies that appeared daily in the dining room of her childhood home.

"I waited for you all the while." Kuei appeared at the kitchen door. "I thought you were washing yourself or something, so I didn't come to disturb you." He came over, stood behind her, and put his arms around her waist. "Never mind the cooking. I'm not hungry at all."

She didn't speak. She knew he was lying. He was always hungry. So was everyone else.

He buried his face in her hair. "You smell so good," he said, sniffing, rubbing his nose against her earlobes and then her neck.

It tickled her and she giggled. "You're smelling the flower you gave me," she said, taking the wild winter blossom from her hair and laying it on the table. "I don't smell good at all. I worked all the time and haven't washed myself for a week."

"Nor have I," he mumbled, nibbling her ears first, then her neck. "Why are we standing here and wasting our valuable time, my foolish little bride?"

He moved his hands to her breasts. He held them gently at first, kneaded them in his palms, then began to squeeze them. It hurt a little, but

Qing didn't want him to loosen his grasp. She closed her eyes, tilted her head back to rest against his chest. As she leaned her body against his, she felt something hard poking her backside.

"What's happening?" she whispered, then blushed at the answer that came from her imagination.

His mouth left her neck. His hands moved away from her breasts. "I've waited for this moment since you were sixteen. That was the first time I noticed your womanly figure," he said, turning her around to face him. "Baba has always been with us in the house. There are always watchful eyes everywhere in the village." He took her face in his hands.

"You are so beautiful," he whispered, then raised a hand to rub a speck of dirt off her forehead.

"I am so dirty," she said, laughing softly. "Please let me wash my face—" Her mouth was covered by his hand.

"I've seen you much dirtier than this." He moved his hand away from her mouth and stroked her cheek tenderly. "The little girl chasing after my wagon was filthy."

He smiled as he looked into her eyes. Then the smile was gone and his expression became serious. "I loved that filthy little girl when I helped her to climb up on my wagon. I've loved her all these years."

He moved quickly without giving her any warning. She found herself swept off the floor, clutched in his arms, being carried out of the kitchen.

"Kuei, the door is open," she mumbled in his embrace. "The children may peek in."

The villagers never liked to close their doors. But a year ago it had become compulsory for doors to remain open during the day, unless it was raining. One of the many jobs of the village children was to peek into people's homes to see what they were doing and to hear what was being said within each family. The children would then report to the authorities, often exaggerating and distorting what they had heard and seen.

"To hell with the little devils with long ears!" Kuei said. He marched to the front door with Qing in his arms, gave the door a hard kick, and closed it with a bang.

Kuei stood between two inner doors, debating whether to take his bride to the room he shared with his father or to Qing's room. He decided on the first, because Qing slept on a narrow cot. He carried her to the big wooden bed, put her on it, then sat beside her.

He smoothed her hair away from her face, looked from her parted lips to her heaving chest, then back to her lips again. "Your lips are trembling and you are breathing hard. Are you all right?" he asked with concern, as naive as she.

She nodded. He lowered his head toward hers and kissed her. His mouth was warm, his lips firm and aggressive. There had been many kisses between them during stolen moments, but his lips had always been soft and withholding.

Now his suppressed passion was freed. He kissed her hungrily, took her upper lip in his mouth and sucked on it, then moved to her lower lip with thirst.

"Qing, my Qing, you're all mine now!" His voice quivered. The tip of his tongue pried open her clenched teeth. As his tongue roamed everywhere in her mouth, his hands worked on the buttons of her blouse and then the tie string of her pants.

Evening light poured in through a high window, illuminated Qing's naked body. She lay quietly on her back, trembling as she watched her groom stand up to undress. No one had ever told her how to behave on her wedding night. Should the bride close her eyes? But she was full of curiosity for her groom's nakedness. In the past nine years she had never seen him without his pants. She had no idea what a man's sex looked like.

She stared at his erect penis. So this was the difference between him and her. She looked away quickly, moved her eyes to his narrow hips and flat stomach, his broad chest and strong arms, then his wide shoulders and handsome face. She saw him smiling at her and she felt her face burning.

"It's all right," he said gently, sitting beside her again. "You want to look at me, just as I want to look at you. We can look all we want, now that we are married.

"Your body is so white," he said, savoring her nakedness from head to toe. "I guess if you had never worked in the field, your face and arms would be just as white as the rest of you." He put a hand on her foot, playing with her toes one by one. "You would look like an ivory doll . . . my precious doll," he teased.

He put both hands on her, feeling every inch of her flesh, moving from her ankles to her calves, then to her knees and her thighs. He cupped the small dark triangle in his hand, and at the same time leaned forward.

As his fingers massaged her, parted her, and gradually entered her, his mouth was busy also. His lips caressed and kissed her breasts. His teeth nipped at them lightly. His tongue licked her nipples.

"I feel funny, Kuei!" Qing moaned. "I think I'm running a fever!"

Her inexperienced groom looked up and frowned. "I hope not. This is no time for you to be sick. It feels so good to touch you. Do you want to touch me too?"

"I don't know," Qing twisted from side to side. "Maybe I do . . ." She touched his chest quickly with the fingertips of one hand, then moved her hand to his back. He was right. It did feel good to touch those hard muscles. Her other hand joined the first one. She rubbed his back for a while, then began to pull him toward her.

"I still feel funny," she whispered, lifting her buttocks off the bed. "I feel an itch inside me, but don't know how to scratch it."

Kuei stetched out next to her in bed. "I feel the same itch. But I think I know just the way to scratch." He knelt over her, kissed her lips, and kneaded her breasts with his hands.

They were both surprised that everything fell into place so perfectly. Their bodies knew what to do. Their senses relished every moment of newfound ecstasy.

Afterward, they lay in each other's arms their skin sweaty and hearts pounding . When their heavy breathing returned to normal, Qing giggled.

"It's funny . . . I'm itchy again," she said, blushing and rubbing her young body against his.

"So am I!" He gave her a loving kiss, and was ready to take her again.

They were sleeping in each other's arms when the door burst open.

"Get out of here, you filth!" shouted the people as they charged in. "This is not your home anymore!"

Kuei grabbed his clothes and dressed quickly. He threw Qing's things to her so she could get dressed under the quilt.

There were about ten intruders, men and women, all grinning and staring at Qing's useless efforts to conceal her naked body.

"What do you mean, this is not our home anymore? My father and I have always lived here," Kuei said as he put on his pants. "The house was given to us by its original owner—" He didn't have a chance to continue.

"We know all about that!" shouted one of the men. "The original owner is an imperialistic pig! He had no right to give away the people's property! Your father was a good party member, so we ignored the whole thing until now."

A woman pointed a finger at Qing. "We cannot allow an enemy of the party to live in a brick house like this. Only a family with pure background deserves such a good home."

Kuei said, "Qing received official permission to live here—" Once again he was interrupted.

A man in party uniform stepped forward. "Ma

Qing was being punished for belonging to a family of oppressors, and the Fan Shen policy was carried out by making the landlord's granddaughter a servant to the gravedigger and his son. But since you two have become lovers, she has become the woman of the house. There is no more Fan Shen policy, and the whole thing has become unacceptable!"

Many hands grabbed Kuei and Qing and dragged them out of the house, although Qing was only half-dressed and Kuei had on only one shoe.

"You must talk to my father!" Kuei shouted as he struggled in the hands of the mob. "He is working in the crematory!"

Someone laughed. "No, he is not! We arrested him before coming for the two of you! Fan Kuei, can't you see that by marrying Ma Qing, both you and your father have become undesirables?"

Qing and Kuei were pulled and pushed, pounded and kicked all the way to the White Stone jail.

PART III

16

In the spring of 1959 Ma Te started his first class in sociology.

He looked around curiously.

The dozen chairs in this classroom were arranged in a circle, all on the same level. The professor's chair was also made of hard wood, no different from all the others.

There were two things wrong with this picture, Te thought. The professor did not have a pedestal, for one, and his chair was not covered with a thick cushion.

Then he heard his name being called.

"Ma Te, am I pronouncing your name correctly?" asked the professor, a white-haired man in gray pants and an open-necked white shirt.

Te stood up immediately as he observed two more mistakes. The first was the professor's clothes. The Taiwan professors always wore dark suits, although they might be tattered and ill-fitting. The second thing was the professor's question: a teacher should never ask a student if he was doing things correctly.

Te nodded, although his professor did not say his name correctly at all. What was supposed to be Righteous Conduct was now pronounced as

Peculiarity. Te couldn't help smiling at the funny sound.

The professor went on with another question. "Te, why don't you participate with the rest of the class?"

Te was quickly angered. How could the professor accuse him of being lazy, since he had been working so hard? "I . . ." He pointed at his notebook and textbooks. "Sir, I am participating the best I know how. I already wrote down every word you said. I will memorize the textbook word by word. You'll soon find out that I am not a lazy person at all!"

The professor noticed the fury in Te's eyes and asked himself: Why were the Asian students always so touchy? And why did they like to stand up when being called on? He softened his voice and smiled at Te as reassuringly as he could. "Please sit down. You make me nervous standing there. And I never said you were lazy. All you Asians are hard workers. I know. Almost all of you can finish both your bachelor's and master's degrees in less than five years, and it'll take us Americans much longer."

The professor waited for Te to sit. Te sat hesitantly, with his back stiff and feet together. He stared at the man and couldn't hide his wounded feelings. "I am Ma Te, not just another Asian student. Please don't categorize me with all the others," he said loudly.

The professor was surprised by the amount of anger in Te's voice. He looked at Te's rigid posture and noticed the knuckles on Te's right hand were white from gripping a pen tightly. "Please don't be so indignant. My comment about the

Asian students was meant to be a compliment. But I guess I should not have made it. And all I want to know is why you have not said anything. I don't want you to memorize the textbook or record my words. Did you understand what I said in the beginning of this class?"

Te answered quickly, "Yes, I did understand. Just give me one moment, and I can prove to you that I have done so."

In the silent classroom everyone heard Te reading from his notebook. " 'Today is the first day of my sociology class, and these are my professor's words.' " Te cleared his throat, then continued: " 'I welcome you to my class. During this semester we will list the many problems in our society. We will discuss them honestly. We will find the true causes of these problems, and come up with ways of solving them. Each class will be a group discussion. Every person is encouraged to participate. I hope the rain will stop soon. The windshield wipers on my car don't work too well. On my way here I almost skipped a stupid stop sign—' "

Te stopped reading when he heard the whole class laughing. He looked up with a red face. What had he done wrong now? He had taken the notes exactly as he would have done in Taiwan.

The professor stared at Te in disbelief. "Don't tell me you wrote down every single word that came out of my mouth!"

Te was extremely angry for a brief moment, then realized what he had done: the professor had lost face because Te had mentioned that his windshield wipers didn't work. Te answered apologetically, "I'm sorry, sir, for having offended you.

I'm sure your car is an expensive one, and your windshield wipers are working perfectly by now."

The class roared. The professor shook his head while laughing just as hard as the students. The feeling of being made a fool was like a fire ignited within Te. He glared at the whole class and raised his voice, "Don't you dare laugh at me because I am a Chinese!"

The laughter died down quickly, and a female voice could be heard from the far end of the room. "No one laughed at you because of your nationality, Ma Te. You're being overly sensitive. My God, I didn't know anyone else could be as sensitive about racial differences as I am."

Te followed the voice and saw the most beautiful girl he had ever laid eyes on. Only recently he had watched an opera on TV—*Aïda*. This girl reminded him of that princess, in a much smaller frame and with a more delicate face. Like Aïda, she looked proud and fearless. She was smiling at him broadly, revealing perfect teeth.

"My name is Delia Porter," she said to him from across the room, then looked away from him and glanced over the other students and the professor. "I'm sure you have all realized by now that we have just witnessed one of the most serious problems in our society."

Te tilted his head to one side, studied the girl with deep interest. She wore a short-sleeved sweater, skirt and loafers. Her hair was curly and short, her skin smooth and the color of dark chocolate. The gold loops hanging from her earlobes danced beside her long neck as she turned her head from side to side, glaring at everyone.

She said, "We Americans are the most self-centered people in the world. Because America is a rich country, we think we have a model society, a perfect example for the human race." Fire sparked in her large dark eyes. Rage parted her natural-red lips. Even the nostrils on her upturned little nose flared in exasperation as she continued. "We laugh at people from societies dissimilar to ours because their behavior seems strange to our ignorant eyes."

Delia Porter paused. Her eyes kept defying the others, daring them to disagree. Everyone avoided her challenging eyes; even the professor seemed embarrassed. She continued. "I laughed with you a while ago, but I've also been laughed at enough. The Asian culture is many thousands of years old, just like the African culture of my people. But in the eyes of white men, Ma Te and I are second-class citizens." She raised her voice. "It is an undeniable truth that the Chinese, the Negroes, and all the other minority races are rejected and ridiculed by white America!"

As soon as Delia finished, Te took a deep breath and began to talk. "Miss Porter is right. She and I are not second-class citizens. You must not laugh at us. We will not allow it!"

The other students looked away from the challenging eyes of Te and Delia. Some of them murmured their displeasure, but no one argued. After a long silence, the professor cleared his throat. "I think we owe Te an apology. I shouldn't have made an issue of his taking detailed notes, and we certainly shouldn't have laughed. It's just that we are very ignorant of the study habits of students from foreign countries." The professor smiled at Delia and said, "Delia, you've made a good point. Our society *does* have a tendency to expect everyone to behave exactly the way we do. And we like to tag all things foreign to us as 'bizarre,' 'odd,' 'funny,' or 'absurd.' Now, let's see what we can do to correct our mistake."

Te couldn't believe it was so easy to fight authority in the USA. "America is truly a great country!" he said to himself, then looked across the room at Delia Porter. She smiled at him, and their eyes held for a long time.

Te unlocked his mailbox and found a letter from his father. He opened the envelope and a check fell to the floor. He picked it up and smiled at the amount. Baba must be doing extremely well to be so generous. Te pocketed the check and went to one of the tables beside the Coke machines.

". . . Taiwan is becoming more prosperous with each passing day. It's a shame that people are starving on the mainland. You mentioned you are still trying to contact Qing. Your Mama and I want you to be very careful when doing it. If the Americans should frown upon your writing to someone in a communist country, then forget about your sister.

"Your mother and I gave up Qing a long time ago—when we gave her to her grandmother. Your mother missed her very much in the beginning, but then she gave all her love to you, and Qing became merely a memory.

"We were poor once, when we first arrived in Taiwan. It wasn't easy for me to become rich. Now that I have regained my wealth, I don't want to do anything to jeopardize it. The government would take away all my trading privileges if they knew I was communicating with anyone on the mainland; that is how the Chiang Kai-shek regime is. Qing is a girl, and we can't let a girl endanger the Ma family's future. . . ."

Te finished reading the letter but continued to sit in deep thought. Being an ocean apart from his parents had enabled him to look at them more objectively, and he didn't like what he saw:

With age, Mama had become even more docile than she used to be. It was a mother's nature to love all her children, but since Baba said they couldn't afford to love Qing, Mama held back her love. Baba had changed a great deal through the years. When his pockets became loaded with more money, his heart turned colder.

Te put away the letter and walked across the campus. He was hungry. He thought of the food in the cafeteria and frowned.

"Ma Te!"

Te turned. Delia Porter came running from the administration building, waving at him and smiling broadly.

Te could hear his heart drumming when Delia came closer. She was like a ray of sun shining through the campus, bringing illumination and warmth. She looked extremely beautiful today. Her white slacks and blouse contrasted her dark skin. She always wore colorful looped earrings; they were red ones now. Te had noticed that all her colors were strong and definite, just like her: no shades of gray, no in-betweens.

"I just won a battle, you'll be delighted to know." Delia stopped beside Te and smiled brightly.

"What was the battle?" Te asked, admiring the beam of victory in her eyes.

"I went to the placement center and told them that right now the black and Asian students only get cafeteria jobs and jobs that the white students don't want. I demanded that changes be made. At first they pretended that they didn't notice such things. Then they gave me many ambiguous excuses. So I finally asked them: how would you like to see all the minority students marching on campus and holding signs?"

She tilted her head back and laughed proudly. "After I said that, it didn't take them long to promise me that more library and office jobs will be given to minority students in need of financial aid."

"You fought with the school officials?" Te was instantly excited. "Why didn't you tell me? I would have joined you to fight against the unfair rules I'm running into. Did you know that with my student visa I am not allowed to get a work permit? This is why the Asian students can't find jobs any better than dishwashers, waiters, and waitresses?"

"I didn't know that. It seems you and I are being mistreated in this country in different ways, and we should exchange information," Delia said, and began to laugh again. "What a team we'll make, and what a problem we'll create for the administration!"

Te discovered that when she laughed, the sun moved closer to earth, and the whole world became brighter and warmer. Bathed in such powerful light and heat, his shyness was dazzled away. He heard himself asking, "Would you like to celebrate the beginning of our troublemaking team with a dinner in Chinatown with me?"

Delia agreed immediately, and an hour later they were at Jade Garden.

"It looks like a fancy place." Delia admired the gilded dragons curling on the thick posts and the green tiles shining on the pointed roof. "Are you sure we can afford it?"

"Yes," Te answered proudly. "Don't worry. You can order the most expensive dinner and the best imported wine."

He didn't notice the strange expression that suddenly appeared on Delia's face. He was busy acting the part of a man used to taking pretty girls to restaurants.

A waiter greeted Te with familiarity as he took them to a table near a small empty stage. "It's clever of you to come early, Mr. Ma. In a little while the place will be crowded and the entertainment will begin," the man said. "Tonight we have a young female singer from Hong Kong." He pulled out chairs for Te and Delia, then stood waiting.

Te looked at the wine list and asked Delia, "Would you like to try the plum wine? It's sweet and mild and made in Taiwan. Or do you prefer something from Europe—?" He stopped.

All the light and warmth had disappeared from Delia's face. She was frowning with disapproval. She gave the waiter a hard glance of dismissal. "Give me a beer that's made in this country."

When the waiter was gone, Delia leaned forward and said with a scowl, "I am disappointed in you!"

"Why?" Te was puzzled.

Delia stared at Te and her dark eyes were piercing like sharp knives. "I liked you very much when you were angry with the professor and our classmates for laughing at you. I came to dinner with you because I thought you were not only a handsome man but also a big man. But now I realize you may still be handsome, but you are certainly not very big at all."

"Why am I suddenly reduced in size?" Te asked angrily.

The waiter arrived with their drinks. Delia waited for him to leave, then began to talk. "I know you are about my age, and not working. It's evident you come here often. One of the things I can't stand is a jobless young man wasting money on useless things. Are you spending your father's money?"

Te narrowed his eyes, studied Delia for a while, then answered with pride. "Yes. My father is a wealthy businessman in Taiwan. He pays for my schooling, living expenses, and gives me a good allowance. I am his only son and he wants me to live well. Do you have a problem with this?"

"I sure do. I'd be very ashamed if I were you," Delia said with a sneering look.

Te's face became the color of Delia's scarlet earrings. "Ashamed?" He raised his voice. "Why should I be? It's not only a son's right but also his obligation to be supported by his parents. Someday the parents will be old and the son will be the rice-winner, and then it'll be the son's turn to support the aged ones—that, too, will be not only a privilege but also a duty."

Delia stared at him. She seemed intrigued by his theory. After a while the hardness on her face softened. Her cold eyes were warm again. A smile appeared slowly, curling her lips. She opened her mouth, showing her gleaming teeth and filling the quiet dining room with her roaring laughter. "I'm so sorry!" she said while laughing, offering her hand to Te from across the table. "I'm no better than any of the arrogant white Americans!"

Te cocked his head to one side, studied her with amusement. Did all African princesses change their moods with the speed of lightning? A sunny day could suddenly become a stormy night, and then the next moment a killer typhoon could turn into a gentle breeze. It took time for the damaged trees to recover from a hurricane, and his wounded feelings could not heal at her command. He wouldn't take her extended hand.

"I already apologized!" Delia said. "Shake my hand or I'll throw the beer in your face!"

She just might carry out her threat, Te thought, so he took her hand reluctantly and murmured under his breath, "What a way to start a friendship!"

"As long as we're friends, I'll explain why I was so disgusted with you," Delia said, still holding hands with Te. "My home is in Mississippi. My parents were born in a small town where higher education was beyond their reach. They went to New York together and received their degrees in elementary education. They were married in New York, then went home to teach. In a school for Negroes, naturally. I grew up in a comfortable home. I had more things than my friends. But I always knew I had to stand on my own, work and fight hard so I could earn a place for myself in a world that is filled with injustice."

Delia paused to take a swig of her beer. "In this country we encourage independence. Whether black or white, we want our children to be strong individuals. As soon as our children are old enough, they'll try to earn their own money—delivering newspapers, selling lemonade, whatever they can do. Once we reach eighteen, very few of us can feel comfortable living as freeloaders in our parents' homes. We'll either move out or pay our parents something for our room and board—"

Te interrupted her. "You are joking! No parents will accept money from their children for living under their roofs and eating their food! A child renting a room from his own father and mother? Nothing that ridiculous can exist under the sun!"

Delia gave Te's hand a firm squeeze. "Listen to yourself, Ma Te. You are no better than I. You, too, are expecting the whole world to do things only one way . . . your way."

They continued to talk. Delia complained about things in the USA, and Te told her that in Taiwan things were much worse. "People are pushed around by the government," he said, then told her about Tan Yen. "I have had enough. I will fight with the world from now on."

Delia said, "When we were in class, I felt the fighting spirit in you, and it attracted me immensely—that and your good looks. You remind me of my people who finally decided to fight. Ma Te, let us fight side by side." She took both of his hands.

"I thought our team was already formed a while ago," Te said, smiling.

His smile faded when he noticed the waiters

and Chinese customers looking at four hands entwined on the table. He ignored the loathing stares of his fellow countrymen and continued to talk with Delia.

Te had never known that he could talk to a girl as freely as he could to a boy. He described to her his childhood days, his parents, and his sister. "Someday I'll find her . . ." he went on, until the waiter arrived to take their orders.

Te looked at Delia mischievously and said, "I would like to treat you to something nice, but then, I don't want you to be angry with me for wasting my father's money. The cheapest thing is a bowl of plain noodles, and the most expensive is lobster. I guess I'll let you decide."

Delia threw her head back and laughed. "If we want our friendship to last, we better learn to accept our different ways. If it's your right and obligation to waste your father's money, who am I to save it for him?" She pointed at the menu and said, "I usually order chicken chop suey, but lobster Cantonese sounds great!"

Te sighed with relief. He would have lost much face in front of the waiter if she had ordered something cheap. He ordered lobster for Delia and crab for himself.

The band began to play. A young girl in a tightly fit long shining gown appeared onstage, started to sing a popular Chinese song in a thin squeaky voice.

Neither Te nor Delia noticed that all the other Chinese were watching them with the same question written clearly in their eyes: Why was a nice Chinese boy holding hands with a Ha Gui—a Black Devil?

17

TIME HAD STOOD still in Hana for many decades. It was 1960, but no city signs had arrived to change the picture of a paradise.

It rained every morning. The misty shower never lasted long. When the sky was still gray with clouds, the sun began to shine. Two rainbows appeared. One bright, the other a shade paler. They curved side by side across the mountaintop.

At the foot of the mountain and in the middle of a banana grove stood a small hut. It had been built many years ago by the Nihoa family, in the traditional way, on a high foundation of bamboo posts and rocks. The door was a draped sheet woven with coconut leaves. Today when it was lifted, a man appeared. He was twenty-five. His tall frame was thin but solid, his handsome face peaceful. The determination in his dark eyes and the perseverance in his firm jawline could be detected only through close observation.

"My home is the home of twin rainbows," Paala Nikoa said, looking up at the sky. "Sumiko, are there many rainbows in San Francisco?"

Lines of sorrow appeared on his forehead. He shook his head, closed his eyes momentarily.

When he opened them again the lines were gone. He lifted his chin, then peeked through the banana trees to look at a narrow path.

"Maybe something good is waiting for me today," he said, and walked away from the hut, wearing only a pair of shorts and sandals. "Maybe today I'll become good enough to go to my Sumiko."

Flowering trees lined the path. Their branches met over Paala's head, entwined, formed a canopy of flowers. "When I am good enough for you, Sumiko, I'll write to you. And then, under a canopy like this, you and I will walk toward the waiting high priest." He began to walk faster.

A breeze passed through the branches, shook the canopy, sent a few wet blossoms dancing. Paala paused, caught a petal, brought it to his lips, kissed it gently. In its fragrant softness he found Sumiko's mouth, in its dampness her tears.

"Forgive me, my Sumiko, if my hiding away from you makes you cry. It takes all my willpower to destroy your letters without reading them. I am afraid that once I read them, I will change my mind. I can't do that, my Sumiko. I have to stay away from you because I am a proud man . . ." His voice shook. He bit his lip, moved on with the wet petal in his hand.

The trees thinned. The path reached its end. Paala continued on a winding road. On both sides of him, mountains rose high. A waterfall poured down from the clouds, ended in a large pool. Two birds, with feathers the colors of a rainbow, perched on a protruding rock, bathed in a mist created by the splashing water. They cocked their heads to one side and looked at Paala, then sang a few notes to greet their old friend.

Paala whistled back a series of notes similar to theirs. "Sorry for returning your duet with a solo," he saluted the familiar birds as he passed them. "Someday Sumiko and I will sing together for you."

A general store appeared on one side of the road, a post office on the other.

"Aloha, Paala!" a woman called from the doorstep of the store. "The mail truck was here just a few minutes ago. I believe it has good news for you."

"Mahalo," Paala thanked her. "I hope you're right."

The post office was operated by an old man. His face was very dark, his hair silver white. He looked at Paala over his glasses and said, "It's a thick envelope, maybe a contract."

Paala's heart beat fast. "I hope so." He extended a trembling hand toward the counter.

The old man handed Paala the brown envelope then turned away. Age had taught him that when a young person was hurt, the pain was easier to endure away from watchful eyes.

"Mahalo," Paala thanked the postmaster for his consideration.

In Hana, very few villagers contacted the outside world. It was customary for people to open their letters in the post office, share their news with whoever was present. The old man had been thrilled by Paala's sending the songs he had composed to the mainland, and was convinced that a contract from an agent would come soon. But so far each letter for Paala had arrived with a rejection. After witnessing Paala's disappointment again and again, the old man no longer wished to watch Paala open his mail.

Paala held the thick envelope next to his heart as he walked to the waterfall. "Please, let this be the long-awaited contract," he prayed earnestly.

The rainbow-colored birds were gone. He sat on the protruding rock, took a deep breath, then opened the envelope.

His eyes fell on the familiar sheets mailed out two months ago—eight songs composed by him either in a prison cell in Honolulu or in the primitive hut in Hana. He had learned the rudiments of composition in an educational program offered by the state, and then continued writing songs in the little hut left to him by his parents. He had decided not to return to singing until he could perform his own songs. His melodies were the themes of his love for Sumiko, the lyrics the pledges of his devotion.

He searched the envelope for a letter, but couldn't find one. The agent hadn't even bothered to scribble a brief note of rejection.

"I know these are good songs!" His voice quivered. Holding the music sheets like a mother cradling her precious baby, he lifted his eyes to the crown of the waterfall.

Thick clouds shrouded the mountain peak, making the origins of the water a mystic land far beyond his reach. "All I need is someone to give me a chance! Please! How can I take my first step toward becoming a songwriter if no one is willing to look at songs written by an unknown?"

More clouds gathered. The magic kingdom was

now concealed by a dense wall. Paala kept staring upward until his neck ached.

Suddenly he shouted, "I'll never get there!" He stood up, let go of the music sheets, and raised his hands to heaven. "Rich and famous? What a hopeless dream! I'll never even become a published songwriter! I'll never have anything to offer my Sumiko!"

The music sheets fell into the pond. The waterfall splashed them forcefully and swirled them about for a moment. Then the sheets began to sink. Paala looked down and saw his hard work floating away. He hadn't even kept copies of these songs.

"No!" A deep lamenting moan came from his heart, reverberated through the valley. "Sumiko! Please wait for me!"

Across the Pacific from Hana, Sumiko was in her room in the Sung house, sitting beside an open window. She could see the gray clouds gathering and hear the wind whistling a sad tune. She looked at the old jewelry box in her hands, opened it, and a soft music began to play. The music box had been made in Japan. The song was "Spring Rain."

Sumiko saw herself and Paala on Waikiki beach in the spring rain. She was sixteen. He kissed her for the first time like a man kissing a woman, and told her that when she reached eighteen they would marry.

In the box white shells lay shining, each the size of a pearl. Nature had put a tiny hole in the middle of every shell and colored its rim with the most beautiful touch of lavender and pink. Sumiko picked up the largest one, held it in the center of her palm, then brought it close to her mouth.

She kissed it tenderly, calling in a tearful voice, "Paala, I still remember the day you gathered them for me. I found them in a coconut shell beside you when you were lying there unconscious. The police took you to the hospital and I took the shells. They've been with me ever since . . ." Her voice faded away.

In her heart the voices of two children clamored in the wind.

A boy's voice said, "I give you this shell, and I also give you my love. Little Sumiko, I am the island's son. Whatever I give, I'll never take back."

A girl's voice answered, "Paala, I'll treasure this shell, and I'll treasure your love . . . forever and ever!"

A tear fell on the shell, turning the lavender and pink more vivid, the shell a splendid jewel. "What destroyed our happy days? What shattered our beautiful dreams? Why don't you answer my letters?" Sumiko began to sob. She closed the box. The music stopped abruptly. The lovely song never reached its end.

"Sumi! Your young doctor is here!" Mrs. Sung entered without knocking. "Come! A woman must never keep a man waiting!"

Sumiko frowned as she hurriedly dried her tears. She knew the woman didn't mean to be rude: Mrs. Sung honestly believed that the elders had every right to enter the room of a younger person without giving notice or asking for permission.

Sumiko put the music box in a drawer and stood

up. "Aunt Sung, Yung Zhang is not a doctor. He is only a medical student."

Mrs. Sung said, "He likes to be called Dr. Yung. He always smiles and answers to that title. Your uncle is not home very often. It's nice to have a man in the house. You and I should do our best to make Dr. Yung happy. Why don't you call him doctor too? A woman must do her best to please her man, you know."

"Yung Zhang is not my man, Aunt Lu-an," Sumiko said, following Mrs. Sung to the living room. "We are only friends."

"A young man and a young woman are never friends," Mrs. Sung said, shaking her head. "A man is an empty cup, and a woman the warm tea. They have to pair up. He holds her and she fills him up."

Sumiko smiled at the philosophy but couldn't help disagreeing. "That's not true, Aunt Sung. Take Ma Te and me: we are good friends."

"Hm! That's because the stupid boy has a Ha Gui Moi already. When a teacup is already full, of course it doesn't have room for more tea."

Sumiko wanted to argue further, but they were nearing the living room.

Yung Zhang had helped himself to the cigarettes in a silver box. He had his feet propped up on a low table and had leaned back and rested his head on the brocade sofa. He was blowing smoke rings toward the high ceiling when the two women entered.

He had followed Sumiko home the first time they went to Jade Garden, and Sumiko had not been able to tell him no. After that Yung Zhang began to visit whenever he pleased. It was easy for him to feel big and important here; it was a feeling he had always relished but seldom captured.

He took his time removing his feet from the table. He stood up slowly, walked toward the two women with a cigarette dangling from the corner of his mouth.

"I'm here to take you ladies to Jade Garden for dinner," Yung Zhang said. He liked to stay in the Sung house for hours, but he had already stayed for dinner on his past several visits. It would be to his disadvantage to wear out his welcome. Besides, when he had either Mrs. Sung or Sumiko with him, he always received free meals in that fabulous restaurant.

Sung Lu-an grinned broadly. "You young people run along. I must stay home and wait." She nodded at the door, said confidently, "My husband may come home today. He just may."

Sumiko put a hand on the plump woman's soft arm. "Aunt Sung . . ." She stopped. It would be too cruel to demolish her aunt's castle of dreams. She forced a smile to her face and said, "Yes, Aunt Lu-an. Uncle Sung just may come home today."

At times Sumiko was glad that Zhang wanted to take her out, because occasionally that would take her mind away from Paala. Today she missed Paala more than usual. Her heart ached so much that she couldn't take it anymore. She turned to Yung Zhang and said hastily, "I'm ready."

He glanced at Sumiko from head to toe. She had on flat shoes, a gray skirt, and a white blouse. Her hair was tied back with a white scarf, and she wore no makeup. Her eyes were red, the lids puffy, as if she had just cried.

Zhang liked girls in bright colors and heavy makeup with strong perfume. He knew he was a handsome man himself, but he also wanted people to notice the beauty of his lady companion and envy him. It was too bad that Sumiko had such attractiveness but always chose to make herself unnoticeable. He asked with a frown, "Aren't you going to change?"

Sumiko shook her head. "Do I look unpresentable?"

Her heart pained when she thought how carefully she used to dress when going out with Paala, and how badly she had always wanted to please him and impress his friends. Since she had parted from Paala, she had lost all interest in making herself look nice.

Yung Zhang quickly disguised his unhappiness. He couldn't afford to hurt Sumiko's feelings.

"You look great." He took her arm and led her toward the door. "You are always the most gorgeous girl in my eyes."

He had found her merely nice-looking in the beginning, and then had felt her good looks greatly improved by the wealth of her guardian, Sung Hwa. But just recently he had discovered another asset that made Sumiko even more valuable to his future. He must hold on to her tightly, whether she looked glamorous or not.

"Sumiko, shall we take your car?" he asked in his gentlest voice. "My car is very old and yours is much newer. It will give us more face if we ride in yours."

Sumiko sighed. She opened her purse and took out a ring of keys. She gave them to Zhang without a word.

"When I become a doctor, I'll buy the most expensive sports car . . ." Yung Zhang chatted happily on the way to Chinatown.

Soon after Sumiko and Yung Zhang had left, the phone rang in the Sung house. It was a long-distance call from Hawaii, from Mrs. Yamada.

Sung Lu-an said, "Sumi went to Chinatown with her boyfriend, the young doctor."

After a brief pause Mrs. Yamada asked, "Mrs. Sung, please tell me how things are between my daughter and this young man. If I ask her, she will say he is no more than a friend."

"Much more than a friend!" Mrs. Sung said positively. "Sumi is too shy to admit that. This Dr. Yung Zhang is very interested in marriage, I can tell. He comes here to see Sumi at least once a week. Every time he is here, he doesn't want to leave. I told Sumi to hold on to him. After all, how many lucky girls get to marry doctors? Sumi is pretty, but not smart enough to please men. If this nice young doctor marries someone else, Sumi will be sad, and so will you and I."

Mrs. Yamada said hesitantly, "I don't want to see Sumiko sad. She's been sad for too long a time. But are you sure she loves this Yung Zhang?"

"Well, I caught Sumi crying a while ago, listening to her old music box and staring at a pile of stinky shells. But then the young doctor came and she stopped crying. What does that tell you? Love or no love?"

After another pause Mrs. Yamada asked, "Do you think this young doctor is a good man? Is he from a decent family? Are his feelings for Sumiko sincere?"

Mrs. Yamada had never met Mrs. Sung Hwa, and Hwa had never talked about his wife in any of his letters. But Mrs. Yamada knew that her old friend Hwa wouldn't marry a stupid woman. She could trust Mrs. Sung's judgment.

"You can't find a young man better than Dr. Yung Zhang," Mrs. Sung answered firmly. She then continued with confidence, "Of course he is from a good family. Have you ever heard of the son of a bad family becoming a doctor? He is very devoted to Sumi, of course. Otherwise, why should he be here so often?" The woman went on in a tone of authority, "Well, I am much older than Sumi, and the older ones are always much wiser: Confucius cannot be wrong. Mrs. Yamada, I love your Sumi. I want her to be as happy as I am. I want her to have a husband as good as mine. I am positive Dr. Yung is the right man. Let's do something to help."

Sumiko and Yung Zhang came home to find Mrs. Sung Lu-an nodding on the living-room sofa. She gave them a big smile. "Congratulations!"

"What for?" Sumiko asked. She had hoped that her Aunt Lu-an had gone to bed. Without this kind woman's overenthusiasm, maybe Yung Zhang would leave sooner.

"Yes, what for, my dear Aunt Sung?" Yung Zhang addressed Mrs. Yung warmly, and the woman's face brightened immediately.

"For a big surprise," Mrs. Sung said proudly.

It wasn't often that she had the chance to announce such important news. It was always other people who had the opportunity to tell her things. "Sumi, your mother called. She and I had a nice long talk. You are graduating soon. She wants to give you a splendid present. I helped her to decide on the gift."

Mrs. Sung paused to maintain the suspense. She giggled like a little girl, then continued. "Surprise! It will be two round-trip tickets"—she looked from Sumiko to Zhang—"to Hawaii for the two of you."

"No! Aunt Lu-an . . ." Sumiko said.

Before Sumiko could object any further, Yung Zhang jumped up and cheered. "I'm going to Hawaii! I'll be on that paradise island that only the rich can afford to see!"

He saw Sumiko frown. He knew instantly that she didn't want to go to Hawaii with him. In that case, he must nail down the deal right now.

"Aunt Sung," he said quickly, "may I use your phone to call Mrs. Yamada? I want to thank her for her kind offer and let her know that Sumiko and I will be there whenever she wants us."

Mrs. Sung smiled her approval of the young doctor's good manners. She answered him by pointing at the phone.

"Wait, Zhang . . ." Sumiko stepped forward, wanting to state her many reasons for objecting to this trip, but she didn't know how.

Soon after meeting Yung Zhang, she had discovered that she could not forget Paala as totally as she had hoped. Regardless of the similarities between the two men, Zhang was not Paala, and she could not love Zhang as she did her first love.

She had not been home for four years now. Her family had visited her several times, and when each vacation neared, they had repeated their request for her to come home. Last year, when Hawaii had become the fiftieth state of the USA, her family had insisted that she join them for the celebration, but she had refused.

She finally continued, ". . . Zhang, let me think it over."

Yung Zhang couldn't allow her time to think. He put on his warmest smile and said in his softest voice, "Sumiko, we mustn't be ungrateful. You don't want to hurt your mother's feelings, do you?"

"No, of course not, but—"

Yung Zhang leaned closer. "Your mother adopted you and has done so much for you—that's what you told me yourself. What did you ever do for her? Don't you think you should make her happy just this once?"

Sumiko stared at Zhang's handsome face and many things flashed through her mind. It had been five years since Paala went to jail. He had refused to see her during visiting hours. His attractive case worker . . . all the unanswered letters! She stepped aside to let Yung Zhang go to the phone.

When he dialed the number given to him by Mrs. Sung, Sumiko stood numbly, listened to Zhang's words as if they were irrelevant to her.

He wanted the trip so badly that he was completely unashamed to be thick-skinned. "Mama Yamada," he addressed a lady he had never met, "Sumiko and I can't wait to thank you in person for your kindness. We'll be forever grateful. . . .

Yes, I'm sorry to hear you'll be tied up in court and unable to attend Sumiko's graduation. . . . Yes, I agree that you and her brothers should wait for us in Hawaii, and we'll celebrate her graduation there. . . . Yes, Sumiko and I have known each other for quite some time. Mama Yamada, to me she is not only the most beautiful girl but also the most priceless one. I will take care of her on the long flight to Hawaii, and I will also take care of her throughout life . . ."

He kept on talking, saying yes to his Mama Yamada, confirming and reconfirming the Hawaii trip. When he was finally through, he gave the receiver to Sumiko with the smile of a man absolutely confident of his victory.

Sumiko heard her mother's voice coming from the other side of the wide ocean, sounding happy and excited. "Sumiko, why didn't you tell me you've got yourself a boyfriend? He sounds like such a marvelous young man! So polite, and devoted to you, not to mention the fact that he will soon become a medical doctor!"

18

LAHAINA WAS AN old capital city on the west end of Maui island. In the center of the town was the office building of Paala's parole officer.

"You are now a free man," the parole officer said to Paala. "You don't have to see me anymore. But you do have to go to Oahu island and bring my signed statement to the main office for your full release."

Paala flinched. "Must I do that?" He had sworn not to return to Oahu without first becoming a success.

The man nodded uncompromisingly.

Paala returned to Oahu reluctantly. He finished his business with the chief parole officer, then went to revisit a few places.

At Hanauma Bay he remembered the childhood days. "You must have thrown away those puka shells already, Sumiko," he said sadly. "I hope you haven't thrown away the love I gave you together with the shells."

On top of the Pali lookout he stood in the thick mist against the howling wind. "Queen Pali, bring me to my Sumiko, please," he whispered with his eyes closed, then added, "But first you must make me invisible. Because I don't want her to see me before I'm worthy."

When he reached Waikiki Beach, it was raining. He walked on the beach, and got soaked. He recalled the spring rain of many years ago when he had kissed Sumiko and told her he would marry her as soon as she was old enough. There was no salt in the rain, but when he licked his lips, he tasted the salt of his tears.

The night before his return to Maui, he decided to pay Mrs. Yamada a visit. "I want her to know how difficult it has been. She should be proud of me . . . or at least agree that I have kept my promise."

On his way to the Yamada house Paala remembered the day Mrs. Yamada had come to see him in prison. Her words had been like a lightning bolt that shocked him into realizing he was bad for Sumiko. He repeated his vow of that day—"I promise you, Mrs. Yamada, I will never try to see Sumiko until I have made something of myself"—now as he neared the house. He looked sadly at the apartment over the garage that had been his home at one time.

The streetlights were dimmed by the thick foliage of a tall coconut palm. In the darkness he entered the garden where his father used to work, moved among the trees and flowers he had helped to care for.

He reached the plumeria tree facing the music-room window. The tree had grown taller and fuller in the past years. He could stand in its shadow and look at the people inside the lighted room.

The room was empty. The piano stood against

the same wall, with the same crocheted white afghan draped over its top. Paala smiled at the same pot of bonsai on the piano. Many years ago he used to stand at this very same spot and wait for Sumiko to finish practice. He could just hear his own voice complaining to her, "By the time you can come out and play, that tiny bonsai will be ten feet tall!"

He started to move away from the window. It was time to knock on the door and pay his brief visit to Mrs. Yamada.

He stopped moving when he saw people entering the room.

Mrs. Yamada was followed by Mr. and Mrs. Sung Quanming. The lady attorney was near forty and the Sung couple about sixty-five. They all looked healthy and successful.

And then came Genkai and Kitaro. Paala tried to remember their ages: twenty-one and twenty-three. He had read about them not too long ago. The Honolulu Star Bulletin always listed the names of the island youth who were doing especially well in school. The paper had reported that Genkai was going on to study law and Kitaro medicine.

Paala felt inferior to them. He was not certain if he should go in or come back another day. He didn't think he could stand it if they should ask him what he had accomplished in the past several years.

He heard himself answering, "I've completed my jail sentence now. I'm living on government aid, struggling to be a published song writer. But all the agents refuse to represent me. I don't know how to open the door to the music world."

He suddenly realized that he didn't know how to open the door to these people's world of prosperity either. He shook his head and was ready to leave.

"Good-bye," he whispered in the darkness to the people in the light. "I'm going back to Maui to work harder. Someday I'll return." He froze.

Sumiko entered the room.

"My Sumiko," Paala called softly, taking one step forward.

He stopped.

A young man appeared. Paala could only see his profile. He could tell the man was handsome. And the stranger seemed to be very proud and confident. Paala watched him pointing at the piano, then saw Sumiko shaking her head.

Kitaro's voice was loud enough to reach Paala's ears. "Sumiko, you must play for Dr. Yung!"

So the man was a doctor! Paala took a step back toward the shadow of the plumeria tree. His heart clenched with jealousy. Had this man kissed Sumiko? He must have, since he called Mrs. Yamada by such a dear name. Was he Sumiko's fiancé? Was he her husband?

Paala turned away. He bit his lip to hold his cry. He must have imagined that Sumiko was thin and miserable-looking. In reality she must be bright-eyed and happy.

Paala ran soundlessly out of the garden, saying silently in his heart: "My Sumiko no longer loves me! I have nothing to live for now!"

Standing on the ferry from Oahu to Maui, Paala leaned against the railing and faced the ocean.

"Sumiko!" he shouted at the waves. "How foolish of me to think you were mine!"

The other passengers stared at him, but he didn't care. Why should a dying man worry if the world considered him crazy?

He knew his preferred way to die. He would go back to his little hut, gather the music sheets that were filled with his songs, then set the hut on fire. He would hold his guitar and close his eyes, play and sing until the flames devoured him.

It was near noon when the ferry reached the east end of Maui. Paala saw almost all the people of Hana gathered on the beach. He tried to remember if it was the birthday of one of the sea gods. When he couldn't think of any, he shrugged. Whatever the reason, it was good to have everyone away from the banana grove. When he set his hut on fire, no one would be there to save it.

No dock had been built for the ferry. Paala waded toward shore in the shallow water of the lagoon.

"Paala! Our Island Son! Paala! One of Us! Our Paala!" All the villagers waved and chanted his name. Most of them had known the Nihoa family for generations.

Two men ran to him. One was the owner of the general store, who also owned the only telephone in Hana, the other the postmaster.

"A New York lady called long distance for you! It was two days ago," shouted the store owner. "She left a message! She wants to be your agent!"

The postmaster yelled, "She also sent you a special-delivery package! It arrived this morning!

I opened it and we all read it! It's a nice thick contract!"

Before Paala could speak, the Hana people laid their hands on him, lifted him off the ground.

"An island son is going to be famous!" they cheered as they carried him through the banana grove.

"Paala's success is the success of the Hana people!" they sang out as they put him down in front of his hut.

They formed a circle and put him in the middle. "Paala has to sing for us!" they shouted. One of them went in the hut and came out with a guitar and ukulele.

Paala chose the guitar, looked at the faces of his kinsmen. He had lost Sumiko's love, but still had in his possession these wonderful people's admiration. Among them there were many young girls. Several were quite beautiful.

He ran his fingers over the strings, gave them a hard strum. He glanced over the lovely girls. He found adoration in their innocent eyes, willingness in their naive smiles.

He gave the strings another loud strum, lifted his head, and raised his voice. "I will live!" he sang, without caring about the tears streaming down his face.

His audiences waited silently for him to go on. Paala played the chords until a melody was born. It was a sad tune intertwined with anger. The lyrics were words of grief shadowed by wrath.

When Paala finished singing, the villagers applauded thunderously. The owner of a truck volunteered to drive Paala to the nearest public notary to have the contract signed, as requested by the agent. Those who could find room in the truck went along, either crammed into the back or jammed into the front. A charming girl, the daughter of the general-store owner, squeezed herself in between the driver and Paala.

She never took her worshiping eyes from his face. There were many turns along the winding road. With each turn, she fell toward Paala, against his chest or onto his lap. Paala soon put an arm around her. It had been a long time since he had touched a girl. It felt good to run his fingers over her soft arm, move his hand up and down her silken thighs. He relished having her hair brushing against his face and her cheek meeting his. He touched her ample breast with his elbow and she giggled.

After the contract was signed, the whole crowd had a few drinks. On the way back to Hana, the girl sat on Paala's lap. He kissed her and fondled her all the way home. He took her hand and led her into his hut. He dropped the coconut mat over the door and pushed the girl to the ground.

The night sky was brightened by a full moon. The birds near the hut thought dawn had arrived and began to sing. In their chirping song Paala heard Sumiko's name.

Moonlight poured in through a hole that served as a window, shone on the girl's naked body. Paala watched her moving under him. On her glistening face he saw the face of his Sumiko. He made love to the girl again and again.

19

The Pearl flowed gently, gleaming in the spring sun of 1961. The riverbank in White Stone rose and fell, in some places as high as a hill, in others as low as the water level. On one of the very lowest points stood a hut; its roof was made of dry grass and mud, its walls scraps of wood.

"I hope the Pearl will not rise any higher, or we'll be flooded again," said a woman as she came out of the hut.

Her baggy pants were all patches. Her tattered blouse barely covered her body. She was barefoot, her face thin and unclean, her hair caked with filth. Ma Qing was only twenty-one, but her youth was buried and her beauty hidden under layers of dirt.

"If the water must wash through our home again, maybe this time it'll leave us a few little fish. It'll be a treat to taste something other than rotted radishes," a man said, moving with difficulty as he stepped over a hole on the ground.

Fan Kuei was twenty-six. His frame was large, but there was no meat on his body—a big kite shaped like a man. His face was deeply lined. On his temples a few white hairs had already appeared. He moved on bare feet toward the river, limping with each step.

Qing and Kuei reached the water and stood looking at it. Not far from them, fishermen were going out on the boats, women doing their daily wash. Some of them saw Qing and Kuei and looked away.

Qing sighed, then whispered to her mate. "They are clever and you are dumb. They don't even want to rest their eyes on a Bloodsucker, but you married one." She pointed at his foot. "I'm so sorry."

Kuei looked around to make sure no one was listening or watching, then took Qing's hand. "The past is behind us. My foot is healed and we are together again."

Qing pressed his hand, kept her trembling voice low. "But you'll always limp, and Baba is gone."

Kuei squeezed her hand back. He couldn't speak until he swallowed the lump in his throat. "It had nothing to do with you, really." His hoarse voice rode on the soft breeze, scattered over the drifting water, and faded away.

They watched the Pearl River flow, shivered at the recurrence of a shared memory.

Fan Yu, Kuei, and Qing had been separated in prison. They labored in different fields, did not see one another. They were neither tried nor told of their crimes.

At the same time, things changed from bad to worse in White Stone. Communes were established soon after the Great Leap Forward began. The movement failed quickly, but the communes continued.

It was a harder blow on the villagers than nationalizing their fishing boats and farming tools. When the fishermen and farmers discovered that they were not working for themselves anymore, their spirits perished, their morale died. The villagers used to chat on their way to work, wishing the Great Buddha would grant them ample catch and good harvest. Now, on their way to the commune they moved silently, their eyes dull, their enthusiasm completely gone.

Soon after the establishment of the commune, White Stone faced another disaster. When all the birds were killed, worms and insects began to devour most of the crops planted by the farmers. It was then that orders came from above to stop killing and chasing away the birds. Mao Tze-dung had made a big mistake, but no one dared to mention it.

Mao had never been a farmer or a fisherman, but his ideas had been many. Each of his notions had been carried out, and every one had ended in disaster. After several of his brilliant suggestions China suffered one of the most severe famines in history, and millions of people died from starvation.

Mao Tze-dung resigned and Liu Shao-chi took over in April 1959. The prisoners in White Stone were released because the jailer had nothing to feed them. Qing and Kuei came out of jail, learned what had happened to Fan Yu: the prisoners were beaten and tortured and humiliated every day. As a result, Fan Yu had died and been cremated. The man who had dug many graves in his life never had one for himself.

Kuei's ankle was broken by one of the guards,

and no doctor was sent for. He could never move as he had before. No permanent damage had been done to Qing's body, but her heart was filled with sorrow and anger.

Her anger was aimed at one man, the man who had married her and Kuei. The greedy comrade had moved his wife and children into the brick house the same day the Fan family were taken to jail by his order.

When Qing and Kuei were released, the man was still in power. The villagers were so afraid of him that no one dared have Qing and Kuei live nearby, so they camped all over the village until they found an unwanted low spot beside the Pearl River.

The famine continued. Qing and Kuei lived on grass roots and tree bark. The willows along the Pearl were soon stripped of leaves and skins. The entire village became a naked land. All the dogs, cats, and rats were eaten. Even the bats, frogs, and snakes disappeared. Before the famine was over, half of the population in White Stone had perished.

Qing and Kuei survived and developed a distinctive view of the world. They were no longer afraid to take chances, because they had learned that in the new China, even if you didn't do anything wrong, your life still could be threatened at any time of any day.

"Well, at least we are together and have a roof over our heads," Kuei said, pressing Qing's hand. "We better go to work now, or they'll take our hut from us too."

They left the Pearl River, began to walk toward the commune.

As they walked near a tall willow tree, the birds perched in the deep foliage flapped their wings and flew high. Qing and Kuei stood still, watched the birds soaring out of sight.

Qing said with a sigh, "In order to prove the birds are harmless, we paid a terrible price."

The sight of the birds stirred such high hopes in their hearts that they continued to strain their ears for the beautiful birdsong left echoing in the lovely spring air.

"It's nice to be alive, no matter how difficult life is," Kuei said.

Qing nodded, "In order to stay alive, it's worthwhile to venture at times."

They stopped walking. Kuei moved very close to Qing and put his mouth next to her ear. "If the birds keep flying northeast, they can cross the border between China and North Korea."

Qing's eyes widened. She turned her head quickly to look over one shoulder, then the other. "But North Korea is also a communist country," she whispered. "Why would the birds want to go there?"

"From there the birds can travel to South Korea, which is not communist."

They resumed walking. They moved in silence for a while, then Qing said, "I still remember the geography lessons from my tutor. If the birds travel toward the southwest, they can fly over the high mountains and land in Vietnam."

Kuei nodded. "The lucky birds have many choices. It's a shame that the Great Buddha can't change you and me into birds. Without road passes, we cannot even leave White Stone."

Qing looked around once again, then stood still and said into Kuei's ear, "If we were birds, should we fly north to Korea or south to Vietnam?"

"Neither," Kuei answered. He made sure no one was near, then squatted and pulled Qing down with him. He picked up a willow twig and began to scratch on the dirt.

A map of China started to appear. "When I was in jail, one of the men in my cell was a scholar. He used to do this all the time," Kuei said as he continued to draw. "He wouldn't tell me what he was doing until he finally trusted me. He said that he wanted to keep the map of China in his mind, so when he dies his spirit will know how to fly away from hell."

When the map was completed, Kuei pointed with the twig. "We are here, and here is the Pearl River. See how it flows into the Deep Bay?"

Qing nodded.

Kuei continued. "On the other side of the bay are Kowloon and Hong Kong, the free world."

Qing sighed. "It's too bad we are not birds. We can't fly from one end of the Pearl to the other. If only Buddha could turn us into two fish . . ." She stopped, her jaw dropping as she stared at Kuei. No, he couldn't possibly be thinking the same impossible thought!

Kuei met her gaze. Without speaking, they conversed in contemplation. Their hearts beat fast when they heard each other's unspoken words. Hope gleamed in their eyes when they silently agreed with what they had heard.

* * *

Spring neared its end, and the weather turned chilly suddenly. Fine rain drizzled in the night, covering White Stone with a wet black net. The Pearl River was cold and deserted. Not a sound was heard on the riverbank, except the soft murmuring from the hut on the low land.

Qing and Kuei whispered cautiously.

"Will they search our home?" Qing asked. "The owners of the bicycles must be looking for their inner tubes by now."

Kuei didn't answer immediately. He was busy piling straw over the hole on the ground that he had just covered. He finally said, "They wouldn't suspect us. We don't even own a bike."

Qing's mind was full of questions, but she kept them to herself as she worked silently beside him. She wondered if in the school gym they would be looking for the basketballs. Would the carpenters be wondering what had happened to their boards? If anyone could figure out that all the missing items could be made into a float, then a search just might be begun. But then, she and Kuei were betting their lives on the people's incapability of putting two and two together. Those who had died in the past years might have gambled, and a few could have won. She and Kuei now had no choice but to gamble, because things in China were becoming worse.

Qing was deeply worried about Kuei's ankle. Could he swim across the Pearl? The riverwater was like ice, but Kuei would risk everything so they would have a chance to reach freedom.

They finished their work and their eyes met. Kuei said, "Don't worry, Qing. Remember how we used to swim when we were children?"

"Yes," she answered softly. "We were so happy then. At the time, I thought things could only become better."

He laughed. "You were so angry when I threw you in the water that day. But then I helped you to float and we had such fun."

They smiled at the fond memory. Kuei forced confidence into his uncertain voice. "We'll make it. We'll feel warm when we swim fast. My ankle will not be a problem as long as our bodies have enough strength to move on."

The year in jail had weakened their young bodies. Ever since deciding to flee, they had tried to make themselves strong. They had not dared to practice swimming, because that would raise suspicion. They had grabbed food whenever they could, devoured it not only to fill their stomachs but also to add fuel to the vehicles that would bring them to a better life.

Qing stood up. "A dark rainy night like this is perfect for stealing." She had become a proficient thief.

"I'm going with you," Kuei said.

"No, your foot will slow us down," Qing said, and was gone.

She moved in the rain, away from the Pearl, into the heart of the village. No dog barked at the soft sound of her footsteps; all dogs had been eaten a long time ago.

She reached the little brick house at the foot of the hill. She tried the back door but found it bolted. The comrade was careful—he didn't believe his own words that in the new China there were no thieves and no door needed to be locked.

Qing walked away from the house and tried not

to remember the years she had lived in it with Kuei and his father: in this house she had grown from a landlord's daughter into a peasant's wife.

She arrived at the biggest mansion in the village—her childhood home. The front door was open. The wind slammed it against the door frame. The banging sound seemed like the furious cries of the two half-destroyed stone lions. One lion had a smashed head, the other a big hole in his back.

Qing entered the garden, ran past the pond, and found her way easily through the various courtyards that were now the homes of many families.

"This is worse than the Japanese occupation," a woman's voice whispered from the courtyard that at one time had belonged to Qing's grandmother. "I've never been so hungry. Not one grain of rice is left in the bin."

From the room that had been Qing's, a man mumbled in a low voice, "The landlords were easier to deal with because they never changed. They were always greedy and cruel, and they had a behavior pattern. The party leaders are harder to handle because they change their minds from day to day. We can get into trouble no matter what we do. The only thing that remains unchanged is that we never have enough to eat. I'm so hungry my stomach hurts—like many little hands are scratching inside my intestines, digging for food."

Qing left her old home without finding anything to steal. The rain was cold, but the drops of water streaming down her cheeks were hot.

She roamed through the village, returned empty-handed to the hut.

She was ashamed to face Kuei with her failure, and could not bring herself to meet his eyes.

But Kuei stood up and came to her, and gathered her into his arms. His strength flowed into her and hers into him, and their hunger temporarily abated.

20

THE CHILLY RAIN STOPPED, but the night sky was a deep river of clouds. There was no wind; the frosty Pearl flowed peacefully, like a dark and untraveled road.

Qing and Kuei had been busy since sunset. They had dug up their stolen goods and made a small float. It was not big enough for them to ride on, but strong enough for them to hang on to. They carried it out of their hut, walked toward the Pearl. Except for a small amount of food, they brought nothing with them.

Around Qing's neck was the single red bead given to her by Kuei many years ago. No one considered it of any value, so even in prison she had been allowed to keep wearing it. It was weightless around her neck, but heavy in sentimental value. She couldn't part from it, no matter what. She touched it now and then, hoping that the dot of red would bring her and her Kuei good luck. Each time she touched the red bead, Kuei smiled at her wordlessly.

They reached the river and placed the float on the water. They held on to it and pushed it to the center of the Pearl.

A gust of wind suddenly blew across the sky,

tossing aside the top layers of clouds. The nearly full moon couldn't be seen clearly, but its brilliant glow brightened the rippling water. In the dim light Qing and Kuei could see the controlled excitement on each other's faces. They had not been certain until that moment that the float would work.

The float drifted, supporting their supplies and a part of their weight, enabling them to go downstream without too much effort. They moved at a steady speed, and soon came to the edge of White Stone.

When the initial excitement was over, they began to feel the iciness of the water. Their teeth began chattering. They moved their feet faster but didn't dare to kick them above the surface. Qing felt the chill cutting into every inch of her flesh. She bit her lip to bear the pain, but was more concerned about Kuei. She looked at him questioningly, and he nodded to reassure her. She wasn't sure his weak nod was telling her the truth.

Kuei was thankful when the moon disappeared behind clouds again. His ankle had never been totally healed, and now the icy water was slicing through it, causing unbearable pain. He used his willpower to hide the anguish, but was sure Qing could see it if there had been moonlight. She was studying him carefully, so he raised three fingers for her to see.

Qing received the silent message: in three days we'll be in Kowloon. Her spirit was uplifted and she nodded with relief as they floated away from White Stone.

The Pearl River turned and twisted its way toward Kowloon, and the total journey from White Stone to the other side of the Deep Bay was eighty-nine miles. Qing and Kuei had planned on hanging on to their float and moving at three or four miles per hour, to travel thirty miles each night. That would give them plenty of time to hide and rest during the day.

Another gust of wind traveled over the river, rippled the water, brightened the sky, revealed Kuei's face to Qing for a brief moment, then returned the whole world into the hands of darkness. During that luminous instant Qing saw her husband smiling at her, and she smiled back at him. Once again they exchanged these silent words: Three days from now we'll travel on land from Kowloon to Hong Kong, and then we'll be free. We will never be afraid anymore, and a fear-free life is a life in heaven.

Just when they were nearing another village, they both stopped moving at the same time. They stared at the far distance and saw the silhouette of a soldier on the riverbank.

Qing gasped, quickly bit her lip. There was not just one soldier, but two. They were not looking at the water, but sharing a match to light their cigarettes.

Qing and Kuei took a deep breath and went underwater. It was terribly cold. They held each other and wished to give their body heat to the other if they could. They hid under the float and came out only when they were out of breath. For a long while they didn't dare to push the float forward, but stayed in the same spot and watched the soldiers.

Even from a distance it could be seen that the

two soldiers were armed. They stayed on the riverbank, smoking their cigarettes, showed no intention of leaving.

Qing and Kuei looked at each other, then nodded their agreement. They pushed the float with the top of their heads, moved soundlessly. The soldiers were about ten yards from them, and then five. And then they could hear the two men talking.

One said, "I wish we were home drinking warm rice wine. It was a silly order to have us standing here waiting for escapees. What fool will swim in this cold water?"

The other soldier said, "Well, an order is an order. They say as soon as summer begins, people try to swim down the Pearl. Although the water is still very cold, summer is only a few days away, and last summer hundreds of the villagers tried—most of them were shot and killed, of course."

Qing and Kuei didn't dare to stick their heads out of the water until their lungs were about to explode. They covered their mouths with their hands, tried to silence their choking. They finally managed to return to normal breathing. They moved with only their noses above the water, and were thankful for the many willow branches floating on the river, hiding their float from the soldiers.

They kept turning their heads to look over their shoulders until the sparkling dots of the soldiers' cigarettes were out of sight. Their limited optimism was now totally destroyed by the words of the soldiers. They no longer dared to feel certain that they would be in Kowloon in three days' time.

Throughout the night they swam wordlessly in fear. When they were tired, they held on to the float for support and rested while treading water. When the sky was turning bright in the east, they were at least thirty miles closer to their destiny, and they were exhausted.

They began to look for some dark corner in which to hide, and after a while they found a shallow creek branched from the Pearl. They pushed their float toward the area where the weeds grew tall from the marshlands. Qing and Kuei struggled in the mud that reached their waist, saw a pile of rocks standing like a fortress.

They headed toward the rocks, then suddenly stopped. Two bodies had been washed up by the Pearl, caught by the rocks. They were a man and a woman, about Qing and Kuei's age. The man still held a stick in his hand, as if ready to fight for his life. The woman had her hands placed over her face, seemed to be afraid to see what she thought was going to happen. Their backs were pierced by bullet holes, but their blood had already dried.

Qing and Kuei stared at the bodies for a long while, then at each other. Kuei saw Qing's tears and came to her. He held her in his arms but didn't utter a sound. When she stopped crying they worked together to push the bodies away from the rocks, and watched the man and woman being carried away by the flowing stream. Both Qing and Kuei held their hands in front of their hearts, palms together, and said their silent prayers for the two dead villagers' spirits.

Qing looked up at the dawning sky and saw a fading almost-full moon. When she looked toward Kuei, she saw him nodding his assurance: Yes, the spirits shall know only happiness in the temple of the moon.

The moon disappeared, the wind became chillier, and it soon started to rain. The sky was gray, but not dark enough to make their dangerous journey safe. Daytime moved slowly as they waited for night to fall. They longed to talk to each other but were afraid to be heard. The water became colder with each passing minute, the mud thicker, their mood grimmer.

They had packed some radishes, carrots, and sweet potatoes on their floats. They ate the wet and muddy food, then continued to wait patiently for the night. Qing didn't know she could sleep standing in cold water, but she dozed off in Kuei's embracing arms. When she woke up, most of the day was over and night was near. They ate more sweet potatoes and traveled on.

They passed several more villages, each guarded by soldiers. They encountered death each time they pushed their float right in front of the soldiers' eyes, and they thanked the Great Buddha when they made it safely. At one point Qing was so tired and cold and hungry and sleepy that she felt she could no longer go on. But then Kuei pulled her softly to him and she felt his love and shared his strength and regained the vitality of her numbed arms and legs.

They made about another thirty miles during the second night, and when daylight came, they found a waterfront gazebo. The land it stood on appeared to be part of a rich man's riverfront garden. The gazebo was half-burned and the statues next to it smashed. There were no signs of life nearby. Qing and Kuei tied their float to a dead tree, collapsed in the gazebo, and slept soundly through the entire day. They woke up to a bright moon, almost full, shining over the gazebo, and Qing gasped when she noticed how weak and pale Kuei was in the moonlight.

She opened her mouth to suggest that they rest another night and day in the gazebo, but Kuei put a finger over her mouth to hush her. They untied their float and began to travel in the cold water again.

Rain had caused the Pearl to rise, and the waves had become more powerful. Their homemade float was soon torn away by gushing breakers. Once they had lost it, they realized how big a help the float had been to them. They swam hard and struggled on grabbing anything to support them. When they neared the end of the Pearl, a full moon appeared on a clear sky.

They looked at each other in despair. For what they were about to do, they didn't need to be in a spotlight.

They swam through the moonlit night accompanied by great tension and fear. When the night was ending and they were at the mouth of the Pearl, strong winds began to blow. Clouds covered the moon for a fleeting moment and then revealed it. Stretching under the moon, the water in Deep Bay looked like an illuminated stage at one instant; the next instant it was a darkened platform.

During the time the moon was shining, several

soldiers could be seen clearly onshore, aiming their shotguns and rifles at the water.

Qing and Kuei hid in a small area darkened by the shadow of a dead willow, then gestured each other to cross the bay in frog strokes. They should not become too noticeable a target for the soldiers, and the sound they made should be minimal. They embraced tightly, gave each other encouraging smiles, then left their hiding place.

A sudden wind sent the clouds flying, unveiled the moon, and silvered the water with light. The soldiers aimed at the two moving dots and fired.

Kuei moaned. He beat his arms quickly in the water, creating a loud splashing sound. Then his fast movement slowed, and he became quiet.

Qing saw her husband sinking. The water closed over him, left no trace of his ever being there. A scream escaped her throat, then was drowned away as she dived into the water. She grabbed Kuei's arms, pulled him out of the water, saw a bullet wound in his left shoulder.

The wind kept blowing and the moon went in hiding. In the darkness Qing put Kuei's arms around her waist and he held on to her instantly. Even in the perilous situation they were in, for a fleeting moment they both remembered the time he had taught her to swim. Then it was she who had put her arms around his waist, and they had been swimming for fun, not for their lives.

A gale twirled the clouds away from the moon, turning the dark water into a mirror-clear pool. The soldiers aimed at the two dots in the water, and their bullets landed just beside Qing and Kuei. The moon shone on Qing's bloodless face. She opened her mouth to speak for the first time in three days.

"We'll make it, Kuei," she whispered without looking back. "My husband, you are a great swimmer. You were my swimming teacher. Now we are both great swimmers. Crossing the bay is like a child's game for you and me. Remember what you told me once? . . . Yes, we are children of the Pearl. We can swim like fish."

The breeze, like a gentle hand, picked up the clouds and wrapped them around the moon. The sky was once again totally dark, and the bay became inky black. The soldiers onshore cursed the sudden loss of their sight. Qing felt Kuei's hands loosening their grip around her waist. She swam with one hand, used the other to put his hands around her waist once more, then continued to swim soundlessly in the frog stroke.

"The wind is on our side. The breeze has put a curtain over the glowing temple of the moon," Qing said as she moved her arms and legs quickly.

"The Moon Buddha has put away all his moonbeams just for you and me, because even the Moon Buddha knows how much we love each other and what a wonderful life is waiting for us in Hong Kong," she said while breathing hard, urging Kuei on.

She felt her arms and legs becoming heavier with each additional stroke. But she was glad that Kuei had not let go of her, had instead tightened his grip on her. His hands around her waist were choking her, and his weight had become as massive as a fleet of fishing boats.

She couldn't keep her head above the waves

any longer. She swallowed a mouthful of the sour-tasting water, choked, and lost her balance.

She struggled to float again. She saw many dots of light shining on the faraway shore. She blinked to make sure they were not a delusion. Once they were confirmed as reality, she acquired a new strength. She recaptured her steadiness and swam on.

She talked to Kuei again. "We're almost there. The clouds are still over the moon. We're still safe. I can already see the lights of Kowloon . . ." She ran out of breath and stopped talking.

She said to him after a while, "Now I can even hear people shouting on the street. Our new life is waiting only a few more yards away. My Kuei, our wonderful life will begin within the next few minutes."

She moved her aching arms and legs with the last ounce of energy left in her numb body. "Kuei, we need to make only a few more strokes and kicks. Let's count them together. Five . . . four . . . three . . . we can almost touch the shore now."

Qing's feet touched the ground. She walked toward shore and then turned her exhausted body around to look at Kuei.

"Let's lie down for a while . . ."

There was no one behind her. What she had thought were Kuei's hands was just a bunch of seaweed twisted around her waist, entwined with the river's flotsam to give them a ponderous weight.

She screamed into the night.

21

Te and Delia's birthdays were only ten days apart. In 1961, when both reached twenty, they went to Jade Garden on a weekend that fell between their two birthdays.

They talked excitedly on their way to Chinatown. This would be their last trip there by bus. Te had learned to drive. He and Delia had put their savings together and now had enough for a used car. They walked into the restaurant while discussing which type of car to buy, and what a wonderful birthday present it was for each other.

"He's here again. Such a handsome Chinese, but always with that Ha Gui Moi," one of the waiters said as soon as he saw the two.

Te glared at the man until the waiter walked away. Delia noticed his anger and asked, "Every time we're in Chinatown, I see people staring at us and hear them murmuring something in Chinese. Among a bunch of singsong syllables, a few words remain the same—Ha Gui Moi, or just Ha Gui. What do they mean?"

Ma Te answered through clenched teeth, "Ha Gui means Black Devil, and Ha Gui Moi means Black Devil Girl."

Delia shrugged. "It's not as bad as I thought."

"It's bad enough. One of these days I'll put an end to it." He then changed the subject. "You look beautiful in every color and everything, but you are gorgeous in a red dress. Thanks for wearing the proper color for this occasion."

In the past two years, besides participating in many protests and political activities, they had continued to try to please each other. Among the many adjustments they had made, Te had started to work in the school library and stopped depending completely on his father's money, and Delia had learned to observe many Chinese traditions.

Delia had on a red dress. It was sleeveless and low-cut, with a wide skirt and a narrow belt tied tightly around the waist. She wore red high-heeled shoes and red earrings. Even her purse was red.

She said, "I like red. Besides, I don't want to make the same mistake I made last year." She laughed.

They had celebrated their nineteenth birthdays together, and Delia had worn white. She had noticed the paling of Te's face the minute he picked her up. He had not told her why, but had stopped on their way to the restaurant and bought a big red scarf to drape over her white dress.

After they were seated, Delia stared at him until he became uncomfortable and rubbed his face with his hand. "Is my face dirty?"

She laughed. "No, not dirty, just extremely handsome. But I wasn't attracted to your good looks. It was your eagerness to fight." Still staring at him, she began to describe him as she would a picture: "Round face with high cheekbones. Large almond eyes. Straight nose and thin lips . . ." She moved her eyes downward. "You have rather broad shoulders, and you are very tall. You are a sexy man, you know—"

Te wouldn't let her continue. "Stop that! You make me feel like a sex object!"

Delia threw her head back and laughed. "Talk about sex—you are the first male friend of mine who is still just a friend after two long years!"

Te leaned forward and said with a frown in a commanding tone, "Tell me about your men friends who have become much more than just friends, and start with the most important one!"

Delia tilted her head to one side. "Are you ordering me?"

Te didn't back down. "Yes!"

She looked at his serious face and answered slowly, "Well, the most important was Roy Jackson. He was the boy next door in my hometown. We played together when we were twelve, then dated seriously when we were fourteen."

The waiter came to take their orders. As soon as he was gone, Te said, "Go on!"

Delia laughed. Her red earrings danced beside her dark face like fire burning against a night sky. "Ma Te, you are even better-looking when you are jealous." She became serious as she continued. "Well, Roy and I were lovers for a year, and then he left town for the nearest city when we were fifteen. I went to Memphis to visit him now and then, but I also dated others when we were not together. Both Roy and I are broad-minded. We never wanted to smother each other, although the understanding was always there . . ." Delia stopped. Her expression changed quickly. Laughter turned into sorrow, then flared into anger.

". . . until something terrible happened, which made Roy and me unable to become anything more than the best of friends." She shook her head violently, as if trying to shake off a painful memory.

Te had many questions, but held them back because of her agony. Their food was served and they talked about things unrelated to themselves and their deepest concerns—such as the low pay and long hours of the sewing-factory workers, and the terrible racial prejudice in the Southern states at this current moment. When they were about to leave the restaurant, Delia asked Te how to say "yellow" in Cantonese, and Te told her: "Won."

On their way out of the door, a waiter thanked them. Delia smiled at the man and said loudly, "You're welcome, Won Gui."

Some of the Chinese customers also heard Delia. They were surprised, then glared at her in fury. She laughed at them and Te laughed with her. "You called the man a Yellow Devil! Good for you! What a fast learner you are!" he said proudly and in pleased surprise.

They continued to laugh as they walked down the street. When they were two blocks from the bus stop, a group of teenage Chinese boys came face-to-face with them on a dark corner piled with garbage cans. There were seven of them.

One of them pointed a finger at Delia and said in Cantonese, "This Ha Gui Moi's lips are thick enough to make two servings of chop suey. And she doesn't seem to be ashamed of them. Look at her! Laughing with those lips wide open to show her big white teeth!"

Another boy made a face at Te. "He must like

dark meat! I wonder if she has a special way to cook it—'' the boy never had a chance to finish.

Te punched the boy to put an end to his comment. The boy stumbled backward. Te took a quick glance at his bleeding knuckles and said, ''I've never hit anyone before, but there is always a first time for everything!'' The next second Te screamed at the sudden pain on his shin.

One of the boys had kicked him. The boys were children of the new immigrants from Hong Kong. After being targets of neighborhood bullies for a while, they had discovered that the best way to protect themselves was to form their own gang and bully others. They were feared by the area's children as well as its adults. While they were foul-mouthing their victims, they never expected to hear people talking back. When they were beating up others, they assumed their targets would take the beatings and run.

Te looked like an ordinary Chinese who would follow the ancient rule of avoiding trouble. How dared he throw the first punch? When they recovered from shock, they decided to teach him a good lesson—they had a reputation to maintain.

Te saw them coming for him and shouted at Delia without looking at her, ''Run! Run away from here as fast as you can! Don't even look back!''

From the corner of his eye Te glimpsed a bunch of bamboo sticks in a trashcan. He reached for the thickest one and held the end of it tightly with both hands. During his schooling in Taiwan he had always hated physical education and military training, the two courses emphasized by the government, but now he was grateful for those courses that prepared the youth of Taiwan to fight the Communist Chinese for liberation of the mainland.

He bent his legs and parted his feet, raised the stick high, and glared at the young gang members threateningly. At the same time, he yelled once more for Delia to run.

"Like hell I will!" She shouted back in a voice louder than Te's.

Te glanced at her quickly. What he saw was beyond his belief. Delia stood with her back against a solid wall, her feet parted and knees bent. Her arms were outstretched and curved. Her hands were positioned one in front of the other, with her forefingers and middle fingers pointing at her opponents. Her chin was held back but her eyes were looking up to focus on one boy at a time.

The boys took advantage of Te's divided attention and began their attack. When they were two yards away from Te his stick landed on their leader's right shoulder with a bang. The beating was so forceful that the boy's right arm was numbed instantly. He cried out in pain as he raised his left hand to rub his shoulder. He stared at Te in awe. Te resumed his position and waited for the next attacker while he continued to keep an eye on Delia.

"Go to hell, you Won Gui!" she screamed, and kicked one of the boys in the groin with the pointed toe of her high-heeled shoe.

The boy cried and doubled over.

"You Won Guis have picked on the wrong Ha Gui this time!" she screamed again, then poked the forefinger and middle finger of her right hand into another boy's eyes. He shrieked and ran away blindly.

Another boy moved toward Te, who raised his stick once more. He tapped it on the boy's head with only half his strength, but the boy screamed and covered his head with both hands, then ran away as soon as he stopped seeing stars in his closed eyes.

None of the boys were trained fighters. Fighting technique had not been needed so far. Until this day they had been able to harass people with nothing but evil looks and threatening words.

The remaining boys looked at one another and silently agreed that they couldn't afford to retreat. Two of them pulled out knives. Usually the mere showing of these shining blades would get them whatever they wanted from store owners and pedestrians.

"You better think twice before you use your knives," Te yelled. "I'll give you a real taste of my stick!"

"This Ha Gui has no time for toys!" Delia held her right foot back to her left knee, then quickly kicked out twice. The knives fell. Her wide skirt was handy for kicking. She stood on both feet again, and again took her defensive position. "Do you have anything more interesting to show me, you stupid Won Guis?"

A siren neared. Te threw down his bamboo stick and the boys found an excuse to save face.

"We can beat you up easily, but we want no trouble with the law!" said the tallest one, and then they disappeared among the crowd.

A police car zoomed by without stopping; it was after someone else. In the fading siren sound Delia and Te walked toward the bus stop, meeting the staring eyes of many Chinese.

Te and Delia asked the same question at the same moment: "How did you learn to fight like that?"

Te answered first. "Kendo is a Japanese fighting technique known by many Taiwanese. The Nationalist government banned most of the Taiwanese culture, but adopted kendo as a part of our curriculum. We had it in P.E. from the sixth grade up. I'm not very good at it. You should see my friend Yen . . ." Te stopped.

Delia was wiping the sweat from her forehead. She didn't notice the sudden sorrow on Te's face. She said, "I want to learn kendo too. Roy taught me kung-fu. He learned it in Memphis when he was working in a gas station in the daytime and going to school every night . . ."

The bus came then. Delia's apartment was on Union Street. The stairway was narrow and dark, but her little room was bright and cheerful. Te had been here many times before, but never stayed long. It seemed that Jade Garden was the only place for the two to sit and talk. The rest of their time together was spent demonstrating and marching.

"You don't have to leave right away," she said, closing the door behind him.

"Great," Te said, throwing himself down on one end of the unmade sofa bed. He patted the bed and smiled at Delia. "Aren't you tired after all that eating and fighting?"

Delia kicked off her shoes and joined Te, and using his lap for her pillow, stretched her long legs out to their full length.

Te had worn a suit and tie to dinner. He hadn't remembered them when he was fighting, but now suddenly felt uncomfortably warm. He loosened the tie, then unbuttoned his jacket.

"Take off whatever makes you feel uneasy . . ." Delia said, paused, then added meaningfully, ". . . including your tradition."

Te smiled. Tradition was definitely losing ground. He took off his jacket and tie, threw them to the floor, then unbuttoned his shirt.

He was undoing the buckle on his belt when Delia raised her arms and circled his neck. She pulled him toward her and they kissed.

A hunger rose from their young bodies, together with a thirst. They tried to curb the desire with their kisses, but the longer and harder they kissed, the stronger the yearning was. When they felt they were about to die from that urge, they stood up from the sofa.

Te threw his shirt to the floor, kicked off his shoes. He then dropped his pants and stepped out of them. Delia undid the hook behind her low collar, unzipped the dress, and let it fall to her hips. She wiggled out of it, tossed it to a chair.

They faced each other. Te looked at her in her bra and half-slip. Delia took his hand, put it on her breast. She moved her upper body, and her breast rubbed against Te's palm.

With a low moan Te bent toward Delia, put one arm behind her knees and the other around her shoulder. He lifted her off the floor and kissed her once more before putting her gently facedown on the sofa bed.

Te sat beside Delia, caressed the silky skin on

her back, then climbed over her. He kissed the back of her neck, behind one ear, then the other.

His feet, still in socks, rubbed against Delia's stockinged feet. He then leaned his face against her back and used his tongue as a soft brush over her spine, slowly and steadily, all the way down. As his tongue touched the back of her bra, then the waist of her slip and panties, he removed whatever was in his way. While taking off her stockings, he turned her to face him.

He took her face in his hands and cradled it carefully. "I love you, Delia."

"And I love you," she answered breathlessly.

He kissed her on the mouth, parted her teeth with his tongue. While kissing her, he tore off his shorts and socks. His naked body joined hers, and as one they traveled to the magic land of ecstasy.

22

SUMIKO, TE, AND DELIA shared a table in Jade Garden. The three of them were together often. Yung Zhang, who was engaged to Sumiko now, seldom joined her friends.

Delia said, "I have the feeling that Yung Zhang tries his best to avoid us. He is afraid that your friends are more clever than you, Sumiko. He thinks Te and I may be able to see something in him that you can't see, something awful—my suspicious mind tells me so."

Te said quickly, "That's no way to talk about Sumiko's future husband."

Delia shrugged. "That's my honest opinion."

Sumiko said with a forced smile, "Thanks for the opinion, but I'm going to marry Yung Zhang just the same." She then lowered her eyes to study the silverware. Their table was netted by silence. There was no live entertainment during the day. The music for lunch came from a radio.

Te tried to break the stifled air. He asked Sumiko, "Are you and Yung Zhang going back to Hawaii during Christmas vacation?"

Sumiko nodded, toying with her teacup. "My mother wants us to get married there and then, in Sung Quanming's house."

Delia leaned closer to Sumiko. "Do you love Yung Zhang?"

Sumiko's voice was louder and harder than usual, "Love? What has that to do with marriage? Zhang will soon be a doctor, and I am already a nurse. We'll make a perfect couple!" Her ire was gone after those words, and she continued softly, "For many of us, life is like the stepping-stones in a garden—each leads to the next one. One stone I was young, the next I was grown. I've graduated from nursing school now, and my next step is to have a husband. Yung Zhang has good looks and a bright future." She pointed a finger at Delia, "You are the only person who doesn't think highly of him."

Delia shook her head. "There is something fishy about a person who averts his eyes from people. Zhang always avoids looking at me directly, but I often catch him studying me when he thinks I don't know. Really, my instinct is usually right. Yung Zhang knows he can fool you, but is uncertain about fooling others. He lies all the time too. For instance, I bet he is not on duty at all today. He just doesn't want to be with your friends."

Te nudged Delia with his elbow. "Hush! You're hurting Sumiko's feelings."

Delia punched Te back. "Don't you ever poke me and hush me again! Aren't we Sumiko's friends? Honesty is an important part of friendship, but I can see it's hard for you to understand." She shook her head at Te. "You have learned to fight the authorities the American way, but are still talking like an evasive Chinese. Do you Chinese believe in connecting two dots with many circles instead of a straight line?"

"Delia," Te said defensively, "there is a difference between honesty and rudeness—"

Sumiko interrupted him. "Please don't fight because of me." She looked from Te to Delia. How she envied those who were in love. She had already told them about Paala. Now she began to tell them what had happened in Honolulu.

She had opened the newspaper and seen a headline: "ISLAND SON SIGNS CONTRACT WITH PROMINENT NEW YORK AGENT." Under the headline Paala smiled at her from a large picture. A lovely young girl had locked her arms around Paala's waist and was leaning her face against his shoulder, smiling proudly.

Sumiko's voice quivered. "The reporter had interviewed them in Paala's hut in Hana, and described the hut as a love nest." She paused to brush off a tear. "It didn't say how long they had been living together. But it's obvious that when I still reserved a corner of my heart for him, he was already in love with someone else."

She went on to tell them that she had dropped the paper and cried. Her mother and brothers had read the same article and seemed relieved.

At the time Yung Zhang had been visiting one of Sung Quanming's coral factories. When he returned to the Yamada house, he was in very high spirits. "You have a mother who is an attorney, two brothers in prestigious professions, a wealthy guardian in San Francisco, and now a powerful friend named Sung Quanming. Why didn't you tell me that the old Mr. Sung is so rich and influential, and treats you like a granddaughter?" he had asked excitedly.

Sumiko said to her friends, "That night he proposed in front of my family. Before I could answer, my mother was already on the phone with the Sungs to make wedding plans. My brothers were shaking Zhang's hands and calling him brother . . ." Sumiko stopped suddenly, tilted her head to one side, listened to the music coming from the radio.

Her eyes widened. She got up, and walked toward the corner where one of the four large speakers stood.

The song coming from the radio was accompanied by a guitar, the sad melody sung by a rich voice, the melancholy lyrics pronounced with deep emotion.

Sumiko sank to her knees and leaned her head against the speaker. She had recognized Paala's voice as soon as the song began. She now listened to his song of a man's first love, likened to the first star of a moonless night, which dominates the sky. But as the night grew deeper and the sky became a sea of diamonds, the first star was forgotten.

When the song ended, an announcer's voice said, "You have just heard Paala Nihoa, new singing star. Until recently Paala was frequently seen in the company of a girl from Hana. But our star has just left his Hana sweetheart for last year's Miss Hawaii. The former beauty queen announced that the two will soon marry and Paala has promised to build her a mansion on top of the Pali Mountain. Now, our next song is . . ."

Sumiko stood up abruptly and walked back to the table. Her face was pale and her lips bloodless. Her cheeks were still wet but her eyes dry.

In a weak but steady voice she said to her two

friends, "I will not only marry Yung Zhang but also have a great life!"

The wedding took place in Hawaii, in the garden of Sung Quanming's house, and the feast was in the banquet room.

The groom was greatly impressed by the social status of the guests: they were either friends of Sung Quanming's or associates of Mrs. Yamada's. Yung Zhang shared one drink after another with them, smiling with deeper and deeper satisfaction as the party wore on. When the guests began to leave and the bride retired to an upstairs guest bedroom, he continued to drink with Genkai and Kitaro.

"You two are my brothers-in-law now," Zhang said. "And you'll soon be a doctor and a lawyer. I'm so proud to be a member of your family." He lifted his eyes to the ceiling. "I am now related to you because of Sumiko. I owe my beautiful little wife a great deal!"

Zhang then raised his drink and toasted himself in his native Cantonese: "To me! I, Yung Zhang, the unwanted bastard from Jasmine Valley, am now among the high and mighty!" He emptied his glass, refilled it, and climbed the stairs to his wedding chamber.

Sumiko stood facing the window. The room was dark except for a lamp beside the bed. The December sky was moonless but filled with stars. Which star had appeared first? She couldn't tell. She thought of Paala's song. Perhaps a person's first love was meant to be forsaken.

The door opened. "Wow! What a sexy nightgown! It's nice to see you in pink for a change, my beautiful bride!'' Yung Zhang said as he walked toward Sumiko with a drink in his hand.

The room was warm, but Sumiko heard her teeth chattering. She was nervous and frightened. Her heart was not with her groom, and because of that, her body was not ready for him.

When Zhang put his hand on Sumiko's shoulders, she shivered at his touch. His hand had held the glass and was chilled by it. Sumiko frowned, and her frown didn't escape Zhang's sharp eyes. He laughed, thinking how shy his little virgin bride was. He had really done well, he thought. How many men could capture a rich, beautiful, gentle virgin with lots of money and good connections?

''My precious Sumiko,'' he called softly, and turned her around slowly, a little bit at a time. His eyes pierced through her thin robe to examine her body, and he whistled at what he saw. ''I would like you to dress like this all the time in our future home. You look much better now than in your usual dreadful dull clothes.''

Sumiko was turned full circle now. She faced her groom once more. Zhang put his chilly hand on her breast and squeezed it tightly.

''It hurts, Zhang,'' Sumiko said, wincing and trying to push him away.

Zhang laughed. ''You are just a little girl. After you become a woman, you won't feel the pain at all. You'll like the things done by a man and a woman, and I'll show them to you one by one. But don't worry, my fragile flower, I'll never hurt you. I'll never do to you anything you don't like. Because you are not only my woman but also a very important person.''

While laughing, he took her in his arms, shook her softly, and leaned his face close to hers. "Do you know how important you are?" he asked. When she didn't answer, he took a deep breath, then said slowly, "You are my whole future, which means my whole life. You are actually my . . ."

He was slightly drunk, but not too drunk to control his tongue. He stopped in mid-sentence, held her tightly. "You are my everything," he murmured, then began to kiss her. His lips burned her like a branding iron. So did his words.

"Your lips are mine," he said, and kissed her on the mouth.

"Your face too," he said while kissing her cheek.

He kissed her neck and then her left breast, and said, "Behind that lovely breast is your heart, and I want that to be mine also."

Zhang lifted Sumiko up and carried her to the bed. He put her on the bed, then took off her gown. He looked at her naked body and his eyes widened. "You are truly beautiful. I am a very lucky man," he said as he shook his head, then quickly removed his own clothes.

He joined her in bed and reached over to turn off the lamp.

Sumiko turned her face toward the window. The curtains were parted. The moonless sky was bright with millions of stars. Where was the star that had appeared first on the night sky? She kept searching as her groom made love to her. There was neither pain nor pleasure. Her body was on the wedding bed, but her mind was on top of the

Pali Mountain, where the clouds were a mattress and the mist a quilt—

"Due-na-ma!" Yung Zhang cursed, and turned on the light.

Sumiko watched him checking the sheet carefully. When he couldn't find what he was looking for, he looked at her with a mixture of many emotions: injury, pain, anger, disgust, and hatred.

"You are not a virgin!" His voice was low and deep as usual, but cold and hard.

Sumiko shook her head.

"Why didn't you tell me?"

"I didn't think it mattered."

He raised a hand, started to slap her with his open palm. His hand stopped only a few inches from her face. "I mustn't hit you. Your family are right in this house and you are important to me, virgin or no virgin," he said, then left the bed.

Sumiko had closed her eyes and waited for the strike. She kept them closed for a long time. When she opened them she saw, in the dim light, Zhang already in a robe and standing facing the window. At his thighs, his hands were clenched into fists and shaking. She covered herself with the sheet and lay wordlessly for a while, then spoke softly. "I'm sorry, Zhang, for not telling you. But I really didn't know it meant so much to you. To most people, it no longer matters—"

Yung Zhang interrupted her without moving. "It matters to me. I am a bastard child, as I told you the first time we met. My mother shamed me. I expected you to bring me honor and prestige and many other things." He laughed sarcastically. "I guess honor will not be one of your gifts." He turned and faced her.

"Zhang," Sumiko said hesitantly, "if it'll make you feel any better . . . there was only one man . . . and we did it only once—"

"Enough!" He raised a fist and took one step forward. "I don't want to hear anything about it! I'll really hit you if you dare mention this again!"

"All right," Sumiko said. The lamplight glowed on Yung Zhang's ashen face, and she felt sorry for him. "Zhang, I'll be a good wife to you. I'll work, and I'll keep house. I won't ask much from you . . ." She paused, thought, then continued. "When I decided to marry you, I also decided to have a great life with you. We can still do that, can't we, Zhang?"

Yung Zhang's eyes moved from her beautiful face to the lovely curve of her body that was clearly outlined under the thin sheet. He tilted his head to one side and listened to the voices of her relatives and close friends coming from downstairs. Color gradually returned to his face, and a smile appeared slowly. He finally shrugged and walked toward the bed.

"Of course we can." He removed his robe and dropped it carelessly. "We'll be the perfect couple, envied by everyone. We'll have money, prestige, and many other things . . . that's what life is all about."

He jerked the sheet off Sumiko, turned off the lamp, and joined her in bed once again.

23

MILLIONS OF STARS shone over the beach of Kowloon. The moon was hiding behind the clouds. Ma Qing lay on the dark beach crying.

"Kuei, Kuei . . ." she called repeatedly. Her body was convulsing, her voice a thin thread vibrating in the wind. She raised a hand to her neck, touched the Lover's Teardrop. The red bead hadn't brought them any good luck. The bead would remain red, but her Kuei was gone.

The wind chased the clouds from the moon. The sky was lighted, the waterfront bright. Qing saw a shadow staggering toward her from the other side of the shore.

"If you are a soldier, you are welcome to shoot me," she said with her remaining strength. "I don't want to live without my Kuei."

"I'm not a soldier. There are no Red Army soldiers in Kowloon," the shadow answered in a female voice hoarse from crying. "I'm a woman escaped from a village alongside the Pearl, called the Willow Place. There were five in my family, but they all drowned."

"My husband is drowned." Qing forced herself up, dragged herself forward to meet the approaching woman. "I want to throw myself back in the water to join him."

The two women met, collapsed on the sand. They lay still and wordless for a long while.

"Would our loved ones want us to die with them?" the Willow Place woman asked Qing.

Qing thought, then answered weakly, "I don't know. Kuei and I never discussed that. We never thought only one of us would survive. It seemed impossible for death to part us when we were still so young."

The Willow Place woman said, "My family and I thought of the possibility, and we did talk about death. We knew some of us would ascend to the Temple of the Moon during the long swim, but we didn't know which ones the Great Buddha had in mind."

"The Great Buddha is blind, and the bullets have no eyes." Qing began to cry again. "I wish I had died and that Kuei had made it. He deserves to live a good life."

Qing pressed her face to the sand, rubbing her cheek against it. She remembered the numerous times she had rubbed her tearful face against Kuei's dependable chest and comforting shoulders, and a choking sob rose from her throat again.

"I think your man would want a good life for you, as mine would for me. Both of them are calling to us now . . . from heaven." The Willow Place woman pointed at the bright full moon. "They'll be very angry if we don't listen. Let's obey them."

Qing looked up and saw on the glowing moon many faces, one overlapping another: the faces of her grandmother, her father-in-law, and her Kuei. Death had wiped away their agony and sorrow; each face appeared to be peaceful and happy. They smiled at her and talked to her in the murmuring wind: Live on, Qing, please live on.

The Willow Place woman was the first to stand up. She gave a hand to Qing.

"I guess we better move away from this beach," Qing said, steadying herself as best she could.

As they walked away from the water, both women looked over their shoulders and whispered good-byes to their loved ones whose bodies were now at the bottom of the sea.

They leaned against each other as they entered the town of Deep Bay. They wavered on like two drunks, zigzagging through a dark street.

After a while the street became brighter and more crowded, and a few houses could be seen only a few yards away.

"Everyone is staring at us," Qing said. "We're dripping and covered with sand and seaweeds."

"We need a change of clothes," said the Willow Place woman. "Shall we beg for money?"

They stood under a lamppost and started to beg immediately.

"My kind Si-san and Tai-tai, please give two poor women a penny or two," said the Willow Place woman with an outstretched hand. "We need rags to cover our humble bodies, so our disgusting filth won't offend your honorable eyes."

Qing felt weak from hunger. She leaned against the lamppost to keep from falling. The night air was warm, but she was shaking and her reaching hand was trembling. "Please spare a penny to save two poor women from starving to death . . ."

Her quavering voice faded in the laughter of the passersby.

Everyone laughed at them, but no one gave them anything. The night grew deeper. The Deep Bay people began to go home.

"Our only alternative is to steal," Qing said.

They reached the first of a cluster of low houses. Bamboo poles were supported on both ends by high tripods made of sticks. Clothes were hung to dry by passing the poles through the sleeves. Qing shivered when she saw a man's shirt hanging with its sleeves stretched. It looked like Kuei standing there, spreading his arms to welcome her into his embrace. "Kuei . . ." she called.

The Willow Place woman said, "We have no time to talk to the dead. We must concentrate on living, so the dead can live through us . . . they do, I know." She quickly lowered one end of a bamboo from the tripod and removed a few pieces of clothing from it. "Catch!" she whispered, and threw something at Qing.

Qing caught a garment. The Willow Place woman's brave and practical action made her feel ashamed of her own sentimental uselessness. She followed the woman's example and grabbed a quilted jacket. She tried to take it from the bamboo pole, but the sleeve was caught on the tripod. Everything fell in the next few seconds, creating noise, trapping her and the Willow Place woman in a net of laundry.

Dogs barked. People shouted. The sound of footsteps neared. Hands landed on Qing. Fear made her roll fiercely on the ground to free herself from their grasp. She kept rolling regardless of the hard rocks and sharp objects on the ground.

She was finally out of people's reach and untangled from the wet sheet. She jumped up and ran from the gathered shouting crowd.

"Another escapee from the mainland! Let's get the police!"

"So many of them are arriving each day, taking jobs and food from us! I'm glad the police will send them back to the mainland and their government will kill them!"

Qing turned only twice to look over her shoulder.

The first time she saw the Willow Place woman struggling helplessly in the hands of two men, being beaten and kicked by those around her.

The second time she saw a police car stopping beside the crowd, two uniformed men twirling their truncheons as they approached the woman.

Qing continued to run.

Deep Bay was only a small town when compared to Kowloon—a city with activities going on twenty-four hours a day.

The streets were brightly lit, although it was past midnight. Food stands were everywhere, each doing a booming business. No vendor provided seats for the customers; many people stood on the sidewalks eating from either chipped bowls or newspaper cones.

The aroma reached Qing's nostrils, deepened the pain of hunger in her abdomen. Her body was numb from exhaustion, but not her stomach.

She stopped at the first food stand, stared at the food. Everything in this world disappeared from her eyes except the steamed buns piled on the wooden table.

She moved like a hypnotized person, took a bun in each hand. She began to eat them in large bites, hearing no protesting words from the vendor, feeling no beating hands from the vendor's wife.

"A crazy woman!" yelled the vendor. "Steals our food but doesn't run away! Let's find a policeman and have her taken to the madhouse!"

"I think she's another escapee from the mainland!" said the vendor's wife as she slapped Qing hard. "The British government hates them as much as we do. Where are the police? She needs to be sent back where she's from!"

Qing took the beating while continuing to shovel the buns into her mouth. She could not run one more step, nor could she live one more second without food. Her mouth was bleeding from the woman's powerful blows, but she swallowed the blood together with the steaming hot bun.

"Aren't you ashamed of yourselves? Look at what you're doing! You are beating a woman who is a human being just like you, and she is obviously starved!" a strong voice shouted.

The slapping stopped when the vendor's wife's hand was held in the firm grip of a middle-aged man.

Qing stared at the man's face. He looked half-Caucasian and half-Chinese. He was well-dressed. Behind him on the road was parked a long black car with its motor running.

The vendor roared angrily, "Si-san, this is none of your business! The woman took buns from us, and my wife has the right to beat her up!"

"Aaron, please give the man whatever the buns are worth and bring the poor woman to me."

From the open window on the passenger side came the voice of a woman. "She looks like she needs help."

Qing looked into the car while chewing the last bite of the bun. The woman spoke perfect Cantonese, just like the well-dressed man, but she was white. Qing had never seen a white person in White Stone. Someone had told her that the language of the white people was the same as birdsong.

The man paid the vendor and came to Qing. He put a hand on her shoulder without frowning at her filth. He smiled kindly at her while pointing at the lovely woman in the car.

He said, "That's my wife, Diana. She and I are on our way home from the theater. We stopped to see what was going on. Please come with me or my wife will yell at me for frightening you away."

Qing took one more look at the woman in the car. The lady had short brown hair and beautiful large eyes. She looked at Qing compassionately. The gentleness in her smile disarmed Qing completely.

Qing let the man escort her to the car. He opened the back door and then put a hand over her head to guide her in. She collapsed on the leather seat.

When the car began to move, Qing turned to look through the rear window. She saw the vendor, his wife, and the crowd staring after her. And then Qing saw a police car coming, slowing down at the food stands. She slid off the seat, ducked to the floor. She crouched so low that her face was against the floor mat, where the design of a red lion was woven into the carpet. She felt dizzy, and in her eyes the lion came to life. It opened its mouth to devour her, and she screamed.

"Please, Si-san and Tai-tai, move faster! Please!" she pleaded with the two people in the front seat. "Death is taking the shape of a lion now! It's coming after me! It'll catch me and give me to the policemen. They'll arrest me and send me back to White Stone. I'll be killed there, I know!"

She heard the woman comforting her in a tender voice. "Don't be afraid, my child. There is no lion. Nor is there death in this car. We'll help you. We've helped many people like you, and we'll make sure that no one sends you anywhere you don't want to go . . ." The woman's sweet voice began to drift away.

The strong smells of the leather seat faded into an indistinct scent. The design of the red lion was now only a blurry splotch. Qing fainted as the car moved on.

"White Stone?" Aaron Cohen asked from one side of the bed.

"Yes," Qing answered, and turned her head on the pillow to study Aaron's half-white and half-Chinese face.

Diana said from the other side of the bed, "My husband and I were in White Stone once. It was many years ago, during the war. We had to run away from that village on bicycles."

Qing felt drowsy, but she felt she owed the nice couple a detailed answer. They had not only saved her life but also taken her home, fed her, and tucked her in bed. "White Stone has always been my home . . ." She told them her life story, paused now and then to rest.

When she talked, the middle-aged couple kept asking questions. As she answered them, she learned to say their strange names: Dah-ah-na and Ah-lon Coo-hen. When she finished, to her surprise, the sorrow in her heart had reduced its piercing power and the heavy burden on her shoulders had lessened its imposing weight.

"I have no home and no one in Hong Kong," Qing added. "My parents and brother are in Taiwan, but I don't know how to find them."

"You have a home with us until you can locate your parents. They'll either come here immediately to get you or send for you to join them, I'm sure," said Diana. "We'll help you to find them. But in the meantime we'll take care of you. Your story has made you more special to us than all the others we've helped." Diana shook her head. "You are a remarkably brave woman. We have never met anyone as strong as you. Besides, you are from White Stone."

Diana looked at Aaron across the bed. Fond memories brightened her lovely eyes. She continued to talk. "When Aaron and I ran away from White Stone on bicycles about twenty years ago, we were not married then. We were two young dreamers ready to conquer the world."

Aaron Cohen nodded. His handsome face was illuminated by the pleasant thoughts of a treasured past. He kept his adoring eyes on his wife's captivating face as he talked to Qing. He told Qing briefly about his own past and his wife's.

Aaron then said, "Diana and I used to live in San Francisco. Since my parents died and left us this house in Hong Kong, we've been traveling between two places, for our jewelry business and also our own enjoyment. When my wife and I were young and foolish, we thought we could turn the whole of China into a livable place. Since we've become older and wiser, we've settled on helping as many Chinese as we can . . . anyway, we'll be your sponsors."

Qing looked at them in puzzlement. They explained what sponsors were.

In the past few years, either by swimming across the water or sneaking across checkpoints, many people had escaped from mainland China to Hong Kong. The British government ordered their police to arrest the illegal arrivals and keep them in camps. Those who could find sponsors were allowed to stay and given legal resident papers. But when a refugee couldn't find a sponsor within a week of his arrest, he would be escorted to the border between Deep Bay and mainland China and handed over to the People's Republic's officials.

Diana said, "We can't blame the British for doing so either. Hong Kong has become almost the most crowded place in the world now. The government can't afford to take in more refugees."

Aaron saw the worried look on Qing's face and added, "My wife and I can keep the police away from you. Our home is yours until you are reunited with your family in Taiwan. All you have to do now is to recover and become physically strong. You need plenty of rest and good food."

At the mention of food, Qing swallowed the saliva that suddenly filled her mouth. The Cohens had already fed her some soup. It would be impolite for her to ask for more. But her stomach was growling again, and she was sure Diana could hear it.

Diana did hear it, and smiled. There was a bell on the wall over the headboard of the bed. Diana pushed it and a maid appeared shortly. ''Bring a tray of food to Miss Ma.'' Diana turned and asked with a smile, ''Or do you prefer to be called Mrs. Fan?''

Qing sighed. Both titles belonged to the good old feudal days. They were forbidden terms in the new China. She had not heard them for a very long time. They made her feel good, as if she had become once again a rich little girl living in a magnificent big home.

''Either name is fine.'' She sighed again, stretched her body in the large comfortable bed. ''As long as you don't call me a Bloodsucker or a comrade.''

The maid returned soon with more soup, half a roasted chicken, a large dish of stir-fried peapods, and a heaping bowl of rice. Qing's jaw dropped. A soft scream of delight escaped her mouth. She couldn't wait for Diana to tuck the linen napkin under her chin. She picked up the chicken by its leg, bit into it, and chewed it, although it burned her tongue. She tore the meat off the bones with her teeth and fingers, then looked at the piled bones and said, ''Mrs. Coo-hen, I mean, Dah-ah-na, please don't throw the bones away. We can put them in a pot of water and make some real good soup.''

Diana shook her head and patted Qing on the shoulder. ''My poor child, haven't you realized your days in hell are over? There are many more chickens in the kitchen. If you want chicken soup, we'll make it with chicken meat instead of bones."

Qing hated very much to see the bones thrown away. She picked up each one and sucked it loudly and thoroughly, saying in between sucking, "The last time I had chicken, I was about nine. Chicken is considered the most nutritious food in China, and only the rich can have it often."

When she was finished with the last bone, she moved the bowl of soup closer. She scooped up rice and peapods and dumped them into the soup, then spooned the mixture into her mouth, making a lot of noise while gulping it down.

Diana and Aaron exchanged a quick glance. Diana cleared her throat and said, "Qing, when you have finished eating you'll take a long nap. When you wake up you'll have a good hot bath, and after that we'll have a lot of work to do."

Swallowing the soup, rice, and peapods quickly, Qing listened to Diana defining "work."

The Cohens didn't intend to hide Qing in their house. But if they should bring Qing to public places and introduce her to their friends, they would prefer that Qing learn to speak some English and have more presentable table manners.

Aaron said, "In Hong Kong, English is spoken by all the people in so-called upper-class society. And those people are very picky about manners. You'll feel them looking down at you if should act beneath their standard. You are a proud person, we can tell. And we don't want your pride hurt."

Diana said, "I'm sure before your home was destroyed by the Communists, your manners were those of a real lady. It won't take long for you to recapture them, so don't worry."

Qing pushed the tray away and slid deeper into the thick quilt. She was well-fed and sleepy now. "What about English? Do you think I can learn that strange language? I can't even say your names right . . ." She couldn't keep her eyes open anymore. Before Diana or Aaron answered her question, she was already sound asleep.

The South China Sea roared far beneath the high cliff. The splashing could not be heard from the top of Victoria Peak.

Standing in a weathered gazebo, Qing stared at the silent waves. She had gained weight in the past four months. The extra pounds had filled her hollow cheeks and erased most of her wrinkles. She had recaptured some of her beauty, and become almost as young as her true age: twenty-one.

The wind blew her hair all over her face. She raised a hand to push it back, feeling the silken strands. Her hair had grown longer, and was the only part of her that had fully recovered; it was smooth and shining again instead of coarse and dry like straw.

She had on new clothes of fine material; Diana had given her many things. But her face was sad and angry; it wore the wounded expression of a person who had been stabbed unexpectedly.

In Qing's hands was a letter. She looked at it and began to read it again. Once more she heard the voice of a stranger, because even in the bygone days her father had seldom talked to her. She had not heard him speak for twelve years now, and had completely forgotten how he sounded.

The stranger said, "Your mother and I were surprised when a man came to our door and told us he was a private detective hired by Mr. Aaron Cohen. You've found us, but our reunion is impossible. Being a refugee from mainland China, you cannot enter Taiwan without a visa. Such a visa can be acquired only if you have a sponsor. I am qualified to be your sponsor, but if I have you under my roof, the government officials will suspect me to a certain degree and take away many of my trading privileges. As a result, I will not be able to make as much money as I am making now. Your brother, Te, is in the USA, and he has been trying to contact you. If you must reunite with your family, perhaps you can write to your brother. Enclosed is your brother's address in San Francisco, and a check of a rather large amount. Please tell the Cohens that if they wish to charge you for room and board, your Baba will be glad to pay. In return, you can do your parents a favor by never writing to us again."

Qing stared at the letter for a while, then loosened her hold on it. A gust of wind carried the papers away. The white sheets sailed down the peak like descending butterflies. Some of them were caught on trees protruding from the cliff and were pierced by the sharp tips of the branches.

Qing watched the torn papers, felt a daughter's heart being torn by the merciless hands of a father. She lifted her head and looked up at the sky.

"So you don't want me, my dear Baba and Mama! Then it's your loss instead of mine!" she said loudly, then left the gazebo, her head high, without one backward glance at the scattered letters.

"I have many things to do," she murmured on her way to the house, "I'll take a hot bath, then study my English book. And then I'll learn the acceptable manners—practice walking and sitting and talking and all the other boring things."

Diana and Aaron were out. As Qing walked through the marble hallway, the servants greeted her with bows. For a fleeting moment Qing had the illusion that she was a child in White Stone, in the Ma mansion that was her own home. She blinked and shivered. She looked at the lovely things around her and whispered, "May the Great Buddha keep communism away from Hong Kong, or this beautiful mansion and this lovely way of life will be destroyed too!"

She reached the bathroom, closed the door, and turned the brass faucets over the bathtub. She poured a generous amount of bath oil in the tub, as Diana had shown her, then undressed while watching the steaming water rise. On the foaming water she saw the bygone days: for twelve long years she had not known running water, and even her drinking water had been from the Pearl River, where people also bathed and dumped garbage and human waste.

She stepped into the filled tub and stretched her body to its full length. She leaned her head against the tiled wall and looked around. She was in the bathroom attached to the guest room for ladies. Everything was either pink, or white, or brass. A crystal vase stood on the vanity table, held fresh night-blooming jasmine, and gave the room a honeyed fragrance that was strong enough to provide her with sweet hallucination.

Qing closed her eyes. But what could she hallucinate? Neither that the days of hardship were erased nor that she could bring Kuei back to life. "But at least I can imagine the future," she whispered softly. She sank deeper into the soothing water and smiled. "I am only twenty-one, and my future can be as great as the amount of work I'm willing to put into it!"

24

ON A BEAUTIFUL spring day in San Francisco in 1962, Ma Te drove away from campus, headed for a new apartment building containing many small units. He and Delia had lived together for almost a year now. He smiled when he thought of their tiny love nest. He drove into the apartment's parking lot, then left his car and rushed into the building.

"I received a letter from my sister!" Te said as soon as he unlocked their door, then continued as he looked for Delia from the kitchen to the living area and then the bedroom. "The first letter in thirteen years! You won't believe what she has gone through. She was deeply hurt when our parents didn't want to see her. She thought I would reject her too. She didn't want to write to me until her friends convinced her to give it a try. Those nice people are bringing her with them to San Francisco soon . . ."

He stopped when he saw Delia sitting on the edge of their bed in her jean jacket, the front of which was covered with small embroidered patches: a fist in a triangle, a torch in a circle, two hands joined in a square . . . It was the jacket she always wore for marches and demonstrations.

"Where are we going this time?" Te asked.

Delia picked up a man's jacket similar to hers and threw it to him, then continued to tie her tennis shoes. "There is a strike in a wire factory at the west end of town. We're going there to root for the strikers. But we still have a few minutes. Please tell me about your sister's letter when we have lunch."

Te put on his jacket and asked, "A wire factory? Are there many black and Asian workers?"

Delia nodded. "The factory pays the black and Asian workers much less than they do the whites. And even the union is not doing a damn thing about it." She stood up and pulled Te with her. "While I fix lunch, you can tell me about the good news from your sister."

Delia moved quickly to make two bowls of instant oatmeal. She put a handful of nuts and raisins in each bowl. Te took Qing's letter from his pocket and translated it to Delia.

When he finished, Delia said, "I'll go with you to the airport when she comes. I believe she and I can become good friends. She sounds very strong. Since the Cohens are teaching her English and I've learned some Chinese from you, she and I shouldn't have a language barrier." Delia shook her head. "When compared to what she has gone through, I guess we don't have much right to complain about the USA. I thought Taiwan was bad enough, from what you said. But after weighing it against the mainland, now I know why Taiwan is called the Free China."

They sat down to eat. When Delia pushed her empty bowl away, she saw that Te had not touched his oatmeal. "Why aren't you eating? It's a nourishing lunch, much better than your oily eggrolls and greasy fried rice."

"I never attack your vegetarian meals, so please don't criticize my Chinese food," Te said, then couldn't help asking: "Delia, you used to like Chinese food. We had so much fun eating together in Chinatown. Why have you become a vegetarian all of a sudden?"

Delia said impatiently while wiping her mouth with a paper napkin, "Because it's cruel to kill the animals and eat their flesh. And also because it's unhealthy to have dead animals in our stomachs. I've explained that before. Being Chinese, you should know all about being a vegetarian. Is it not a part of Buddhist doctrine?"

Te finished half of the oatmeal and pushed the bowl far away. "Let's go!"

They were soon in front of the wire factory, each holding a cardboard sign, walking back and forth among many other demonstrators.

"Equality for blacks!"

"Equality for Asians!"

"We are all created equal!"

"We demand fair pay and benefits!"

They shouted and marched from midafternoon until after nightfall. A truck loaded with torches stopped beside them. The torches were quickly distributed and lit. The spirit of the demonstrators was uplifted when they marched in the torchlight.

"America is home to all of us!" Delia shouted, smiling at Te, thinking that his handsomeness was enhanced by the flames.

"We demand equal rights!" Te yelled, then leaned toward Delia, and kissed her quickly on the cheek, feeling that her beauty was intensified by the glowing torch.

Te pointed at the group of policemen standing in the distance and raised his voice so Delia could hear him. "They have been watching us since we started this demonstration. But they haven't bothered us at all. This sure is different from Taiwan!"

Delia saw the sudden sadness on his face and asked, "Are you thinking of your childhood friend again?"

Te nodded. "I wish he had lived and made it here with me. The three of us could have marched together and made a bigger troublemaking team!"

The night air turned cold. The marchers' voices were hoarse. They left one by one as the police watched quietly. Delia and Te got into their car, exhausted but elated. The result of the demonstration was beyond their control, but they felt they had accomplished something meaningful.

Delia leaned her head against Te's shoulder and said, "I love you, Te. And I have the greatest respect for you. You've come a long way . . ." She giggled. "From the boy who took notes about the professor's windshield wiper, to a brave marcher."

Te kissed the top of her head while driving, then asked with worry, "Do you think your parents will like me when we visit them during our spring break?"

Delia snuggled closer to Te and said, "Everyone in my hometown will like you, Te. Please don't worry."

They drove from California to Little Rock, then to the outskirts of Memphis, Tennessee. Delia pointed at the tall buildings on the horizon and said, "We're only three hours from my home now."

There was a dreamy look on her face. She spoke slowly. "Many years ago Roy and I were two country kids fascinated by city lights. He mowed lawns and I scrubbed floors for white people. We worked so hard to save a few dollars to come to Memphis, to wander around the city in the day, sleep in the Y or on a park bench in the night . . ." She went on.

Roy's parents were very poor. When she was fifteen and he eighteen, he found an auto mechanic's job in Memphis, where he learned martial arts from a Korean teacher. He returned home on his off days and taught Delia everything he learned. He waited for Delia to graduate from high school and join him in Memphis. But when Delia received a scholarship in San Francisco, she changed her mind. She preferred California to Tennessee, and asked Roy to go to San Francisco with her.

She said to Te, "I told him he could find a job near my school and we could share the living expenses. But he insisted on staying in Memphis. Soon after I arrived in San Francisco, he returned home under very unpleasant circumstances . . ." She stopped when her voice became hoarse.

Delia forced away her sudden sorrow. Their little car was once again filled with laughter as they reached Delia's hometown.

In the middle of the town square of Green Hills there was a fountain. The benches around it were occupied by many old men. While chewing tobacco and whittling on small pieces of wood, they took time to spit, talk, and look at every passerby.

"Look at that blue car. It has an out-of-town license plate."

"It's from California. Anyone we know?"

"Two colored folks. One black and one yellow."

"The nigger is the Porter girl. What's in the car with her? A Chink or a Jap?"

The car windows were rolled down and Te and Delia could hear the old men's voices. Delia said to Te jokingly, "Most of them have never seen a Chinese in their entire lives. Maybe we can sell tickets for them to come to my parents' home to look at you."

Te's face was red from anger. "This is the first Southern small town I've ever seen. It sure is different from California. Are these people always so curious?" He frowned and turned to look at the old men once more, then added with animosity, "And so resentful?"

Delia patted Te on the thigh. "Don't let them bother you. They are more curious than malicious. Actually, they are much kinder than city folks. They won't hurt you unless you want to marry into their families."

They passed a paved street with brick houses, entered a narrow dirt road. Delia pointed at the wooden structures and continued to talk. "This is the colored neighborhood. In a Southern town the colored people are treated like dogs. It's not always a bad thing—if you're patient, you'll learn what I mean. You see, we dogs must not share our masters' sofas or dining tables. But as long as we wag our tails and lick their hands, they'll feed us in chipped bowls set on the ground. In Green Hills no one mistreats his dog as long as the dog doesn't bite or bark. But in cities like Memphis, people sometimes like to torture dogs just for fun."

She stopped at a small white wooden house. She said through clenched teeth, "Roy barked too loudly in Memphis, and bit the wrong masters." She opened the car door.

The front door of the house opened and three people appeared: a couple in their forties and a young man. Delia ran to them, laughing and calling out.

Te glanced at the couple quickly. They were neatly dressed and kind-looking, but not eye-catching like the young man, who had skin as black as the darkest teakwood. His face was not only handsome but also powerful. He had the build of an athlete from the waist up. But he was in a wheelchair, and his legs hung lifelessly from the knees down.

"Roy! I knew you'd be here!" Delia got down to her knees, threw her arms around the young man, and kissed him on the mouth.

The man in the wheelchair kissed Delia back. The couple watched with gentle smiles. The four of them weren't aware Te existed, and he didn't want to disturb their reunion.

The sight of Roy made Te's heart beat quickly with compassion. He suddenly found the cause of Delia's determination to slay the mean dragon called Racial Prejudice—the dragon that had destroyed the legs of her playmate and first love.

* * *

Three days later, Te and Delia were on the road again.

"Why didn't you tell me about Roy's legs?" Te asked when they could no longer see the three people waving after them from the house.

"Why should I?" Delia threw him a mischievous smile. "You look cute when you're jealous."

"I was never really jealous of Roy. I was only curious why you loved him so much, yet left him. Now that I've met him, I really like him. I like your parents too. They are intelligent, kind, and just as broad-minded as you." Te shook his head in disbelief. "Not many parents would accept their daughter's male roommate and never even hint at marriage."

He reached to take Delia's hand. "What happened to Roy makes me want even more to do something to change this world."

Four years ago, soon after Delia had left for California, Roy had had a fight in Memphis with several white men. They knocked him down and beat him with crowbars until they smashed his kneecaps. When Roy woke up and learned that his knees were crushed beyond repair and he would live the rest of his days in a wheelchair, he screamed and thrashed about so fiercely that the nurse had to inject him with something to knock out his consciousness.

Delia opened her mouth, then closed it without saying what she wanted to say. It would hurt too much to tell Te that what he had learned about Roy was only half of the story, that Roy had almost gone mad because he had lost much more than his legs—he felt himself to be less than a man because the white men had smashed more than his kneecaps.

Delia said, "Roy is a brave and strong man. He has managed to recover emotionally and now has a job in a machine repair shop. He lives with his parents and a younger brother who drives him to and from work every day. He has accepted fate and readjusted his original plans to suit his new legless life."

Delia continued, "The most difficult adjustment for him was to rule out any possibility of marrying me." She turned to Te. "Someday you and I and Roy will be great friends."

They reached home to find a telegram: Qing would arrive in San Francisco in September.

By September Te and Delia were already in graduate school. They both skipped classes to go to the airport.

Te looked toward the gate longingly. "I haven't seen Qing for thirteen years now. I wonder if she still wears her long pigtails." Passengers began to pour in.

Between a Eurasian man and a Caucasian woman walked a young lady. She was tall and slim. Her hair was straight and hanging loosely, gleaming like a night river flowing under a moonless sky. She had on a short-sleeved white dress and wore very little makeup. A small red bead hung from an invisible thread, like a drop of blood on her chest. She moved gracefully as she looked at the waiting crowd with lips slightly parted and eyes wide open.

When her eyes met Te's, they immediately recognized that they were brother and sister. There was no obvious resemblance, but nonetheless they could see themselves in each other.

"Qing!" Te waved his arms and shouted across the distance.

"Te!" her clear voice rang like a trembling bell over the noise of the crowd.

Delia poked Te in the side with her elbow. "Why didn't you tell me your sister was the most beautiful girl in China?"

Te smiled with tears in his eyes as he moved through the crowd.

25

LOW-FLYING CLOUDS danced around the top of Pali, alternately concealing and revealing the blue tiles on the roof of a newly built house.

The building resembled a giant round hut with a pointed crown. The structure was circled by a porch from which one could enjoy several views: from the city of Honolulu to Diamond Head, then Waikiki Beach and the pineapple fields in the west end.

Walking on his porch, Paala Nihoa didn't pay attention to any of the scenes down below. He looked up at the clouds. "I have a long way to climb before reaching the top," he mumbled, and his jaws tightened, his heart filled with determination. "I'll climb until I reach the summit!"

Keeping his eyes on the sky, he began to search for the lyrics for his new song. He thought of the plumeria trees, the Pali Mountain, the island wind, and the enchanting sea. He left the porch abruptly and entered his music room.

He picked up his guitar, sat on a high stool, and began to strum. When he finally put down his guitar to write the song, he sat at an oak desk. The music room faced the south, so he could look up and see the colorful sails of many sailboats. One of those expensive boats belonged to him.

At twenty-seven Paala had fame, money, and the adoration of thousands of fans. His records sold well—he had one gold one already. When he toured, it was a full house everywhere. After every performance he needed the help of several local policemen to leave the theater.

His agent and public-relations man were clever; they used everything about Paala to his advantage—even his five-year jail sentence.

Paala shook his head when he remembered what was printed in the newspaper:

> Paala Nihoa's songs are songs of anger, sorrow, and love. His anger results from his being accused and convicted of a crime he did not commit. His sorrow is rooted on the fact that when he was in prison, his parents died. Numerous girls are responsible for the love songs he writes. After dating many island girls, including a former beauty queen, Paala has been seen in the company of lovely young ladies from all over the world. The world is eager to find out which lucky girl will capture the title "Mrs. Paala Nihoa."

Paala sighed as he corrected the newsman's mistakes by talking to an empty room, "I wasn't wrongly accused. My parents didn't die when I was in jail. And none of those girls inspired my songs. But most of all, the world will never see a Mrs. Paala Nihoa."

His fingers strummed out notes of wrath. His memory drifted to the past. Notes of anguish poured from his guitar. He had lived in wrath since the moment he had seen Sumiko's wedding photograph in the newspaper, and the only way for him to keep going was to concentrate on his career. He said in a coarse voice, "I must climb to the highest place a songwriter and performer can get, and gain all the material possessions a person can grasp. And then perhaps I'll be happy again."

From Paala's sorrow a melody was gradually formed. He hummed along with it, then sang of a beautiful girl who wouldn't even look at him if he were poor, jobless, and living behind prison walls.

In San Francisco, Sumiko was getting ready for work.

She put on her white uniform, glanced into the mirror, and saw a young woman of twenty-four, thin, pale, with tight lips and a hard glare in her eyes. Her features had not altered, but her softness had gone. And because of that she looked like a different person.

"The difference inside me is greater than eyes can see," she sighed as she brushed her hair, which hung straight to her waist. In bygone days she had worn her hair loose, but now she braided it and then twisted the braid into a tight bun, pinned and secured by a black hairnet.

She put on her white cap. She had stopped wearing makeup since returning to San Francisco. It had been a five-hour flight from Hawaii, during which Yung Zhang had been cold to her but flirted with the stewardesses. By the time the plane touched ground, Sumiko had made a decision: her marriage was a mistake, but she would make the best of it just the same.

There had been a party in her and Zhang's honor, given by Te and Delia. Zhang and she had acted the happy couple, an act that had continued to the present day. By silent agreement she and Zhang always showed up at parties as a perfect couple. Away from the public eye they led separate lives: his was a life of study and playing around; hers was work.

Sumiko arrived at the hospital and headed directly for the rehabilitation center.

Next to the room for physical therapy was a room with many chairs and a piano. Soon after Sumiko entered, her patients began to arrive. Some of them came on their own, but others were accompanied by nurses or pushed in wheelchairs. Their ages varied from under ten to over eighty, but all of them had been hospitalized for emotional problems.

Just as crutches could help people with wounded legs regain the use of damaged leg muscles, so music could serve as a crutch for those with wounded emotions. An experimental job had been created in California so that a few of the more advanced hospitals could share a musical therapist. Sumiko had been given the position because of her nursing degree and her superb technique at the piano.

After greeting each patient, Sumiko went to the piano. She looked at the children in the front row and said, "I'll play for you a waltz composed by a man named Chopin when he was watching a little dog chasing its tail and turning in circles. When you hear me play, use your imagination and you'll see a cute dog spinning around, and you can even pretend that the dog is yours."

As she played the lively music, Sumiko studied the children's faces. Most of them had been abused. Their physical bruises were no longer visible, but emotional ones were hidden deeply in their hearts. Their young features looked old. There were no smiles on their lips, no light in their eyes. But as the music continued, some of the lips curled upward and some of the eyes brightened.

"Hey, I do see a little dog!" a young boy said after listening for a while. "It is brown, with white paws!"

"I see it too!" A young girl clapped her hands. "When my grandparents come to take me home, I'll ask them to get me a dog just like the one I see now!"

Sumiko smiled at the children and then went on to play for the group of teenagers. "This piece was also composed by Chopin. Long after his death, it was turned into a song called 'I'm Always Chasing Rainbows.' The words are beautiful."

She glanced at her young audience. Some of them had been drug users, some suicidal. She said as she played on, "We are all rainbow chasers. Our rainbows take various forms. There is nothing wrong with chasing a rainbow, as long as we know that rainbows exist only temporarily and that after the colorful image disappears, we must face the realities in life."

Some of the young faces looked puzzled, thoughtful. A few of the patients nodded in agreement with Sumiko, but several seemed to be in disagreement with her words. Sumiko continued to play. If her music could bring light into only one of these shadowed young minds, then her work was not wasted.

The next music was played for the emotionally shattered middle-aged group. Then Sumiko played to soothe the battered feelings of the aged. She was totally involved in her work, and found satisfaction in it. When the hour was over she talked with each patient. When they were gone she left this hospital and drove to another to do the same thing. Only when she was on the highway between hospitals was she once again captured by troubled thoughts: she was unhappily married to an unfaithful husband.

She pushed harder on the accelerator. The car's speed diluted her frustration. As she drove on, she remembered that tonight there was a party in honor of Ma Te's sister at the Sung house. Zhang had already said he couldn't make it, so she would have to appear as only half of the perfect couple.

26

DIANA AND AARON COHEN looked at Qing with the pride of two artists who had created a masterpiece by joint effort.

Qing was wearing a white linen suit and white leather high-heeled shoes. Her hair was gathered behind her ears with two small combs adorned with pearls. Her makeup was light, her perfume faint. She turned around slowly with a smile as Diana and Aaron studied her from head to toe.

"Perfect! You are perfect in every way—your beauty, your grace, and most of all your air," Diana said. "You look like a flawless peony blooming in an emperor's garden, never touched by one drop of rain. Only Aaron and I know what storm you have gone through."

Qing looked at Diana and smiled. "This peony would have wilted long ago, if you and Aaron hadn't nurtured it in Hong Kong."

Qing had more gratitude to express, but Diana waved a hand. "Don't thank me and my husband again." She turned to Aaron. "How many times must we remind her that a gardener can give his hardest work to a thistle, yet never turn it into a rose?"

Aaron nodded. "My wife is absolutely right.

The way you look and feel today is a result of your inner strength and your eagerness to learn.''

Qing had learned not only English and perfect manners but also the Western way of showing affection. She hugged Aaron, then held Diana and kissed her on the cheek. ''No matter what the two of you say, I owe my new life to you.''

A slight frown appeared on Diana's face. She pointed at Qing's neck. ''This thing doesn't look right on you. It's the only remaining trace of your being a thistle at one time.''

Qing touched the red bead. Shadow draped her face momentarily. ''It's the only thing left of my Kuei. It's called the Lover's Teardrop. I . . .'' She hesitated for a moment, then reached behind her neck and undid the knot. She gave the bead to Diana. ''You are right. There should be no teardrops in my new life. Kuei lives in my heart, and I don't need to keep this tiny little bead.''

Diana held the bead and looked at her husband. The Cohens were often impressed by Qing's courage, but the giving up of the last memento of her husband overwhelmed them.

A servant came to the door, announcing that Mr. Ma Te was at the door to pick up his sister.

''Have a good time at the party,'' Aaron said to Qing.

''Give our regards to Sung Hwa,'' Diana said. ''Tell him that we can't make it to the party tonight, but would like to see him before going back to Hong Kong.''

Qing left, and the Cohens were ready to go to the opera house with their business associates when the doorbell rang. A handsome gray-haired man walked in.

"Sung Hwa! What are you doing here?" Diana asked in surprise. "There is a party in your house. Shouldn't you stay home and be the host?"

Sung Hwa shook his head. "It's a party for the young. I'm not Lu-an. She has the mentality of a child. I am old. I'd rather visit my old friends. I've been meaning to come over since I knew you'd returned to San Francisco." He looked at the Cohens' clothes. "Did I come at a wrong time?"

The Cohens quickly decided to cancel their opera date, and the three of them settled in the living room and were soon deeply involved in reminiscences.

Sung Hwa pointed at the iron-gray hair on his temples and said to Diana, "When I met your husband in 1937, I was nineteen and he a child. Now I am forty-four."

"Don't you dare talk about age," Diana said. "I'm forty-five." She smiled broadly. "Age is a forbidden subject in our house, because I'm six years older than my husband."

Aaron was sitting on the same sofa with his wife and put an arm around her and kissed her cheek. "You are six years older, sixty times wiser, and six hundred times better in every way."

The affection between the Cohens brought sadness and envy to Sung Hwa's eyes. He could have been this happy too, he thought, if fate had not dealt him a merciless blow.

Diana noticed Hwa's sorrow. She said in a light voice, "If you had come just a few minutes earlier, you would have met Qing. Now she is at your house, and you're here. It would be nice if someday you two can get together."

Hwa asked carelessly, "Qing? The refugee from China? Why would you want me to meet her?"

Diana said, "She is much more than just a refugee . . ." She told him how Aaron and she had rescued Qing from the police and brought her home. She then looked at her husband. "You tell Hwa the rest."

Aaron said slowly, "Qing told us everything that has happened to her since she was nine, but not much that took place before that. We kept asking her questions, but so far we only knew that her maiden name is Ma and that her father used to be the richest man in White Stone. We haven't forgotten what happened all those years ago. We thought that if you could meet Qing, perhaps you would be able to find out if she was related to the girl who still lives in your heart."

"White Stone! A rich man named Ma!" Sung Hwa stood up. "There can't be two rich men by the same name in the same village!"

Diana and Aaron Cohen stared after their friend, who had departed without saying good-bye.

Lu-an, Te, Qing, Delia, and Sumiko were gathered in the Sung house. Because of Delia and Sumiko, Qing tried to speak English, but her accent bothered her. The English-speaking people kept telling her that her accent was "cute." But Qing didn't want to be cute; she preferred perfection.

Lu-an showed her guests around the big mansion. Qing counted on her fingers all the rooms. Besides her accent, there were a few things she could not overcome—awe at the sizes of single-family homes was one of them.

"At least twenty-two families could share all these rooms," she said, sizing up the place with her eyes. "That means homes for about eighty people."

Qing saw the others staring at her and realized what she was doing. "I'm sorry. I've forgotten the size of my childhood home. I can only see all the big houses as places for multifamily dwellings. I did the same thing when I saw the two Cohen houses for the first time."

Te put his arm around Qing, held her tightly. "My poor sister, fate forced you to change so much. You used to be a happy little girl with two long pigtails who thought everyone in this world lived in mansions and had servants."

Qing lifted her head high. "That happy little girl was a silver vase, decorative but not functional. Hot fire melted her, and merciless hands pounded on her. They turned her into a sharp sword." She smiled at Te sadly. "I am prouder of myself this way than I ever was before."

Te looked at his sister's beautiful eyes—two dark pools with incredible strength embedded in their depths. "And I am proud of you too, my sister the shining sword."

"Let's go eat," Lu-an said. "I really don't know what you are talking about. Moving eighty people into this house? I don't think my husband would like it. A beautiful flower vase changed into a sword?" She shook her head and led the way to the dining room.

Lu-an used her own chopsticks to serve food to everyone. She talked loudly and her saliva splashed afar, adding a new seasoning to every dish.

"Sumiko, what's the matter with you? Why do you never have any appetite? Te, you're not eating the way a growing boy should . . . so you *are* twenty-one, but you still look like a child to me. Qing, I like you. You're the only person eating like you are hungry. Dee-lee-ah, do I say your name right? You are strange. Why do you not eat meat?"

"I'm a vegetarian."

"What is that?" Lu-an asked.

"One who eats only vegetables," Delia answered.

"Ah." Lu-an nodded with understanding. "You are a Buddhist. You are afraid to eat a pig who used to be your relative."

"I beg your pardon?" Delia asked, wide-eyed.

Te explained reincarnation to Delia.

Delia laughed. "Come to think of it, some of the people on earth do look like they were either pigs or rats not too long ago."

The words "vegetarian" and "reincarnation" were not yet in Qing's English vocabulary. She was puzzled. She leaned toward Delia and whispered, "You don't eat meat. Are you a Bloodsucker?"

Delia stared at Qing. "Am I a what?"

Before Te could explain, Qing said, "If you don't even know what a Bloodsucker is, then I am sure you are not one." Qing smiled at Delia. "I am very happy for you. For a moment I thought you were being punished by them . . ."

Qing groped through enough words to tell Delia that in White Stone, even when there was meat on the tables of the commune mess hall, the Bloodsuckers were not allowed to eat it.

"It was a very cruel punishment," Qing said, her eyes sparkling in fury. "I still remember once when I had not tasted meat for a long time—actually, I had not tasted much of anything for a long time . . . A pig became sick and was killed. We had a feast. Someone picked up a piece of meat with his chopsticks and dangled it right in front of my eyes. He moved it to my nose and then my mouth. I stared at it, smelled it, and could taste it. My stomach ached for it. I didn't know tears were rolling down my face until I heard people laugh. The Bloodsucker is crying for a piece of meat, they said. The Bloodsucker is shameless, they shouted."

Qing looked up and once again realized what she had done. "I'm so sorry. I didn't mean to ruin the dinner for everyone." She turned to Lu-an and bowed from her chair. "Please forgive me, Mrs. Sung. I will not talk about the unhappy days again."

"My poor child." Lu-an picked up a plateful of beef in oyster sauce, emptied half of it into Qing's rice bowl. "Eat all the meat you want."

While Te and Sumiko sighed over Qing's story, Delia watched Qing eat for a few moments, then made a decision. She picked up her chopsticks and took a piece of stir-fried pork. "I don't think my dead relatives are now pigs. So there is no need for me to be a vegetarian." She put the pork in her mouth and chewed gingerly.

"Hooray!" Te cheered. "No more oatmeal with raisins and nuts! No more salads grassy enough for cows! No more carrot sticks fit only for rabbits!"

When they were laughing loudly, the front door

opened. No one heard the servants greeting their master. Sung Hwa followed the roaring sound to the dining room.

"Ah! You are home!" Lu-an jumped to her feet. She didn't know how to express her thrilling happiness, so she talked nervously like a clucking hen. "What a nice surprise. It's so kind of you to give us your valuable time. I am so sorry for starting dinner without you . . ." She went on and on.

According to old Chinese custom, when the man of the house enters a room, all women must stand up. Diana had taught Qing the Western ways. But when Lu-an was so high-strung and eager to please, all of Diana's teachings had been forgotten. Now Qing stood up hurriedly.

Hwa saw a girl in white.

White was the favorite color of the girl in his memory.

Hwa glanced over Qing's full white skirt. He took in the wide black sash around Qing's narrow waist.

It was the fragile frame he used to embrace. It had disappeared from his arms but never his heart.

He brought his eyes up to Qing's face and was unable to look away.

Her face was exactly the face of the girl who had lived in his soul all these years.

Sung Hwa didn't answer his wife. He didn't respond to Sumiko's greetings. Te stood up politely, but Hwa didn't glance at the young man. Delia made a face, but Hwa didn't notice. Hwa saw no one but the girl in the white dress. He heard nothing except his own heart drumming.

His heart drummed out these words: How could she be in my house right now, since she died seventeen years ago?

As Sung Hwa stared at Qing, she studied him curiously. The man framed in the doorway was tall and lean in a light gray suit. He had the air of a lord, but his face was as dark as the face of a peasant. His hands on the door frame were the hands of a rich man before liberation, but he was as muscled as a coolie. Qing remembered what Diana had told her: the rich in America would pay to labor in places called health spas. She was amused by this wealthy man's purchased tan and muscle. She smiled.

Even her smile belonged to his beloved! Sung Hwa had to hold on to the door frame very tightly to keep himself from falling. His legs were weak and his knees about to buckle. He could hear blood rushing to his head and feel it burning his face. But at the same time beads of cold sweat stood out on his forehead. His mouth was dry and something hot was pricking his eyes.

For seventeen years a name had continued to exist in Hwa's every drop of blood and flow in all his veins and echo in his every heartbeat. But he had never vocalized it, not even once. Now, as he stared at Qing, he felt that name stirring within him, trying to escape his throat and fly out of his mouth.

Qing bowed politely to the master of the house. "Mr. Sung," she called softly.

Her voice was the voice of Hwa's eternal love! She had just addressed him the very same way his love called him the first time they were introduced to each other.

When Qing finished bowing and straightened herself, she looked at Sung Hwa again. She saw him taking his hands away from the door frame, bringing them to his throat. And then, without moving his eyes from her, he stumbled forward and opened his mouth. But from his quivering lips no sound came. It seemed that whatever Mr. Sung wanted to say was confined within him by his restraining hands.

Sung Hwa began to shake violently. His hands were on his mouth now. He was doing his best to stifle whatever words were trying to burst out of him.

And then Sung Hwa dropped his hands. He looked like a soldier at the end of a losing battle, now totally exhausted, with no more strength to fight. Standing there with his feet parted, shoulders drooped, and arms hanging limp at his sides, he ran the tip of his tongue over his lips and took a deep breath.

"You . . ." he whispered, gazing at Qing.

That single word crumbled his dam of self-control. Suddenly something inside him exploded. Sung Hwa's lifeless arms became vigorous clubs raised over his head. His feeble hands were now strong fists waving in the air.

Blazing fire flared in his wet eyes as he screamed in a ripping voice, "Melin! Melin! My Melin! Why did you hide from me all these years?"

PART IV

27

As spring 1963 neared its end, the Cohens were ready to go back to Hong Kong. In their living room they discussed Qing's future.

"You'll continue to live in this house, of course. And you can go to school," Diana said.

"I've never had much schooling in my life. Even before I was nine, I was taught only by a private tutor. I'm certainly too old to start school now," Qing answered. "I want to work."

"You can't find any decent job without some schooling or a special trade," Aaron reminded her.

"Then I'll start a business of my own, if you'll lend me the money." Qing looked at the Cohens. "My business will be a success, and I'll pay you back."

"I'm not worried about the money. But what kind of business do you have in mind?" Aaron asked with an amused smile.

"A restaurant," Qing answered quickly. "You've taken me to every restaurant in Chinatown, but I've not found one that served the dim sum my grandmother loved. I'm sure many Chinese are hungry for it, and if there is a dim-sum restaurant, it will have a booming business."

"No one here knows how to make those complicated delicacies," Diana said. "You'll not be able to find a cook."

Qing said with a smile, "I'll be the cook myself."

"You?" The Cohens stared at her.

Qing nodded confidently. "I cooked for Kuei and his father when I was only a child. Even the peasant food I cooked for them can be on the menu."

Diana looked at Qing with disbelief. "Your peasant days are over. Won't you feel degraded going back to cooking for others?"

Qing shook her head. "As you said, I learn fast. I've learned that no job is considered degrading in the USA. As long as a person is making good money, he'll gain people's respect. No, I will not be ashamed to be a cook." She looked from Diana to Aaron pleadingly. "I really would like to own a restaurant that serves something more than food. The old China is gone, but it can be recreated in my restaurant. I don't need a big place. I'll fill the small area with the beauty of old China. It will stand out in Chinatown like a beautiful little ivory pagoda."

When the Cohens agreed to help with the other aspects of starting a restaurant, Qing experimented in their kitchen. She had used to watch her grandmother sitting on a sofa or propped up in bed, her long-nailed white fingers lingering over a large tray of dishes whose secret recipes were handed down from the cook to his number-one son.

Using her memory as a guidebook, after many failures Qing finally mastered the craft.

Ivory Pagoda opened in the autumn of 1963. Qing was so proud to hear her employees call her Ma Lau-ban.

Ma Lau-ban decorated her place with paper lanterns and artworks imported from Hong Kong, and in her dining room traditional Chinese music played softly. Her waiters and waitresses wore either red or dark blue peasant blouses with black wide-legged pants, and on their feet were white cotton socks and soft black shoes. In one corner of the dining room a statue of Buddha sat cross-legged with a serene smile. Once they came into Ivory Pagoda, the customers unconsciously lowered their voices to a whisper. Throughout their meals they lived in a faraway land of ancient days that contained only art, poetry, music, and peaceful thoughts.

On this colorful autumn morning Ma Lau-ban was busy preparing Yuan-shaws for the approaching Yuan-shaw festival.

Around her, her employees worked quietly, chopping vegetables and meat, cleaning fish and shrimp. Like her waiters and waitresses, many of her kitchen workers were college students. American law forbade people without green cards to hold work permits, and it was illegal to hire anyone without such a permit. Some of the boys felt unmasculine washing dishes, and some of the girls felt it was beneath their dignity to wait on tables. Qing treated them with respect, tried her best to lift their spirits.

Qing's working area was a large stainless-steel table facing the back window. She worked silently, occasionally looked at an alley where a row of garbage cans stood beside two rusted refrigerators and a stack of wooden crates. A large white bird circled the garbage cans, then landed slowly. Qing had never seen a bird so big and fat before. She stared at it, thought of the legendary Bird of Destiny.

Her grandmother used to tell her, "We all fly on wings of destiny. We want to go one way, and others want us to go another. But only the big white bird knows where it's going, and our destiny is never predictable."

How true the saying was, Qing thought. No fortune-teller could ever have foretold that the girl from a rich family would first become the wife of a peasant and then the Lau-ban of a Chinese restaurant in America.

Qing mixed red-bean paste with sugar and sesame seed in a bowl until they were perfectly smooth and just right in moisture. She then pinched a small piece from it, rolled it into a ball the size of a marble, and put the ball on a round platter covered with sweet-rice flour. When there were about a dozen balls on the platter, she took it in her hands and began to shake it horizontally in a circular motion.

A thin layer of flour coated each ball. Qing removed the balls to an empty plate, picked up a sprayer, and stepped a few feet from the plate. A fine mist sprayed out, barely reached the plate, and moistened the balls to the right degree.

Qing put the balls back on the platter and started to shake it again. After she had repeated the process several times, a dozen Yuan-shaws were made. They would be either deep-fried or boiled in water—and the customers would never know how the stuffing got into such a paper-thin dough.

Just when Qing had enough Yuan-shaws made for the day, she heard her employees saying, "Good morning, Sung Lau-ban."

Qing turned and saw Sung Hwa. He looked extremely handsome today in a blue shirt, gray pants, and a white sweater. Qing's heart beat fast at the sight of him. This happened each time she saw him, and she couldn't explain why.

News traveled fast in Chinatown. It didn't take long for the bachelors to know that a beautiful young widow had arrived from China to live in the house of her wealthy sponsors. Qing's becoming a Lau-ban and her success with the Ivory Pagoda enhanced her desirability in the eyes of many men, and they approached her either by formal introduction or by self-advance—but none of these meetings was as dramatic as the first one between her and Sung Hwa.

Hwa was twenty-two years older than she and the other suitors much younger, but none of them could make her heart beat the way Hwa could. Now she looked into his eyes and suddenly found the reason: since the death of Kuei, no man had ever looked at her with such tenderness.

Looking at Qing like the most precious thing he had ever seen, Sung Hwa said gently, "Good morning, Qing. Would you like to go for a ride with me on this lovely autumn morning?"

In the car, Hwa reached over to take Qing's hand.

She tried to withdraw her hand. "I left in a

hurry. The rice flour from the Yuan-shaws is still caked in my fingernails.''

Hwa held her hand firmly, brought it to his lips, and kissed it with affection. ''Tell me about the Yuan-shaw festival,'' he said softly.

Qing sighed helplessly, then began to talk. ''I can still see the last two Yuan-shaw festivals in my childhood days . . .'' She went on as the car glided smoothly.

The importance of the Yuan-shaw festival was great during China's good old days. On the fifteenth day of the first month of the year, in every household, dumplings called Yuan-shaws were made. The outside was made with sweet-rice flour and was sticky, the stuffing sweet. It was said that after eating them, all gossiping lips would be sealed by the stickiness, all bitter tones replaced by honeyed sounds.

In every kitchen a large bowl of Yuan-shaws was presented to the statue of Kitchen Buddha, whose job was to go up to heaven once a year at midnight on the day of the Yuan-shaw festival to tell the Supreme Buddha all the happenings in each family. Being posted in the kitchen, the Kitchen Buddha could hear all the women talk and learn all the domestic events—among which were many not decent enough to please the ears of the Supreme Buddha. After eating the sticky Yuan-shaws, the Kitchen Buddha's lips would be sealed. Because of the sweet taste in his mouth, the few words he uttered would be sugary.

When Qing finished her story, Hwa said, ''Maybe we should all eat Yuan-shaws every day. We'll talk very little then, and every word we say will be sweet.''

Suddenly he shivered and tightened his grasp on Qing's hand.

"Is something wrong?" Qing asked anxiously.

"This is just like the old days," Hwa said, his voice trembling with emotion, "when she and I talked about the Chinese festivals, traditions, and fairy tales. She taught me Chinese calligraphy. Our classroom was in a deserted temple. We could hear an old monk tapping on his wooden fish, talking to the Great Buddha through his endless prayers . . ." His voice faded away and he swallowed hard.

Qing looked at the lines of sorrow on Hwa's face. Her heart ached for him. She leaned closer. "Are you speaking of Melin, the girl you called out to when you saw me the first time?"

Hwa nodded but didn't speak. He continued to hold her hand tightly until they reached the Japanese Garden, a place they had visited many times before.

Holding hands, they walked past the gazebo and pagoda, stopped on the arched bridge to look at the golden carp in the pond. Despite the lively fish, the deep water was tranquil enough to reflect a clear image of Hwa and Qing.

Looking at their reflection, Hwa resumed. "In 1937 I went to White Stone and met Ma Melin. We fell in love with each other and planned to elope. I waited for her beside the Pearl River, but she never came. We were both tricked by fate. The war parted us for eight long years. I rushed back to White Stone as soon as I could, but I was too late. I was just in time for her funeral."

A bird flew overhead, carrying a flower petal in its beak. The petal dropped into the pond, and the water rippled, the reflection shattered. Hwa turned to face Qing, released her hand, and took her in his arms. "Melin drowned herself in the lotus pond inside her walled garden. The best part of me died with her. I dragged through each day, used other women to numb my pain, waited for death to reunite me with my Melin. Until I saw you, Qing. You look so much like her."

Qing stared at Hwa. "Ma Melin . . . drowned in a lotus pond . . . looked very much like me . . ." She frowned deeply as she tried to remember. "It's been a long time since I was a child. And I've been through too many things in the past years. But back in my memory there was an aunt . . . I think her name was Melin."

Qing's eyes brightened when she finally remembered. "Yes! Melin was my father's sister! She died when I was only four or five. I don't remember her, but I do remember people talking about her." Qing flinched when memory took her back to 1949, when she had stood in the lotus pond and worried about being caught by the attacking villagers.

Qing shook her head. She didn't want to think of the terrible bygone days. She looked at Sung Hwa and asked accusingly, "What took you so long to tell me about my Aunt Melin? Why didn't you ask me that night when you saw me for the first time?"

Sung Hwa was just as astonished as Qing by the discovery. Holding her even tighter now, he said, "That night I felt like a fool after I shouted Melin's name. Everyone was staring at me. So I quickly made an excuse and detoured people's attention to something else. After that I was busy following you around and helping you to start the restaurant. When a man is courting a girl, he doesn't usually ask her if she is related to his first love."

Qing shook her head sadly, tried to push Hwa away. "You have been courting a memory and a ghost, not me."

Hwa pulled her against his heart, embraced her as if he were holding on to life. "You're wrong. You look like Melin, but are completely different from her. I've been watching you closely. If I had been looking for Melin in you, I would be long gone."

"Really?" Qing moved her head away from Hwa's heart, looked at him challengingly. "What did Aunt Melin have that I don't?"

"Weakness," Hwa said, then quickly explained. "Melin was a fragile butterfly. She couldn't make it through a storm. Her wings were torn, but she wouldn't have had to die if she were stronger. If you had gone through what she did, you would have lived, I'm sure."

Qing lowered her head. "I shouldn't be jealous of my own aunt. Especially when she died in such a tragic way. But I can't help it."

Sung Hwa lifted up her chin with his fingers and forced her to meet his eyes. "Say it again!"

"Say what again?"

"That you're jealous of your aunt."

Qing blushed. "Well . . ." She searched Hwa's eyes and was touched by what she saw. She said softly but quickly, "Yes. I'm jealous of Aunt Melin because you love her and I love you."

All the birds in the Japanese garden were frightened by the loud cheer that came from Sung Hwa.

They flew into the sky and left a series of chirping notes of complaint.

"You love me!" Sung Hwa continued to yell. "I fell in love with you the moment I saw you, and I've been worried to death that you may not love me! With all the younger men after you, still you love me! Tell me again, Qing, please."

Qing said while laughing at Hwa's childlike behavior, "I love you."

Hwa's face suddenly darkened. "Why do you love me? Are you pitying an old man?"

Qing pounded him on the chest with a soft fist. "What a fool you are! Don't you ever look at yourself? Can you find any man, young or old, as handsome as you? And, yes, we must not overlook your money. Very few men in San Francisco are as rich as you." Qing saw Hwa's expression and laughed. "Don't worry, Mr. Sung Hwa. I love you neither for your looks nor for your wealth. Even if you were penniless and ugly, I'd love you just the same."

Qing studied Hwa's face carefully. "You don't believe me, but I'm telling you the truth." She paused then continued in a voice that was sad and sincere. "I've gone through a lot in life. I may be strong, but I am tired. I can still work hard in my restaurant, but hard work is nothing like the emotional struggle. Emotionally I need someone to take care of me, pamper me, baby me, and spoil me in every way. And that's exactly what you've been doing. Do you understand me? I love you not only because of your numerous good points—your handsomeness, wealth, intelligence, sensitivity, and honest sentiments . . . and on and on—but also because I love the way you love me. Have I made it clear enough for you, Mr. Sung Hwa?"

Sung Hwa laughed so loud that the birds had to take another brief flight.

One winter day Sung Hwa and Qing were in the deserted Japanese Garden again.

"I have something for you, Qing," Hwa said, reaching into his pocket.

The black onyx earrings were circled with diamonds and matched by a necklace and a bracelet. Their glistening beauty took Qing's breath away.

"Hwa!" she gasped. "They are beautiful!"

"Not quite as beautiful as you are," Hwa said, took the earrings out of the box, and put them on Qing.

He then turned Qing around to fasten the necklace around her delicate neck. He turned her to face him once again and took her hand. He slipped the bracelet over her small hand, watched the diamonds glistening around her tiny wrist, then glanced at her naked fingers.

"Someday I'll buy you a set of wedding bands, and may that day come soon." He took her in his arms and began to kiss her.

The carp continued to swim as the two reflections in the pond combined into one. Over the bridge a pair of songbirds sang cheerfully.

A cool breeze swept over the garden, sent a few leaves flying, but was unable to blow away the rising passion of a healthy man and young woman. With their arms around each other, Hwa and Qing left the bridge, walked out of the garden.

Hwa drove with one hand, used his other to hold Qing in a tender embrace. Qing laid her head on his shoulder and closed her eyes.

Hwa was a married man, and he would never be able to buy her the wedding band. But she preferred to block out that fact. They enjoyed traveling life's path side by side. It would be too cruel to remember that at the end of the path was a sign that said the Dead End.

However, as she moved her hand to her earlobes and touched the earrings, in her fancy each earring had suddenly acquired the talking ability of a woman. "You're taking my husband away from me! And I've treated you so nicely!"

Qing sighed deeply. She shook her head, trying to shake away her illusion. She knew the wail of the earrings could never put an end to her loving Hwa. She might as well turn a deaf ear to Lu-an's cry and walk toward the unavoidable future, even though every step would be a step of guilt.

They stopped at Hwa's apartment. He looked at her questioningly. She nodded. No words were needed. They knew where they were heading.

Hwa took Qing's arm as he guided her through the white living room. "I want to be honest with you. Please don't think badly of me. I rented this place right after my wedding day. A son's obligation was carried out in the house where Lu-an lives. But a lonely man's fun-searching continued in this apartment."

Hwa held Qing in his arms when they were in the bedroom, where everything was either black or red or adorned with leopard skin. "I have brought many women here. They gave me fun, but not life. With you here I shall begin to live again."

They stood beside the king-size bed. He pressed her against his heart. They listened to the sound of traffic many stories down on the street. The noise was much softer than the clamor of their heartbeats. After a long while Hwa held Qing away to look at her, then cupped her face in his hands.

"I love you and I want to marry you someday, although it cannot be done right away," he said as he kissed her.

"You are mine, with or without marriage," he mumbled when he began to undress her.

Qing let herself be undressed like a child. It felt great to be doted on. "I love you, Hwa," she said as she removed the jewelry he had given her. "And I want to be your woman even if I can never become your wife."

Hwa finished undressing Qing, removed the combs from her hair. Qing's long hair spilled to her naked shoulders like black water from a broken dam, splashing over her bare back. Hwa stood looking at Qing, was mesmerized by her beauty. She smiled, moved to the bed.

The bed was covered with a black quilt and piled with leopardskin pillows. Qing stretched on it, felt the cool silk under her nude body. She toyed with the pillows as she watched Hwa undress. When his naked body covered hers, she felt like the earth lying in the warmth of a spring sun. His fingers were the fingers of an experienced farmer, kneading and compressing, agitating and inspiring. Qing was the rich soil, fully awake and ready to absorb Hwa's planting.

The spring shower fell gently for a while, then turned into a blustering thunderstorm. Lightning inflamed the world. An earthquake reverberated the whole universe. Millions of multicolored magic flowers bloomed for Qing and Hwa, dazzling them with beauty. Qing and Hwa shared the delight of stepping into their garden of paradise hand in hand.

28

ONE MORNING IN the beginning of spring 1964, Delia Porter and Ma Te sat on the campus on a stone bench beneath an old tree.

"I've been to the doctor," Delia said without looking at Te. "I'm pregnant."

"What?" Te put his hands on her shoulders and turned her to face him, knocked their books to the ground, and left them there.

Delia repeated her statement.

Te stared at her one moment longer and said, "Let's get married."

Delia tilted her head to one side, looked at him doubtfully. "Do you really want a baby? Are you ready to be a father and a husband?" She added, "Give me an honest answer!"

Te thought for a while. "Honestly, I don't want a baby more than I want a cold. And I'm about as ready to become a father as I am a tight-rope walker. But since it's our baby, I'll be very happy to walk the rope with a cold. How about you?"

Delia shook her head. "Well, I'm not ready to become a wife." A bright smile spread over her face and a gleam appeared in her eyes. She looked softer and more beautiful than Te had ever seen. "But I'm ready to become a mother."

Te was puzzled. "Isn't marriage a prerequisite to motherhood?"

Delia laughed. "According to the general public's opinion, yes. But according to my belief, no." She then added, "We'll be married someday, but not forced into it by our baby."

Te thought, agreed, but still had one more question. "What will your parents say?"

Delia shook her head again. "They have no more control over my life than does the baby." She looked at Te. "How about your parents? Are you going to tell them that your black girlfriend is about to give the Ma family an heir?"

Te laughed hard. "For quite some time now I have told my parents only the weather in San Francisco. I'm no longer a good Chinese son. Their attitude toward my sister turned me off, I suppose. No, I'll not tell them about you and our baby. I know what they'll say, and I don't want to hear those insulting words."

They picked up their books, walked around the campus, and made plans. They had received their bachelor's degrees in less than four years. Being hardworking students, it was easy for them to accumulate the required thirty graduate hours in two semesters. By the end of summer they would receive their master's degrees in sociology. They had already been accepted for postgraduate studies in the same university. They both had part-time jobs, and so far they were managing to pay their bills. But now they must give up summer school and find full-time jobs somewhere, to save money for the hospital expenses and future costs of their baby.

Delia said, "We'll resume our studies in the fall semester, and graduate in December." She stopped, smiled at Te. "Our baby should be born around Christmas. What a graduation present we'll give each other."

They went to Qing and Sumiko with their good news. Both offered financial support, but Te and Delia turned down their offers.

Delia said, "I've always paid my own way throughout my entire life."

Te said, "I can still hear Yen calling me my father's crybaby. I feel him watching over me from the Temple of the Moon, and I must prove to him that I am a man."

Te and Delia received their master's degrees in the middle of December, and a week later the baby boy was born. He had Te's features and Delia's color. He was named Todd Porter Ma.

In two weeks' time Delia was doing everything she had done before giving birth. In the middle of January 1965, on a Saturday, Te baby-sat and Delia went to a meeting. She came home excited. "We're taking a trip to the South," she said. "There are two important demonstrations we must attend. The first one is next Monday in Memphis, the second takes place three days later in Mobile, Alabama. We'll leave tomorrow."

School wouldn't start until January 23. The timing was perfect. They could participate in both demonstrations and then come back for their first classes.

"And we'll take Todd with us," Delia said.

"We'll go to Green Hills first, leaving him with my parents. We won't pick him up until returning from Alabama. This trip will be like a honeymoon for us!"

The word "honeymoon" made Te think. He wouldn't tell Delia anything yet, but when they reached Green Hills he would definitely have a long talk with Delia's parents. With their help, he should be able to convince Delia that Todd's parents really ought to be married soon.

That night, when they were packing, a telegram came.

"My parents are arriving Sunday afternoon!" Te exclaimed, looking at the sheet of paper. "And they plan to stay until Friday morning!"

They dropped the things they were packing and had a long discussion. Te knew the reason for his parents' sudden visit. His letters had been too vague to ensure them that their precious son was safe and sound. They had to come and see for themselves. And they must be curious about Qing too. In one of Te's letters he had exaggerated the wealth and power of Qing's very special friend Sung Hwa, purposefully skipping the fact that Hwa had a wife.

"I guess I can still leave town, and let Qing and Hwa meet them in the airport," Te said hesitantly.

Delia shook her head. "I know you better than you do yourself. You are a liberated Chinese son, but still a Chinese son after all. All of us must die sooner or later. At the death of your parents, you'll be haunted by guilt—you'll always regret that when they traveled thousands of miles to see you, you skipped town."

"Why are you always so damn right?" Te raised his voice, shouting angrily. Delia laughed. Todd cried.

They decided that Delia would go to the demonstrations alone, taking Todd on the trip. Her parents would meet her in Memphis, then take Todd with them to Green Hills. Te would try his best to persuade his parents to leave early, or let Qing keep them company toward the end of their visit. "I'll join you in Green Hills," he said. "I'll miss the demonstration in Memphis, but hope to arrive in Mobile in time."

Te and Delia found a sitter for Todd, then went to Ivory Pagoda to tell Qing the news.

Qing's face whitened. "I'll see my parents for the first time in fifteen years!" she said.

For the next few moments, excitement, sorrow, happiness, love, and hate all appeared on Qing's beautiful face. Just as multiple colors on a palette produce gray, so the combination of all the emotions gave Qing a gray look. She said slowly, "Well, I guess I'll know how I feel when I face them. My feelings toward them will be a reflection of their feelings toward me, I suppose."

Qing sat with Te and Delia, told the waiter to bring out a tray. Delia took one look at the food and opened her eyes wide. "I don't have the heart to eat them," she said, pointing at the tiniest cookies she had ever seen.

Every cookie was handmade, shaped like a flower, an animal, or a human being, then painted with food color.

"But you must," Qing said, searched through the tray, and found two horses, each the size of a grape. She gave the cookies to Te and Delia and said, "Eat these and you'll both gallop toward a bright future."

"The horse melted in my mouth!" Te exclaimed. "I'm glad I'm not riding on it!"

Qing ignored his comment, found two cookies that looked like men in armor carrying swords. "The warriors will help you fight all the battles in life."

Delia put the entire cookie into her mouth. "Thanks, Qing," she said while chewing. "Mm . . . my little soldier is delicious."

Qing then held up a cookie that looked like a water buffalo. "Eat this, and one of you should gain the patience of this persistent animal. That's what Hwa and I need right now—patience. We love each other so much, but we can't get married. We must wait. Someday, somehow, we'll come up with the courage to tell Lu-an. Maybe she'll give Hwa a divorce . . ." She took a small bite of the cookie, chewed, looked at Te and Delia. "I moved out of the Cohen house and into Hwa's apartment about a week ago."

Delia grabbed Qing's hands and said quickly, "Congratulations! I'm so happy for the two of you!"

Te also congratulated Qing, then laughed. "Our poor parents! Just wait until they hear about your good news. I also plan on telling them about Delia and me and their grandson. Do you think they can take so much excitement at one time?"

The Ma couple's visit was a disaster.

They had never given their daughter much but were quite ready to claim their positions as in-laws to a rich and powerful American citizen—

Sung Hwa. They were impressed by Sung Hwa's wealth, but ashamed of the fact that Qing was Hwa's mistress. The aged Mr. Ma had no objection about men having mistresses, provided that none of the mistresses was his own daughter. In the past years he and his wife had cared little about Qing, but now they both developed a sudden concern about her reputation. "Words may travel across the Pacific to Taiwan," Mr. Ma said. "I'll lose much face if people find out my daughter was once a communist and now a whore!"

Sung Hwa wanted to hit the old man. Qing pulled Hwa away. Te had to entertain his parents all alone for the rest of their stay. He couldn't persuade them to leave early. He never told them about Delia and Todd. He was not afraid of trouble. He just felt them unworthy of sharing his happiness, since they had treated Qing so heartlessly.

The Mas left California on Friday morning. The earliest plane for Memphis wouldn't leave until that night. As soon as his parents were out of sight, Te raced from the airport back to Chinatown.

He circled the crowded streets until he found a parking space. He walked from one store to another, searching for a piece of jewelry for Delia. He wanted something that was one of a kind. "First I'll talk to her parents in Green Hills, then I'll go to Mobile to propose marriage," he said as he continued searching.

He stopped in front of an antique store at the edge of Chinatown. A brooch, sparkling red, caught his eye. Red was Delia's favorite color. He felt the cash in his jeans pocket. He had taken all he had in the bank.

An old woman in a blue silk pajama suit stood at the shop door glaring at Te. "We're not buying!" she said in Cantonese, and tried to wave Te away. "Plenty of things already!"

Te had worn his usual faded jeans, old tennis shoes, and torn T-shirt to make a statement to his parents. He met the jeweled woman's narrowed eyes. The animosity in them stabbed him. "Why do you yell at me and look at me like that?" He stepped toward the short woman. "Only because I look poor? Are poor people necessarily bad? If I were indeed poor, since it's obvious we are both Chinese, don't you think you owe a little sympathy to a poor Chinese boy?"

To his disbelief, the fat woman opened her yellow-toothed mouth and spat on the pavement. "I don't have time for crazy talk! Just get away from my window if you don't have money to buy!"

Te was so angry that he reached into his pocket and took out a handful of cash. He waved it at the ugly woman and shouted at her face, "I'm here to *spend* money, you old fool!"

Regardless of his rudeness, the oily haired woman smiled. Her eyes were no longer narrowed to resemble two grains of rice. They were widened and focused on Te's money. "Why didn't you say so? Come in! Please!" She stepped aside, bowing slightly.

Once inside the shop, the woman explained to an old man behind the counter, "I thought he was another study person trying to pawn things. But he wants to buy, for a change." The uneducated Chinatown people called the exchange students study people; it was a name born out of jealousy and resentment.

The man was thin as a stick. He looked at the stack of cash in Te's hand and smiled to show a big gold tooth. "Which item in my humble shop is of interest to you?"

"The red brooch," Te said quickly. He wanted to buy that unusual piece of jewelry for Delia and leave the shop as soon as possible.

The old man brought the brooch out of the window and placed it on the counter. "The ruby is from India, the setting done in China." One claw-like finger pointed at the brooch. "See how yellow the gold is? It's rare to see a precious stone set in twenty-four-karat gold these days. Today's jewelers are all using sixteen-karat gold or less. This is a priceless antique piece—"

Te interrupted the man, asked for the price, counted out the money, grabbed the brooch, and left in a hurry.

Te arrived in Memphis late at night. He checked into an inexpensive hotel. Early Saturday morning he rented a car and left for Green Hills. He arrived before noon, dashed past the town square, ignored the staring eyes. He sped along the bumpy road, found the Porters' house, then brought the car to a sliding stop.

A dark face appeared at the lower part of the window, then quickly disappeared. The door opened. Roy Jackson sat in his wheelchair, holding Todd. One look at his face and Te knew something horrible had happened.

Without greeting Te, Roy said quickly, "You

better go to Mobile right away. A friend of Delia's called from Mobile General Hospital yesterday morning. Delia is hurt. Her parents tried to call you but couldn't get an answer. Then they left and asked me to take care of Todd. I've been calling you every few minutes, but you were not home."

Te said, "I was showing my parents around San Francisco, and then shopping for . . . Never mind. How is Delia?"

Roy shook his head. "You better go to her right now."

Roy's voice sent a chill down Te's spine. He nearly dropped the bag he was holding.

"Go!" Roy commanded. "If I could walk, I'd be there with her already!"

Te took one more look at the baby in Roy's arms and left the Porter house.

"I'll take care of your son!" Roy shouted after Te. "I'll guard him with my life!"

Te sped back to the Memphis airport, hoping that he could immediately board a flight to Mobile. He left the rented car in the parking lot, quickened his steps toward the terminals. He felt something cold falling on the back of his neck, melting and becoming drops of water. He looked up and saw snowflakes dancing slowly in the air.

"The first snow I ever see, and you are not with me!" he cursed. Delia had told him about the occasional cold winters in the South. She had tried hard to describe snow to Te, who had lived only in south China, the tropical island of Taiwan, and then California.

The snow was falling harder now. The sky

was gray, and something dark and threatening lingered in the chilling air. Te began to run toward the terminal building. He was just in time for a plane for Mobile, leaving in twenty minutes.

The taxi sped down Station Street, stopped at Mobile General Hospital.

Te paid and ran into the lobby. Around him, many hallways spread out, leading to different departments. He looked at the signs but didn't know where to go. He saw an information desk and charged toward it.

A silver-haired lady looked at him over the top of her glasses and smiled. "Can I help you? I'm a volunteer worker and my name is—"

Te didn't let her finish. "I must find Delia Porter. She was wounded in the Thursday demonstration. The police brought her here. Please tell me where she is."

The lady shook her head, sighed, and then said with a heavy drawl, "Demonstration . . . those ignorant fools! They ought to stay home and mind their own business. They wouldn't get hurt then, and we wouldn't have so much trouble."

"Please!" Te said.

She looked at him curiously. "You are Chinese, aren't you? What did you say your friend's name was? If she is one of your own people, then it's very strange, because you Chinese are not troublemakers like the blacks—"

"Please tell me where Delia is!" Te pounded his fists on the desk.

The lady gasped, and her politeness vanished, her face turned red. "Mind your manners, you rude Chinaman!'' She pointed a finger at a hallway. ''Take one of those elevators to the third floor. All the demonstrators wounded on Thursday were brought up there that night.''

As soon as Te stepped out of the elevator, he saw Negroes everywhere. Some of them wore bandages and slings, and all wore the same expression: hurt and anger.

Te stepped into a nearby room. There were eight beds, each surrounded by many visitors. The loud talking was disturbing and the sound of crying distressing. Delia must be in some other room, he decided, since the first two beds were occupied by men. But the next two patients were women. Te frowned. The hospital authorities hadn't even bothered to separate male patients from female ones. They were all blacks, so they were thrown together like animals.

Another man, another woman. And then he saw Delia's parents.

The Porters had aged unbelievably. Their faces were colorless and stained with tears. Mr. Porter got up when he saw Te, pointed at an empty chair. Te sat without taking time to greet the old couple. He fixed his eyes on Delia.

She was covered to the chin by a white sheet, and she looked no bigger than a child.

''My Delia!'' Te bent toward her, looked her over carefully. What he saw made his heart sink. Delia was hurt badly, he realized.

He couldn't find any wound, but he knew it would be a long time before he could take her home. There was no tube in her nose, no needles in her arms, but her face was gray, her lips pale, her eyes closed.

As if sensing his presence, Delia opened her eyes.

"Delia, my love," Te called softly, then waited for her to focus her eyes on him.

At the sound of Te's voice, a dim luster brightened Delia's eyes. Her nostrils flared and her lips trembled. She gathered her remaining strength and strove to talk. The whispering sound from her mouth was only a single syllable.

"Te . . ."

She seemed to have so much to tell him, but her energy failed her. Her voice faded, and after a brief moment she closed her eyes again.

"Delia!" Te bent closer. He had never seen her so weak before.

He must give her all his own strength. Very carefully he reached under the sheet with his hand. There was a thin layer of plastic under the sheet, rustling at his fumbling. He touched Delia's upper body under the plastic cover. She was wrapped in layers of bandages that were wet and sticky. He knew it was blood but didn't want to look. He found Delia's hand. It was ice cold and damp. He squeezed it gently.

"I want to give you my energy and my life," Te said. "Let them flow out of me, go through our clasping hands, and enter your bloodstream."

Delia's father tapped Te on the shoulder. Delia's mother sobbed on the other side of the bed. Te ignored them both, continued to hold Delia's hand in his, concentrated on willing his vitality into her.

A nurse appeared, checking each patient. She glanced at Delia over Te's shoulder, then shook her head and walked away, mumbling under her breath, "It's a miracle that one is still alive!"

"Delia!" Te cried in a hoarse voice, and shook his head vigorously. "That stupid woman has not seen any miracle yet, but we will show her when we leave this hospital hand in hand."

Delia opened her eyes again. The glassy emptiness in them stabbed Te and made his sunken heart continue to descend. He kept blinking away tears while staring at her and calling her name again and again, "Delia, my love . . . Delia . . . my Delia . . . please get well. I've brought you an engagement present. . . . We'll get married and have other children than Todd . . ."

At the mention of Todd's name, Delia's body jerked. She opened her eyes wider and struggled with all her willpower to center her eyesight once again. Finally a faint glow appeared on her face, and she looked at Te with concentration.

That touch of a gleam and the focused look gave Te great hope. He used his free hand to reach into his pocket for the ruby brooch. He brought it up to Delia's eye level and began to talk quickly. "Delia. Look. Red, your favorite color—and the color of good luck. You and Todd and I will live happily ever after . . ." He stopped when he saw Delia trying to talk.

She labored to twist the corners of her mouth, then fought to part her lips. She used all the life left in her to pour from her heart a series of sluggish sounds barely perceptible as words.

"Te, please take care of our son . . ."

An invisible force wrenched her body and jerked it with intense power. She convulsed, then became silent in the middle of her last word.

While still gazing at Te, her eyes turned dull and her pupils began to dilate. In Te's loving grip, the last trace of warmth began to disappear from her fingers.

29

Sung Lu-an walked around the mansion and listened to the echo of her footsteps.

Her loneliness was unbearable. She decided to go out for a while.

Lu-an couldn't drive. She called a taxi. ''Take me to Chinatown,'' she said to the cabdriver.

Lu-an had not been to her childhood home for a long time. The dingy laundry looked darker than she remembered. Her entire family was busy washing and ironing in a room filled with smelly hot steam. Their faces were shining with sweat and their wet hair fell over their foreheads.

Standing on the customer's side of the counter, Lu-an realized how fortunate she had been—her husband had saved her from all this and placed her in luxury.

Her older brother's wife came to her. The woman glanced over Lu-an, took in the expensive clothes, neatly combed hair, and costly jewelry. Envy, hatred, and anger appeared on the woman's face instantaneously.

''How are you, my elder sister?'' Lu-an greeted the woman with a respectful bow and a big smile.

The woman narrowed her eyes, thought

quickly, and found a way to wipe that happy smile off Lu-an's face.

She said proudly in a cheerful tone, "Thanks to the Great Buddha, I am enjoying a perfect life. My man is right in the next room working—that's where he is all the time. And we're expecting our fourth child." She then curved her mouth downward and continued in a pitying manner, "It's too bad that the Great Buddha is not very kind to you."

"Wh-what do you mean?" The smile froze on Lu-an's face. In her mind's eyes she could see herself shrinking both in size and in status, quickly changing from a rich grown woman to a young girl living in the shadow of her bossy sister-in-law. "Hwa is good to me . . . he doesn't care that we don't have any children . . ." she mumbled uncertainly.

"You poor thing!" The sister-in-law shook her head and sighed, trying her best to conceal the pleasure of deflating Lu-an's pride. "The whole of Chinatown knows it, but you don't!"

"What do they know? Please tell me," Lu-an pleaded humbly.

Lu-an's humiliation satisfied her sister-in-law. The woman sighed once again. "Well, it hurts me so much to be the bad-news carrier. I really wish I could bite my tongue. But then, what are families for?" She paused for suspense, then continued slowly, "Your husband has a mistress. They have a love nest in his fancy apartment. All the employees in Jade Garden know where it is."

Lu-an tried to sound indifferent. "My husband is rich and handsome. Women are attracted to either his money or his looks. Mistresses come and go. Only the number-one wife stays on with her honorable title."

The sister-in-law said, "This woman is much more than a mere mistress. She has moved into your husband's apartment. He doesn't have any other mistresses anymore. It's obvious that he is truly serious about this one. He takes her everywhere, while you stay in that big empty house like a widow." She watched Lu-an's face turn white and couldn't help smiling at her success.

Lu-an saw that smile. She wanted to save face, so she forced herself to square her shoulders and hold up her head. "I'm sure this woman is nothing but a tramp."

The sister-in-law's smile widened. "You are a fool!" she then began to laugh. "But you've always been an idiot. I still remember when you worked in our laundry, you could never do anything right."

It seemed to require all her effort to stop chuckling. She then said, "Your opponent is a beautiful young woman with the air of a true lady and the mind of a shrewd businessman. Do you know that she is the Lau-ban of a new restaurant? And her restaurant is as successful as your husband's. People are saying that Jade Garden and Ivory Pagoda are a perfect pair, just like their owners. . . ." She went on to tell Lu-an what the people in Chinatown knew.

"Qing?" Lu-an lost her composure. She stood shaking, holding on to the counter to keep herself from falling. "She is Sumi's friend . . . I treated both of them like my daughters . . . Hwa met Qing in our home . . . not all that long ago. He acted very strangely that night . . ." Lu-an began to cry.

The sister-in-law was not totally satisfied. She turned back to her ironing and stabbed Lu-an one more time. "You better think of a way to keep your title as Mrs. Sung!"

Qing hummed a happy tune as she dusted the furniture in every room. Hwa's apartment looked completely different now. A playboy's hunting ground had been changed into a contented man's comfortable nest. The once-white living room was now beige and brown. The leopardskin pillows and rugs were gone from the bedroom. The bar's liquor supply had been reduced, but the cooking utensils and supplies had greatly increased in the kitchen.

Qing straightened Hwa's desk in the study, smiled at the picture of the two of them in a silver frame.

The doorbell rang. She ran to open the door, then dropped the dustcloth at the sight of Lu-an.

"May I come in?" Lu-an asked with a pleading smile.

"Of course, Mrs. Sung." Qing stepped aside, and was hit by many emotions all at once.

Leading Lu-an to the living room, Qing concluded that since Lu-an had found this place, she must know everything. But why was she here? Had she come for a fight?

After seating Lu-an in the living room, Qing went to the kitchen and made tea. She wished Hwa were here to shield her from this embarrassing situation. But she was also glad that Hwa was in a business meeting. He was so protective of her, he just might rudely throw Lu-an out of the apartment.

Qing served tea with a fast-beating heart. "Mrs. Sung . . ." She held her teacup in both hands and raised it to her eyebrows. It was a humble gesture of great respect.

She took one look at Lu-an's sad face and her heart was filled with guilt. "Please forgive me for what I've done. I didn't mean to steal your husband. It just happened . . ." She had to stop when hot tea spilled from the agitated cup and poured over her shaking hands.

"Don't be ridiculous," Lu-an said, forcing herself to smile.

Lu-an held her cup with both hands also. Which meant she didn't intend to humiliate Qing in any way. She then raised the cup to just below her eyebrows. It was a proper gesture, because after all she was the number-one wife. She lowered her cup and took a sip of the tea. Which was a good sign—she would not have done that had she not wanted to accept Qing's apology.

Lu-an then said slowly, "Why should you need my forgiveness, since you've helped me to take care of our man?"

As Qing stared at her dumbfounded, Lu-an opened her large purse: She had gone to an antique store in Chinatown and bought a back scratcher with a jade handle. She gave it to Qing with a smile.

Qing held the back scratcher and felt totally lost. "What do you want me to do with this?"

"Keep it, of course!" Lu-an stared at Qing. Why had her sister-in-law said Hwa's mistress was clever? She shook her head. "Aren't you familiar with the meaning of this Joo-yee?" she asked, calling the back scratcher by its Chinese name.

Qing nodded. "I've heard my grandmother talking about it."

Lu-an put her hands on Qing's hands, which were holding the back scratcher. "I give you this Joo-yee, my sister, because I want that beautiful tradition to continue its existence among us three—you and I and our man."

Qing's jaw dropped.

"Joo-yee" meant "Your Heart's Wish." It was a fancy name for "back scratcher." A man's number-one wife was like his hands. His many concubines were his back scratchers. There were certain spots on a man's back that were not reachable by his hands. With the help of a Joo-yee, his itchy areas could be scratched, and he could sigh with pleasure and relief.

Qing lowered her eyes. She didn't know whether to laugh or cry. She couldn't look at Lu-an. She kept her eyes on the jade handle and the red silk tassels hanging from it. She said, "Mrs. Sung, even my grandmother wouldn't give a Joo-yee to any of my grandfather's women. I think such tradition died with the Ching dynasty."

Lu-an laughed. "Tradition is like a millipede. Have you ever watched a millipede die? Its many feet never die at the same time. The custom of Joo-yee may have expired in some of the families—like a departing millipede's first few lifeless feet—but in other families those feet have kept kicking stubbornly and living on."

Qing still couldn't raise her eyes. She looked at Lu-an's hands. It was hard to believe that the owner of these living hands had a mind that belonged to the long-dead.

Lu-an grabbed Qing's hands and shook them eagerly. "We do want our man to feel satisfied, don't we? I, the number-one wife, have given you my consent together with this Joo-yee. What is your answer? Do you agree to be Hwa's concubine and scratch all the itchy spots that are beyond my reach?"

Qing looked up slowly, observed the tightness of Lu-an's jawline and the anxiety in her eyes. She saw the face of a frightened woman behind the mask of a generous wife. Her heart ached for Lu-an.

She freed her hands from Lu-an's grasp and in turn held Lu-an's hands in a reassuring grip. She swallowed, then said with a forced smile, "Mrs. Sung, I thank you for this Joo-yee. You will always be the only Mrs. Sung Hwa, I promise."

Lu-an's hands stopped trembling. She breathed with relief and didn't press for what Qing really meant. As long as her title was secure, she was gratefully satisfied.

After Lu-an left, it began to rain. The soft shower soon turned into a thunderstorm. With all the windows closed, Qing felt smothered in the apartment. She grabbed an umbrella and ran out of the building. A taxi stopped for her, but when the driver asked her where she wanted to go, she didn't know what to say.

"The Japanese Garden," she finally told him.

The driver looked at Qing in the rearview mirror, then shrugged. Driving a taxicab in a big city, he had seen too many strange things to be surprised by a woman going to a park in the pouring rain.

Qing was almost alone in the park. She wandered through puddles to reach the bridge. Her umbrella was soon turned inside out by the gale. She cast the broken umbrella aside, walked to the middle of the bridge.

She stood watching the rain splashing down on the pond. The golden carp were hiding somewhere, but she herself had no place to hide.

"I've been hiding from the truth," she said, shivering not from the beating rain or the abusing wind, but from the unavoidable reality. "I'm a thief who has stolen the husband of a kind woman who has just offered to let me stay as her husband's concubine."

Qing looked up at the grim sky that showed no hope of sunshine. "I should give Hwa back to his wife! I should leave him! But I love him so much! What can I do?"

Sung Hwa parked his car in front of the house, then raced to the door in the gushing rain.

He felt strange as he looked for his key. He had always felt this place was Lu-an's home instead of his, and now that feeling had become extreme. When today's talk with Lu-an reached its expected result, he would leave his key; if he should ever come again, it would be as a guest.

Hwa was surprised to see Lu-an standing in the entrance hall, soaking wet. He had not called for an appointment because she was always home.

"How nice of you to come home in this weather." Lu-an looked at Hwa in disbelief, then smiled and nodded her understanding. "Ah, so she has told you already."

"I have to talk with you. Never mind the weather . . ." Hwa stopped.

He never paid attention to Lu-an's words. He had come home to ask for a divorce. He had lied to Qing about the meeting; he wanted to bring Lu-an's positive answer back to Qing as a pleasant surprise.

"What did you say?" he asked after catching a word or two.

Lu-an came to Hwa, helped him take off his wet jacket. "You better have a cup of hot tea right away. You may catch a cold. Please sit and let me take off your shoes. Maybe I should draw you a tub of hot water—"

"What did you just say?" Hwa interrupted her loudly. "Who told me *what* already?"

Lu-an shook her head and smiled. Clearly Hwa couldn't believe what a wonderful, understanding, and clever wife she was. He had rushed home to hear her tell him the good news with her own mouth. How good of him to value the statement of his number-one wife over the hearsay of a mere back scratcher.

"Well, what your concubine told you is true," she said with an air of great importance. "My sister-in-law told me about her. I went to Jade Garden and forced the address of your apartment out of the manager. I went to see Qing and gave her a Joo-yee. It is the most expensive one I could find. It has a jade handle. Anyway, she accepted the Joo-yee and agreed to be your concubine openly and all the time. She and I are sisters now. The three of us will live happily ever after. When the two of you have children, I'll be the mama and she'll be the aunt. Now you can relax and let me take off your wet shoes and socks and draw you a hot bath—"

Lu-an screamed when Hwa slapped her hard across the face. She stumbled and then lost her balance. She fell against the hall tree and knocked it over. She covered her burning cheek and watched her husband storming out of the door.

The servants came rushing at the scream and the crash. "Tai-tai, what happened?" a maid asked, looking from the mistress on the floor to the open door and the master speeding away in his car.

"I don't know," Lu-an sobbed, rubbing her stinging face. "He hit me. He never hit me in all these years. Not even when the doctor told him I could never give him a son. Why did he hit me now? I spent a lot of money to buy that Joo-yee. I've just paid a courtesy call to his concubine. He should be happy that his two women will call each other sisters from now on."

She pushed away the maid's helping hands, stayed on the floor, and continued to cry. She had never felt her efforts so unappreciated in all her married life.

Sung Hwa cursed Lu-an all the way back to his apartment. "Stupid woman! How could my poor Qing take such an insult?" he asked again and again.

He ran from one empty room to another, calling Qing's name. He saw the teapot and two cups on the low table in the living room, and the back scratcher beside them. He picked it up and threw it across the room. The jade handle shattered against the wall.

Hwa panicked when he saw the broken pieces fall to the floor. "No! Qing!" he screamed.

When a Chinese woman was so severely insulted that she felt death was better than life and decided to commit suicide, she would quote an old saying: I would rather be the broken pieces of precious jade than a whole piece of worthless brick.

Now Hwa knew why he had slapped Lu-an: he was afraid that Lu-an had insulted Qing to the degree that Qing would want to take her own life.

"Take her own life . . . just like Melin!" Hwa cried. "No! No! No!"

Hwa left the apartment in a flash and drove around at high speed without knowing where to go. The windshield wipers couldn't move fast enough to clear the water. All he saw was surging water drowning out the dark world.

"Drowning . . . the pond . . . the bridge . . . the Japanese Garden!" he shouted, and floored the accelerator.

The garden was a gloomy gray cell, the overhanging sky its low roof. The falling rain looked like thousands of steel beams slanted by the wind into interwoven bars to imprison whoever entered.

Sung Hwa saw from a distance a small figure in a green dress caught in the gray cage. She stood helplessly on the highest point of the curving bridge. Why was she leaning over the railings? Why was she bending so close to the water?

"No! Qing!" he shrieked, and jumped out of

his car without waiting for it to come to a full stop.

"Qing! Don't do it! You are my whole life!" he shouted as he ran toward her in the coursing rain.

Qing neither answered his call nor looked at him. She was mesmerized by her own rippling image in the pond. When Hwa took her in his arms, she was startled.

"Qing, I'll never make you a concubine!" he shouted. "Don't be insulted by Lu-an's crazy talk. I'm glad I caught you in time. If you had killed yourself, I'd kill her!"

Qing stared at Hwa in confusion. She then asked him slowly, "What are you talking about? Killing myself?" She shook her head firmly. "That thought never crossed my mind. I lived through hell in China. Why would I want to die now?"

"But the way you were bent over the railings," Hwa said, "and you were so close to the water . . ."

Qing shook her head once more. "I was not thinking about suicide. I was merely studying my own reflection."

Hwa kept his tight grasp on Qing as he looked into the water with her.

The rain-splashed pool showed the wavering likeness of a man and woman. The man was definitely Sung Hwa. The woman had Qing's face but different hairstyle and clothes. Qing's hair was down, while the woman's was up. Qing had on a green dress today, but the woman wore a white skirt.

The wind kept toying with the water. The pond

rippled, the picture moved. Qing didn't wave or smile, but the woman in the water did both.

Both Hwa and Qing shivered. They held each other tighter, and the woman in the pond smiled fondly as she waved good-bye. The wind continued to wail, and the raindrops gushed on.

Lu-an finally picked herself up from the floor. She sobbed her way to the bathroom, peeled off her wet clothes, and stepped into a tub of hot water. The pain on her cheek had eased, but the ache in her heart only increased its force.

"I don't understand," she murmured as she soaped herself.

"I simply don't know why he is so upset," she kept muttering when her right hand squeezed the suds from her left breast.

"I thought he would be so pleased," she murmured when she felt a hard swelling under her armpit.

"I was looking forward to being the mama of their many children." She started to cry again as she ran her fingers over the lump that was the size of a cherry.

When she finished washing herself, she stepped out of the tub and looked at her naked body in the mirror.

She glanced at the lump nonchalantly. It had no color. It couldn't be a bruise from her falling against the hall tree a while ago.

When she dried herself, she rubbed the towel against the lump heedlessly. It didn't hurt, and it didn't itch either.

Had it always been there? She couldn't remember.

30

IN THE AUTUMN OF 1965 Sumiko was in a small shopping arcade, searching for a wedding gift for Qing and Sung Hwa. She was happy for them, but sad when she thought of Lu-an.

Lu-an's breast cancer had been rooted in her a long time before she discovered it at the beginning of the year. She had died in the summer.

Soft music poured out of hidden speakers, reverberated within the dome-shaped building shared by many stores. A new song had just begun, and Sumiko recognized Paala's voice.

Grief and pain echoed in each syllable, turning every word into the grasping fingers of a lonely man reaching for his love. Those same fingers touched Sumiko's heart and refused to let go. Sumiko pressed a hand to her heart because she couldn't bear the sorrow and pain. She was drowning in a voice that was a part of her soul.

Sumiko leaned against the wall as she listened on. The melody finally ended, and a woman's voice filled the shopping center with a cheerful song. Sumiko entered a store near her, a boutique for arts and crafts. She was instantly surrounded by jewelry, statues, and ornaments of silver, brass, crystal, and fine china. She looked around. An item on a low stand caught her eye.

The pot was brass, and the soil was white gravel. There were half a dozen stalks made of silver, shaped like swords; they burst forth in all directions like fireworks. In the center of the tall stalks bloomed a flower of purple and yellow; the petals were semiprecious stones.

"Love-of-my-life!" Sumiko gasped.

"You are right." A well-dressed salesgirl appeared beside her, greeted her with a bright smile. "Many people admire it, but you're the first to know its name." The salesgirl continued, "The artist's model is a flower that grows in the volcanic earth of Hawaii, near the valley of the House of the Sun . . ." She went on to tell the beautiful story.

Living on the rich volcanic earth of the Haleakala, this plant had leaves resembling silver swords. Each leaf could grow more than six feet tall. The fierce island sun couldn't wilt the plant nor could stormy weather. When the plant was many years old, a bud would sprout from its heart. A delicate flower would bloom in yellow and purple. All the leaves would curl toward the flower to embrace it and protect it, using themselves as shields from the sun, the wind, and the hands of passersby.

For seven days the magnificent flower would brighten the mountain with its exquisite color, fill the valley with its divine fragrance. On the eighth day a shadow would fall on the petals to take their brilliant hue. At the same time, an invisible hand would come in the wind to snatch the ravishing scent. With the falling of each petal, a leaf would begin to droop. When the last petal left its stalk, the entire plant would crumble. The brown leaves would lie enfolding the dead flower, holding it persistently as they both gradually became a part of the volcanic soil.

"You don't have to continue," Sumiko interrupted the girl. "I'll take it. It'll make a perfect wedding present for my friends. They really love each other."

Carrying the plant to her car, she looked at her watch. It was almost one in the afternoon. She had to go home to leave the plant and change into her uniform, then be at the hospital at three. All the way home she glanced at the rearview mirror. Speeding had become her habit. She had already received several tickets, and she couldn't afford to lose her license.

She was surprised to see Yung Zhang's car parked in front of the house. He had started to practice general medicine half a year ago, and had been extremely busy. He seldom came home even at night, and never during the day.

Sumiko parked on the sidewalk, left the key in the ignition and her purse on the seat. She must change quickly and leave as fast as she could.

When she rushed past the expensive new sports car, she shook her head and mumbled, "If you can afford this thing, why can't you afford to pay back some of the money you borrowed from Sung Hwa and Sung Quanming?"

Zhang had used every reason he could find to persuade Sumiko to borrow from the Sungs. First for buying their house, and then his well-equipped clinic. Sumiko knew of no other young doctor or nurse who lived as well as she and Zhang.

She entered the living room through the back door, looked around, but couldn't find her husband. The bedroom door was closed. Zhang must be taking a nap. Sumiko put down her package soundlessly, then suddenly remembered that she was working until eleven tonight and should make herself a sandwich. She tiptoed to the kitchen, took out the bread and meat. When her sandwich was made, she moved quietly to the bedroom for her uniform.

She opened the door and froze.

Two people were sleeping soundly in the bed. The sheet was pulled up to their shoulders. Their heads were touching; one was Zhang's, the other a young Caucasian woman's.

Sumiko screamed. Zhang and the woman sat up. The sheet fell from their naked bodies, revealing the woman's large breasts. The woman jumped out of bed, bent toward the clothes scattered all over the carpet, and picked up what were hers. She ran toward the bathroom. Sumiko stared after her narrow waist and broad buttocks until the door shut with a bang.

Sumiko turned to Yung Zhang, who was still sitting in bed. He opened his mouth to say something, then looked at Sumiko's fuming face and changed his mind. He shrugged. "So you caught us," he said casually.

Sumiko waited for him to say more, but he didn't. He took his time getting out of bed, picked up his clothes, then put them on slowly. He finished tying his shoes, then went to the dresser to knot his tie in front of the mirror.

Just then the bathroom door opened. The young woman was fully dressed now. She saw Sumiko by the door, turned toward Zhang for help. Zhang met her frightened eyes in the mirror, waved at her without turning. "See you in the clinic," he said, and continued to straighten his silk tie.

The girl looked at Sumiko pleadingly. "I'm sorry, Mrs. Yung. I . . . I work for Dr. Yung. And I couldn't . . ." Her young voice quivered, then turned into a whimper.

Sumiko stepped aside to let the girl pass. After she heard the girl running out the front door, she said to Zhang calmly, "I want a divorce."

"A divorce?" Zhang took another look at himself in the mirror and raised his hand, touched his hair carefully with his fingertips. He then turned to look at Sumiko. "Don't be ridiculous. I'm not through with you yet."

"What do you mean?" Sumiko felt her fingernails digging into her palms. She would like to use those nails to scratch Zhang's handsome face and scoop out his shining black eyeballs.

Yung Zhang walked toward Sumiko, stopped to face her with a grin. "What I mean is you are still very useful to me. I married you for two things, and so far I have received only one—the money." He grinned broader. "I consider the loans from the Sungs your dowry. Quite a large sum, I must admit. But in China people usually give extremely large compensations to the men who marry the girls they want to get rid of . . . the ones who are no longer virgins."

He leaned closer. "Well, I'm still waiting for the second thing to happen—my citizenship. I've come to the USA on a student visa. Because I married you, an American citizen, and also because your mother is a good attorney, I've become a permanent resident in this country. But that's not enough. We must stay married for quite a while before I can become a citizen. Until then, I won't have a green card, and my right to stay in this golden land is not guaranteed. If we are divorced now, I can still be deported. And I certainly won't allow that to happen."

Shaking his head slowly, Yung Zhang continued, "You don't want a divorce either, Sumiko. You'll lose so much face if you let people know what happened . . . I mean starting on our wedding night. I know you, Mrs. Sumiko Yung. You are a proud person. Divorce is nothing to be proud of, especially for an Asian woman. So just forget what you saw a while ago, and let's keep living the way we've lived since we became husband and wife."

Sumiko gathered all her strength into one hand, then raised that hand and slapped Zhang across the face. She didn't wait for him to react. She turned and ran from the house, dashed across the lawn, and reached the sidewalk.

She got into her car, turned the key.

Her hands shook on the steering wheel. Her vision blurred.

"Calm down, you stupid fool!" she yelled at herself as she turned the corner.

"Don't you dare shed tears because of that bastard!" She blinked her eyes again and again after she entered the highway.

"Instead of shaking and crying, you should do something positive . . . that's what you'd tell a patient if she married a jerk." She kept on talking to herself. "You'll call your mother and ask her to arrange a divorce. You'll tell her everything and ask her to make sure that Yung Zhang is deported from this country. And in the meantime you'll drive to work collected and composed and enjoy this beautiful California sun."

The California sunshine was bright and cheerful. Bathed in it, Sumiko continued to tremble, cry, and feel burning humiliation. She tried to deny it by pretending that reality did not exist.

"I'm driving in the lovely sunshine of Hawaii. Yes, I'm in Hawaii, and I am only a young girl. I know no one by the name of Yung Zhang . . ." Sumiko pressed her foot on the accelerator, stepped all the way down.

She saw in the blinding rays a girl with hair flying behind her running to the waiting arms of a tall handsome man.

He lifted her up high and turned her around while the plumeria petals rained down on them from the surrounding trees.

"My Paala, so you still love me!" the girl said while laughing.

"Of course I still love you! I'll love you forever!" He lowered her to the ground and began to kiss her.

Sumiko was smiling when she ran through a red light.

She heard thunder crack and the golden sky turned black. The flower petals continued to fall on her, but somehow they were no longer soft and fragrant—they felt more like sharp glass and metal, and they tasted like her own blood.

* * *

The plumerias had changed into banyan trees. The flowers had become the banyan's long vines, the soft petals numerous strong restraining ropes. Sumiko found herself in a banyan grove so deep and dark that her body was wrapped and knotted and restricted by branches, her face covered by leaves, and she could hardly see.

Sumiko tried to free herself. She felt severe pain. The imprisoning banyans were much more powerful than she.

She heard a stranger's voice. ". . . three days now. Her family has arrived from Hawaii and has been waiting . . ."

Sumiko stopped struggling with the banyans. She gave in to their bridling arms, let them pull her down farther toward the bottom of a black sea. She stayed there powerlessly, knowing that she was sinking deeper into the dark water.

She stayed in the cold and murky terrain until she heard from far above a woman crying and calling, "Sumiko, my daughter, please put up a fight."

And then she heard a young man's voice. "My dear sister, you must fight for your life!"

And there was also the voice of a woman with an accent. "If I can fight my way out of Communist China with all things against me, of course you can fight your way out of the land of death with everyone on your side."

And after that there was a young male voice that was also accented. "Please fight, Sumiko, my dear friend. My poor Todd has already lost his mother, please don't let him lose his brave Aunt Sumiko too."

Sumiko heard other voices. They all wanted her

to fight her way out of the sea of blackness. But their voices were not enough. She needed much more than that to help resist the strong desire to sink to the bottom of that restful sea. She drifted back into unconsciousness.

While she slept, operations were performed on her, fluids injected into her to give her strength. Several days later, Sumiko woke up again.

She found herself hooked to tubes and wrapped in bandages. Most of her face was covered, and she could open her eyes only with difficulty.

In her unclear vision she saw many faces: her mother's, her brothers', Lu-an's, Sung Hwa's, Qing's, Te's, and even Sung Quanming's and his wife Laurie's.

Her eyelids weighed tons. An invisible hand was pulling her back to that unlit land. Just before she closed her eyes and surrendered to that powerful hand, she saw Yung Zhang's face behind the faces of all the others.

Fury was a strong force. It made Sumiko's weak heart beat faster. Her hands jerked and her mouth opened a little.

"Go away!" she tried to scream, but made only a muted moan.

She heard her mother's concerned voice. "What did Sumiko say?"

She heard Yung Zhang's voice of pretense. "She asked me not to go away."

Anger gave Sumiko enough energy to raise her voice. "Liar!"

This time everyone in the room heard her clearly.

The old but still-powerful voice of a man said,

"Dr. Yung, I think something strange is going on. You'd better remain silent while our Sumiko talks, or I'll have you thrown out of here."

"But, Mr. Sung—I mean, dear Uncle Quanming, Sumiko should not talk," Yung Zhang protested in a hurry. "She needs to be put back to sleep. I'll call the nurse and ask her to give Sumiko a shot. And you people have stayed too long here. The visiting hour is over—"

Sumiko heard Sung Hwa's angry voice interrupting Yung Zhang. "Your license to practice general medicine doesn't make you a king in all hospitals. You are not Sumiko's doctor. You have no right to give her nurse any orders. And if you think you can push us around, then you are very wrong."

"You misunderstood me," Yung Zhang argued in a voice of faked worry. "I have only Sumiko's best interests in mind."

Hatred was a miracle drug of incredible impact. With her eyes closed, Sumiko opened her mouth once again. "Yung Zhang never cared about me. He married me to become a U.S. citizen. He also married me for money."

Sumiko poured out all her grief and wrath. Yung Zhang tried to stop her, but her family and friends wouldn't let him. At last all the anger and sorrows and pain were discharged from inside her, and Sumiko's heart became empty.

She ached to have the emptiness filled. Only one person on earth had that magic power. Sumiko called, "Paala!"

Right after the name left her lips, Sumiko lost consciousness once again. She returned to her dreamland, slept peacefully. When she woke up, she took the first bite of food since her wreck. Her family and friends watched the nurse leaving with the nearly empty tray and breathed in relief.

"We'll find Paala for you," Mrs. Yamada said with a smile. "It won't be hard. He is so well-known. All we need to do is give his record company a call and ask them to give him your name."

The summer of 1967 arrived gloriously in Hawaii.

The shorelines of Hanauma Bay curved softly, like two loving hands cupped together holding a precious bowl of turquoise water.

A young woman walked barefoot in the midmorning sun, her face uplifted to enjoy the caressing rays.

Sumiko had on a short pink muumuu that reached only her thighs, revealing legs that were dark and well-shaped. Her long hair hung to her waist, adorned by a pink plumeria pinned casually behind her right ear. As the wind blew and her hair flew, Sumiko raised a hand to push it away from her face, then turned to look at the hill.

She saw a man run through the plumeria grove, zigzagging his way down the descending path known only to the islanders.

Sumiko walked toward the foot of the hill to meet the emerging tall figure.

Paala ran through the flowering trees, kicked off his shoes as he reached the beach. The distance between him and Sumiko disappeared quickly. With each passing second she could see him more clearly. His long muscled legs were exposed in a pair of white shorts. His tanned strong arms were revealed by his short-sleeved Aloha shirt. His black hair reached the nape of his neck and fell over part of his forehead. Sumiko could see his deep-set dark brown eyes now. And now also his straight nose, and his coral-red lips that were too beautiful for the mouth of a man.

"Paala!" She waved at him. "What took you so long? You called me at my mother's place, told me to meet you here. You said you were leaving our home right away. I shortened my visit to rush over. I've been here for almost an hour now."

"It's not my fault!" Paala explained as he ran toward his wife. "You left me and our baby to visit your mother, and I felt terribly lonely. I called the baby-sitter, and she promised to come over immediately. But then, after you had already left your mother's place, she called again. She had some urgent matter to attend to, so I had to find another sitter—I couldn't leave our baby girl home alone, could I?"

Epilogue

Autumn 1977

THE GREAT PROLETARIAN CULTURAL REVOLUTION had ended a year ago, after Mao Tze-dung's death. Tourists had poured into China ever since then.

A full moon shone over the Pearl River, revealing a wide and endless body of water. The sparkling river flowed past the capital city of Kwangchow, then through many ancient villages: Jasmine Valley, Willow Place, and White Stone.

White Stone Hotel was an old building containing very few rooms. The facilities were outmoded, the efficiency minimal. The employees were not used to seven outsiders who conversed among themselves in a foreign tongue. In the eyes of the porters, the six adults looked at least normal, but the teenage boy appeared dreadfully strange.

"What is he?" one porter asked another. "He looks like a Chinese who has painted his face black."

The other porter was about to say something, then stopped at the sight of the seven guests descending the stairway.

"We're going for a walk," said a man in his

mid-eighties, the oldest of the group. His Cantonese was perfect. He sounded like a native son of the Pearl.

"Yes, Mr. Sung." The porter had remembered the name of the leader of this group because of his generous tip. "We'll turn down the beds for you."

"Are you sure you want to do this, Baba?" asked the second-oldest man, who was in his sixties. His Cantonese was accented and not fluent. It sounded as if he had learned it many years ago, then not used it for a long time. "We've just arrived. You were already exhausted when we were in Kwangchow. Don't you think you need to rest?"

The older man shook his head. "I don't want to rest. I left White Stone sixty-five years ago. Over forty years ago I came back for a brief visit, and haven't returned until now . . ." Sorrow crept into his voice as he continued. "I only wish Laurie had lived long enough to see it with me."

Sung Quanming, Sung Hwa, and Qing led the way. Behind them walked Ma Te, Paala Nihoa, and Sumiko. Todd bounced around them, looked at everything wide-eyed, and wouldn't stop talking.

"So this is the hometown of the Ma family," the tall, lean, almost-thirteen-year-old boy said. "My name is Todd Porter Ma. Perhaps I should move back here someday and live the life of a landlord like my grandfather and great-grandfather did." He laughed, delighted at the idea.

At thirty-six, Te's temples were already streaked

with silver. He shook his head. "There is no more landlord in China, my son."

Qing was a year older than her brother. Age had not yet marked her appearance, but as she walked beside her husband and looked around carefully, she sighed like an old woman.

"I left White Stone fifteen years ago," she said in a quavering voice. "For fifteen years I saw this village in my memories . . . sometimes fond ones, most of the time bitter. But even in my worst nightmares it never looked as horrible as this." She turned toward Hwa and said, "In a way, I'm glad our son and daughter didn't come with us."

Paala, a striking man in his early forties, said, "And I'm glad Sumiko and I didn't bring our children. When we joined you for this trip, I thought I could compose a song or two, using China as a beautiful theme. But from what we've seen so far, I can't compose anything of beauty."

Sumiko, a stunning woman of thirty-nine, agreed with her husband. "What we saw in Taiwan can only be told in songs of anger, and what we've seen in Beijing, Shanghai, and Kwangchow should be described through songs of sorrow."

In Taiwan they had visited Te and Qing's parents. The aged Ma couple had rejected Te's half-black son and made it obvious to Qing that she was good enough to be their daughter now only because she had married a rich man. The seven of them had soon discovered that the tiny island was loaded with wealth, but totally lacking humanity and true freedom. After being the president continuously for almost three decades, Chiang Kai-shek had died two years ago. But his son was now in power, and the young Chiang was a duplicate of the old. Te had searched for the grave of his childhood friend, but was unable to find it.

"I have a better name for Taiwan," Todd laughed. "It is a tyrant hiding behind a smiling mask. As for mainland China, Beijing is a smashed Ming vase, Shanghai a bolt of dirty old silk, and Kwangchow a torn paper lantern. And White Stone, well . . ." He waved a hand around. "The dead trees, crumbled houses, wasted farmland, and deserted streets. Where are the people hiding? Are they all ghosts? It's like in the movies I saw, when the world reached its end." He pointed at a half-crumbled platform that protruded from the ground. "What's that?"

Qing held on to Hwa tightly and answered in a shaky voice, "That's the stage they built for the trials of the Bloodsuckers." She looked around and found an old willow. She pointed at its branches. "That was where I hid when they tortured my family."

She trembled as she listened carefully. "Is it the Pearl River rippling? Or is it my grandmother crying?"

She suddenly jumped and looked over her shoulder. "Is it the wind blowing through the grass? Or do they still have spies watching everyone?"

Sung Hwa put his arm around Qing. "If White Stone frightens you so, perhaps we should leave as soon as possible."

Qing lifted her head, raised her voice to reassure her husband. "I managed to escape from White Stone. Why should I be afraid of it?"

To prove that she was unafraid, Qing led the

others forward. Time had not changed the country road. She could still find her way after all these years, by the guiding light of a radiant moon.

It was a long walk from the town square to the Ma house. A narrow path led east to west. When they were tired and slowed down, the moon moved ahead impatiently, casting their shadows behind them.

Te looked back, pointed at Todd's shadow, and said to his son, "You are almost as tall as I am. I hope your life will be easier than mine and your Aunt Qing's."

There was innocent joy in Todd's voice as he answered, "With the color of my skin, my life will be difficult in America—even though I'm a professor's son. That's why I thought of moving back to White Stone to become a landlord . . ." He stopped when he heard Qing gasp.

The once-glorious building was now a skeleton in tattered clothes. The woodwork was stripped, the window glass substituted with cardboard, the paint had flaked away. The seven of them wandered from one shattered courtyard to another, finally entering the garden.

The place was piled with rubbish. They made their way through the waste to the pond, stood on a nearly collapsed bridge. They looked down and saw in the moonlight a mudhole filled with trash and lotuses that were long dead.

The many families living in the house peeked at them from behind plundered pagodas, lifeless trees, and headless statues, and talked loudly.

"I heard that some descendants of the Ma family have returned from America," a man's voice said with clear animosity.

"Since China is on good terms with the Americans again, they say that if the Ma children want, our government will give this house back to them," said another man, obviously resentful and worried.

"Then we'll have no place to live!" a woman shouted with frustration and fear.

Qing, Te, Hwa, and Todd—the four who could claim this house either directly or indirectly—looked at one another. The luminous moon revealed the same expression on their faces as they shook their heads.

"Qing, you tell them that we don't want this place," Hwa said. "Your Cantonese is better than mine."

"Yes, Qing, you tell them," Te agreed.

"But I'm only a girl, Te, and you have more right to this place than I," Qing said to her brother.

As the discussion continued, Sung Quanming stepped forward. "I'll tell them."

Quanming had been quiet all this time. The rest of them had thought that seeing his hometown had made him too emotional to speak. But as soon as he did, everyone noticed that his voice was unusually weak. Even in the silvery moonlight they saw that his face was drained of color.

"Baba!" Sung Hwa took Quanming's arm. "We should go back to the hotel . . ."

Quanming raised a shaky hand to stop his son. "Let me talk!"

With the support of his son, Quanming walked toward the people in the shadows. As soon as he started to move, several men and women in rags emerged from the darkness and revealed themselves. They greeted Quanming with narrowed eyes and tightened lips. Quanming studied their faces, then sighed deeply. Their hard, cold, distrustful, frightened, and suffering expressions stabbed through his heart.

"Don't worry," he said in the Pearl River dialect. "My family and friends are here to see our homeland. We have no intention of taking anything away from you—your homes, or whatever you own."

Quanming leaned against his son as he continued. "We children of the Pearl have never had much, except love for our land . . . and for one another. We do love our people. But life is always so hard along the Pearl, and we are forever forced to fight among ourselves simply to survive . . ." Quanming's voice shook, and his knees buckled. He sank to the ground and couldn't stand up.

"Baba!" Sung Hwa squatted beside his father on one side, Qing on the other.

"Don't worry," Quanming struggled to say weakly, "I'm tired . . . very tired . . . that's all."

Todd, Te, and the Nihoas went to look for means of transportation. They came back with a wheelbarrow. Quanming was lifted onto it and pushed all the way back to the hotel.

A local doctor was summoned to his bedside. The man couldn't find any sign of illness in Quanming. "Like Mr. Sung said, he is very tired," the doctor said. "You should let him have a good night's sleep, and he will be just fine."

Sumiko and Paala left with the doctor. Todd, Te, Qing, and Hwa stayed with Quanming for a while longer. When they were also ready to leave and almost out the door, Quanming called feebly. "Please . . ."

They rushed back to Quanming, asked if there was anything he wanted them to do.

"Yes . . ." he answered in a frail voice.

After a long pause, Quanming gathered his strength and continued, "Please love China. The Nihoas are not Chinese. They won't understand. But . . ."

He looked from Hwa to Qing and then to Te. "The three of you have your roots in China. It doesn't matter where you live now, or how long you have lived in your adopted homes. It doesn't even matter what shape China is in . . ."

Quanming took a deep breath. "China is your country. You should love her just like a son should always love his mother, whether she is near or far, beautiful or not."

Quanming looked at Todd and smiled. "You are half-Chinese, and you should love China too, with at least half of your heart."

Quanming struggled to breathe as he went on. "I have complained about China throughout the years. I'm sorry for all the negative things I said about my motherland. But most of all I regret that I lived too far from her for too long . . ."

Quanming closed his eyes. The four people waited until Quanming was asleep, then tiptoed away. Hwa stopped at the door and looked back with worry. "Maybe I should stay with Baba," he said.

Qing listened for a moment. "Baba is breathing evenly. Let him sleep."

When morning came and Hwa went to check

on his father, he found that Quanming had died in his sleep, a peaceful smile on his lips.

They talked about the funeral arrangements, and Hwa was deeply troubled. When Laurie had died a year ago in Hawaii, Quanming had purchased a cemetery plot next to her grave. "From what Baba said last night, maybe he would prefer to be buried right here in his hometown. But then, he wouldn't want to be parted from Laurie. What shall we do?" Hwa asked Qing.

Qing thought for a while, then answered, "Graves are often dug up in China. It's safer for Baba to rest in San Francisco." She patted her husband on the shoulder. "Spirits are not confined to where their bodies are buried. No matter where we lay him to rest Baba will be free to visit White Stone, maybe even bring Laurie with him."

After arrangements were made to return immediately to San Francisco, the group was ready to leave China. The night before their departure, the moon was full and bright. They walked around White Stone for the last time, and stopped at the riverbank.

They stood silently, looking at the Pearl River. The moon descended in the far west and began to pale. The night was almost over. The ancient Pearl glittered in the moonlight, carrying in its current the tears and laughter of its children, flowing toward eternity.

Afterword

LIFE IS LIKE a flower garden. Traveling through it, each of us follows a different path. The blessed encounter roses and peonies, while the cursed see thistles and weeds. Only from the Temple of the Moon can a complete panorama of the garden be observed.

On Wings of Destiny is fictional. Through the imaginary characters and historically based events I described the garden of life I've seen during the years as I walk along a path assigned by fate. Those taking another route may have a different view of the garden, and my pricking thorns may be fragrant petals according to their beliefs.

Like Sung Quanming, I feel sad at having to point out all the dreary occurrences in my motherland. And through Quanming's last breath I'm saying what many of the wandering Chinese want to say: We love China as a son loves his mother, whether she is near or far, beautiful or otherwise.